E1

A Valley Dream

ANNA JACOBS

A Valley Dream

Backshaw Moss Saga Book One

HODDER &
STOUGHTON

First published in Great Britain in 2021 by Hodder & Stoughton
An Hachette UK company

1

A CIP catalogue record for this title is available from the British Library

Hardback ISBN 978 1 529 35348 8
eBook ISBN 978 1 529 35349 5

Typeset in Plantin Light by Palimpsest Book Production Ltd, Falkirk, Stirlingshire

Printed and bound in Great Britain by Clays Ltd, Elcograf S.p.A.

Hodder & Stoughton policy is to use papers that are natural, renewable
and recyclable products and made from wood grown in sustainable forests.
The logging and manufacturing processes are expected to conform to
the environmental regulations of the country of origin.

Hodder & Stoughton Ltd
Carmelite House
50 Victoria Embankment
London EC4Y 0DZ

www.hodder.co.uk

Dear readers,

This is the first book in my new series set in Backshaw Moss. It will be the last series set in Ellindale, my imaginary Pennine valley. I really enjoyed writing this story and working out how to finish the whole group of series.

This time, it's Bella's story and it's what is often called a 'coming of age' story, which means someone is changing their life for the better. Her name is short for Arabella, but that was too much of a mouthful, so Bella she became.

Whenever I try to find names for characters it always reminds me that I can see some names being suitable for heroines and heroes, others only for villains, and others only for very minor characters. Why that is, I've never been able to figure out. I do know that I have trouble calling any character 'David' as that's my lovely husband's name and I can't see anyone, even a hero, wearing it.

I love designing the houses my characters inhabit, too. People's homes are so important, don't you think? This time we're not using two-up, two-down terraced houses, but a group of three detached houses built roughly three-quarters of the way through the nineteenth century.

These were solid houses built to last, but in that era houses didn't usually have bathrooms and certainly not amenities like electricity or even gas. Gas lighting was used in some urban streets in the early nineteenth century, but wasn't thought suitable for indoors until much later in the nineteenth and early twentieth centuries. This story is set in 1935 and the modernisation process is an integral part of the story.

I was born at the beginning of World War 2 and as I

grew up, I watched poor-quality housing being knocked down and modern estates replacing the terraced streets. For most of my childhood, my maternal grandparents lived in a one-up, one-down back-to-back house, i.e. it only had frontage on one street, and its back abutted the house behind it.

My granddad set up his home workshop in the cellar, and I remember sitting down there watching him make things. He was very good with his hands, had been trained as a fitter and turner. When he bought his first car (an Austin 7, before I was born) he pulled the whole thing to pieces, literally, so that he would know how it worked, then rebuilt it. After that he was able to repair anything on it himself. He was a very clever man in many ways.

I do wish I'd taken better note of what was going on around me with regard to housing in the post-WW2 housing boom, but my head was full of school, boyfriends and the books I was reading – at the rate of at least eight books a week while I was at primary school, reducing to four books a week while I was at grammar school.

What can I say? I'm a story addict, whether writing them or reading them. We currently have about fifteen bookcases full of 'keepers' and research books in our house and a burglar would be very disappointed at what is to be found, because books quickly lose their monetary value when they've been read – but not their 'love' value if it's a story that is dear to one's heart.

Happy reading, everyone! I certainly had a happy time writing this story and hope you enjoy it.

Anna

A Valley Dream

Prologue

1933

James Beaton stared at his godmother's lawyer in shock. He'd just been told that he'd been appointed sole executor of Sarah Jane Chapman's estate.

To his surprise the lawyer added, 'You are apparently the only relative of hers whom she felt she could trust to carry out her wishes, sir.'

'And she was – well, in her rightful mind?'

'She may have been old, but there was nothing wrong with her brain, I promise you. She asks that you read her diaries to gain a clearer insight into why she's chosen these relatives to inherit and why the bequests have been made in such a way. In summary, it's to nudge those who inherit into finding the courage to make changes to their lives.'

'Well, well.' James sat thinking for a moment or two, then shrugged. He had no pressing reason to go straight back to London. In fact, he'd been rather bored lately. 'Then I shall stay here as she requested and find the best way to carry out her wishes.'

'I've had her house prepared for you to live in. Her house-keeper and maid are happy to stay on for a while.'

James ended up spending longer in Rivenshaw than he'd expected to – several weeks, in fact. It was a pleasant little town and he'd never visited the Lancashire moors before.

During this time he went through every cupboard and

drawer in his godmother's house, finding it unexpectedly intriguing to see in intimate detail how someone else had lived, having been a reclusive bachelor all his life.

He found Sarah's diaries and read them all. She had a telling way with words. She'd been concerned that while the employment situation had improved in the south and Midlands in recent years, in Lancashire times were still hard. Not only were the poor struggling to put food on the table, but even those who normally would have made an adequate living were struggling.

He explored the area of the valley she had felt needed support. Much of the hamlet of Backshaw Moss was a slum, but the part near the larger village of Birch End was much better, and he chose to make a start on doing as Sarah had asked there, combining her wishes with his own desire to leave the world a better place.

As the train rattled its way back to London, James couldn't help thinking about his own situation. He wasn't in good health so could no longer travel, and sorting out Sarah's bequests had made him look at his own will again.

From then on he surprised his family by attending most of their social functions, and he was distressed to find out that the nephew he'd once thought a decent chap and worthy heir was anything but.

As a consequence, Thomas Beaton was no longer going to inherit anything, and the first person to benefit from his own and Sarah's legacies would be his great-niece Arabella Porter, who went by the name of Bella. Why hadn't he noticed what a miserable life the poor woman had been leading since the Great War, thanks to his nephew, on whom she was totally dependent?

James trusted his lawyer enough to tell him the truth. 'It must be impossible for my nephew Thomas to overturn my will. He is not a good man.'

The slight smile Albert Neven couldn't quite hide suggested that he was already aware of this fact. 'It's entirely your choice who inherits, Mr Beaton. He has no claim on you.'

As he sat sipping a glass of cognac the evening after he'd signed the will, James wished he could be there to see what the beneficiaries made of their legacies.

He'd asked for Bella to be dealt with first, because she was the one he knew personally. He hoped she wouldn't give way to Thomas's bullying. He was quite sure his nephew would try to take her legacy from her, but he trusted Albert Neven to prevent that.

He raised his glass in a silent salute to her. Only time would tell whether his bequests would achieve their aim. He was at least giving Bella and the others a chance for a better life, and that thought gave him great satisfaction.

In the end, it was up to them what they did with it.

I

London: 1935

The lawyer shuffled his papers and cleared his throat and the small group of family members sitting in the drawing room fell silent, looking at him expectantly. Albert Neven, who had drawn up the last will and testament of the late James Beaton, studied the group, frowned, and looked at his host.

'Mr Beaton, I particularly requested that Miss Arabella Jane Porter be present today, since she is also a beneficiary of your uncle.'

All heads turned to Thomas Beaton, now head of the family.

'I'm representing her.'

'Did she ask you to do that?'

As Beaton harrumphed, his elder son gathered his courage together and said loudly, 'No, she didn't. When I spoke to her a short time ago, she wasn't even aware that she was a legatee.'

His father glared at him and said scornfully, 'I didn't need to discuss it with her. It's only fitting, since she is totally dependent on me, that I take care of whatever this legacy is. Women do not understand business.'

At least two of the women present glared at him and the lawyer ignored him completely, inclining his head towards Stephen Beaton. 'Thank you for clarifying this, sir. You will appreciate that I am legally obliged to carry out the wishes of your late uncle.'

Bella was standing outside the small side door of the drawing room, which was usually used by servants entering and leaving. Over the years she'd found it a useful place to find things out when excluded from a family gathering. It had saved her a lot of trouble.

Unfortunately she'd been totally dependent on her cousin Thomas ever since the death of her parents a few years after the Great War ended, and still was at thirty-six, sadly.

The slightly open door gave her only a limited view of the room, but she had heard clearly what the lawyer said and was now feeling angry. Why had she not been told about this legacy?

How much had she been left? Could it be enough to live on independently? No, independence was too much to hope for. She not only didn't have a penny to her name, but lacked any skills that could earn her a wage.

Thomas had deliberately kept her helpless over the years, not even allowing her to do a typewriting course, claiming it 'unladylike'. In reality, she was sure that was because he found it useful to have another pair of hands around the house without needing to pay her any wages.

Even if she had found a job, women were always paid far less than men, anyway. The ladies she met at church worked as clerks or typists, earning wages of a mere twenty-five or thirty shillings a week. That was not enough to live on decently. One of them had gone hungry last winter, missing lunches for a month in order to buy a new winter coat.

At least by living with Thomas she got enough to eat and was warm in winter. And best of all, she'd had the pleasure of helping to raise his children, something he'd had little interest in.

As if in answer to her prayers, she heard Mr Neven say, 'Your uncle specifically asked that Miss Porter be present to hear the details of her legacy. I cannot therefore continue to read the will without her.'

'Why did James do that?'

'I can't tell you his reasons, I'm merely carrying out his orders. If Miss Porter is not able to be here today, I shall have to come back and read the will another time when she is at home.'

'I think I heard her come in a short time ago,' Thomas's wife Muriel said hastily. 'Shall I go and fetch her?'

Thomas sighed irritably. 'If we must. But warn her that she had better not interrupt.'

Bella didn't need to see his face to know he would be glaring at the lawyer.

She could see dear Stephen's face, though, and he was scowling at his father from across the room. They clashed regularly now that Stephen had got a job, married a wife with a little money of her own, and left home.

Bella realised Muriel was standing up to come and fetch her so hurried off to the small parlour at the rear of the house where she spent most of her days. She only had time to go and stand by the window before her cousin's wife came into the room.

'Idling again, Bella. There is always the mending to be done, you know.'

She didn't attempt to defend herself, simply waited in silence.

'Your presence is required in the drawing room at the will reading. James has apparently left you some trifling bequest. You need not say anything except to express your gratitude. My husband will deal with it for you, since it's family money.' She turned without waiting for an answer.

Bella followed her into the drawing room and took the seat Thomas pointed to, a hard chair at the back of the main group. Only the lawyer nodded a greeting.

Mr Neven began to read the will and list the bequests. There was nothing for Cousin Thomas except James's wishes for a long and happy life.

Thomas glared at the lawyer. 'I can't believe he would have left me out. You must have got it wrong.'

The lawyer breathed deeply. 'I can assure you, sir, that our accounts are quite accurate.'

'I suppose he spent a lot when he was gallivanting all over Europe in his younger days. A fool and his money are soon parted.'

The lawyer ignored this and went on in a chilly voice. 'To continue, apart from minor bequests to his servants, the rest will be divided between three family members. Two recipients are not to be named here, only Miss Arabella Jane Porter.'

'But surely this is—'

Mr Neven interrupted Thomas without hesitation. 'Please allow me to finish, Mr Beaton. Miss Porter, my client has left you a cottage in a small village called Backshaw Moss, which is in Lancashire.'

Thomas interrupted before she could ask what sort of property, speaking loudly and slowly. 'I don't understand, Mr Neven. How could he own property there?'

'The cottage was left to him by his godmother, I gather. It would, he thought, provide Miss Porter with a little pin money of her own. It upset him to see her so shabbily dressed. He felt it didn't reflect well on the family.'

James had told his lawyer to say that, if Thomas quibbled. He'd tried to cover every eventuality in his verbal instructions before he signed the will, sure that his mercenary nephew wouldn't willingly accept Bella receiving money from his uncle, when she was only a distant cousin.

'I must insist that you name the other two beneficiaries. I now have a duty to ensure that James's wishes are carried out.'

'No, sir, I have that duty, and you can be sure I shall carry it out faithfully.'

Bella was grateful to be left anything, of course, but her heart sank at the words 'pin money'. Not enough to make her independent, then. And the remark about her shabbiness would infuriate her cousin, who would no doubt blame her for not paying more attention to her appearance. As if she had any choice about what she wore. She dressed mainly in hand-me-downs from other family members.

'How much exactly is this property worth if I sell it?' Thomas demanded.

'That is not up to you.' The lawyer looked across at Bella. 'I'm not sure of the property's value, Miss Porter, but it is rented out in three separate flats and brings in a total income of around £200 per annum. Your cousin called it a cottage, not a house, so I doubt it's very big. Oh, and the legacy also includes a few trinkets that belonged to Mr James Beaton's godmother. There is nothing particularly valuable, but he thought you might like to have some jewellery to wear. He had noticed when he saw you at church that you seemed to have none, and the other ladies did.'

Bella's breath caught in her throat and hope began to rise in her. She could live in one of the flats, and even two thirds of £200 would be enough to live on if you didn't need to pay rent and were frugal in your ways. And the trinkets might be worth something, too. Even a small amount of money in the bank would be a comfort.

It gradually sank in that she would be able to leave here, she really would. Only, did she dare do it? Because she was very sure that Thomas would try anything – including force – to stop her.

Before she could say anything, Thomas turned to her. 'You can be sure that I'll manage the money very carefully for you, Bella. It'll give you a little more pin money if carefully invested.'

Which meant he intended to keep most of it, she was sure. All the years of humiliating and patronising treatment suddenly boiled over, and she jumped to her feet. 'I would prefer to manage it myself, thank you, cousin. I shall go to Lancashire and look at this cottage. If it's suitable, I shall move into part of it and continue to let out the rest.'

There was a very brief silence, then Thomas stormed across to stand over her, dominating her five foot two inches with his six foot of generous flesh. 'You will do no such thing! I'm not having an unmarried female relative of mine living on her own in such a ramshackle way. Goodness knows who the other tenants might be. Why, they might even be men, which would not be at all respectable. Besides, you have a perfectly good home here.'

She took an involuntary step backwards and it took all her courage to say, 'I'm grateful for that, Thomas, but I've always longed for a home of my own, even though it might only be a cottage.'

If the kitchen cat had got up and done a dance, Thomas could not have looked more astonished. For a moment he gaped at her, then he shouted, 'I will not have it! I warn you now, Bella, that if you leave this house and go to Lancashire, you will not be welcome to come back here again, what-ever you find there.'

Mr Neven moved quickly across to stand beside her. 'Mr Beaton, please. I'm sure you don't mean that.'

Thomas glared at him. 'Oh, but I do! I always insist on being obeyed in my own home. Besides, what does a foolish spinster know about managing money? She'll only waste it and end up as a burden on me again.'

He thumped his clenched fist down on a nearby side table, setting the ornaments rattling. 'Go to your room at once, Bella! And don't leave it till I send for you.'

The lawyer gaped at him in utter amazement.

That gave Bella the courage to say, 'No. I shall only go there to pack, and then I shall leave the house for ever.'

She was proud that she'd not let her voice wobble, but she was shuddering with fear inside and guessed she'd need help to actually get away. 'I'd be grateful if you could wait for me, Mr Neven. I, um, need to ask you about some of the details.'

Mr Neven was shorter than Thomas, but somehow his self-control made him seem more powerful as he turned to Bella and said gently, 'If that's what you truly wish to do, Miss Porter, you are of course free to leave at any time. You are certainly not a prisoner here.' He didn't even look at Thomas as he added, 'Go and pack all your things, my dear lady. I shall be happy to wait for you and take you somewhere you can spend the next few days till we can finalise the financial details and make arrangements for you to go to Lancashire.'

But even then, Thomas had to add insult to injury. 'Go with her, Muriel. We must make sure she doesn't take with her anything to which she is not entitled.'

This time the shock on Mr Neven's face at such an insult was echoed on the faces of the other family members. Stephen even took a hasty step forward, then stilled as the lawyer spoke loudly and clearly to his elderly clerk.

'Penscombe, please go with Miss Porter and make sure that she isn't bullied or coerced as she packs. Fetch me at once if anyone attempts to do that. And you'd better make a list of everything she takes with her in case anyone claims afterwards that something is missing.'

Bella's voice came out as a shaky whisper. 'Thank you, Mr Neven.'

Muriel stood up and led the way out without a word. Bella and the clerk followed her.

Bella felt sick with disgust at how Thomas had treated her. No one except Stephen and the lawyer had spoken in her defence, and she knew she couldn't expect any help from the rest of the family later if things went wrong.

But to treat her like that! And in public, too. Shame upon him.

She wasn't staying here one second longer than necessary

after such insults, let alone pleading to be allowed back if things went wrong. She'd throw herself off a cliff first.

The next hour passed in a blur of activity as a battered old trunk and two equally worn suitcases were brought quickly down from the attics by two of the servants and dumped in her bedroom.

'These came with you and they can leave with you, too,' Muriel said. 'We would never use such shabby luggage. These were only kept in case one of the servants needed some luggage to accompany us on a trip.'

Bella didn't comment, simply started taking her things out of the drawers and wardrobe.

The clerk pulled out a notebook and began to enumerate and list each item. 'So that you can see they don't belong to you, madam.'

'Do you think we'd try to steal such pitiful possessions from her, Mr Penscombe?' Muriel demanded

'I'm sorry if what I'm doing upsets you, Mrs Beaton, but I'm only doing as instructed. Mr Neven doesn't want there to be any grounds for claims that Miss Porter took anything from here which didn't belong to her.'

'It's rank impertinence to send you up to watch me!'

Penscombe didn't bother to hide his disgust at her attitude and continued to take notes.

The trunk was found to contain some old clothes which smelled strongly of mothballs.

When Bella started to pull these out, Muriel said sharply, 'These must have come here with you when your parents died, so they can leave with you as well. Not even the servants would wear such shabby garments, and long skirts like that haven't been in vogue for years. They must have been forgotten or they would have been torn up and used for rags. They're even longer than your frumpy clothes.'

There was no need for this gratuitous insult. It was Thomas who had decreed that Bella cover her legs 'decently', as became her age and position in his household, completely ignoring the fact that his wife, who was older and plumper than her, wore the shorter, more modern skirts.

Bella was embarrassed to have all her faded and worn underwear exposed, but she kept her expression calm as she pulled the rest of her things out of drawers and cupboards, packing them any old how, desperate to get away.

She did allow herself one act of satisfying defiance: she took the basket of family mending from the bedside table and said, 'You'll have to do this yourself now.' She thrust it into Muriel's arms, making her cousin squeak in shock and dump it quickly on the windowsill.

Bella hadn't expected to have enough possessions to fill the three pieces of luggage, but by the time she'd put in her books, her sketching materials, and some packets of miscellaneous papers, they were all full.

Muriel insisted on checking the papers. 'What on earth are these scribbles? You don't need bits of scrap paper.'

When she screwed one bundle up and tossed it in the wastepaper basket, the clerk said hastily, 'I don't think Mr Neven would wish you to destroy anything belonging to Miss Porter.'

'This is merely rubbish.'

'Nonetheless, it belongs to Miss Porter. Shall I fetch Mr Neven so that you can ask him about it?'

'No, you shall not. But I shall tell him how impertinent you've been when we go down.' She stepped back and folded her arms.

Bella put the papers into her suitcase. They were only little stories she used to make up for the children of the house. 'I keep them for sentimental reasons, cousin Muriel. I've always been fond of your children.'

'Ah. I see.' For a moment even Muriel looked shamefaced.

Bella turned to the clerk and said apologetically, 'I'd better pull that old coat out from the bottom of the trunk and put it on top to protect my books and papers.'

'Here, take this. And keep it.' Muriel picked up the old travel rug Bella had used to keep herself warm when sitting in her room reading, because heating wasn't often allowed on this upper floor of the house or in the servants' attics.

When the clerk immediately wrote that down, Muriel recovered rapidly from her one kind gesture and went back to glaring at him.

After Bella had finished, she checked every cupboard and drawer one final time, with Muriel peering over her shoulder, then said, 'I can't carry these cases down by myself.'

'I'll send someone to do it,' Muriel said.

'I'll wait until they arrive then come down with them to rejoin Mr Neven,' Penscombe said quietly.

Muriel's voice was a near screech. 'Do you think my servants are going to steal something?'

'Of course not, madam, but I cannot disobey my employer's instructions.'

Muriel let out a choked sound and turned to Bella. 'Come back downstairs, you ungrateful wretch!' She set off, once again not waiting for an answer because she knew she would be obeyed.

'Good luck, miss,' Penscombe whispered to Bella.

She mouthed 'Thank you' at him and left the room, not pausing for a final look around. This bedroom might have been hers for many years, but she'd often wept herself to sleep here and would be happy never to see it again. In fact she hated the whole house, but not as much as she despised Thomas and Muriel.

She found that her cousin and the lawyer were the only ones left in the sombre, book-lined room.

'This is your final chance, Bella. Have you come to your senses?' Thomas demanded.

She raised her chin. 'Yes, I have. That's why I'm leaving. I should have done it years ago.'

Thomas just about spat words at her. 'Don't ever dare try to return.'

'I won't.'

The only thing she'd regret was that she'd never see the children again, Bella thought. Though they weren't really children any longer, but young men and women. They'd given her a lot of pleasure when they were younger. She'd been the only adult to play with them and read to them, apart from the nanny or the nursery maid – and definitely the only person ever to cuddle them.

How Thomas and his wife could have created such nice children she would never understand. Sadly, once they'd grown up, she'd become totally superfluous here and recently had started secretly looking for a post as a lady's companion. It hadn't been a prospect that she relished, and she was delighted that it would no longer be necessary.

The two boys had started work a few years ago. Stephen had left the household when he married, associating more nowadays with his wife's family than his own. Oscar was engaged, at his father's command, to a rich but rather stupid young woman with whom he never looked comfortable.

Penelope had been married off at nineteen to a much older man chosen by her parents, and had wept in Bella's arms at the prospect of it. She was now a shadow of the vibrant young woman she had been, and after two years was showing no signs of bearing a child to her husband.

Alma, now almost eighteen, had joined her mother recently in social engagements designed to find her a suitable husband as soon as possible. She'd been looking pale and unhappy most of the time since that had started.

If a woman didn't have a husband she was nothing to people like the Beatons, Bella thought in a sudden surge of bitterness. Yet she'd read in the newspapers about modern women doing all sorts of things, including becoming members of Parliament, engineers, and scientists. Was it too late for her to achieve something, however modest? She hoped not.

'If you're ready, Miss Porter, I'll take you wherever you wish to go,' Mr Neven said.

'I just need my outdoor things.' When the maid had brought them, she took a deep breath and said quietly, 'I'm ready now.'

Thomas remained where he was near the fire. He'd glared at her as soon as she entered the room, but now he began to read the newspaper, ignoring her completely.

Bella had nothing to thank him for, so she didn't say anything. Head held high, she led the way out. And if her stomach was churning with nervousness, he couldn't see that.

2

Not until the trunk and suitcases had been dumped on the pavement and the front door closed did she confess to Mr Neven, 'I don't have any other relative who would dare take me in after Thomas has thrown me out. And . . . and I don't have anything but a few shillings, which won't pay for lodgings and expenses for more than a day or two.' She could feel her cheeks burning with shame as she added hesitantly, 'Do you think you could advance me some of my inheritance, just a little?'

The clerk tactfully moved a few paces away.

Mr Neven blinked at her in shock, then turned to stare back at the house. 'My dear lady, I didn't realise—Your cousin is quite a wealthy man. Did he not know how short of money you were?'

'Of course he did. It's how he's kept me captive for years. I was nothing more to him than an extra servant to whom he didn't need to pay wages.'

He shook his head slowly. 'That settles it. I have been uncertain about his, um, let us say, his general moral attitude towards the world.'

She nodded, but she'd have put it more strongly.

'I've been thinking of asking him to find himself another family lawyer once I've settled this will, and today has decided it. Turning you out on the street is the most unchristian act I've ever seen – and him a so-called pillar of society! Miss Porter, I'm quite sure my wife will be happy for you to stay in one of our spare bedrooms for a few days until we can arrange for you to travel north to this village. And of course I'll advance you some spending money.'

Her relief was so strong, it was a few seconds before she could string any words together. 'Thank you. I shall be extremely grateful – for your help.'

A passing cab was hailed. Bella and the two men got inside while her luggage was being strapped to the rear rack. She didn't look back as the large Humber was driven away.

She wasn't upset about leaving, she was furiously angry with Thomas's attitude – but she was afraid of facing the world on her own and felt ashamed to feel like that at her age. She had led such a sheltered life until now, learning about the modern world mainly from the newspapers and magazines the servants slipped to her for a few days before using them in the house cleaning.

But one thing she did have a great deal of experience of was living frugally. Surely that would see her through? Two hundred pounds a year seemed a large amount of money to her. Thomas had only allowed her two guineas a quarter, which had to cover clothes as well as incidental expenses such as church collections.

She turned to the lawyer, who was sitting beside her in the back seat of the car. There were so many things she needed to find out, and quickly. 'Backshaw Moss, did you say this village is called?'

'Yes. I'm afraid I know very little about it except where it is on the map. The nearest town is called Rivenshaw, which is in Lancashire near the border with Yorkshire. I can lend you a book of road maps so that you can find out exactly where your new home is situated, if you like?'

'That would be most helpful, thank you. I've never heard of either of those places, I must admit. Do you have any further details about the property itself?'

'I'm afraid not.' His client had forbidden him to disclose that information. 'But there is an agent, Mr Welch, who collects rent from it for its owner. I'm sure he will be able to show it to you when you get there. His office is in Rivenshaw.'

'Yes. Right.'

'You can't go there till the money side of your inheritance is settled, but once we've done that, we'll book you on a train. My clerk will phone this Welch and tell him when to expect you.' He nodded across at Penscombe.

'Thank you.'

'It'll take me a few days to finalise everything, but you'll be safe with my wife and me, my dear lady. Now, just let me stop at my rooms and get the rest of your inheritance. I won't keep you waiting long.'

Rest of her inheritance? What did he mean? Oh yes, he'd said something about jewellery.

She watched as he and his clerk got out, leaving her sitting there. She appreciated a few minutes' peace.

It wasn't long before Mr Neven came back alone. As the taxi set off again, he handed her an old-fashioned leather-covered jewellery box, rather plain and scratched. 'Here you are, my dear. These pieces might not be valuable, but Mr Beaton said they had belonged to his godmother and would give you some pretty bracelets and brooches to wear.'

'Thank you.' She clutched the box without looking inside. What did she care about cheap trinkets? It was money to live on that she needed.

Mr Neven fell silent, frowning in thought, and she didn't like to interrupt him with more questions though her head was teeming with things she wanted to know.

When they got to the lawyer's house, he paid the taxi driver and left Bella sitting in the hall, sending out a buxom maid to help the driver bring her trunk and suitcases into the house.

Bella didn't have long to wait until the lawyer brought his wife out to meet her. She stood up, hastily putting down the box of trinkets on a nearby table as Mrs Neven came forward.

The older woman clasped her hand in a comforting, motherly gesture. 'My dear Miss Porter, I'm sorry you've been treated so badly. You can be sure we'll look after you better here.'

The unexpectedly kind welcome brought tears rolling down her cheeks and Mrs Neven put an arm around her shoulders, leading her gently into a cosy sitting room which had a cheerful fire blazing in the grate. The lawyer followed them, then stood staring down at the flames, leaving his wife to deal with the tears.

'Take your time to settle down, my dear. You've had a nasty experience which would upset anyone. I'm so glad my husband brought you here.'

It was a few moments before Bella managed to calm down again, after which her kind hostess sent for a tray of tea and biscuits. Mr Neven drank three cups of tea and ate several biscuits, then said he had work to do in his study.

His wife showed Bella up to a very comfortable bedroom where her suitcases and trunk were already waiting for her. They looked even shabbier in the luxuriously furnished room.

It wasn't till she went to bed that she remembered the box of jewellery, which she'd left in the hall. Someone had kindly placed it on the dressing table.

She checked the contents and, as Mr Neven had said, they didn't look particularly valuable. But they were pretty pieces, and might bring in some much-needed money if she was ever desperate. Even a few pounds would come in useful. What might be a trivial amount to others could mean months of security to her. She pushed the box into the trunk, tucking it under one of her threadbare petticoats.

Over the next few days she felt rather disoriented, suspended in a blur of uncertainty between her old and new lives. Here she had the freedom to come and go as she pleased. Mr Neven went to work each day, and his wife continued with her engagements and charity work.

This freedom made a wonderful change and, as the March weather remained fine if cold, Bella was able to walk where she pleased and enjoy staring into shop windows or walking around department stores.

She didn't spend more than a few pennies on these excursions. It was enough to be able to go where she pleased, to have no one nagging her to do something, to have a warm bedroom.

The anxiety about her future was still there, of course, but this time there was also hope for a more pleasant life to come. That made all the difference.

Two days after her arrival, Bella was getting ready for bed when she suddenly remembered her mother's jewellery pieces. How could she possibly have forgotten them? Because she hadn't seen them for fifteen years, that was why. Thomas had taken the pieces from her when she first went to live with him, saying she wouldn't need them 'in her position', and that he'd 'keep them safe' for her.

They were the only things she had left from her parents, apart from a few photographs and some dog-eared books, because her cousin had sold the contents of their small house lock, stock and barrel after her parents had died. They had, he insisted, left a lot of debts, which the money the furniture and other items brought in had only just paid off.

Bella doubted that. Indeed, she couldn't imagine her parents running up any debts at all, just couldn't.

She broached the matter of the jewellery with Mr Neven the next morning as the three of them were having breakfast. 'I'm afraid I forgot to tell you something.'

He listened, then gaped at her. 'Beaton took your mother's jewellery away from you?'

'Yes.'

'He didn't mention it to me when you left, nor has he contacted me since! That is rather surprising. Do you have a list?'

'I can remember her jewellery quite clearly. There were only eight items. Mother used to let me have them for a treat sometimes to play at dressing up, so they can't be valuable. They have great sentimental value to me, however. Shall I make a list for you?'

'If you would, my dear. With a brief description of each. They belong to you, and you have a right to them.'

'The one I care about most of all is my mother's gold locket with photos of her and my father in it. Are you still my cousin Thomas's lawyer?'

'Yes. I consider it prudent to stay in that role until your future is sorted out, but after that is done, I shall ask him to find someone else to deal with his legal affairs. Please make that list for me immediately and I'll ask him to return the items.'

'I doubt he'll do it. He'll probably claim to have sold them.'

'Oh, I don't think he would dare do that with me.'

Mr Neven came home after work that day looking smug. He put a small wooden box on the table, a box Bella recognised. 'Could you please check that these are the pieces you remember, and that none is missing?'

She opened the box with fingers that trembled. She looked inside and nodded, fighting against tears at the mere sight of them after all these years. 'Yes. They're all here. Thank you so much. How on earth did you manage to get them from him?'

'I threatened to call in the police to look into the matter

when he claimed he couldn't find them, and that they must have been lost or stolen.'

'I should imagine he was furious at that.'

'Yes. He turned deep puce. I thought he was going to have a seizure. When his clerk brought the box in, the poor man got scolded for mislaying them.'

'Nothing is ever Thomas's fault.'

'He should be deeply ashamed of himself, trying to steal from an impoverished relative. I wasn't going to let him get away with that.'

Mr Neven smiled at the memory of his encounter, and it was a few moments before he added, 'May I have a good look at them and the pieces that James Beaton left you as well? He said they weren't valuable, so I didn't examine them as carefully as I perhaps should have done.'

'I'll go and get the others.' She ran up to her comfortable bedroom, which was situated near the family, not the servants.

When she brought the box down, she found Mrs Neven with him.

'My wife has more knowledge of jewellery than I do.'

Bella took the items out of both boxes and spread them out on the table.

'These don't look like cheap pieces to me,' Mrs Neven said after picking them up and checking for hallmarks. 'Some are definitely gold.'

'I hope you're right, my dear.' He turned back to Bella. 'From what James Beaton told me when he said to include them in the will, I'd thought they would be silver. Yes, and if that's not a diamond in this ring, I'm a Dutchman. As for your mother's pieces, they are of such fine workmanship I suspect they're going to prove even more valuable. I could show them to a jeweller friend of mine, if you like, and find out for sure?'

'Yes, please.' Because of how kind he'd been, she dared ask,

'May I come with you?' This could make such a big difference to her life, and she would prefer to hear the facts from an expert so that she knew exactly where she stood.

'I'd be happy to have your company.'

The jeweller was a rather plump gentleman with a smiling face. He listened to Mr Neven's explanation of how these items had come from 'two separate legacies' and then asked them to take a seat while he gave the pieces a preliminary check in the rear workshop.

When he came out to join them, he was smiling broadly. 'I think you're right, Mr Neven, though actually, these are even more valuable than you had supposed. Some of what you thought was silver is actually platinum, and one of the makers is a well-known eighteenth-century goldsmith whose pieces are always sought after. And the diamond in the ring is indeed a very fine one with no flaws. No wonder they set it in platinum.'

Bella's breath caught in her throat and she had to press one hand to her mouth to hold in a sudden surge of elation, quickly followed by deep, shuddering relief. They were valuable. If she sold them, she'd have some money in the bank, and that would make her feel so much safer.

Once again, she marvelled at cousin James's generosity. He'd hardly ever spoken to her at family gatherings, so why had he chosen her to inherit? Whatever the reason, she'd be grateful to him for as long as she lived.

She smiled at the two men, who were still looking at her in concern. 'I should like to sell all the pieces I inherited from James Beaton immediately, as that would give me some financial security. They have no sentimental value whatsoever to me, and I doubt I'll ever be in a position to wear expensive jewellery. Perhaps you two gentlemen can advise me how to sell them to best advantage? And I should also like to sell most of the ones from my mother, just keeping the locket and its chain, and perhaps the gold bracelet?'

The jeweller gave her a kindly smile. 'Bless you, I'd be happy to buy them all myself. They're of very fine workmanship, if a trifle old-fashioned and in need of cleaning properly. You can be sure I'd give you a fair price.'

She glanced at Mr Neven, who nodded encouragement, so said, 'Thank you. I shall be happy to sell them to you.'

'It'll take a couple of days to make sure of their exact value.'

'That's fine by me.'

'I'll send word to you via Mr Neven of the amount I'm offering. I should advise you to keep the remaining three pieces in the bank, just to be safe until you're settled somewhere.'

'Yes, I'll do that. I must find out if there is a branch of my bank in Rivenshaw. It's at the lower end of the Ellin Valley and looks on the map to be a reasonably sized town.'

When they were outside, she turned to her companion. 'Would you act as my lawyer from now on, Mr Neven? Just in case I . . . need help. Thomas can be . . . difficult.' She could see by his expression that he understood what she wasn't saying.

'I shall be very happy to do that. I'm about to tell Mr Beaton I can no longer retain him as a client.'

'He'll be furious.'

'Let him. I consider it my duty to behave according to Christian principles and take that duty very seriously. He clearly does not.'

'Thank you. I'm more grateful than I can say to you and your wife for the way you've helped me.'

When she went to bed that night, Bella shed a few tears of thankfulness to have that extra money behind her. But she smiled later as she drifted off to sleep. Whatever happened, she'd escaped from Thomas and Muriel for ever, something she'd dreamed of for years.

And if the cottage she'd inherited wasn't suitable for her to live in, she'd find somewhere else to make a new life for herself. She would have claimed her mother's jewellery back and done that long ago if she'd known how valuable it was.

Years of bullying had sapped her of the willpower to take any action that put her own safety at risk, and so it had never occurred to her to do so. This legacy had jerked her out of her apathy.

Thank you, Cousin James!

She had to learn to stand on her own feet from now on without flinching at what the world might offer her. And she would, she vowed. Whatever it took.

Of course, Bella's stay in this pleasant home couldn't continue and, two days after the visit to the jeweller, Mr Neven came home early and said he needed to speak to her. His wife stayed with them and, when Bella saw him hesitating, she guessed it wasn't good news.

'My clerk telephoned Mr Welch and this time caught him in his office. He asked him about the last quarter's rents, which are late being paid into James Beaton's bank account. He was apologetic that he'd not been able to keep all the flats fully occupied, so there will be a little less money than usual, I'm afraid.'

She held her breath, dreading to think what this might mean.

'It's not too bad, Miss Porter. He says the house you've been left does indeed bring in £200 a year, give or take, and he'll pay the money into the bank now he knows you've taken charge of your inheritance.'

'Oh, thank goodness.' But she could see that there was more bad news to come, so she waited.

'He seemed surprised that Mr Beaton had left the house to an unmarried lady. Apparently it's situated in a poor area which might not be suitable for you to live in. He'll be happy to continue collecting the rents for you, however.'

She took a moment or two to think this through, then asked, 'What does he mean by "poor area"?'

'Hmm. I don't know exactly, since I've never been to that part of Lancashire. Why do you ask, Miss Beaton?'

She'd thought about this, because her wide reading of anything and everything had included articles on how the poor lived. She wasn't a fool – at least, she didn't think she was – and hadn't expected a cottage that was split into several lodgings to be located in a part of town where the gentry lived. 'There are areas that are poor and yet remain respectable, and there are slums where life can be violent and where it would indeed be dangerous for me to live on my own. But would James Beaton's godmother have bought a cottage in a bad slum, do you think? It seems unlikely.'

He looked at her in surprise, then nodded slowly. 'My dear lady, you may have a very sensible point there. You must make sure of the area's safety before you decide to live there, however. If necessary you could sell that cottage and buy another one somewhere more respectable.'

'But I won't necessarily accept the word of a man whose living would be taken away if I moved into the cottage.'

'Ah yes. Another good point. We can't know exactly what he means from here. You must investigate it carefully before you do anything, and it might even be better for you to find yourself a lawyer in Rivenshaw itself. I should not be at all offended by that, I promise you, although I shall always stand ready to help you, in memory of James Beaton, whom I greatly respected.'

'Yes. I'll definitely consider that, thank you.' Since she'd found out yesterday that she would get over £400 from the sale of the 'trinkets', she had been working out what to do. 'I think the best thing would be for me to go ahead and visit

Backshaw Moss, as I'd planned, and move into some respectable lodgings for a while. I can then find out for myself
whether I should be able to live in this cottage safely or not.'

'And if you are at all unsure, don't move in.'

'I'll take care. I'd be able to buy a small dwelling without
spending all the money I've made selling the jewellery. I could
even take in a lodger or two myself. Respectable female lodgers
only, of course. The income from that, together with the rents
from James Beaton's cottage would keep me in modest
comfort, which is all I ask.'

He looked surprised. 'Do you have the household skills to
look after lodgers?'

'Oh, yes. I've had to do many mundane jobs while living
with cousin Thomas. I ran the nursery for a time. Most of
the servants were very helpful and they used to show me the
best way to do such tasks. Well, they didn't want to face an
angry mistress about work poorly done, did they?'

He looked at her sympathetically. 'The Beatons may be
related to you, but they've made your life miserable for many
years, haven't they?'

'They made use of me, certainly. But I quite enjoyed the
earlier years when I was looking after their children. Even
after the boys went away to school, they would try to spend
time with me during the holidays – only when their parents
were out of the house, of course. And the other servants have
continued to treat me as kindly as they dare.'

He frowned at her. 'Well, you sound to be thinking about
it all very practically, but I still don't like the thought of you
going to Lancashire on your own. The trouble is I'd have to
charge you to send someone with you, and they wouldn't
know the area even so. One thing I can arrange for you,
however, is to have the gas and electricity switched on in your
part of the house. The others use coin meters for theirs, but
for some strange reason the ground floor flat has the gas and

electricity charges included in their rent, my clerk tells me. And even then, the rent isn't very high. You should definitely increase it.'

'Thank you. That information is very helpful.'

'Have you thought of hiring a maid when you get there, someone older and sensible like yourself?'

The way he described her was the way most people saw her, but not the way she felt inside her head. Thirty-six wasn't old, and she was in excellent health. But she knew he didn't mean to offend her, so she didn't quibble. 'I can't afford to hire one.' She smiled ruefully. 'A scrubbing woman perhaps, if I take in lodgers, not a maid.'

'I suppose you're right.'

She felt to be coming to life again since she'd left her cousin's house, but she had a long way to go to feel secure in her new freedom.

If truth be told, she didn't like the thought of going to Lancashire on her own either, especially after spending nearly a week in this comfortable household, but needs must. 'I have to learn to fend for myself from now on, Mr Neven. Other women do it and, now that I have a little money behind me, I am determined to become a more modern woman – in every way.'

'I certainly wish you well. Only, you won't hesitate to contact me at once if there is any trouble or if you need some sort of character reference, will you? I'm always at your service.'

Mrs Neven smiled at her. 'And do come back to us if you ever need temporary accommodation in London. You've been a very easy and pleasant guest.'

Tears came into her eyes at their kindness. 'Thank you. It's good to know that I have a fall-back, but I shall try very hard not to need it. You've both been so very helpful and I shall always be grateful. If you hadn't been there the other day, I think Thomas might have prevented me from leaving by force.'

Mr Neven shook his head sadly, not commenting, but her plucky approach to the situation would have pleased James Beaton, he was sure. The legacy had pushed her into action, as his client had hoped. He would be interested to see how she continued to react to her new life.

That night as she lay in bed, Bella was both fearful and excited about the future. The only thing she considered to be unreservedly good about this situation was getting enough money to escape from Thomas Beaton.

From now on, her fate would be in her own hands – but also in the hands of blind chance. You couldn't foresee every possibility, however carefully you proceeded on your journey through life.

Tomorrow, she thought as she yawned and snuggled down, tomorrow my new life will really begin. Whatever happens, I can but do my best.

Would that be good enough? Only time would tell.

3

Ryan Cornish was glad when his wife started to have the baby, and so was she. She'd been dragging herself around for weeks, not coping as she had during her other pregnancies.

'Oh, thank goodness it's begun, Ryan, love. I've had enough of this.' She paused to gasp and wince. 'It's hurting more this time.'

He felt so helpless as he watched Deirdre ease herself up from her chair then begin walking slowly to and fro. He'd had enough of seeing her suffer. Besides, she'd been even harder to live with for the past few weeks, complaining about anything and everything. Their three kids, even the baby, had been shouted at for the slightest thing.

Unlike some men, Ryan helped with anything he could when he came home from work, and he loved playing with his three children, which was a good thing at the moment.

He was working all the hours he could, and fortunately even in these hard times, a plumber could find reasonably steady work – enough to get by, anyway. He'd done a few jobs for Roy Tyler recently, and he was the best builder in the valley, folk reckoned. He hoped that might lead to better things.

Deirdre yanked at his sleeve. 'Are you listening to me, Ryan Cornish? Typical man. Get all the pleasure and none of the pain. Fetch the midwife first, and when she gets here you can take the kids across the road. Maggie said she'd look after them when my time came.'

He looked at her in concern. Her face was chalk white and her breathing sounded laboured. 'Are you all right?'

'I shall be as soon as it's over. Get off with you!'

'I won't be long.' He hurried out to fetch Mrs Britten, who only lived a couple of streets away. She'd delivered most of the children in Birch End during the past ten years, including his first three. She was a proper certified midwife, which doctors wanted these days, and everyone liked her, said she was good at her job and worth the extra money.

Ryan sighed. He always felt helpless and guilty at this stage.

He was glad when Mrs Britten arrived a few minutes after his return and took charge upstairs in the larger of the two bedrooms. He left her to settle in and went across the road, carrying little Nelly on his shoulder, with the other two trailing behind. Maddy, at barely five years old, was holding three-year-old Devin's hand and telling him to watch where he was walking. She was already learning to be a 'little mother'.

When he got back, the downstairs of the house felt empty without the kids. He made himself a slice of bread and jam, pushed half of it away, then pulled the plate back and forced the rest down. You didn't waste good food.

Then he tried to read the newspaper, but couldn't settle to it, not with the sounds of his wife's travail coming more regularly from upstairs.

His wife always screamed and yelled during the births. Was it his imagination, or was there a shriller agony echoing in the sounds this time?

After another hour or two, with nothing happening, he got so worried he went up and tapped on the bedroom door.

'How are things going?'

The midwife frowned and shook her head slightly. 'Not as quickly as usual.'

Two more long hours later Mrs Britten came down from the bedroom and asked him to send for the doctor. 'And tell him I said he's needed quickly. She's not getting it out, and we may need the forceps.'

Ryan's heart sank as he ran to the corner shop to phone. McDevitt was a good doctor, he told himself. He would sort out whatever was wrong with Deirdre.

He sighed guiltily at his feelings towards his wife. He'd been bowled over by Deirdre's lush femininity and they'd got married quickly, even though he was several years older than her and had been trying for years to avoid getting tied down by marriage. But she'd fallen pregnant the second month and suffered badly from morning sickness, so their early married bliss hadn't lasted long.

She seemed to have been expecting or recovering from it for most of the time since, and she'd changed in her attitude towards him. She'd got what she wanted by marrying him, hadn't she? A steady wage earner. And now she was creating the big family it seemed she'd longed for even more than a husband.

By then he knew her a lot better and was regretting his rash marriage for other reasons. He hadn't realised how slow-thinking she was, not at all interested in the wider world, only in her home and family – and her church. He did his best to make her a good husband, though. He'd made his promises in church and would keep them. Besides, he loved his children dearly. How could you not?

Ryan was what people called a lapsed Catholic, but Deirdre was a fervent believer and dragged him and all the children to church every Sunday, complaining if he had an emergency job to attend to instead of his appointment with the Lord.

After she'd produced three children in just under five years Ryan had suggested using protection when they made love, as some of the other men did. He and Deirdre had had fierce rows about that because she'd refused point-blank to consider doing anything to limit their family size. The priest said it was a mortal sin. If the priest said the sun was blue, she'd believe him.

Ryan reckoned it was a far bigger mortal sin to bring more children into the world than you could afford to feed and clothe decently.

He winced. Poor lass! It must be going badly from the sounds echoing around the house.

He had stopped wanting her, too worried about the consequences – well, most of the time the worry held him back. But after one careless night – just the one, dammit! – when she'd teased him into loving her, she'd fallen for another child.

She'd been triumphant; he'd been in despair. He could see nothing but years of poverty and struggle ahead for his family, for all that he'd been in steady work – as steady as it got for most people these days, anyway. He might not be having trouble feeding the mouths he already had, but there were problems putting shoes on their fast-growing little feet. He hated to see the two older ones sluthering around, as his mother would have called it, in ill-fitting shoes that rubbed blisters on tender toes, but they didn't always have the money for new shoes that fitted properly.

He heaved a sigh of relief when the doctor arrived. 'Can I do anything to help?'

'Just stay out of the way, Mr Cornish. Let me do my job.'

Dr McDevitt came down ten minutes later. 'It'll be a while yet, I'm afraid. The baby's a big one and I may have to use forceps. I'm afraid Mrs Cornish is rather tired.'

After the doctor went back upstairs Ryan began pacing up and down, hearing fainter moans instead of screams now, wishing he knew what was going on, wishing he could do something, anything to help her.

An hour or so later Dr McDevitt came down and stopped in the doorway. 'I'm sorry. I did my best but – your wife has just died.'

Ryan gaped at him, unable to speak for a moment or two, so shocked was he. 'She can't have. She was yelling and screaming not long ago.'

'It happened so quickly there wasn't even time to fetch you up to say goodbye. I was trying to stanch the bleeding when her heart stopped and I couldn't get it started again. I'm really sorry.'

'And the baby?'

'It died too, I'm afraid. A boy.'

Ryan couldn't speak for a moment or two, he was so shocked. 'How is that possible?' he whispered at last.

'It happens. Not often, thank goodness. Nothing would stop the bleeding, you see. I was going to ask you to phone for an ambulance, when she simply – well, stopped breathing. She must have had heart problems that we didn't know about. Did she ever get breathless for no reason?'

Ryan nodded. 'Yes. Especially walking uphill. And sometimes she got tired for no reason too. She used to say she was having one of her "turns". She'd been having them quite often recently.'

'She should have come to see me about it.'

'That's what I said, but she wouldn't. Deirdre didn't like men being involved, doctors or not, said they didn't understand women like midwives did. Mrs Britten told her she should see you, too, just to be sure everything was all right.'

'If I'd been worried about her heart, I'd have sent her to hospital for the birth. No one fully understands these things, though. Bearing children is a complex process and every woman is different.'

After Dr McDevitt had left, Ryan sent a neighbour for the priest, more because Deirdre would have wanted it than because it'd comfort him. Father Joseph didn't arrive until an hour later. He prayed over the body and mumbled something about God's will.

In which case, Ryan thought rebelliously, he wanted nothing

more to do with a God who'd willed his poor wife to die so young, and when the priest repeated those useless words, he said as much.

'You don't mean it, my son. It's grief speaking.' Father Joseph didn't wait for a reply, he rarely did, just churned out a few platitudes and waddled slowly out of the house.

Ryan held the door open and watched him disappear down the street. 'I'm not your son and I do mean it,' he muttered.

The midwife waited with him for Owen Jeavons, the undertaker, to arrive. 'He'll do a good job for you,' she said quietly.

'It'll have to be his cheapest funeral.'

'I know. Most of them are these days. What do you intend to do about the children?'

'I don't know yet. I didn't expect – this.' He gestured upwards, didn't want to see his wife again. Without the liveliness that had been present in life, Deirdre's body already looked as if it belonged to a stranger.

'I'll tell you what I tell other husbands who've lost their wives. You need to face the fact that you'll have to remarry. It's the only way you'll manage with three children to look after. Unless you've family who'll take them in?'

He shook his head. All his cousins and his aunt and uncle were struggling to survive. His parents were long dead, and his only brother was living over in Rochdale and busy raising his own children.

'Give it a month or two and keep your eyes open for a likely mother for them. I'll let you know if I hear of anyone.'

He gaped at her. 'You say that, and my wife not yet cold?'

'I know it sounds cruel, but someone has to tell you so that you can get used to the idea.'

'I'm never marrying again. Never, ever.' Look where this marriage had led him. Widowed at thirty-four with three young children to care for and bring up. He loved them dearly, but the thought of being the only one responsible for every aspect of their lives from now on was terrifying. But that didn't mean he intended to marry again out of mere convenience. How could you even begin to share your life with a woman if you didn't care about her?

The midwife's eyes were old and wise as she patted his cheek. 'I've heard that many times, son, but it rarely happens. You'll find you have to, in the end. It's too hard to do it on your own, especially with such little ones. You'll need to keep working to earn the money, so you'll have to find someone to look after your children.'

He didn't have to find a wife to do it, though. And he wouldn't even try. Definitely not. He didn't argue, though, because he knew Mrs Britten meant well.

After the funeral, Ryan found out that the midwife had been right about one thing. It was very hard indeed for a man to manage on his own. Even with his neighbour minding the children during the day, he couldn't care for them and the house properly after work, let alone go out to answer the better-paying emergency calls. He'd had a little money saved, was proud of that, but it was gradually being eaten away to pay for the washing and for help with the cleaning.

As for cooking, thank heavens for fish and chip shops and bakers who sold pies. And apples. The kids got through pounds of apples.

To add to his woes, the landlord suddenly gave him notice to leave the little house with only a week's notice because he wanted it for a nephew who had just got married, and accommodation was scarce.

Ryan had to move his family from Rivenshaw to a two-room flat in Backshaw Moss, which was near the village of Birch End, halfway up the Ellin Valley. Not a place where he'd have chosen to live. The move also meant he had to find a new childminder.

The neighbour didn't seem to care to be losing the children. Wouldn't she even miss them a little bit? Not that he could see. He gave them a few extra hugs at the thought of how unloved they were. Deirdre's family had moved away from the valley, so it seemed that he'd be the only person to love his poor little dears now.

The flat he found wasn't at the worst end of the Moss, thank goodness, but it wasn't in the part of the valley where he wanted to bring up his children. Only, both the other places he'd looked at had been in an even worse state. At least this house had been well built originally, with proper drains, or would have, once he'd fixed a couple of things. Unfortunately, though, it had an outside lavatory and only one sink in the flat.

The rent collector refused to pay him for his suggested work on the drains and the flat – said the landlord hadn't authorised it and didn't have money to waste. Ryan scrounged around for bits of pipe and other materials, and got rid of the leaks under the sink at least.

In the end he could only afford to hire an old woman to look after the three children and see to the housework. He had to sleep in the room they used for a kitchen and sitting room, while she shared the bedroom with the children.

Hettie was honest and kind and he could see she did her very best and was desperate to keep the job. But she was old and tired, struggling to keep up with the work, and he still had to send some of the washing out to the laundry.

At least she grew fond of the children and they of her. He felt sad sometimes that the baby had died with Deirdre, but Hettie had more than enough on her plate with three little ones to care for.

Ryan lay awake many a night, worrying, not knowing what to do for the best. Had the midwife been right? Would he be forced to marry again for practical reasons?

No, he couldn't face it. If he ever considered marrying again, he was going to have a long courtship first, to make sure the woman wouldn't drive him mad once they started living together. And he wasn't going to marry anyone so mindlessly religious as Deirdre, either. He hadn't set foot in the church since the hasty funeral. He refused to let the children go to Sunday School, and turned the young curate away when he found his way to the new flat to ask why they were missing their classes.

After that they left him alone.

At least Hettie didn't push religion at him. He reckoned she was too tired to bother about that, poor creature. She often followed the children to bed as soon as tea was cleared away, or fell asleep in front of the fire on the old wooden rocking chair she'd brought with her. She'd brought a bed and bedding too, thank goodness. That wasn't much to show for sixty-four years on this earth, though, was it?

What sort of life was this? he wondered sometimes as the weeks passed. All he could hope was that things would get better when the children grew a little older and could do more for themselves. Better for them all, not just himself, he hoped.

At least he was getting occasional bigger jobs from Roy Tyler, whose building business was picking up nicely.

Ryan had got to know one or two other chaps since he'd come to live in the Moss, which was the only good thing about living here. They hated the slums as much as he did, even though like him they were living at the better end of the district. They were able to form a group of families that the rougher inhabitants didn't dare pick on, which helped.

And he was closer to the moors here. The views across them on the few occasions he'd been able to get out for a walk on a Sunday were a real treat. He loved the moors. When the kids were bigger he'd take them for walks there, too.

4

The mayor invited some of the members of Rivenshaw's Town Council to gather at his house before the official meeting, because the special grant offered to the town and its two nearby villages would expire if not used within a certain period – and there wasn't much time left. Reginald Kirby welcomed them and looked around, counting heads. Yes, his supporters on the council were all here now.

'I just wanted to make sure we're in agreement before the meeting. Backshaw Moss is an eyesore in the valley, but I reckon we're going to have a hard time getting any useful work done on it even with this special grant, unless we push for it good and hard. Some of Higgerson's cronies will probably want to spend it improving their own properties because they're as corrupt as he is.'

'No probably about that,' Todd Selby muttered.

'Well, you're right, lad, unfortunately. But gaining agreement to use the money wisely has to be our priority tonight. Quite apart from the time problems, the grant is only supposed to be used to start work on slum clearance.'

'Aye. And we all know what Higgerson and his cronies will vote, the greedy sods,' Charlie Willcox said.

There were murmurs of agreement and Reg waited for them to die down before continuing. 'Apart from anything else, the work will provide a few extra jobs for a while. The grant is a one-off, so I doubt there will be anything else like it for a while.'

'All of Backshaw Moss is a slum,' Todd said gloomily. 'The grant money will hardly allow us to make a dent in it.'

'Ah, come on,' Charlie said cheerfully. 'Any progress has to be good. We've got rid of a couple of the worst houses in the past few months without outside help.'

'We only got rid of those houses because one of them fell down and made the one next door unsafe,' Leah Selby said, supporting her husband.

'But we refused permission for them to repair the second house, and insisted on that whole piece of land being cleared, didn't we?' Charlie added. 'And we said they couldn't rebuild there until the whole street was demolished.'

Todd shrugged. His business partner always looked on the bright side of life. Todd had strolled through the Moss a couple of days ago, wishing to get an accurate view of how it was going, and he'd been horrified at how bad some parts of it were now. He exchanged glances with his wife, remembering their discussions.

Like all of them, Leah knew that getting rid of two slum houses was a poor effort when there were several streets and alleys in the Moss that were an utter disgrace and a health hazard too, especially those at the lower eastern end.

When she rubbed her belly without realising it, the men all stiffened and Todd hid a grin. He knew they were afraid of her giving birth at a meeting. It was unusual to have a younger, pregnant woman on the council, or in any public role, and they weren't quite sure what to expect from her sometimes. But things were changing, even in the valley, and they'd have to get used to women being around more. When he'd travelled abroad after the war, he'd seen women playing a much more open role in the world in some countries, pregnant or not.

Progress, some called it. Outrageous, others said, that a woman in her condition should carry on as a council member. The more conservative inhabitants muttered this regularly, but not where Todd could hear them. Or Charlie Willcox, give him his due. He was her brother-in-law from her first marriage.

Reg tapped the table with his pen to get their attention. 'We're all agreed, then, that we'll take Roy Tyler's advice and make a start at the west end of Daisy Street? Roy is the valley's best builder, after all. That little row of houses there is a crying shame and should have been demolished years ago. The others nearby are in a reasonable state of repair, if in need of modernisation.'

'Those three detached houses at the very end were well built and could set a good example to the rest. We need to chase up the owner, but someone said he'd died and left them in his lawyer's care.'

'I'll follow that up,' Henry Lloyd said. 'Neven, he's called. He lives in London, and I've never met him. He leaves it to Welch to collect rents and see to repairs, which just shows how unaware he is of what's really going on.'

There were several scornful exclamations at that name.

'Welch will get caught stepping over the legal lines one day,' Henry said. 'And that day can't come too soon for me. He might claim to have mended his ways and turned honest, but he hasn't really. All right, let's go and fight the good fight.'

They made their way to the Town Hall and found to their relief that the others who would join them in voting for a proper slum clearance programme were there, giving them a slender, one-person majority.

It was the leader of their opponents who broached the problem they'd wanted to leave till after the decision to demolish some other houses had been taken. Trust him.

Higgerson raised one hand and stared across the room at the mayor, who gave him a reluctant nod of permission to speak.

'What I want to know, Mr Mayor, is what's going to happen to the people living in those houses you're intending to condemn and knock down? There aren't a lot of rental houses lacking tenants in our valley at the moment, as we all know.' He leaned back and gave them one of his wolfish smiles. 'Do enlighten us on how you can continue to knock down houses.'

Leah leaned forward. 'I've taken it upon myself to check around. The old Ebenezer Chapel is still watertight and it wouldn't take much to make it fit for habitation. We can rent it or, if necessary, requisition it temporarily once we really get going.'

'Even living there communally will be far healthier than living in some of those hovels,' her husband put in, glaring at Higgerson.

The builder scowled back. 'And where is the money coming from for that? People won't want an increase in their rates, you know.'

'The grant will cover most of this first project,' the mayor said and continued talking as if the matter had been sorted out. 'We need to find someone to do the demolition and rebuilding work, and I propose Roy Tyler for the job.'

'What about Gareth here?' one of Higgerson's friends asked without even signalling for the mayor's permission to speak. 'He's the biggest builder in the valley, has much more expert-ise than Tyler.'

Higgerson shook his head and waggled one hand in a negative gesture. 'No, thank you. There's no profit to be had from helping the poor.'

'You could consider it helping the town,' Todd said.

Higgerson rolled his eyes. 'I prefer to help my fellow citizens by building good houses for decent, hard-working people who can afford them and who will look after them.'

Todd breathed deeply, but Reg shook his head in warning, so Todd didn't say what he thought and knew, which was that

Higgerson's houses were the slums of the future, so shoddily built were they.

Charlie was looking grim too, because his house in the better part of Birch End had been built by Higgerson and had needed a lot of repairs and re-finishing to bring it up to scratch quite soon after they moved in.

Reg held up his hand for silence and frowned at Higgerson. 'I expected you to say that, and since there's no one else in the valley capable of taking on such a big job, I'll speak to Roy and Ethel Tyler. If they're agreeable, the council will contract them to take on the work of demolishing the slum houses at the east end of Daisy Street.'

'That'll cost a small fortune,' someone growled.

'That's what the grant money is for. If we start immediately we will not need to ask the ratepayers to fund this. Now, those in favour?'

The vote was carried.

'Can we now deal with my original question: how do we pay for further improvements to the area afterwards, and where do we put those displaced by demolitions?' Higgerson asked.

'Mrs Selby has offered to help find placements—' the mayor started.

'If she's available!' Higgerson interrupted, looking at Leah's stomach as if disgusted by its fullness.

The mayor ignored him and carried on speaking, 'And perhaps Charlie will help Mrs Selby, just in case she's, er, indisposed for a while.'

'It doesn't do to pamper the poor,' Higgerson said loudly to the man next to him.

His friend nodded. 'There will be trouble about this, mark my words.'

The meeting broke up shortly afterwards.

5

The morning she was due to travel to Rivenshaw, Bella woke far too early and felt it polite to stay quietly in her bedroom to let the servants get on with preparing breakfast. It seemed ages until it was time to join her kind hosts downstairs.

Mr Neven accompanied her to the station in a taxi, wished her well, and walked away briskly.

She stood watching him till he was out of sight, then shivered. From now on she would be completely on her own for the first time in many years. It felt terrifying.

She had some money behind her, she told herself. She'd be all right. She wasn't stupid, had enough common sense to manage whatever came her way. She'd been telling herself that for days, but it didn't stop the fear.

She dealt with her luggage, seeing the trunk and second suitcase stowed in the guard's van, then got on the train with the other suitcase. She wasn't tall enough to put it in the rack, but a kindly gentleman helped her.

The journey seemed to take for ever, even though she'd bought a newspaper to while away the time. Yet when she arrived in Rivenshaw after successfully changing in Manchester to a local line, she didn't feel quite ready to leave the second train.

Oh, she had to stop being so silly, she thought as she waited for the porter to get her trunk and suitcase out of the guard's van. She'd made a mental list of how to start her new life and just had to work her way down it.

The first step on arrival in Rivenshaw was to leave her trunk and one suitcase in the left luggage office at the station. They ought to be safe there and it would be easier just to lug one suitcase around with her for the first few days.

She'd packed this one very carefully, putting in the necessary clothing and toiletries for a few nights. The obliging porter then took her and the suitcase outside to where a taxi was waiting for hire.

First step completed without trouble, which was a good omen, surely?

Her second step would be to find somewhere respectable to stay that night and probably for a few other nights as well. Mr Neven had suggested asking a taxi driver, because most of them knew their towns better than any newcomer could.

She studied the man waiting for a fare. He was older than her and looked honest, so she tipped the porter threepence and smiled at the driver.

'Where can I take you, missus?'

'I need to find some temporary lodgings, somewhere respectable. Would you know of somewhere in or near Backshaw Moss?'

He studied her for a few moments before answering. 'There's nowhere suitable in Backshaw Moss. Have you ever been there before, missus?'

'Um, no, but I have business there.'

'Well, to be frank, most of it is a slum, no place for a lady like you, my dear. The only lodgings you'll find there are shared rooms for labourers, and women who are not respectable.'

Her heart sank. What did that suggest about the cottage she'd inherited? 'Are there any lodgings in Birch End, then? I believe that's the next village.'

'Not that I know of. It's only a small place, though it's not a slum like the Moss. Some younger professional people live at one end of it, and decent, working folk in the rest. But no one offers lodgings for ladies.'

'Oh dear.'

'From down south are you, missus?'

'I'm a miss not a missus, thank you. And yes, I am from the south. But I hope to live round here from now on.'

He smiled approvingly at that remark. 'It's a good place to live, the Ellin Valley is, most of it anyway. I've lived here all my life, I have. Wouldn't live anywhere else. Look, I know a woman as keeps decent lodgings in Rivenshaw. That'd give you a start.'

'Thank you. Could you take me there, please?'

'Happy to. You won't be disappointed. Mrs Tucker keeps a clean, respectable house and sets a good table too.'

As he started the vehicle and drove off, Bella sat worrying. Had her worst fears been realised already? Had she only inherited a slum dwelling? But surely the kind old man who'd left her a legacy wouldn't have owned a really bad place, or if he had, he wouldn't have passed it on to a respectable single lady? That didn't make sense – unless he hadn't realised that this Backshaw Moss village had gone downhill?

The taxi stopped and the driver said, 'Here you are, miss. You'll be all right here. I'll wait while you check that Mrs Tucker has a room free. She takes mostly permanent lodgers and just keeps a couple of rooms for ladies staying in town for a short time only. I can take you somewhere else if she's full, but this is the best.'

The minute Bella saw her, she could tell that Mrs Tucker was respectable, which was a relief. The landlady studied her as carefully as the taxi driver had, then nodded, as if she'd passed some test.

'How long were you wanting to stay, Miss Porter?'

'A few nights. I'm not sure exactly how long.'

'Visiting someone round here, are you?'

She hesitated then thought, why not, so said, 'No. I've inherited a cottage nearby.'

'Ah. Very nice for you, I'm sure. You're not wearing mourning. Not someone close to you, then?'

'No. A distant relative. I'd only met him a few times, so it was a pleasant surprise.'

'You must tell me about the cottage later. I'm well acquainted with our valley. Let me show you the room and, if it suits, we can bring your luggage inside.'

The room was small but adequate, and Bella tactfully took the time to admire the quality of its furnishings before agreeing to take it for a few days.

They went back down and she paid the taxi driver before carrying in her own suitcase.

This time, on the way through the hall to the stairs Mrs Tucker indicated two doors, pushing each one open to give a glimpse of the room it led to. 'This is the guests' sitting room, which you're free to use in the evenings, and this is the dining room where all meals are served.'

Dusk was falling and Bella was glad she'd planned to wait until the following day to inspect her inheritance. She'd not have seen much in the dark anyway and she was tired.

When Mrs Tucker asked where her inheritance was, she again responded frankly. 'Somewhere called Backshaw Moss.'

'Oh.' The tone was flat, disapproving. 'Whereabouts exactly?'

'On Daisy Street, Number 23. Do you know it?'

'I don't know the Moss well, but I believe one end of Daisy Street is much more respectable than the other. I can't say which end yours is at, given only the house number. People who live there call it the Moss, by the way. It isn't well regarded, though I've heard that the town council is about to take steps to clear up the worst of the slums there.'

'That's very forward-thinking of them.'

'Well, I heard they'd been offered a special grant to help the town get started, but they have to do something quickly or they'll lose the money. There are some councillors objecting to the changes, yet the whole valley will benefit from clearing up those slums. It might help you with your cottage, too.'

'Why would anyone not want to clear up a slum area?'

'Some would rather use the money to improve their own properties in the area and cram more tenants in, leaving the worst of the slums to fester. It's been talked about a lot recently.'

Clearly Mrs Tucker was well abreast of all the latest gossip.

The older woman moved towards the bedroom door. 'Anyway, what am I nattering on for? You must be tired after such a long journey. I'll leave you to get settled. The evening meal is served at half past six. You'll hear the dinner gong. I have some very nice ladies staying here permanently, so you won't lack for company.'

Well, Bella thought as she washed her hands and face in the nearby shared bathroom, that sounded more optimistic than what the taxi driver had said about Daisy Street.

Whatever her inheritance was like, she'd have enough money to manage. Thank heavens for that jewellery. Had cousin James known it was valuable? She had to wonder. She'd only met him a few times but he'd come across to chat to her each time, which had made Thomas scowl across the room at him.

Bella looked round the plainly furnished little room. Always other people's rooms. She was longing to have a place to call home, a whole house if possible. Even the smallest cottage would be sheer luxury to her, a place where she could do as she pleased. She'd been living under other people's rules for so very long.

When she went downstairs, Bella found herself sharing an evening meal with a group of women of all ages, most of them spinsters like herself, but one a widow. All of them had just returned from their day's work in shops or offices.

She did indeed find them friendly and welcoming, as the landlady had said, and far more modern in attitude to women's roles in the world than anyone at her cousin's house. The conversation ranged over all sorts of topics, and she sat in fascination, not joining in much but simply enjoying listening.

Afterwards she joined the other ladies in the guests' sitting room, where they continued to chat. She not only learned about what was going on in the valley, but about how ordinary women who weren't under the thumb of bullying relatives lived and thought.

She'd been right about one thing, though. It was as difficult here as it was in London for a single woman to manage on a clerk or shop assistant's wages and there was much talk of economies and bargains. But there was also hope for a better life in future. Two of the women were studying to improve themselves at a night school that had been started up recently in Rivenshaw, with classes for both men and women.

She was envious of them. For all their low wages, they dressed as smartly as they could manage, some basing their clothes on those worn by their favourite film stars, like Claudette Colbert or Katharine Hepburn.

Her own skirt was far too long for current fashion and when one of them looked at it and grimaced, she said openly that she'd been living with an elderly relative who didn't allow her to dress in the modern fashion.

'I'm going to shorten my skirts as soon as I settle down,' she said recklessly. 'And I'm going to have my hair cut shorter, too.'

'I could cut your hair for you now for a small charge,' one of them said. 'Don't feel obliged, but it's what I do for a living and Mrs Tucker lets me trim the other guests' hair in the scullery because I do her hair for free.'

'I could shorten a couple of skirts for you,' another offered. 'I'd not charge much.'

Rashness seized her and she didn't think twice about accepting the offers. 'That would be wonderful. Thank you so much, um— I'm sorry. I've forgotten your names.'

The first young woman smiled. 'I understand – too many introductions at once. I'm Julie. No time like the present, if that's all right with you? We'll just have time to do your hair before the cocoa is brought up.'

'And I'm Louisa,' the other reminded her. 'I could come up with you and check what's needed, then start on one of the skirts tonight. If it only needs the hem taking up I'll have finished the first one by tomorrow evening, then if you like what I've done I'll do any others you have too.'

'Thank you so much.'

Julie came across to finger Bella's hair, which she'd washed only two nights ago. 'It looks as if it has a natural wave.'

'It does. It was my relative who insisted I wear it smoothed back in this bun.'

'It doesn't suit the shape of your face. Naturally wavy hair will be easier for you to look after. You won't need to get it permed. I can't do that here anyway. I don't have all the equipment to heat the perm rollers just so, let alone all the rest of the gadgets. I'll nip down to the kitchen and check with Mrs T that it's all right to trim yours now.'

'While she's doing that, let's measure your skirt,' Louisa said.

They hurried up to Bella's bedroom and Louisa took a little box of pins out of her handbag and knelt to put some in the hem, then took it away while Bella changed into another skirt.

When she went down again, Julie was back from seeing Mrs Tucker. She beckoned. 'Mrs T says to be quick, but I don't think your hair will be hard to cut. Have you any idea how you want it?'

The rashness continued. 'No, none, except shorter. Do what you think will suit me and make me look more modern.'

Bella sat with half-closed eyes and let Julie do as she willed. When she peeped, there seemed to be a lot of hair falling on to the floor and for a moment anxiety ran through her, then she thought of how old-fashioned and unflattering that dratted bun was, and how hard to keep tidy. Nothing could look worse than that.

When Julie had finished, she stepped back and beamed at Bella. 'I knew that would suit you. Aren't you going to look?' She indicated a mirror on one wall.

Bella took a deep breath, stood up, and went across to stare at the stranger in the mirror. 'Oh!' Her hair, still slightly damp, was curling nicely around her face in a jaw-length bob which made her look younger, somehow.

'Don't you like it?'

'Of course I do. It's absolutely wonderful! Julie, you are so clever!' She went across to her handbag. 'How much do I owe you?'

'Two shillings.'

She gave Julie half a crown and said to keep the change. The extra sixpence made the younger woman beam at her, then she called, 'Mrs T, come and have a look. I'm just going to sweep up the mess.'

The landlady peered around the door and she too beamed. 'It's lovely. You're so clever with hair, Julie.'

'One day I'll have my own shop. You'll see.' She slipped the silver coin into her pocket. 'This will go towards it. It's not the rent that's hard to find, but the money to buy all the equipment, you see.'

When Bella returned to the guests' sitting room, everyone *ooh*ed and *aah*ed over how much the shorter hair suited her. She couldn't wait for Louisa to shorten that skirt to match the new hairstyle. She'd have stayed up late and done one skirt herself, but she was suddenly feeling utterly exhausted so she just sat and listened to the others chat. It had been a very long day.

When she was settled in her own home, she hoped to make a few friends, perhaps some of these women. There were so many things she wanted to do now, not just big things like setting up a home, but small things like going to the cinema any time she fancied a particular film.

Well, the haircut made a wonderful start. Who'd have thought she'd get that done on the very first night?

Tired as she was, she felt sorry when the nightly cocoa was brought in and the gathering broke up. It had been many years since she'd spent such a pleasant evening.

In her room she wrote a quick postcard to Mr and Mrs Neven, telling them she'd arrived safely and giving them the address of her lodgings. She'd post it first thing tomorrow.

Then she snuggled down in the comfortable bed and let herself slide quickly into sleep.

6

After an excellent breakfast the next day, the other lodgers all hurried off to work and Bella asked Mrs Tucker for directions to Carrier Street.

The landlady gave her a strange look. 'What would a stranger like you be doing in that part of Rivenshaw?'

She decided on the truth. 'I need to see a Mr Welch, who has been collecting the rents for the cottage I've inherited.'

'Oh dear.'

'Could I ask what you mean by that? If you know anything about him, I'd be really grateful if you'd tell me.'

Mrs Tucker gestured to one of the dining chairs. 'Let's sit down and chat in comfort, dear. I heard how well you got on with my young ladies yesterday, and I must say you seem respectable, but—'

'Isn't Mr Welch respectable?'

'He treads the borders of respectability now, but was rather notorious at one time. And Carrier Street isn't a nice area. I wouldn't want my daughter going to that street on her own.'

'Oh dear. I thought his office there would be all right to visit since he manages people's properties.'

'He doesn't manage any properties in the better areas of town that I know of, just several in the poorer areas. And to get rent money out of people who live in such places he has to act in a bullying way at times. He doesn't usually deal with the better class of people and I wouldn't trust him to take my money to the bank.'

She stared at the landlady in dismay. 'I don't know what to say or do. I'd better be very careful how I go, and I'm grateful to you for warning me, but I do have to see him.'

Mrs Tucker hesitated, then said, 'Are you going to see him on your own? Only I've lived in Rivenshaw all my life and been running a guesthouse here for over twenty years so I hear things others might not find out about. We still have a shortage of regular work in the north, so people get desperate. You don't want any rough lads snatching your handbag, do you?'

'I was intending to go on my own, yes. What else can I do? I don't have any family here, or even any acquaintances.'

Mrs Tucker hesitated again, then said, 'You'll probably be all right, but you're a slip of a thing and you might be better spending a few shillings on hiring a strong man to keep you safe in that part of town. Not just to keep safe, but in case Mr Welch tries to intimidate you.'

Shocked, Bella swallowed hard, then realised having someone with her would indeed make her feel better because apart from anything else, she still didn't know her way around the town. 'Would you happen to know a suitable man?'

'I know half a dozen who'd jump at the job and whom I'd trust.'

'So you can find me someone?'

'Easily. I know of several decent chaps in our valley who are still looking for any odd job they can find. Let me think for a moment about which one would suit you best.'

'Is there someone nearby who could come straight away? I really do need to get on with sorting out my inheritance, and Mr Welch has been told to expect me today.'

'Hmm. Oh, I know. My son has a friend called Gabriel Harte. He's a nice lad and his whole family are well thought of. My Peter mentioned only last night that his friend is looking for work, said if I heard about any odd jobs to let him know. Gabriel lives in Birch End, so he may know more than most about Backshaw Moss. I could telephone the shop in Birch End and they'll send a lad to let him know there's a day's work on offer. He could be here within half an hour at most, even sooner if he borrows his brother's van.' She looked expectantly at Bella.

'How much will he charge?'

'He'll look after you all day for a few shillings, and be able to drive you round if you pay a bit extra for his brother's van. Jericho Harte works for Tyler's, a local builder, you see, and mostly uses their bigger vehicles for work.'

Bella hid a smile at this torrent of gossipy information. Mrs Tucker would no doubt be telling people about her arrival in town soon. She contented herself with saying, 'Having a vehicle to drive round in would make everything much easier on my first day or two here. Could you please get a message to him?'

Mrs Tucker went up to the hall to use the phone and came back smiling. 'Gabriel had just walked past the shop, so they called him back and I asked him there and then. He'll do it but will have to charge an extra four shillings for the van to pay for a day's petrol and use. He can be here in fifteen minutes or so if that's all right? I said it would be. I hope I did right.'

It felt strange but nice to be able to afford to hire someone. 'Yes, that's fine. Thank you very much for your help.'

'We women have to stick together, my dear. It's a man's world out there, so I keep an eye on the young women who stay here and help them out when I can. That doesn't always go down well with some folk in town.'

'I'm sure the lodgers appreciate your kindness, as I do.'

Bella smiled as she went back to her room to put on her coat and hat. Even her lumpy felt hat looked better with the new hairstyle. And she would feel so much safer to have someone with her today given all she'd heard about Backshaw Moss so far.

As she was tucking her woollen scarf round her neck, she paused to grimace again at her reflection in the mirror. She'd buy a new hat as soon as she could, and hang the expense. This one had been given to her by Muriel, and deliberately chosen to be as unflattering as possible, she had no doubt. Only, if you didn't wear a head covering to go out, people didn't think you were respectable. There were some stupid unwritten rules about how women should dress.

When she heard a vehicle stop outside the boarding house, she went to peep through the window. A young man got out of it, tall and dark-haired. He was shabbily dressed, but looked full of life and energy. As he came closer she wondered if he was as young as he looked. He had a serious expression on his face, as if he'd experienced some hard times. You got to know that look. Poor lad, if she was right.

She heard Mrs Tucker open the door to him and went down to join them.

'Miss Porter, this is Gabriel Harte.'

'I'm pleased to meet you, Mr Harte.'

He nodded to her and the landlady took over again. 'Gabriel's a man of few words, so don't expect him to gossip, but he'll stay by your side for as long as you need him today, and you can trust him with your life.'

Bella had already decided that she liked the look of him. 'I'd like to hire you for the whole day, then, Mr Harte. And the van. Would that be all right?'

Another nod was accompanied by a simple, 'Yes.'

Mrs Tucker gave him a nudge. 'Tell her the cost, you fool. Oh, I'll do it. Five shillings for half a day, eight shillings for a full day for Gabriel, and for use of the van all day, four shillings more.'

'That'll be fine.'

He bobbed his head and said, 'Good. I'm ready when you are, Miss Porter.'

'We'll go and call on this Mr Welch straight away. He collects the rents for a cottage I've inherited.'

He frowned and this time he didn't need urging to speak. 'Better get someone else to do that.'

Mr Neven had wondered about that, too. 'Mr Welch still hasn't sent an accounting for the last quarter's rents or paid the money into the bank, so I intend to check what he's been doing very carefully, believe me. I haven't even seen the property I've inherited yet.'

Gabriel gave her an earnest look and made his longest speech yet. 'Don't let him fool you. He tells lies as soon as look at you, that one does.'

As he led the way outside to the van, Mrs Tucker said, 'That's a lot of words from Gabriel. He must feel at ease with you.'

She felt at ease with him, too. It was like that with some people you met. If she'd ever had a brother, she'd have wanted one with that sincere, caring look on his face.

By the time she got into the van Mrs Tucker had gone inside. Bella felt very much on her own, but she would manage somehow to sort out her inheritance, and with it, her whole future. She glanced sideways and added mentally, helped by a complete stranger.

'I think we'll go to the bank first, Mr Harte. I need to check that my account has been transferred to Rivenshaw and find out whether the money has been paid in.'

'I'd rather you called me Gabriel, if that's all right.'

'That's fine.'

He asked which bank and had her outside it within five minutes, which just showed it was worth spending the money to speed up all the things she needed to do.

Mr Neven's clerk had helped transfer the account a few days ago and the bank manager himself came out of his office to meet her when he was told her name.

'We like to get to know new customers,' he said cheerfully.

When she came out again, Gabriel was leaning on the van and moved quickly to open the door on the passenger side for her.

'I'd like to go and see Mr Welch next. He's been collecting the rents of my house.'

Five minutes later they drew up outside a house and he gestured with one hand. 'This is it.'

She looked at it in puzzlement. 'It doesn't look like an office.'

'It isn't. Welch lives here and rents out some of the rooms.'

'You seem to know a lot about him.'

'Everyone knows what he's like.'

'Except my late cousin and his lawyer, apparently.'

'Yes. Bad choice of agent.'

She looked around. The street was shabby but didn't seem to be a slum. Well, not quite. The house was in the middle of a terrace of similar two-up, two-down dwellings with a shop on the far corner.

'Shall I come in with you, miss?'

She didn't want to appear weak, so she said, 'I'll go in alone, but perhaps you could wait somewhere within earshot. Just in case.' She smiled. 'I have a very loud voice when I wish to be heard.'

He gave another of his firm nods.

The front door of Number 17 was propped open, so she went inside, looking around for an office. All she saw were three closed, scuffed doors, none carrying a business sign.

Gathering her courage, she knocked on the nearest and said to the harassed-looking woman who answered it with a baby in her arms, 'I'm trying to find Mr Welch.'

'Upstairs, to the right.' The door was immediately closed again.

There were no signs upstairs either, but as there was only one door to the right, she knocked on it.

She was just about to knock again when an older woman opened it, this one better dressed and looking well fed.

She scowled at Bella by way of a greeting. 'Yes?'

'I'm looking for Mr Welch. He should be expecting me. My name's Porter. Mr Neven's clerk phoned to say when I would be arriving in Rivenshaw late yesterday.'

The woman eyed her up and down rather scornfully, then turned and called into the room, 'Vince! She's here.'

A man came to join them at the door, middle-aged and neatly dressed in a rather loud, checked suit. He gave Bella what she would call a 'false smile', one that didn't reach his eyes let alone disturb the wrinkles around them.

'Miss Porter, is it?'

At least his tone was more polite than the woman's. 'Yes.'

'Please come in. I'm Vincent Welch and this is my wife. Do sit down.'

The office seemed to consist of only one large, cluttered room with a sink, cooker and table to the rear and a faint smell of fried bacon lingering in the air. There was another larger table piled with papers and oddments near the door, and a closed door to the rear at the left. The woman had to lift some papers off a chair to give Bella a seat.

Bella didn't like the way Mr Welch left it to his wife to do the lifting while he turned back to study his client again. His eyes ran up and down her body in a way she considered extremely offensive. When she stiffened and looked at him indignantly, he stopped looking at her breasts and his expression changed back to that false smile.

'I'm pleased to meet you, Miss Porter. I hope I shall have the pleasure of collecting your rents for a long time to come.'

'I have no idea what my plans will be until I've seen the cottage I've inherited. I'd like to do that today. If you can't show it to me, I'll go on my own.'

'I'll be happy to show it to you. I'm busy this morning, but I can drive you out there this afternoon.'

She nearly accepted his offer, but the thought of sitting in a car close to him made her say hastily, 'Thank you, but I've hired someone to drive me around, so I'll meet you there.'

He exchanged glances with his wife, and she could tell that he didn't like this idea of her going there independently of him, but he said, 'Good, good. I'll meet you in Daisy Street at two o'clock, if that suits.'

'Two o'clock will be fine.'

He stood up as if expecting her to leave, but she stayed where she was. She'd expected him to mention the rents and when he didn't, she waited him out. If there was one thing in which she was an expert, it was waiting for someone else to say something.

'Um, was there something else, Miss Porter?'

'Yes. I'd like to see the accounts for the last quarter, Mr Welch. I gather from my lawyer that your payment of rent money to his former client for that quarter is overdue, so I'll expect it to be paid into my bank account here in Rivenshaw by tomorrow morning at the latest.'

That remark seemed to unsettle him. 'Mr Neven is your lawyer still? I'd have thought you'd look for someone in Rivenshaw.'

'Not until I've settled in and know my way around.' Something impelled her to add, 'I'm very satisfied with Mr Neven's help so far. He's very efficient and knows some important people. I'm sure I can trust him to make sure I'm not cheated. I'll be obliged if you'll pay in the money at once. The account is now in my name, Miss I J Porter.'

Welch chewed one corner of his mouth and frowned, so

she said firmly, 'You'll need to write down my name so that you can pay in the rent money.'

He looked at his wife, and Bella watched the woman scribble it down on a writing pad.

'Yes. Right. I'll have the accounts ready for you tomorrow. My wife will need to get them up to date first. She acts as my clerk, but she's been ill, you see, so there are a few entries still to be made. I'm mostly out and about collecting the money for all my clients and managing any necessary repairs to their properties, you see. But Mrs Welch is very capable, so we'll soon sort it all out.'

'I see.' Bella studied the woman, feeling increasingly suspicious of both of them.

'Let me show you out.'

When she went outside, Gabriel was leaning against the wall of the house, and he straightened up when he saw her.

Welch scowled at him and tugged her arm to stop her moving. 'Is he with you?'

'Yes. He's driving me around.'

'A word of warning. You can't trust a Harte. They're a tricky bunch.'

'I'll take great care whom I trust, you can be sure of that,' she said pointedly.

His ghastly smile flickered off for a moment, then turned back on again. She definitely didn't like him, didn't want him working for her for a day longer than was necessary. But she'd not sack him till he paid her money into the bank.

When he went back into the upstairs room, Vince crossed to the window to watch his new client get into the van. 'She came with one of them damned Hartes.'

'If she's new to the town, how the hell did she meet him?'

'I don't know. I thought the new owner would have his own lawyer, and we'd be rid of that Neven chap and his nosey clerk. They've been asking some sharp questions since they took over managing the house after Beaton died. Better sort out the accounts a bit before we hand them over, Clara love.'

'Pity. We could have creamed off some more from the next lot of rents.'

'We've done all right and we can still keep back a little each week, eh? She won't know exactly how much should be coming in. Beaton wasn't all that sharp about money even before he fell ill. And that lawyer chappie lives in London, so he won't know whether a room has been empty or not over the past few months.'

'Or whether the repairs we've claimed for have been made recently.'

They laughed heartily at that, then Clara waggled her forefinger at him in warning. 'You see you treat her nicely, Vince. Even without our little extras, it brings in steady money, that house does.'

He tapped one finger to his nose. 'Leave it to me. I'm good with older women.'

'Older? She can't be more than thirty-five, and I'm a fair judge. She's a typical spinster, though. Dowdy.' She shuddered. 'I'd not be seen dead in an outfit like that, even though it's good quality material.'

'Never mind her clothes. The important thing is to keep her happy with our services, so you take care of those accounts, just a few little tweaks.'

She tossed her head. 'I'm better than you at them so I don't need telling how to do it.'

'Yes, yes. We make a good team, you and me. Higgerson married money and added to it. We've had to get ours from scratch, where and how we could. She'd better not upset me, though. I'm not letting a frumpy little mouse like her mess me around.'

Clara looked at him anxiously. 'Don't talk like that, Vince.

We said no more violence when we moved to this house. We want to turn respectable, remember.'

He shrugged. 'You need to do what's necessary if you want to get on, and above anything else you need to make money. That's what makes you respectable: money in the bank.'

She was still looking anxious.

'Leave that side of things to me and you stick to the paper-work. I haven't got in trouble with the law for a long time now, have I? I've learned how to tread carefully.'

7

As Gabriel drove away he glanced at Bella, opened his mouth, then shut it again.

She waited, then prompted, 'What did you want to ask? I'd rather you talked to me.'

'I was wondering how it went.'

'Could you find somewhere to stop? I'll tell you what happened and I'd be very interested to see what you think. Your honest opinion, please. I don't take offence easily and there's so much I need to find out here. Afterwards I'd also like to discuss with you what I'm thinking of doing next. You know how things are done in the valley, so you may have some better ideas.'

He cast her one quick glance of surprise, then shortly afterwards pulled over to a wider piece of verge at the side of the road and stopped the engine. 'Don't you have any family to help you?'

'None that care about me.' She stared at him, wondering if she dared use him as a confidant, and he gave her a faint smile.

'Tell me, then. I'm a good listener, better than I am at talking.'

He had such a nice smile, she relaxed. 'I think you're a kind man, too.'

He flushed slightly and waved one hand as if to tell her to go on.

As she went through what had happened, he began to scowl.

'The Welches must be fiddling the accounts.'

'I guessed that from the way his wife smirked, and he must think I'm stupid because he spoke slowly and patronisingly to me. But how can I check their figures? My lawyer is in London. I don't know anyone here.'

He stared down at his hands, then took a deep breath and said slowly, 'Sergeant Deemer is a good policeman, in charge of the whole valley. Tell him. He'll listen and remember, even if he can't do anything now.'

That was a long speech. But was Gabriel giving her good advice?

'I might speak to him once I have something to back up my suspicions, but no one would listen to me now.' She stared down at her horrible skirt. 'They think I'm stupid because I wear frumpy, old-fashioned clothes. I don't have any others yet.'

'It's faces I look at, not clothes.'

His words were comforting and he seemed an honest soul. She considered herself a fair judge of character. 'Mrs Tucker said you were sparing with words, but you've talked to me.'

'I don't talk for talking's sake.'

'You've made sense.'

'Good. You've hired me, and you need help.'

'Thank you. And if I have any more work to offer, I'll come back to you. I very much appreciate your honesty.'

Another nod was her only answer.

'Now, let's plan the rest of the day. I want to see the whole valley. Can we drive right up to the top of it?'

'Yes.'

'Afterwards I want to go and look at the cottage I've inherited.'

'Don't you want to see the cottage before we drive around?'

'No. I want to understand the whole valley. Besides, I'm not sure whether I can just go straight into the cottage, since it's rented out. I can only look at the outside.'

'Yes. Good idea.'

'You used three words then,' she teased.

His smile was genuine. 'I sometimes use four or five.' He started the engine again.

She leaned back as Gabriel drove up the hill from Rivenshaw, mentally following their journey on the map she'd bought.

He slowed down again and pointed to the right. 'Birch End village. Backshaw Moss is beyond it.'

'Those houses look nice.'

'New houses, those, for better-off folk. Not well built, though. Higgerson built them, and he always skimps on something.'

She'd expected to turn off there, but he continued up the slightly twisting road.

'Ellindale is at the top. Small village. Road ends there. Coming down we can go and look at Backshaw Moss.'

She couldn't help but wish she'd inherited one of the better modern houses she'd seen, shoddily built or not. Would her cottage even have a garden? She did hope so. Before her parents died, she and her mother had loved gardening.

The road climbed more steeply, with a drystone wall to the right and beyond it the moors rolling in great curves towards the far horizon.

'Do people go walking across the moors, Gabriel?'

'Yes. We're lucky here; no barriers to our moors.' He suddenly began to sound enthusiastic and continued without prompting. 'Rich men tried to put up barriers in other places, but people protested.'

'I think I read about it in the newspapers. There was a mass trespass by the public at Kinder Scout in Derbyshire – two, no, nearly three years ago now – because ordinary people and hikers were denied access to the open countryside. I was on their side.'

'I'd have protested too, but I hadn't the money to travel

there. We're luckier here and can go walking on the moors. There are several well-used paths.'

Was it her imagination or was he speaking in longer sentences? Perhaps he felt as comfortable with her as she did with him. She couldn't work out why she felt so at ease with him. She just did.

He stopped the van and gestured. 'This is Ellindale village centre.'

She stared around, thinking how pleasant it all looked. There was a little shop to one side and a village green at the centre of the open space, with all sorts of houses and cottages set higgledy piggledy around it, as if they'd been built at different times and tossed into place by careless children.

'There's a fizzy drink factory at the top where the road ends, and then only the moors beyond it.'

'What sort of fizzy drinks?'

'Mrs Selby – Leah – started off with ginger beer, but now she does several sorts. She's a clever woman.'

Bella consulted her fob watch. 'We'd better not go any further today.'

'You can buy a sandwich at the village store for your dinner.'

'I'm not hungry. Are you?'

'I can wait.'

But she'd heard his stomach growl a couple of times so said, 'Mind you, it'd be wise to eat something now, wouldn't it?'

She bought them a pie each and a bottle of the local lemonade with paper cups to drink it from. He didn't protest and she guessed she'd been right and he was hungry. Well, he had a big, strong body to sustain.

They didn't linger over their picnic but neither left a crumb, because she'd suddenly found her appetite.

She wished she had a brother or cousin like Gabriel.

She'd brought up two young men. Would Stephen and

Oscar be this kind to a stranger? They were rather guarded these days, even with her. But it was the best way to deal with their father: keep their thoughts and plans to themselves.

Would she ever see them again?

Gabriel drove back down the hill and turned left towards Birch End.

'The village is in two halves – new!' He indicated the modern houses visible on the left. He stopped the van a little further on to the right near a strip of green with a few small shops and miscellaneous homes. 'This is the old part of Birch End. And Backshaw Moss is beyond this.'

He slowed down. 'I need to know the house number.'

'Oh, sorry. It's 23 Daisy Street. Is that . . . ' She hesitated, then said it aloud, 'Tell me the truth, is it in the bad slum area?'

He let out a small murmur of thoughtful sound. 'Daisy Street is at the better end of the Moss, on the edge of Birch End.' After a pause he added, 'For what that's worth – because there are still problems round there, it's not as bad as the rest of the Moss.'

She crossed her fingers in the desperate hope that she'd be able to live in her cottage.

Of course he noticed it, slowed right down and took one hand off the steering wheel to pat her hand. 'I know the poorer area quite well. My family and I had to live there after we paid the hospital for Ma to be looked after when she was ill.'

'But she's better now?'

He grinned. 'Aye. Back on form.'

'I'd like to meet her.'

'Really?'

'Yes.'

'She likes to meet new people.'

'I need to make new friends.' She waited a minute, then spoke her thoughts aloud. 'Most of all, though, I want my own home.'

'Nowhere in the Moss is a good area for a lady like you to live in.'

She didn't care if he saw the tears in her eyes. 'Everyone pulls a face at the mere mention of Backshaw Moss.' He waited for her to gulp back incipient tears and continue.

'I have nowhere to go back to, Gabriel, no family who care about me, no friends.' She wouldn't dare try to contact the Beaton children again, didn't want to attract cousin Thomas's attention. 'If it's at all possible to live in my cottage, I shall.'

'Let's see which house it is, then. I'll tell you straight out if it's not going to be safe for you there.'

What a nice young man he was. Kind underneath that quiet exterior. The women at her lodgings had been kind to her too. Oh, if only she could make a few friends here! She'd been achingly lonely for too many years.

As they left the village centre, Gabriel slowed down to a walking pace so that she could have a good look around. 'Most folk reckon this is the last street in Birch End. Beyond this is where the Moss begins, at Daisy Street. Your cottage should be one of the first few houses there.'

Bella could hardly breathe as he turned into it, then stopped almost immediately to look for house numbers.

A slovenly woman with a sacking shopping bag slowed down to stare at them before continuing to move stiffly past the van. Two men sitting on a crumbling wall further along stopped chatting to peer across the street at them.

He pointed. 'Here it is!'

Number 23 was on the left. To her astonishment it was three storeys high and the middle one of three identical detached dwellings.

'This isn't a cottage! It's a house, and quite a big one too!'

'Aye. I wondered why you kept calling it a cottage.'

'That was what it was called in the will.'

She looked at the other side of the street and grimaced at the small terrace of six sagging houses opposite hers. 'Those look ready to fall down.'

'They are. They've got too many people crammed into them.'

'Poor things.'

She turned back to her own house, frowning. 'Why did the will say I'd inherited a cottage?' she wondered aloud, not surprised when he didn't comment on that. She was getting used to the way he only spoke when he had something pertinent to contribute to the conversation.

Had James Beaton called it a cottage to fool Thomas? She'd never know now. If that was the reason, she could only hope it would work. Her cousin would take her last penny from her if he could. No. Even Thomas wouldn't come all the way to Lancashire to inspect a 'cottage', surely? He despised places outside London, and never even went away on holiday. She was counting on that to help keep him away. And Mr Neven would be able to protect her legally, if the worst came to the worst, surely?

She turned her attention back to her inheritance. Unlike some of the smaller houses on the opposite side of the street, which looked ready to fall down, Number 23 and its two neighbouring dwellings looked to be solidly built.

'I always liked these three houses,' Gabriel said suddenly. 'They're quite old, you know, over a hundred years. See.'

He pointed and she saw a small stone panel above the front door with 1822 carved on it.

'They'd be pretty if they'd been looked after properly,' that quiet voice continued.

She shook her head sadly. 'Only they haven't been well maintained, have they?' The more she looked at her house, the more problems she could see. Everything about it seemed to need attention: the paintwork, the filthy windows, the gutters, a drainpipe lacking its bottom section and ending at shoulder height, which had left stains on the wall from water splashing out of it. And who knew what the interior would be like?

The only thing that seemed to have been maintained was the roof, with its grey slate tiles.

Narrow gardens ran along the front of the houses, with low walls separating them from the pavement. When she studied hers, it had no plants growing in it, just a patch of bare earth, stamped hard and flat. The other two gardens were even worse, full of rubbish. Who had cleared hers up? There were chunks of stone in a neat pile at one end, as if a job had been planned but not carried out.

In the centre of each garden, right next to the house, there was an oblong row of small paving stones around a hole with an iron grill covering it. That must be an air well to let light and fresh air into a cellar, she guessed. There was also a wooden trap door to one side of it. A coal chute?

Gabriel was right. It must have been quite a nice house when first built, but it had clearly been neglected for years. The houses on either side were in a similarly poor condition. Who owned those? she wondered. They didn't even look to be occupied.

As they sat looking at the house she voiced her regrets. 'This could have been a nice home if it'd been properly cared for. So could the others.' She studied the next set of houses on her side of the street. They were a mixture of semi-detached houses and old-fashioned cottages from the last century, well built in their time but most seemed to have been let run down.

Gabriel's voice interrupted her thoughts. 'The three houses could be made good again with a bit of work. Pity they haven't been better looked after.'

Some yells and shrieks made her look across the street and she saw two women screeching insults at one another from their front doorsteps. 'The slum houses opposite are in a shocking condition. What if they get worse?'

'They will. They've been badly built. Higgerson's earliest houses will look like these in a few years.'

'You've mentioned his poor work before. Why does no one complain about it?'

'They do. But he's one of the richest men in the valley, so he does a few token repairs if pushed, and that's it.'

She couldn't resist saying, 'You know what, Gabriel? Mrs Tucker said you're noted for being taciturn, but you've spoken to me and given me a lot of information as well as much to think about.'

'You're easy to talk to. And you talk to me, not at me, like some folk.'

'You're easy to talk to as well, Gabriel. And I'm grateful for your help today.' She waited, sensing he hadn't finished speaking.

'I'm interested in what you do with this house.' His voice went lower, and he stared blindly out of the van window as he went on. 'Eh, if I were from a rich family, I'd have learned to design houses that are modern, well built, and pretty to look at. Whoever designed these thought of their outside appearance and I bet they're nice inside, or at least, could be made nice again.'

She guessed he'd been voicing his dearest dreams, so she waited a moment or two before carrying on the conversation. 'Money shapes all our lives, Gabriel, whether we have it or lack it. Until now I've lacked it, and though I've inherited this house, I didn't inherit a lot of money to repair it and look after it properly. If I came to live here, I'd still have to let out rooms to give me something to live on.'

She'd already decided that she wasn't going to tell anyone

about having over £400 in the bank from the sale of the jewellery, for safety's sake, nor was she going to spend a penny of it she didn't need to once she'd sorted out where she was living. That money would represent security for the rest of her life if she looked after it carefully.

Gabriel seemed to shake off his dreams like a dog shaking off water. He gestured towards the house. 'Shall we see who lives here?'

'Can we do that?'

'You own it.'

'It seems – rude just to barge in, I mean.'

'Rent collectors do it all the time.'

Before they could move, the front door opened and a tall man who looked frazzled and weary came to stand in the doorway. He had a small child in his arms, was jiggling it about as if trying to stop it crying.

He jerked around suddenly to look back inside the house and they too could hear a faint voice calling for him. He glanced around then across at them, looking desperate.

'It's Ryan Cornish,' Gabriel said. 'We know him. Nice chap. It looks as if he needs help. Do you mind if I see what's wrong? I know you're paying me but—'

'Go on. In fact, I'll come with you. We may both be able to help. That young child looks feverish to me. I don't like to see children suffering.'

'He's a good father.'

She could guess that, see the love in the man's face as he looked down at the tiny child, who couldn't even be two years old.

Was he one of her tenants? It'd be nice to have children in the house.

8

Ryan swayed Nelly to and fro in his arms as he went downstairs to stand in the doorway, hoping the cooler air would reduce the heat that seemed to be consuming her little body. He'd gone against Hettie's urgent pleas not to take off the blanket the child had been wrapped in because it didn't make sense to him, as it was making her even warmer.

He was desperate to know what else he could do to help her and the other two, who weren't well, either.

Suddenly voices echoed down the stairwell. Devin had started crying loudly and saying he was too hot, and Hettie was calling out for Ryan to help her because Maddy was getting worse, too, and wouldn't keep her blanket on.

The old lady had already suggested fetching the doctor, and Ryan agreed that it was a good idea, but who would look after the children if he went to phone for Dr McDevitt? Poor Hettie would never be able to manage all three children in this state, so he looked around to see if there was someone passing who could make the phone call for him.

He looked across at the van parked outside the house. Two people had been sitting in it, but one of them was opening the door. Surely that damned agent wasn't going to try to cram another family into this house?

Then he realised it was Gabriel Harte getting out of the van and coming towards him, Jericho's brother. He'd go and phone for the doctor, surely? The Hartes always helped folk when they could.

'What's wrong, Ryan lad?'

'All the children have a fever and we don't know what to do. Hettie can't cope alone so it's lucky I didn't have a job to go to this afternoon. I'm that worried about them! I want to phone for the doctor, only I daren't leave her with all three of them to look after.'

A woman he didn't recognise followed Gabriel across the street, listened to what he'd said, then moved close enough to feel little Nelly's forehead. After that she lifted the tiny child's clothes to check her stomach. He didn't try to stop her because she seemed to know what she was doing and any advice would probably be more worth listening to than Hettie's suggestions for old-fashioned remedies.

The stranger looked up at him, not much taller than his shoulder but about his age, he'd guess. For all her plain looks, she had lovely eyes, full of compassion and kindness. He didn't normally notice clothes, but why any woman would wear that sack-like beige garment, he couldn't think. Perhaps it was all she owned, except she spoke with a posh accent and – ah, what did he know about anything lately?

He was still struggling to cope without Deirdre, who might not have been the world's most capable housewife, but who'd done far more than he realised to keep the family fed and clothed.

'I don't think it's measles or anything serious like that,' the woman said. 'Your little girl has no spots or rash on her body, so it's probably just a fever. They can be passed on quickly from one child to another. The doctor would know whether there's something going around and how serious it is, so you should definitely send for him.'

'I've two other children inside and they've got it too.'

'Let's get this one back into the house, then. If we take off more of her clothes we can cool her down. You shouldn't keep the warmth in.'

He was glad she'd said that. It seemed so obvious, whatever Hettie said, only he was still learning about children's needs so hadn't trusted his instincts.

'You should just leave her nappy on and cool her down with wet cloths. Is there someone who can help you with that? Is your wife not at home today?'

'My wife died a few months ago. There's an old woman who looks after the kids while I'm at work. Hettie does her best and she's kind to them, but she's panicking at the moment.'

'Let me see the others, then. Perhaps I can help.'

He didn't care who she was, she seemed to know more than he did about sick children, so he led the way inside carrying Nelly. The lady followed him up to their flat. Once there she took charge, seeming quite confident about what needed doing, which was more than he was. He'd let her give the orders as long as they made sense.

She left him holding Nelly and scooped up little Devin from the rug, sitting on a chair with him on her lap, talking soothingly. The little boy seemed to respond to her soft voice and let her start taking his clothes off without resisting. She stopped doing that to say, 'Your older daughter is too hot as well.'

Then she turned to Hettie and said, 'Could you get us some cold water and damp cloths, please?'

'Yes, miss.'

From her tone Hettie recognised the voice of authority, and he looked at the stranger with more respect before turning to Maddy, who was sitting listlessly on the rug, looking flushed and uncomfortable. He got down beside her, still holding Nelly.

'I'm too hot, Daddy. Why does Hettie keep trying to cover me with a blanket?'

'Sometimes that helps with sick people. But not this time, the lady says.' Maddy at once began to remove her outer clothes, rejecting any help. 'Good girl.'

As Ryan continued to rock Nelly to and fro, he said soothingly, 'We'll soon get you cooler, my little love.' He wasn't
sure she was listening, though, because she hadn't stopped
crying miserably. She was so young, still, only eighteen months
old, and looked so vulnerable today, he was terrified of losing
her, too.

Who was the stranger? He looked across at Gabriel and
jerked his head towards her in an unspoken question.

'This is Miss Porter – Miss Porter, Ryan Cornish.'

'Pleased to meet you.'

But she didn't look at him as she spoke, was concentrating
on the little boy on her lap, so Ryan checked that Maddy
wasn't shivering or anything, and simply waited. Who'd have
thought that such a meek-looking lady could take charge like
this? Or inspire such confidence?

Hettie dipped some water from the clean water bucket with
the jug they kept just for that, pouring it into a big bowl. She
opened the cupboard door and produced a couple of clean
rags, dampened them and handed him and Miss Porter one
each, then got one for Maddy.

When the stranger started sponging Devin down, Maddy
did the same, and Ryan dealt with Nelly. And it did seem to
help, thank goodness. When Nelly sighed and stopped griz-
zling, closing her eyes and not pushing the cool wet cloth
away, he began to feel more hopeful.

'I was looking after some children a few years ago when a
similar thing happened.' Miss Porter was still concentrating
on cooling Devin, not even looking at Ryan. 'This is what
the doctor suggested we try first then, and it helped a lot.'

'Do you still want me to go and phone for Dr McDevitt,
Ryan?' Gabriel asked.

He looked automatically at his visitor for guidance.

'It'd be wisest to get your doctor to check them,' she said.
'You can't be too careful with little children.'

Ryan nodded agreement. 'If you don't mind, lad.'

Gabriel looked at Miss Porter for permission. 'The nearest phone is at the grocer's in Birch End, so I'll be away a few minutes if that's all right, miss?'

'It'll be fine. Sick children are far more important than driving me around.'

'I won't be long, then. You look after Miss Porter, Ryan.'

Ryan turned back to the lady. 'Thanks for your help, miss. They're looking more comfortable already.'

Devin was lying limply in the lady's lap, letting her rub a cool wet cloth across his thin little body. She bent down and dropped a kiss on his cheek, smiling at him. Ryan didn't think she even realised she'd done that. Her smile made her whole face beautiful. She must love children.

Hettie was helping Maddy, who was, as usual, trying to do everything for herself and pushing the old woman's hand away. He smiled as he watched. As usual, Maddy won, so he continued to work on Nelly. 'There's a good girl,' he said encouragingly. 'Are you all right, Maddy love?'

'It feels better, Daddy.'

'Good, good.'

Gabriel hurried out of the house and drove back to the main street in Birch End to pay his tuppence to the shopkeeper and phone the doctor from the grocer's, as folk around here did.

Mrs McDevitt answered the phone, said there was definitely a fever going around and to cool the children down till the doctor could get to them. 'A wet cloth would be the easiest way probably. He's going out on his rounds in a few minutes, so you've caught him just in time.'

So that confirmed it: Miss Porter did know what she was doing. Who'd have thought it of such a quiet, spinster lady? Eh, she certainly loved children, that one did. You could see it on her face as she cared for them.

The more time Gabriel spent with her, the more he'd liked her, and this incident with the children had set the seal on it.

When he got back to the house, the little boy was lying in his father's arms looking exhausted, and Miss Porter was cuddling the smallest child. Hettie had one arm around Maddy's shoulders. It was a cosy domestic scene.

All three children were looking weary but far more comfortable, so Gabriel said quietly, 'Maybe while we wait for the doctor I should explain why we're here today, Ryan. Miss Porter is the new owner of this house and therefore your landlord, and—'

His friend stiffened and turned to glare at her, interrupting Gabriel. 'Then you ought to do something about the drains here and stop charging such extortionate rents for hovels. If I could find anywhere else to live, I'd move out quick smart, believe me, and then maybe my children wouldn't have got ill like this.'

She gaped at him, then frowned. 'How much do you pay in rent? What do you call extortionate? I've only just inherited the house and the rent agent hasn't got the last quarter's accounts ready yet.'

There was dead silence, then Ryan said stiffly, 'Oh. Sorry, then. But now you do know, I hope you'll do something about it all. I have to pay ten shillings a week for this place.'

Gabriel looked at him in surprise. 'That's a lot for two rooms in Backshaw Moss.'

'I agree, but it was that or live in the street after the landlord gave us notice to leave our other house. Six years we'd been there, and never once late with the rent, which was hard at times, but he gave me only a week to move out!'

'Ryan, it's not Miss Porter's fault that the drains need sorting out here.'

'And the rest of it! There are other problems too, like that missing drainpipe.'

'Aye, well, just listen instead of interrupting, will you, lad? She's trying to find out if Welch is doing an honest job.'

Ryan let out a scornful laugh.

'She doesn't know him like we do,' Gabriel added sharply. 'Give her a chance. She hasn't even seen around the house yet, let alone found out any details of how much it's being rented for. She stopped looking round to help you with the kids. That alone tells you what sort of person she is.'

There was dead silence again, and Ryan bent his head for a moment, trying to gather his thoughts. 'Oh. I see.' But though he tried to speak in a conciliatory manner, every time he looked around he felt angry, and all he could manage was, 'Well, I'm sorry if I upset you, Miss Porter, but you're in for a few shocks with this place. And I suppose you'll throw me out now for complaining.'

She folded her arms and scowled back at him, speaking sharply with her fancy southern accent. 'I wasn't intending to throw anyone out, let alone someone with three sick children. But you'll have to give me time to investigate.'

He suddenly remembered the kiss she'd given Devin and that calmed him a little more. 'Sorry. But they're all I have now.'

'Any father would be anxious. I'd be grateful if you keep it to yourself that you've met me already, though, Mr Cornish. I want to see what Mr Welch says is happening here when he shows me around later today.'

'I'll do that. And, well, thank you for your help with the kids. I'm grateful.'

Ryan was feeling guilty for lashing out at her without finding out the facts first, only he was so tired after a disturbed night that he was finding it hard to think straight. All he knew was that his kids were ill and he hated living here, was ashamed not to be able to provide a better home for them. But that wasn't her fault, was it? He owed her an apology.

'I'm really sorry for snapping at you, Miss Porter. I didn't get much sleep last night because there was a fight down the street and the kids were upset by it and didn't settle again. They must have been sickening for this fever. But still, that's no excuse for being rude to you.'

Her expression softened visibly, so he added, 'Look, I can tell you anything you need to know about the real state of this house, as well as about my own situation. I can't help overhearing what Welch says when he collects the rents because he has such a loud voice. I know exactly how much the other tenants pay. And he's crammed in more of them than is safe. He put another family in the cellar last week, and that isn't fit for habitation by animals, let alone human beings. They have to pay five shillings a week for it.'

'He rented out the cellar? Good heavens. That will be useful to know.'

She didn't seem to realise that she'd dropped another of her tender kisses, this time on Nelly's cheek, and was still rubbing the child gently with the wet cloth.

Ryan watched his baby daughter nestle against her trustingly and his heart clenched. His children needed loving, and he was working such long hours it was hard to give them as much attention as he wanted to.

The midwife had been right, damn her. A man needed a wife to help run a house and bring up his children, however little he wanted another one.

'There are five sets of people in the house at the moment, and—'

She interrupted, 'What? Are you sure? I was told three?'

'There were always four, though the attic rooms aren't really fit for habitation either because the roof leaks. He's got two lots up there. The house will get worse and worse if something's not done about the leaks. Welch won't get anything mended. When it rains, the folk in the attics have to set buckets to catch the drips.'

'I'll definitely see to that. Five lots of people! The list the clerk at my lawyer's in London gave me said there were three tenant families here.'

Gabriel whistled softly. It looked as if Welch was cheating his client. Which didn't surprise him with that sod.

Miss Porter was looking thoughtful. 'We need to find out the facts before I change anything. If you're going to be all right with the children, Mr Cornish, as soon as the doctor arrives, I'll leave. I'll come back at two o'clock as arranged to go around with Welch, but I won't let him know I've been here already.'

'I hope you can sort it all out. This must have been a nice house once, but there really shouldn't be so many people crammed into it. There's the danger of fire from the cooking, and the sewage system keeps getting blocked. I've had to sort it out twice this month, and Welch refuses even to pay for the materials.'

'Ryan's a plumber,' Gabriel put in. 'So he knows about such things.'

'I'll pay you for your work and we'll talk about repairing the plumbing properly at another time. If you can do that job, it's yours. First of all, however, I need to deal with Mr Welch.'

'He can be violent if he's upset,' Gabriel warned her. 'Don't confront him on your own.'

'No. I'd better be careful. If you don't have any other jobs booked, could you stay with me for another two or three days?'

A voice called up the stairwell, 'Where are the sick children?'

Ryan called out, 'They're up here, Dr McDevitt.'

The doctor's footsteps sounded on the stairs and when he came in, he went straight across to the three little ones.

Ryan watched Gabriel usher Miss Porter out, after which he turned his attention to what the doctor was saying about his children. Thank goodness it wasn't a bad fever that was going around.

9

Gabriel took Miss Porter for a drive around Birch End, stopping to show her a path that led up to a walk over the moors. At just before two o'clock, they came back and he parked the van outside Number 23 again.

It was ten past the hour before Welch drove up and got out of his vehicle. He stood waiting as if he expected Miss Porter to come to him.

'Let him wait,' she said to her companion. 'Pretend we're chatting.'

Gabriel winked at her. 'Well, we are. Even me.'

She chuckled. It was nice that he could laugh at himself. Strange how comfortable she felt with this young man, as if she'd known him for ever.

Welch began frowning and eventually came across to the van, bending to speak to her through the open window. 'Are you not joining me, Miss Porter?'

'I was finishing a conversation. Since you were late, our meeting was clearly not important to you, so I was asking Gabriel to explain a few thing about the valley. I can always look round the house on my own if you're too busy to get here on time.'

She could see that her response had surprised him.

'I was delayed by a traffic hold-up in the town centre. Not my fault, I assure you. You'll need me to show you round because I know more about the house and its tenants than anyone else does. I can explain anything that puzzles you.'

She eyed him, head on one side. He clearly thought she was stupid. He'd spoken to her in a slow, patronising voice, which annoyed her.

'Shall we go inside then, Miss Porter?'

She got out of the van. 'Wait a moment. I want to take a good look at the house from the outside first and I may have some questions. That drainpipe needs repairing for a start. Why has it been left so long?'

'What? Oh, that one. It's been repaired once. The lads playing in the street must have pulled it off again.'

'I'm not blind, Mr Welch. That pipe must have been lacking its bottom length for weeks if not months to have caused that much staining on the wall below it.'

He looked at her sharply, as if seeing her for the first time.

She stared straight back at him. She'd just caught him lying to her before they even went inside. What other lies was he intending to tell her today? 'How many tenants did you say there were, Mr Welch?'

'Um, three families.'

'You sound uncertain.'

'Well, there's one temporary group who were homeless. My wife was worried about the poor things so she let them have a room just for a little while. They'll be moving out once they've found somewhere else to live, by next week at the latest.'

'I hope they're paying rent while they're here. Temporary payments can so easily be forgotten in the accounts.'

'Oh, yes. Just, er, five shillings a week, I think my wife said.'

'I shall be interested to see the accounts. Do you have them with you?'

'Er, no.'

'Then I'll come to your office and pick up the account book and other paperwork after we've finished here.' She watched his false smile vanish completely.

'It'd be better if I brought them to you tomorrow. They're rough and untidy at the moment. You'll have trouble understanding them.'

'Nonetheless, I'd like to have them today so that I can find out how I stand financially. I'm sure I can cope with the arithmetic involved and there will be similar accounts in the books from previous quarters to guide me. How long have you been collecting the rents for this house?'

'Um, is it two or three years? I forget.'

She raised an eyebrow at him and waited.

'Nearly three years,' he said hastily. 'Miss Chapman bought these three houses a few months before she died and Mr Beaton decided to keep them. He asked me to continue collecting the rents because he was satisfied with how I was dealing with the properties.'

She continued to study him and he wriggled uncomfortably, as if caught out in a lie. She didn't allow herself to smile, but she wanted to. She'd used this severe look on the Beaton children when they tried to lie to her. She hadn't realised it'd work on a grown man as well. She doubted Welch realised he'd betrayed himself.

She looked back at the houses. 'Who owns the other two houses now? Do you collect their rents too?'

'Um, no. There's no one living in either of them at the moment but I'm paid a small amount to keep an eye on the outside of the buildings.'

'You haven't said who owns them now.'

'Mr Neven says the owners wish to remain anonymous and deal with me through him.'

How strange! The lawyer had said nothing about the other houses to her. 'All right, Mr Welch. Let's go inside my house. Tell me about the ground-floor tenants.'

'Um, it's a widow with two grown-up children, or is it three? I'm afraid I can't be sure of that. She pays the rent regularly, keeps the place clean, and has the whole of the ground-floor flat. Those are the best rooms in the house.' He moved towards the stairs.

She stayed where she was in the hall. 'I'd like to see them and meet the tenant, if she's at home.'

'She values her privacy, so as long as she pays the rent I leave her be. I always find it best to leave good tenants in peace.'

'The situation has changed now, though, has it not? I wish to see my inheritance and meet the occupants. Where does that door on the other side of the hall lead to?'

'Oh, it's blocked off on the other side. When this house was divided into flats, they made the door at the right of the hall the only entrance to the ground-floor flat.'

'I see.' She waited.

He sighed and knocked on the door to the right. A woman answered, looking at him as if annoyed to be disturbed.

'This is the new owner, Miss Porter. She's come to inspect the building.'

The woman scowled at Bella then turned back to him. 'You said you'd give me notice of anyone coming to see the place, Vin— Mr Welch.'

'I didn't find out myself till this morning that Miss Porter had arrived in Rivenshaw.'

'Well, it's not tidy because I've had one of my headaches. So if you can come back another time, it'd be better.'

Bella was getting annoyed at her presence being ignored. 'You still haven't introduced this lady to me, Mr Welch.'

He paused, blinked as if he'd not expected her to join in, then gestured to the woman. 'This is Mrs Goodby.' He reached out and pushed the door open. 'We'll just have a quick glance round, eh, Pammy?'

So they were both on first name terms, were they?

'Can't you come back after I've cleared up?'

Bella grew angry. 'No, we can't.' She went in past him.

The flat was definitely not tidy, nor was it all that clean. In fact, it had a sour smell to it. There were four main rooms and a kitchen from whose window a big tin bathtub was visible hanging on the outside wall in what looked like quite a large backyard.

She turned to Mr Welch. 'Isn't there a bathroom in the house?'

'No. It's very old-fashioned. And it'd be a waste of money to put one in. It'd not be kept clean by our sort of tenants.'

'I'd use one!' Mrs Goodby protested. 'I enjoy a good lie in a warm bath.'

She didn't look as if she did that very often, Bella thought – and neither did Mr Welch, come to think of it. In fact, he had an unwashed smell to him that she found offensive now she was at close quarters.

She wrinkled her nose at the strong smell of unwashed bodies in one bedroom, then studied it. There were clearly several people sleeping in it, using mattresses on the floor, and battered cardboard boxes here and there. She was beginning to wonder whether this flat was being used as a lodging house.

She didn't voice her suspicions, but made a mental note to ask Mr Cornish about who came in and out of it at another time. She didn't think he'd lie to her. He'd probably err on the side of bluntness in everything he said or did, she'd guess. He had that sort of look to him.

When they'd finished inspecting the rooms, she knew she couldn't leave the situation like this, so said firmly, 'I'd prefer you to keep the place cleaner than this in future, Mrs Goodby. I shall come back in a couple of days to check that you've cleaned it up . . . properly.'

The woman breathed deeply, glared at Mr Welch, but said nothing.

He winked at her, not seeming to realise Bella could see that too. This man wasn't nearly as clever as he thought he was, as well as being dishonest.

As they went upstairs Welch said, 'A Mr Cornish lives here. He's only been a tenant for a few weeks. He's a widower with three children. Pays his rent on time, which is the main thing.'

Mr Cornish came to answer the knock on the door, giving no sign that he'd met her before, thank goodness.

He put one finger to his lips when Welch started to speak. 'The children are poorly and I've only just got them off to sleep.'

'Nonetheless, your new landlady wishes to see her property. We needn't take long.'

Why did Welch always speak so loudly? Bella wondered. Was he going deaf?

Mr Cornish sighed, stepped back and gestured to them to enter.

When Mr Welch opened his mouth to speak again, Bella took it upon herself to shush him, saying in a whisper, 'If there are sick children we should keep quiet. I can look round without speaking.'

She studied the second room, which was being used as a bedroom and where the children were lying in one big bed. There was also a narrow single bed and another single mattress leaning against one wall, with a neat pile of bedding beside it.

She said nothing, but it was light enough for her to see how clean the whole place was compared to the ground-floor flat. Untidy, yes, but someone obviously scrubbed these wooden floorboards regularly, right to the edges.

They went back into the main room, where there was a sink in one corner and next to it a gas stove, also clean, and a small table.

She was sure she'd caught a glimpse of shame on Mr

Cornish's face as she studied the rooms. The poor man must be struggling to cope without a wife, had probably had a better home before this.

Mr Welch hovered impatiently near the door and Bella realised he was trying to get her out of there as fast as he could. Well, she'd oblige him this time because Mr Cornish needed peace and quiet for his children.

Once they'd left, she said, 'I was pleased to see that those rooms are being kept clean.'

'They weren't till I told him a couple of weeks ago that he'd be out if he didn't clean up.'

She didn't believe that. You could tell when cleaning had been skimpy and infrequent. 'Then why didn't you tell Mrs Goodby the same thing?'

'She's been a tenant for a long time, pays her rent on the dot, doesn't damage the property, so I give her a bit of leeway.'

The top-floor tenants weren't at home, so Welch unlocked the doors to show four small, untidy rooms with low ceilings. They were clearly split into two dwellings, which made it four sets of permanent tenants, not three.

They shared a sink and gas cooker on the landing, and these rooms, too, smelled of unwashed bodies and clothes. She would, she decided, get the whole house scrubbed and cleaned properly before she moved in.

'Which of these rooms is being used by the people your wife felt sorry for?'

'Um, those two.' He pointed to the left.

'Were they empty before that?'

'Have been for a while.'

Strange, she thought. Mr Cornish had said it was hard to find rooms to rent. She'd have to ask him and Gabriel about that.

With a sigh, she turned to follow him downstairs again. She was definitely going to find another rent collector.

10

Welch tried to lead her straight out of the house, but she stopped him on the first-floor landing. 'Where does that door lead to? It wasn't part of Mr Cornish's flat.'

'It's a room that needs a few repairs before it can be rented out.' He started down the stairs.

'Come back and open the door. How many times must I tell you that I wish to see all parts of the house?' She'd need copies of all the keys, too, since this one had a separate lock.

His hesitation was accompanied by another scowl.

She folded her arms and waited, staring at him steadily and seeing the moment he gave in.

With a sigh he pulled a jingling key ring out of his pocket again and sorted out a large, old-fashioned key. When he opened the door she was surprised to see that the inside was crammed full, stacked past shoulder height with pieces of furniture and cardboard boxes or tea chests containing who knew what else.

'To whom do these things belong?'

'The room's been used for storage for as long as I've been collecting the rents. I was going to clear it out after Miss Chapman died, but that London lawyer told me to leave it as it was.'

Was that another lie? Surely Mr Neven would have told her about it if he'd known about this? She came to what she hoped was the obvious conclusion. 'Then the contents must be mine now. Give me the key and I'll check with Mr Neven. Since it seems to be mine, I'll do the clearing out myself. I might find some things I can use.'

She turned the key and pulled it out of the lock with the other keys jangling on the key ring. When he would have taken it from her, she took a step away from him and started to slide the keys round till she could get this one off it, then stopped to compare it to the next key. 'Oh, look. There are two identical ones. How useful!' She removed them both and dropped them into her handbag, then had a thought and looked at the key ring again.

'Which one is the front door key?'

He stiffened.

'I'll naturally need my own key.'

He scowled even more deeply and indicated a key further along the row. 'That one.'

She checked it and nodded. 'And there are two keys again, so I'll take one.' She twisted it off and dropped it in her handbag.

He tried and failed to hide his annoyance.

Could he have been planning to steal the contents of this room now she'd taken over? She wouldn't be surprised. And did he really expect that she'd not want her own keys? Now she came to think of it, she was surprised that Mr Neven hadn't given her one.

'That's it, Miss Porter. You've seen everything.'

'No, I haven't. I saw from the road that there's a cellar. I'd like to see that as well.'

She said nothing as she followed him down into the dark, stuffy space illuminated only by the air well she'd noticed in the garden. The cellar contained mattresses and a table with two rickety chairs. She peered into the coal cellar next to it, but there was no coal there. There were rat droppings, though. She shuddered and made a mental note to call a rat catcher in as well. There must be one in such a poor area.

When they got outside, Mr Welch said with false brightness, 'There you are, then. It might not be the sort of place a lady like you would live in, but it'll bring you in a good return on the money invested and you can be sure I'll keep the tenants up to date on payments.'

She didn't comment on that. 'We need to go to your office now to pick up the account book. I'll follow you straight there.'

'But I've already told you that Mrs Welch hasn't had time yet to finish the accounts properly.'

'Then I'll take the unfinished ones and finish the totals myself. And I'd like the previous years' account books too. I'm sure you have them still. The lawyer will have wanted to see them when Miss Chapman died and the houses were transferred to Mr Beaton, won't he? Your wife will presumably have shown in it the times someone hasn't paid the rent.'

'Um, right. Yes, of course. Only I usually make sure they all pay, or else I throw them out. That's why I'm hired. But it sometimes takes a while to get new tenants.'

That was not what Mr Ryan had said about finding accommodation and she knew who she trusted.

'I'll see you at your office, then.'

He nodded and got into his car, setting off immediately, driving like a man in a hurry.

When she got into the van, Bella felt all the energy drain from her and sat for a moment or two, trying to calm down. She wouldn't have thought she'd have had the courage to stand up to Welch, yet she had done it. Only she felt rather shaky now that the anger at his cheating had subsided a little.

'Are you all right?' Gabriel asked.

'Yes . . . no.' She didn't have to pretend with this man. 'I'm rather upset at what I found. I'm sure that man's been cheating on the rents.'

'Wouldn't surprise me.'

'And I think the ground-floor tenant takes in lodgers.'

He looked at her in surprise. 'It's well known. Didn't anyone tell you?'

'No, they didn't.'

'Hmm. I wonder if they have a council licence for doing that?'

'I'm wondering about a lot of things. Anyway, let's get on with it. Could you take me to Mr Welch's office next, please? I'm going to get hold of those account books today if it's the last thing I do. And I think you'd better come in with me this time, please.'

He was still looking at her in a slightly anxious way, so she said baldly, 'I've not had to stand up for myself like that for many years. It was – difficult for me. That's why I needed a minute or two to calm down afterwards.'

'I hate cheats and thieves.'

'So do I. I shall have to find a new agent to collect the rents or perhaps if I move in, I'll be able to collect them myself, especially if I find some more pleasant tenants for the attic flat, ones who keep it clean.'

Gabriel gave her a look that said he wasn't certain that was a good thing for her to do and didn't start the van straight away. He was looking thoughtful now.

'I'm not sure you should move in. Hey, I know what. Why don't you talk to my mother before you do it? She'll advise you better than I could. As I said before, we had to live in the Moss when she came out of hospital because we'd spent our last penny on getting her medical help.'

'Would she mind?'

'Not at all. She'd be happy to help.'

Bella was still upset enough to blurt out how she felt. 'You must be a kind family, then. You're even being kind to me, like the brother I never had and always wanted.' She hadn't meant to say that last part aloud. Oh dear. What must he think of her?

'You remind me of my sister, especially when you smile. She doesn't live in the valley now and I miss her. Shall I adopt you as an extra relative? Cousin Bella, perhaps?'

She gaped at him, thinking he was mocking her, then realised he wasn't the sort of person to do that. And he was talking easily, not in short jerky sentences. 'You mean that, don't you?'

'I usually keep my thoughts to myself, except with people I trust absolutely.'

'I've had to keep my own feelings to myself for the past few years, but I'm going to say what I think now. So yes please. I'd like to ask your mother's advice, and I'd like to be someone's cousin, even if it's only pretend.' She sighed and added before she could stop herself, 'I've been feeling very alone lately.'

He took his hand off the steering wheel for a moment to pat hers as it lay on her lap. 'I'll tell Mam, and introduce you to her and my brothers.'

'Won't they think it ridiculous when you and I have only just met?'

'Not them. We all have friends who are closer than relatives, and Mam likes helping people.' He smiled. 'She collects them.'

Then his smile faded. 'Why didn't you have any friends?'

'I wasn't allowed to bring strangers into the house, and there was always some reason why I couldn't keep an engagement to meet someone. I stopped trying.'

He gaped at her for a moment. 'Eh, lass, lass! Your real cousin sounds to be a horrible man.'

He patted her hand again then started the van and set off. 'And just to make things clear, when I do speak, I never say anything I don't mean. So I meant it when I offered to make you our honorary cousin.'

She gulped and felt tears well in her eyes. 'Thank you.'

She mopped her eyes quickly, then said what she had been

thinking aloud. 'Gabriel, I think I'm going to move into that house whatever your mother says. After all, it's right on the edge of Birch End, so it can't be as bad as the poorer parts of Backshaw Moss. I'm going to get rid of all the tenants except for Mr Cornish. His rooms are kept nice and clean, and those children need a home. Then I'm going to find someone to scrub the place out thoroughly before I move in. And I'll make the top floor one flat again and get a clean, reliable tenant.'

'He's a good man, Ryan is. Struggling at the moment.'

'Yes. I could tell. They're lovely children. I'll live in the ground-floor flat. If I put someone honest in the top floor, maybe I can collect the rents myself.'

'It won't be easy, especially at first.'

'Nothing's easy. You can only do your best. I'm going to fire Welch today. Then will you help me give notice to the tenants?'

'Yes.' They drew up outside Welch's so-called office.

She took a deep breath. 'Let's get this done, then. I'm glad you will be coming in with me.'

'Wouldn't miss it. I'm looking forward to seeing his face.'

'I'm also glad that I can hire you for a few more days in case I need protecting.'

'Yes.' He grinned and added, 'I'm always ready to earn money.'

'Thank you. You're very kind.' But she knew he wouldn't just be looking after her for the money. She was so lucky to have met him.

Bella braced herself and got out of the van. She could do this. She must. There was no one else who could do it for her, however kind they were.

Her inheritance wasn't just giving her money, but making her take charge of her life. Which was just as important.

Thank you, Cousin James, she thought. I wonder if you knew what a difference this money would make to me.

11

That same afternoon, Roy Tyler took a stroll along Daisy Street. He needed to decide whether to suggest to the council that they make this the first area to be 'improved' under the conditions of the special grant. And if so, how best he could organise the first stage.

His friend Charlie Willcox, who was on the town council, had discussed the job with him 'in theory'. Then later the mayor had asked officially for his expert opinion on doing the work needed, and some idea of the cost. Apparently, a certain group of council members wanted to use the money to improve their own slum properties, which were scattered here and there around the Moss.

Roy hadn't needed telling who would be leading the opposing group: Higgerson, one of the worst builders he'd ever encountered.

Doing it piecemeal, Roy was certain, would be highly inefficient. You had to go about it in an organised way, as you'd approach any job. And if you couldn't afford to clear out the entire slum, then you should do it in logical parcels, so to speak.

It'd be a shame for the grant to be forfeited, especially when so much needed doing to Backshaw Moss's narrow streets and alleys. And just as much a shame for it to be used for the benefit of certain slum landlords rather than for the hapless slum dwellers struggling to cope with appalling living conditions.

He'd love to get stuck into the job. Apart from anything else, it could provide employment for men who'd been out of work for years, and give a start to younger lads who had nothing to look forward to but idling around and filling the long hours as best they could.

Eh, hard times seemed to have settled on the north in the long years since the Great War ended. Was it really almost seventeen years since the lads who'd survived its horrors came home?

He saw Ryan Cornish standing at the doorway of one of the better houses near the end of the street, and stopped to have a chat.

'You're looking tired, lad.'

'Short of sleep. The children have had a fever. Dr McDevitt says it's a mild one that's going round, thank goodness, and they'll be right as rain in a couple of days. They've settled down and they're sleeping now, so Hettie's keeping an eye on them while I get a breath of fresh air.' He was overtaken by a huge yawn.

Roy took a step backwards and studied the house. 'What's this place like inside? And the other two houses? They're of a very similar design and look nicer than most buildings round here. But faults can lie hidden. Are they worth saving, do you think, or are they all three ready for knocking down?'

'Well worth saving if the new owners do it properly. They were well built, so they're basically sound, but there are a few things that need sorting out, like that damned drainpipe outside, and the outside plumbing.'

Roy made a mental note to give any plumbing jobs to Ryan in return for this information. He'd used him a few times and found him very thorough.

'I've met the new owner of our house, Mr Tyler, and she seems an honest woman, but whether she'll do something is anyone's guess. Maybe she won't be able to afford it.'

'Who is she?'

'A Miss Porter, but she only owns this middle house. You'd have to contact the lawyer who handled Miss Chapman's estate to find the other owners.'

'Will this woman be able to see through Welch? Because he doesn't believe in repairs, let alone improvements, from what I've seen.'

'Oh, she can see through him all right. She's a bit timid until she gets angry, which she did with him. Then bam! Her voice changes and you should see her eyes sparkle. I heard her tell him and that Goodby woman on the ground floor that she wanted the place cleaning up properly and would be back to check that it had been done in two days.'

Roy chuckled. 'I'd like to have seen their faces.'

'So would I. I only overheard the conversation because sound echoes up that stairwell. Gabriel Harte has been driving her around today and he seems to like her, too. You get a feeling for some people, don't you?' He was still surprised at how much he'd liked her himself.

'Yes, you get a feeling either for or against some people quite quickly. I agree. Welch won't like having an owner living locally and seeing what he gets up to.'

'He's always been a rogue, that one, and he's only playing at being respectable. He's misjudged Miss Porter, though. She's shrewder than she looks.'

'Older lady, is she?'

Ryan shrugged. 'Hard to tell her age, she's so old-fashioned looking. She speaks with a posh southern accent. You'd recognise her as a dyed-in-the-wool spinster the minute you clapped eyes on her. She's only just inherited and was shocked at how bad a condition parts of the house are in. Miss Porter has been hoping to live here herself, Gabriel said. I'm a bit worried that I'm going to get thrown out so she can have our two rooms. She won't need the biggest flat downstairs for just herself, will she?'

'Who knows? Do you know where she's staying? I think I might send my wife round to speak to her about the house, see what her plans are now she's had a proper look round it. Women usually find it easier to talk to other women.'

'She's probably staying at Mrs Tucker's. That's where the taxi drivers usually take respectable ladies looking for accommodation. Gabriel Harte could tell you for certain. He seemed to be on good terms with her, was chatting away.'

'Gabriel Harte was chatting away to someone?'

'Yes. Surprised me too. I know he's usually quiet, but every now and then he starts talking and he's worth listening to. But that's only when it's something he really cares about.'

Roy continued to study the three end houses, then ambled off to finish his casual survey of the area. The information he'd gained from Ryan had been very helpful. He drove home via the house where Gabriel's mother was the resident housekeeper. Her two younger sons were living with her in a separate dwelling at the rear, so he went around to knock on that door. He'd organised the building work at the back and he gave the new wall a proprietorial pat as he passed by. Good bricklaying, that. There were some good tradesmen underemployed in the valley. Such a waste.

'Hello, Gwynneth. I was wanting to catch your Gabriel to check something with him.'

'He's out on a job.'

'Still out, eh? I'm looking for the woman who hired him today. And I'd like to ask him what he thinks of her before I say anything to her.'

'Well, she's staying at Mrs Tucker's, so she's definitely respectable. That's where he went to pick her up this morning. I can't tell you what he thinks of her till he comes home. He'll be out all day with her.'

'I'll get Ethel to phone and leave a message at Mrs Tucker's, then she can go to speak to Miss Porter later. Thanks for your help.'

He ambled off again. You couldn't keep anything secret in the valley for long, so he needed to act quickly before Higgerson got to hear exactly what was being planned by those on the town council who were determined to use the special grant money to get rid of the slums.

This time he headed for the newsagent in the village to buy a paper. Best to make sure people didn't realise he'd only been interested in seeing Daisy Street today.

'Out for a walk, Mr Tyson?' the shopkeeper asked.

'Yes. You know me. I get twitchy if I have to stay indoors on a fine day. I thought I'd walk across from the office to pick up a newspaper.'

'Well, you shouldn't let yourself get too chilled. It might be fine but it's still a bit cold. How's the baby?'

Roy beamed at the question. He loved the baby he and his wife had adopted recently. 'Robbie's doing really well. He's a grand little chap.'

'That's good to hear. It was kind of you to adopt him.'

'One of the best things we ever did. I haven't seen my wife so happy for years.'

Another customer came in just then, so Roy went on his way, thinking about his family. He'd been doubtful about adopting, if truth be told, but it'd made Ethel so happy, he'd not regretted it for a moment.

There was nothing like having a baby in the house for making you feel like a family again. Their own son might have died just as he reached manhood, but Roy had a new son now and hoped to live long enough to see Robbie grow into a man and continue the family building business.

Bella got out of the van in Carrier Street, feeling as if she were about to walk into the lion's den. When Gabriel locked the van doors and waited for her to lead the way, she breathed a sigh of relief that he was with her. 'I'm going to tell Mr Welch that the rent money for the last quarter must be in the bank by the end of today. Do you think that's asking too much?'

'No. It's your money and it's owed to you. He has no excuse for holding on to it.'

She nodded, gathered up all her courage, and walked inside. She knew where to go now, so knocked smartly on Welch's door and, when no one answered, she simply pushed it open.

Welch and his wife looked up from the desk, and if ever guilt had been written on someone's face it was staring at her from both of theirs.

She moved forward, looking down at the papers and the heading Daisy Street. 'My accounts?'

'They aren't finished,' the woman said, her voice sharp and her tone insolent. She even splayed her hand across the top of the pile to prevent their new client from seeing what was scribbled on them in pencil.

That was just what was needed to give Bella the final push to act. She looked down at the pile of papers with scribblings all over the top one and whipped them smartly sideways from under Mrs Welch's hand, taking her by surprise.

'Our accounts are not finished!' The woman tried to grab them back.

'My accounts, you mean.'

As Mr Welch took a step towards her, scowling and clearly intending to take the papers back, Bella clutched them to her chest and Gabriel came to stand beside her, towering over everyone. She hadn't realised how threatening he could look.

He glanced quickly down at the desk, picked up another couple of pieces of paper and handed them to her. 'You'll want to study these at your leisure now, won't you, Miss Porter?'

He nudged her gently away from the table, then turned back to say slowly and emphatically to Welch. 'Miss Porter asked me to tell you that if the money owed to her for this past quarter isn't in her bank account by the end of the afternoon, she'll be going to see Sergeant Deemer and ask him to find out where it's got to.'

Both the Welches gaped at him and edged closer to one another.

Bella felt relief shudder through her. She'd been trying to pluck up the courage to say this and, to her shame, failing. She was so lucky to have Gabriel helping her.

'I should have been firmer with Welch from the start,' she muttered as she got into the van. 'Only he's a bit frightening. So is his wife. She looks like she'd scratch your eyes out if you upset her. But I'm disappointed in myself.'

'He and his wife were two to your one today, and you're not a big woman, so it's a good thing you had the sense to take me with you. You were right to be wary. Welch has been known to get violent at times, though the police have never been able to pin down any proof.'

Bella nodded, unable to speak for the shudders still roiling around inside her. 'I saw his fists clench and wondered if he was going to punch me – or you.'

He shrugged. 'He's getting a bit old and fat for fighting, usually hires others to do that for him. He could have tried, but I know how to defend myself and my friends. I've never been able to stand bullies, so I'm glad to help, apart from the money you're paying me.'

'You're well and truly earning it.' She studied his face. He was at least a decade younger than her, she suspected, but he was much wiser in the ways of the world. He wasn't only good-looking, he also had kindness in his gaze somehow. Had he meant it about his family adopting her as a cousin? People didn't usually do things like that, not in her experience, anyway.

She'd lived with unkind people for so long, she didn't know how to begin to judge kind ones.

Mr Neven had been kind to her too, taking her into his own home.

'Ready to go now?'

'Yes.' Gabriel drove back up the hill to Birch End and Bella looked down as the various papers crackled in her hands. She would learn a lot from them, she was sure.

This time, Gabriel turned off to the left before they got to the main street of the village and stopped outside a large detached house that looked as if it was well cared for. Even the garden was attractive, with clumps of early daffodils dancing happily here and there.

Gabriel gestured to the house. 'Mrs Pollard bought this place, then soon afterwards she married Wilf, who was a widower. He and his children came to live with her here. It's even bigger than it looks from the street. Me and my younger brother Lucas live in a separate part at the back with our mother, who acts as their housekeeper. Our elder brother Jericho got married recently and moved out.'

He studied Bella intently. 'I'll go in first, if you don't mind, and tell Ma about you. Any road, you look as if you need a minute or two of quiet time.'

'I do. Thank you.'

When he came back, Bella opened the van door and got out. Gabriel was accompanied by an older woman, who came straight across to her side, smiling.

She didn't wait for him to introduce her, but said, 'I'm Gwynneth Harte. Come in and have a nice cup of tea, Miss Porter. It sounds as if you've been having a bit of trouble and I'm so glad my Gabriel brought you back here. The kettle boiled recently and it won't take me a minute to brew us a pot of tea.'

Bella was swept inside on a sea of trivial but somehow

comforting words, which didn't seem to need answers other than murmurs and nods.

When they were all seated round the kitchen table, Gwynneth looked at her with a kind expression very like her son's, and said softly, 'You've been on your own for a long time, haven't you, love?'

'Yes. After my parents died I cared for my cousin's children for a few years and I loved doing that, though I couldn't stop him being cruel to them sometimes. But since they've grown up and gone out into the world, I've been used as the family drudge, and my cousins have tried to prevent the children from seeing me.' She smiled sadly. 'They didn't always succeed, thank goodness.'

'Well, if you can put up with us, we'll adopt you as a cousin and then you'll always have someone to turn to here in the valley.' Gwynneth chuckled. 'Mind you, I give you fair warning: that also means we'll be poking our noses into your business.'

She waited and when Bella gulped and fought against tears, she jerked her head to her son and he left them alone.

'Cry it out, love,' Gwynneth said softly, moving to put her arms around the younger woman. 'Me an' my lads have had bad patches too, so we understand.'

And Bella did cry, easing the big lump of sadness and who knew what else that had been weighing her down for years.

When Gabriel came back, he knocked loudly on the door before coming in and said apologetically, 'Sorry to interrupt but we need to get to the bank before it closes to check that they've paid in your money.'

'Oh, my goodness, yes. Only my eyes will be red.'

'No one will care even if they do notice, which most people won't,' Gwynneth said. 'The important thing is not to let Welch get away with cheating you. Shall I come with you?'

'Would you?' She found Gwynneth as comforting as a plump pillow.

Her companion seemed to read her mind. 'People helped me when I was in a bad way. Now I help others in my turn. One day you'll be able to do that too and you'll relish the opportunity, as I do.'

Bella nodded, weary now, but determined to stick with this and finish it properly.

She'd pretend they really were family from now on. How wonderful that would be.

12

The bank manager was standing chatting to another customer but recognised her at once and greeted her with a smile.

'How may we help you this afternoon, Miss Porter?'

'I need to check that the rent money for the past quarter has been paid into my bank account this afternoon. I'd like to know exactly how much there is so that I can make sure the accounts have been done . . . um, properly.'

He stilled, gave her a searching look, then nodded. 'Very wise. Please come into my office and I'll get you the information.'

He seemed surprised when she asked if Gabriel and his mother could accompany her.

'Our cousin is a little tired today,' Gwynneth explained in her soft voice. 'She's tried to do too much.'

'She's a cousin of yours, Mrs Harte?' He seemed to know Gwynneth and be faintly surprised at this.

'Second cousin, more like. A bit distant, but still family, eh?'

'Yes, of course. Still family.'

He turned back to Bella. 'And that sheds a little light on what happened today. The person who paid in the money was a Mr Welch, who is not one of our customers, and he asked to see me privately. He told me he was worried with you being new to the town that you might be taken advantage of by strangers. But if this is a family matter, I can see why you and your companions are here. Family should always help one another, in my opinion.'

He paused and then went on, 'This Mr Welch . . . well, let's just say that he didn't make a good impression on me – or on my staff, who have dealt with him at the counter occasionally. They consider him lacking in manners. Ah, here's Pearson with the figures.'

A middle-aged man nodded to the two ladies, handed the manager a sheet of paper, and left.

When she saw the totals, Bella frowned. 'I've seen the previous quarter's accounts and there was more money paid in then.'

'That shows you were right to be suspicious, and that he is cheating you,' Gabriel said quietly.

'Oh dear!' The bank manager stared at her, then said, 'You'd best hire another rent collector straight away, my dear lady.'

She was thinking hard. There was significantly less money this time. Mr Cornish had said it was difficult to find decent accommodation in the valley at present, so the flats couldn't have been empty for several weeks as shown in the accounts. And hadn't Mr Cornish said he was paying ten shillings a week? The accounts showed only eight shillings from him.

'I'll definitely find another rent collector.' She'd have another word with Mr Cornish as well. He'd been living in the house for most of that quarter so he'd know whether any flats had been left unoccupied.

They went back to Gwynneth's home where Gabriel, who seemed good with numbers, helped her check the accounts more carefully.

'The Welches aren't very clever at cheating, are they?' he said when they'd finished.

'No. It's too late to do anything today and I'm getting tired, but I'll sack him first thing in the morning.'

'You might want to hire a night watchman to help you keep the property safe until the unwanted tenants leave,' Gwynneth suggested. 'My son can find someone. You don't want them damaging the building out of spite.'

'Would they go that far?' Bella asked in dismay.

'And further. Remember, my sons and I lived in the Moss for a few months. There are some bad people there, not just dishonest, but violent, and your ground-floor tenants don't sound to have made a good impression on you, for a start.'

'I took an instant dislike to Mrs Goodby,' Bella admitted.

Gwynneth shook her head and made a tutting noise.

Gabriel drove Bella to Mrs Tucker's in time for the evening meal. She felt tired but happy to think she'd stood up for herself and made some new friends. She must be the luckiest woman in England today to have met Gabriel and his mother.

She turned to him before she got out of the van. 'I'll need you to help me and drive me round for the rest of the week, if you're free. And once we've given these people notice, can you find someone to guard my property till they've left?'

He nodded at once. 'I'm definitely free. And I'll find someone you can trust to stay there.' He frowned. 'You'll need to go round early tomorrow to catch the people on the top floor and give them notice before they go to work. Do you have any idea who they are exactly?'

'None at all. Mr Welch didn't even list their names. But I want them out because they're dirty, and also I want to turn it back into one flat. I don't want to cram people into my house like sardines.'

'I think you're right. I'll pick you up tomorrow morning at seven then, shall I?'

'Yes, please. I'll set my alarm clock and mention it to Mrs Tucker.'

★

There was another surprise waiting for Bella inside her lodgings. Her life seemed full of surprises lately. The landlady passed on a message from Mrs Tyler, wife of the builder Gabriel's brother worked for. She'd phoned to say she'd like to pop in after tea for a quiet chat about something of mutual interest. Miss Porter should phone her back if that wasn't convenient and they'd arrange another time, otherwise she'd just turn up at half-past seven.

'Mrs Tyler is a very clever woman,' the landlady said. 'She runs the office for her husband's business. They're both well thought of in the valley and they're really nice to deal with. If it's known you're working with her, people will be quicker to trust you, and that'll make it easier for you to settle into the valley.'

Bella was tired, but she could see the sense in summoning up the energy to meet her tonight. 'I see. Thank you for that information. Is there somewhere I can see Mrs Tyler privately? My room isn't big enough.'

'Oh, goodness, you wouldn't want to take her up there! You can use a little room I have at the back of the hall. I let my lodgers have it sometimes for family meetings. You'll be quite private, and there's a gas fire. I'll turn it on just before she's due, to warm the place up.'

'Thank you so much. Um, did Mrs Tyler say anything at all about what she wanted?'

'No, she only said she'd explain it when she got here. Now, you've just got time to take your coat off and wash your hands before I serve tea.'

Once again, the meal was a very pleasant affair and Bella enjoyed listening to the other lodgers chatting as they ate.

Then it was time to go and wait for Mrs Tyler.

'I'll have your skirt finished with another half hour's work at most,' Louisa called across to her as she stood up.

'Thank you so much. I can't wait to wear it.'

Mrs Tyler was on time, and turned out to be another person with a warm smile that made Bella immediately feel at ease with her.

'I'll get straight to the point, Miss Porter. My husband is going to be working for the council, which intends to clear up the slum areas of Backshaw Moss gradually. Parts of it are really bad, a disgrace to the valley. The town has been given a special grant to make a start on the job, and the man in charge of organising this has asked for my husband's advice. They're thinking of starting with Daisy Street, the part of it nearest to Birch End.'

'Oh. What do they intend to do?'

'Well, that little row of houses opposite yours is appalling, and a danger to health as well given the state of their drains. The houses are beyond repair and must be knocked down.'

Bella's stomach clenched. What if they were going to knock her house down, too? She'd be in trouble then. She was counting on it to provide her with both a home and an income.

'Your house is a bit different.'

'What exactly do you mean? Is my house in a worse condition than I'd thought?'

'My husband says your house and the two others like it are well built, but they need modernising. They're over one hundred years old and don't have proper services, for a start. I gather there isn't a bathroom or lavatory inside them, just the privvies in the yard and cold water to one sink on each floor.'

Bella's heart sank still further.

'And some of the exterior needs immediate attention: the roof tiles are mostly all right but there are a couple of leaks, and the drainpipes and gutters need attention. My husband was looking at the outside today.'

'Yes, even I could see some of the problems. I've only just

inherited and I was sorry to find such neglect. I intend to do some repairs, I assure you.'

'How would you feel about getting involved in more extensive improvements?'

'What do you mean?'

'If the council uses some of the grant money to pay half of what it'll cost to update your house and put in plumbing and other modern services, would you be prepared to pay the rest? It's a good offer.'

She didn't have to think twice. 'That's very tempting. What about the other two houses, though? Would the owners do the same? I'm not paying for their improvements.'

'I gather your London lawyer is handling all three properties.'

'Apparently.'

'So we'll ask him about those. And the next few houses along on the same side are owned by people who say they'll be happy to share the expenses. Their houses aren't as nice as yours, or as big, but they would be well worth improving, unlike those on the opposite side.'

'What will happen to that bit of land after the houses have been demolished?'

'My husband says the council would use the rest of the grant money to build a new row of six houses opposite yours, and will give the job to him. If this goes well, they're hoping for more government grants in the future to carry on making improvements further and further into Backshaw Moss till it's all done. They'll be using some of the rates money as well, of course. But that will probably take years. Your improvements would be the first to be done.'

'That sounds a good offer, only how much would it cost? Just approximately. I have a little money that I was going to use on repairs, but not a huge amount.'

'Your share would probably come to about forty pounds

if you just put in one shared bathroom, and a little more, say just around fifty pounds, if you gave each flat its own bathroom. Can you find that much?'

'I could just about afford that. I'm going to throw out the current tenants on the ground floor anyway, and I intend to move into it myself once it's been thoroughly cleaned. I wouldn't want to share my bathroom with tenants.'

'My husband had guessed the new owner might do that. It's obviously the best use of the building. And if you give each flat its own bathroom, you'll be able to charge higher rents, so you'll gradually make up some of the money you spend. He says it wouldn't be too expensive or difficult to put them in because the stairs are in a very convenient pattern for such changes.'

'Oh, that'd be wonderful.'

'Are you turning all the current tenants out?'

'No. I'll leave the middle floor tenant in place, because Mr Cornish keeps it clean and he seems respectable. There are his three children to think of, such little dears. But the family will have to live with the mess of the improvements if they stay.' And so would she if she moved in.

Mrs Tyler nodded. 'I know Ryan Cornish because he's done a few jobs for us. He's definitely decent. Since his wife died, Hettie Lambert has been doing her best to look after everything. She lost her husband years ago. She's always been a demon scrubber of floors, but she's getting on in years now and finds it all a bit too much with three young children to look after as well.'

'I noticed how clean that flat was. I shall have to hire someone to clean the whole house out after the tenants leave.'

'I can find you a couple of excellent cleaners.'

'I'd be so grateful for your help.'

The two women looked at one another, then smiled at the same time.

'You'll fit in well here, Miss Porter. My husband and I will enjoy helping you to get your new home sorted out. But I warn you, if you move in you'll have to put up with a lot of noise and mess from the building work opposite as well.'

'It'll be worth it to have a home of my own. That's been my dearest dream ever since my parents died.'

'It's what most people dream of, my dear. They don't have big dreams, just a comfortable home to live in and enough money earned to put bread on the table each day.'

When Bella had seen Ethel Tyler out, she went back into the guests' sitting room, where Louisa was working on her skirt in a corner set up for sewing with a tall standard lamp shining down on the work area. The other lodgers were chatting animatedly in two small groups.

Louisa greeted her with, 'They let me use the sewing machine at work to oversew some edges during my lunch break. So I've just had to finish the hem by hand tonight. It's nearly done now.'

'That's wonderful!' Bella caught a glimpse of her new hair-style in the mirror and turned from one side to the other, pleased with it. 'I need to buy myself a more flattering hat, though. I felt awful with that lumpy old thing on today. Is there a good milliner in Rivenshaw?'

'Why don't you buy a beret to be going on with? In fact, I can lend you one for tomorrow if you don't object to wearing mine. Even a beret would be better than that hat you were wearing today.'

Bella said frankly, 'It was chosen by my relatives, like all my clothes until now. I think they deliberately chose things that would make me look ugly.'

'How unkind.' Louisa nipped off the thread and held out the skirt. 'There. It's done. Use the little sitting room to slip it on, then come and show me and we'll see if it's all right or if anything else needs adjusting. While you're doing that I'll run up to my room and get the beret. Afterwards I can help you decide which way is more flattering to wear it.'

When Louisa came back down Bella was wearing the skirt. She twirled around and beamed at Louisa, aware that the others were watching her and nodding approval. 'That's just right.'

'It's nice material. You'll have to dress it up with a bit of colour, though, and don't buy anything else beige. A soft blue would suit you best, I think. You've got nice ankles, so you should be showing them off.'

Bella peered down. 'Do you think so?'

'Definitely. Mine are too thick and they swell a bit by the end of the day.' She stuck her legs out, stared down at them, sighing and shrugging as she drew them back.

Bella got the money out of her purse and paid for the alterations. 'I have two other skirts that I'd like shortening as soon as possible. Would you have time to do those for me as well? This one' – she pointed to the one she'd taken off – 'and another. There are two other skirts I hate so much I shall use them for cleaning rags.'

Her companion beamed, well pleased with the prospect. 'Happy to do more for you. I like to earn a bit extra whenever I can.'

Bella thrust the skirt she'd been wearing into Louisa's hands. 'I'll go up and fetch the other one straight away.'

When Bella went to bed half an hour later she was still smiling as she snuggled down in the darkness. What could have been a terrible day had been brightened from start to finish by the kindness of others.

And she wouldn't look quite as frumpy tomorrow.

She wondered if anyone would even notice the changes, apart from her fellow lodgers. Well, she would know. She'd feel better, as well as looking better.

13

Bella was outside the house just before seven the next morning, waiting in the chilly grey light of dawn, with her borrowed beret at a jaunty angle. She had the heavy, old-fashioned keys to the front door of her house and the storeroom in her handbag and was jiggling it about for the childish pleasure of hearing the faint clunking sound they made.

When Gabriel drove up, she hurried around to the passenger side and slipped quickly in before he wasted time getting out and opening it for her.

He was staring at her as if he'd never seen her before.

'You look different.'

'I'm trying some more modern clothes and hats now I'm not living with my cousins. Did you ask your friend if he'd help keep an eye on my house?'

'Yes. I called in on Ed last night and he jumped at the chance of some work. He'll be waiting for us in Daisy Street.'

'Times have been very bad here in the valley, haven't they?'

'Aye. They still aren't good, but we're coming out of it slowly. I've read about things being better in the south. It sounds like a different world. I'll go and see it one day.'

'You could have gone and got a job there already.'

'And leave our mam on her own? Nay, I couldn't do that. None of us could. She's the best mother in the world. But I will go and see more of our country one day and maybe some other countries too. France isn't all that far away, is it? I read in the paper that they do day trips across the Channel. You should hear Todd Selby when he gets talking about places he visited after the war. He's even travelled to Australia. Just imagine that.'

She didn't ask who Todd Selby was because her brain was overloaded with new names and information, but it felt good that Gabriel was at ease enough with her to chat. 'I'm sure you'll get your wish in time. And I'll give you one of my suitcases when you do go off on your travels. They're shabby but sturdy.'

She added before she could stop herself, 'Personally, I just want to get a home of my own, make it cosy, and stay there.' Maybe, if she was very lucky, one or two of the Beaton children she'd helped raise might come and see her once in a while. She doubted that horrible husband would ever allow Penelope to come, though. Her heart broke sometimes when she remembered how the lively girl had changed into a pale shadow of herself. Being rich didn't make you happy, did it? She shook away those unhappy thoughts to listen to Gabriel again.

'All right, cousin Bella. It's a bargain. I'll take your suitcase travelling one day and once you're settled in, I'll bring Mam to christen your new home for you with a cup of tea. We won't have to wait as long to do that.'

She smiled. He was beginning to feel like a real relative, especially when he gave her that teasing grin. He reminded her of Stephen Beaton, her cousin's elder son – such an enthusiastic young man. He'd got away from his father by marrying a wife with money of her own. Bella had seen him a couple of times at church, but he hadn't come across to chat. He probably guessed it would cause trouble for her if he did and his father heard about it. But he'd winked at her, and his young wife had smiled. That might seem nothing to other people, but to her it had meant a lot simply to be acknowledged.

Whenever she thought about the girls she'd helped raise, she hoped that Alma hadn't been forced into a marriage and that Penelope was staying strong. But there was nothing she could do to help them now.

The van came to a halt just then and she had to give the present her full attention. This wasn't going to be a pleasant start to the day, she was sure, but it had to be done.

Poor house, Bella thought, so much in need of care and attention. Then a young man moved forward to join them and she let Gabriel introduce her to Ed.

'Stay inside the front hall and come running if either of us calls,' Gabriel told him.

'You can count on me, lad.'

She was still surprised that Gabriel and his mother had been so emphatic about the possibility of them needing Ed's help, because the street seemed peaceful at this hour of the morning, with just a few people walking briskly past, on their way to work presumably. But she supposed the tenants might make a fuss about being given notice, especially that woman on the ground floor, so better safe than sorry.

She used her front door key for the first time, resisting the temptation to pat the door as she opened it and promising herself that she'd do whatever was necessary to make this into a decent, modern home.

The door to the side of the hall opened as she went in and Mrs Goodby peered out.

'Oh, it's you.'

'Good morning. I'm glad to have caught you. I'm here to give you notice to move out as soon as you can.'

The woman's mouth fell open in shock, then she glared at Bella. 'You can't do that. Mr Welch promised me I could stay here, promised faithfully he did. It's my home. And I've never missed paying my rent, not once.'

Bella could see past Mrs Goodby to where three scruffy-looking young men were standing, clearly people who lived there. They were listening to the conversation and grinning as if expecting trouble to erupt. 'It looks as if it's home to several other people as well.'

'So what? They're family.'

Bella studied the young men, who bore no resemblance either to Mrs Goodby or to one another.

Two more men appeared in the doorway of the bedroom and another peered out from the kitchen at the rear, a tin mug with steam rising from it in his hand.

'You must have a lot of male relatives! But you're wrong. As it's my house, I can give you notice any time I choose.'

'Have you told Mr Welch you're doing that? He won't like it. Good, paying tenants are hard to find these days.'

One of the young men sniggered. 'You tell her what's what, Mrs G.'

Bella's anger at the woman's rudeness boiled over. 'What's more, I think you're using this as a common lodging house. Do you have a council licence for that?'

The noise Mrs Goodby made sounded more like a growl than a word, and the expression on her face was now thunderous. 'You'll regret doing this. Mr Welch will see to that.'

'It's not up to him. As I keep reminding you, I'm the owner. I think you'd better be out of here by this evening. If not, I shall call in the police to check how many people you've crammed in.'

Mrs Goodby lost her aggressive look and now it was panic on her face and she whipped back inside, slamming the door hard and shooting the bolts so that Bella couldn't follow her in, even if she'd had a key. Which, Bella realised in that moment, she didn't.

Bella went close to the door of the flat and yelled, 'We don't want to have any damage, Mrs Goodby. I remember clearly what everything was like in your rooms and won't hesitate to call in the police if I find damage.'

There was silence from inside.

Her heart was beating fast with the stress of doing this and she felt a bit shaky, but when she turned to Gabriel and Ed, they both nodded at her and grinned. That cheered her up a little.

'I've never behaved like that in my whole life,' she confessed. 'But that woman made me so angry. Only – perhaps we'd better find another man to keep watch with Ed for a night or two.'

'Good idea,' Gabriel said quietly. 'You don't want to take any risks.' He turned to Ed. 'Go and see if one of your cousins is free. Quick as you can, lad.'

Ed left and Bella gave Gabriel a shaky smile. 'Let's go and see the top floor people before I lose what's left of my courage.'

'You'll manage it. And when you see another Hartley you'll know why I sent for Ed's cousin. They're all big lads in that family. They don't start fights, but if someone else does, they've never lost one yet, so it's not often they're challenged round here.'

The two families on the top floor hadn't left for work yet. Both groups turned surly when she gave them notice to leave.

Gabriel took a step forward to her side, tall and strong compared to the group of people on the landing.

She saw them eyeing him a bit nervously but carried on with what she'd planned to say. 'There shouldn't be two families crammed in up here. If you behave and leave the place clean, you can have a few days to find somewhere else. Mrs Goodby will be leaving by tonight, because she's been awkward and rude to me. What is it to be for you?'

One man's shoulders sagged. 'We'll do our best to find somewhere quickly, miss, but it'll help to have time to look.'

The woman next to him muttered, 'Thanks, miss.'

The wife in the other family nodded, her face set in grim lines of what looked like endurance. 'We can go and stay with my sister, so we can be out by tonight. Rent's due tomorrow. I haven't got it anyway this week, whatever he threatens me with.'

Bella felt sorry for her. 'You can both have two more days here rent free,' she said quietly. 'Mr Welch is no longer collecting my rents, so don't give him any more money.'

Silence, then resigned nods, and the woman said, 'Thanks, miss. That'll make the move easier.'

'Make sure you do right by Miss Porter in return, and leave the place clean,' Gabriel warned them, and they nodded again.

'I feel guilty,' Bella whispered after their doors had closed. 'They looked so beaten down by life. But I'll be making big changes up here, and they'd just be in the way. And afterwards – well, to be frank, I want cleaner tenants.'

'We can't do anything about how life is treating them. There's a lot of folk in the same boat round here. You did what you could, at least, gave them time to move. Come on. We need to catch the people in the cellar.'

'Oh my, I'd forgotten them.'

But they found no one now living in the cellar. They must have already left, sharpish.

She wrinkled her nose in disgust. 'They've left it filthy down here. I'll have to get it cleaned out.'

When they came back to the hall, Gabriel waited, then prompted, 'You need to see Ryan Cornish now. He'll want to know what's going on.'

'Oh, yes.' She braced herself. She didn't want to appear to be a nosy, interfering landlady, but at least she wasn't giving him the same bad news as the other tenants. But would he want to stay in her house? She did hope he would. She'd really enjoy having those delightful children nearby.

★

Mr Cornish opened the door of his flat, looking at her with a grim expression. 'I heard what you said to the others. As I told you, sound echoes in the stairwell.'

'Can I come in, then? I don't want everyone else listening to what I have to say to you.'

She followed him inside and said it baldly. 'I haven't come to turn you out because you've kept your rooms clean, as well as paying your rent on time.'

Relief washed over his face and he closed his eyes for a few seconds, then thanked her. 'You won't regret it. I get enough work to pay the rent.'

The old woman was standing in the bedroom doorway and she too looked relieved. What a tired face and work-worn hands she had, poor thing, not to mention nearly ragged clothes. It suddenly occurred to Bella that she had two perfectly good skirts that she loathed. She'd offer them to Hettie.

The eldest child was standing slightly behind her babysitter, watching what was going on.

Bella turned back to Mr Cornish. 'I'm going to be doing some necessary repairs and work on the house, so you may decide to leave anyway and find somewhere quieter, but if you can put up with mess and noise, you're welcome to stay. And the rent will be eight shillings a week, not ten.'

'We'll stay. I hope you're going to improve the plumbing.'

'Yes, I am. In fact, I'm going to have a bathroom put into each flat. Nothing fancy, but it'll be an improvement.'

Hettie brightened. 'Eh, that'll be grand for the children.'

'How are they today?'

He looked towards the little girl standing in the doorway. 'Maddy's a lot better, but the other two are still a bit listless.'

'That's good. The doctor said it wasn't a bad fever.'

There was so much to do and Bella was feeling so weary and— Suddenly the room started wavering around her and she clutched the nearest thing, which happened to be Mr Cornish's arm. 'I'm sorry. I feel – a bit dizzy.'

He scooped her up into his arms and, before Gabriel could get to her, he'd set her down gently in the wooden rocking chair, kneeling beside her to steady her.

From that position she couldn't help gazing straight into his beautiful eyes, and she drew comfort from the kindness in his expression. 'Thank you. I'm not usually so – so stupid.'

Gabriel was standing next to Mr Cornish. 'It's a reaction. Miss Porter stood up to that witch downstairs like a good 'un, then calmed down what could have been an unpleasant situation on the top floor.'

'I'm not used to standing up to anyone,' she admitted. 'I'm learning, but it makes me feel a bit wobbly afterwards.'

'It'll get easier. And that Goodby female's a nasty type, so you did well. We'll have to keep an eye on you for a while. She might try to get back at you.' He looked at Ryan as he said that, and the other man nodded.

Hettie came across to join them. 'How about a nice, sweet cup of tea? That'll set you right, miss.'

Bella was starting to feel more herself, but nodded. Apart from anything else, if she was coming to live here, she wanted to be on good terms with all these people. 'Thank you. Very kind of you. And after that I need to get back to my lodgings for breakfast. I've paid for it, so I might as well eat it.'

Hettie nodded vigorously. 'Never waste the chance of good food.'

From that, Bella guessed that the old woman had gone hungry often.

Gabriel also accepted a big enamel mug of tea, drinking it on the landing so that he could keep an eye on the entrance.

Bella turned to Mr Cornish. 'For how long did the upstairs flat stay empty?'

He looked surprised. 'Neither of them has been empty since we came here, and that's nearly two months ago now. What made you think it had been empty?'

'Mr Welch's accounts show it as having been empty for weeks.'

'It's a lie.'

By that time, Gabriel had finished the mug of tea and he called out that Ed had come back with his cousin Steve to help him keep watch, so they could leave now.

Bella turned to Hettie. 'Thank you for the tea. You were right. It did the trick, and you make a good cup.' She was glad to see the old woman's face brighten at this compliment.

As she was going downstairs, she smiled to see how big her new watchman was, over six foot tall. However, her mood darkened again as she saw Welch arrive. She guessed Mrs Goodby had sent for him, so braced herself to do battle again, then had a sudden idea and as he turned towards her, she took the initiative.

'You're fired, Welch, because you've been trying to cheat me, pretending the flat at the top has been vacant. If the rest of the rent money owing isn't paid into my bank account today, I'll be asking the police to look into where the missing money has gone.'

He gaped at her, taken by surprise at this sudden attack, then snapped, 'I was going to resign anyway.'

'Good. Now, give me the keys and kindly leave my premises. And don't come here again.'

'I've come to see Mrs Goodby, not collect your rents.' He turned towards the door of the flat.

Ed moved forward and his friend joined him. They were both taller than Welch by several inches, even if thinner. 'The lady asked you to leave now.'

'And don't forget to pay the rest of the money into the bank,' Gabriel added from the landing, moving down a couple of steps as he spoke.

Welch moved backwards, glowered round at them all, then turned to leave.

There was the sound of a bolt being slammed back and Mrs Goodby opened her door to screech, 'She's throwing me out today, so I need somewhere to move to, Vince.'

'I'll find you somewhere better than this hovel to live in,' he yelled back, gave a final glare at the group in the hall, and strode off down the street.

Gabriel was watching Bella warily, but she said, 'I'm not going to turn faint again.'

'Then let's get you back to Mrs Tucker's for your breakfast. She'll stop serving soon.'

As they drove off, she said thoughtfully, 'I don't understand why he was so keen to keep her in the ground-floor flat.'

'She was probably paying him to let her cram too many people into it. If she has to move somewhere else, she might have to get council permission to run a lodging house.'

'The whole place smelled horrible.'

'Yes. But it can be scrubbed clean.'

When they got back to Mrs Tucker's, Bella thrust a florin into Gabriel's hand. 'Buy something to eat for Ed and Steve. This is on top of their wages. They both look deep-down hungry.'

'They are. Thank you.'

She went straight into the dining room for breakfast and was the last to arrive. She ate her meal with relish, suddenly ravenously hungry herself, and by the time she'd finished, the others had gone off to work.

Fancy nearly fainting, she thought as she drank the last mouthful of tea. What an idiot she must seem!

But she hadn't felt faint till after she'd dealt with that horrible woman and the people on the top floor, so that was something. She'd held firm till the crisis was over and was rather proud of that.

She enjoyed finishing her meal without having to rush, and relished a few moments' peace and quiet.

Since she'd inherited the house, she'd felt as if she'd been caught up by a whirlwind, so much had happened in a couple of days. Where would it spin her away to next?

Well, whatever was to come, she could only take things one step at a time. That was all anyone could do: move forward in life towards what they wanted at whatever speed they could manage, and if things went wrong, find another path.

14

In London, Alma Beaton stared at her mother in horror. 'You can't mean that?'

'I never say anything I don't mean.'

'But Maxwell Greene is sixty if he's a day. And he's nearly bald, and – and shorter than me! It'd be like marrying a – a corpse!'

'Nonetheless, it's an advantageous match for the family, so you will do as we tell you, and you will smile as you accept his proposal.' She waited for a moment, then added, 'Think how rich you'll be.'

Alma bent her head, but the tears would flow and even when her mother slapped her on the side of her head, she couldn't stop weeping. 'I can't do it,' she whispered at last, desperation giving her the courage to speak out. 'I won't.'

'You will do as you are told.' Another slap sent her tumbling sideways on to the sofa.

She could only shake her head and cover her face with her cupped hands to ward off further slaps as she sobbed.

'I thought we'd taught you to obey us. It seems you need another lesson. Go to your room and take off your clothes, then put your nightgown on and wait for your father to come up. He's busy at the moment, but you'll wait till he can spare the time to deal with your impertinence.'

Alma gaped at her. They hadn't treated her like this since she was a small child. You didn't spank grown-up daughters on bare flesh. But her mother's gaze was unflinching. She meant what she said.

'Do I have to hit you again?' Her mother raised her hand.

Sobbing even more loudly, Alma ran out and stumbled up the stairs, bumping into her brother Oscar at the top.

He caught hold of her arm. 'What's the matter, Ally?'

She glanced over her shoulder and put one finger to her mouth, then led the way to her bedroom.

They both checked carefully to make sure no servants were around to see him going in, then he asked again what was wrong.

'They're going to force me to marry Maxwell Greene.'

He was nearly as horrified as she had been.

'When I—' she gulped, 'said I couldn't, Mother told me to come up here and take my clothes off. Father's going to spank me.'

'Dear heaven, he hasn't done that to any of us for years. It's disgusting to do it to anyone, let alone a grown daughter. What's got into them to force you into a marriage like that, anyway?'

'What always drives them to act? Money. Advantages for the family.'

'You can't do it. The man's vile.' He didn't dare tell her how vile, but Maxwell Greene's behaviour was notorious among men who were acquainted with him.

'I'll be too sore to do anything but lie here in agony and scream yes by the time Father's finished with me. You know how he enjoys hurting people.'

There was dead silence, then her brother said in a quiet, firm tone, 'You must run away before he can come up here.'

'Where can I go? I've no money and no friends that they don't approve of. I daren't go to Stephen. That'd expose our brother to Father's anger as well.'

Oscar stood there thinking hard, then snapped his fingers. 'I know. You must go to Bella. She'll shelter you.'

'I don't even know where she lives now.'

'Mr Neven knows where she is, and he'll help you get to her, I'm sure. He's stopped acting for Father because he disapproves of how he treated her. I have some money I can give you, not much, but enough for you to get there and manage for a while. Pack some necessities in a bag quickly and we'll sneak you out by the back stairs. Wait for me in the park up near the top, and I'll join you there as soon as I can. We don't want them to see us leaving together.'

'I daren't.'

'Then stay here and be beaten till you can hardly move. I still remember Father's beatings.' He shuddered. 'I'm as big as he is, so he wouldn't dare touch me now, but he's a lot bigger and stronger than you.'

She stared at him numbly, then the thought of what would happen if she didn't escape sank in and she whispered, 'I'll do it.'

'Pack a bag quickly.'

She started stuffing a few clothes and underclothes into a bag she used for shopping.

'Jewellery?' he asked. 'You can sell it if you need more money.'

She got out her jewellery box and emptied its contents into the bag. 'It's not very valuable. Mother keeps the better pieces and only brings them out on special occasions.'

'The money it brings could still come in useful.'

She saw her toiletries on the washstand and shoved them into the bag, too. 'That's it. I can't fit anything else in.'

'Coat, hat?'

'My outdoor clothes are in the hall cupboard. I daren't go down for them. Oh, I know. I have some old clothes here waiting to be sent to the church's charity box.' She fumbled in the wardrobe and took out some shabby outer garments.

Then she looked at her brother numbly, finding it hard to think or move.

Oscar plonked a kiss on her cheek. 'You can do it, Ally. I know you can.'

She nodded. She had to try at least.

'Come on! There isn't much time.' He led the way down the servants' stairs, held up one hand till the coast was clear at the bottom, and then pushed her outside.

'Hurry up! Stay close to the garden wall behind the bushes so they don't see you leaving.'

She left by the rear gate, stumbled up the back alleys to the small park, and found a bench out of sight from the street, collapsing on to it. She was beyond tears now. Terror filled her in great, shuddering waves and she kept glancing around to make sure she was alone. She was quite sure that her parents would kill her if they caught her.

It was over an hour before her brother came for her, according to the little gold fob watch pinned to her bodice. How much would that fetch if she sold it?

At last a cab drew up in the nearby road. When Oscar got out of it and beckoned to her, she couldn't move for a moment, then grabbed her bag and ran down to him, almost tumbling into the vehicle.

'Crouch on the floor,' he whispered. 'I've told the cab driver we're eloping.'

She did as he asked, then said breathlessly, 'Do they know I've gone?'

'Yes. And all hell has broken loose. I started work on that job for Father. I peered out of the office and asked what was going on. When I offered to help search for you, they told me to go to work and behave as usual. Father said you couldn't have got far and that he'd soon find you.'

As the cab turned a corner sharply, she squeaked and was thrown against his knees.

He stopped her falling sideways. 'It's all right. I've got you. I have to take you to Mr Neven as quickly as I can, then go into work as usual.'

'What if he won't help me?'

'We'll think of something else. But I believe he will. He's a gentleman.'

And when he told the lawyer what their father was really like, including describing matters Alma was too naïve to understand, surely he'd not refuse to help them?

Once they got to Mr Neven's rooms, Oscar pulled his hat down to hide his face and murmured, 'Walk in quietly and calmly, keeping your head down. Wait for me in the lobby.'

He paid the cab driver and gave him an extra five shillings on the promise of keeping quiet about ever seeing them.

'I never seen a lass as frightened as that one,' the cab driver muttered.

'Her father beats her if she displeases him – hard enough to draw blood.'

'Well, I never. His own daughter. And them gentry, too. Should be taken out and shot, men who beat young lasses should.'

'I agree.'

As the cab drove off, Oscar hurried inside and caught the head clerk just crossing the lobby towards his sister. He grabbed Penscombe's arm and said, 'If you have any pity in you, please hide Miss Beaton from public view while I speak to Mr Neven, because if our father finds her, he'll beat her senseless – literally.'

Penscombe gaped at him for a moment or two, then glanced at the terrified young woman and said, 'I'll hide her in the records room. No one will know she's here, I promise you. You go and tell Mr Neven what's happened. He'll be free for a while.'

He beckoned to Alma and when she didn't move, he said

gently, 'This way, miss. You'll be safe with me. I've got a granddaughter your age.'

Oscar knocked on the half-open door of Mr Neven's room. 'Penscombe said I should come in. There's a – an emergency and I need your help.'

'I'm no longer acting for your father.'

'That's why I've come to you.'

'Ah. Please sit down and tell me what exactly is wrong.'

Oscar turned to shut the door, then sat down, clutching his cheeks with his hands for a moment as he tried to think how to say what he needed to, then he straightened up and began to explain the situation.

'Unfortunately, a father has the legal right to beat his children,' Mr Neven said.

'It's not just a beating. He . . . ' It was a moment or two before he could put the shameful situation into words. 'He gets great pleasure from hurting people. Who's to know how far he'll go now – with a pretty young girl? Naked.'

There was dead silence, then Albert Neven shuddered. 'You mean—'

'I mean something so bad I can't put it into words. He's attacked maids in that way before now.'

'Heaven deliver us from monsters like that!'

'I didn't know where to turn for help, but I remembered how you do a lot for charity, so I thought perhaps you'd advise us. Should we take refuge with Bella, do you think? I'm sure she'd help us if she knew.'

Albert shook his head. 'No. Your father would find her quite easily. Look, I'll do what's necessary. We'll discuss exactly what that will involve later. Where is your sister now?'

'Penscombe said he'd hide her in the records room.'

'Good. My car is parked in the backyard. I'll just phone my wife, then I'll drive you and Alma to our house.'

And Oscar, for all that he was a man grown, burst into strangled sobs of sheer relief.

'My dear boy.' Albert Neven went and patted his shoulder awkwardly, suddenly wondering how bad things had been for this unhappy young chap as well as his sister over the years.

When his visitor had calmed down, he said, 'From what you've told me, perhaps you should get away from your family as well.'

'I'd love to. I don't want to marry the woman they forced me to propose to. She's a shrew. How can I get away, though? I've very little money because I'm working for my father. And I'll need to give most of my savings to Alma.'

'We'll consider the whole situation for a day or two and come up with a long-term solution. Will you be all right staying on at home for that long?'

'Yes. I'm sure they believed me today. I pretended I'd been working on some accounts Father brought home yesterday, and hadn't seen my sister.'

'Then let's get Alma to my wife before we do anything else.'

'I can't come to your house now, Mr Neven. I have to get to work as quickly as I can or Father might suspect something. I daren't even come around tonight, but perhaps early tomorrow evening?'

'Come any time you like. And Oscar, if you need to flee as well, come to me. I mean it.'

'Thank you. I don't think they'll guess what I've done, but your offer gives me great comfort. I'll just have a quick word with my sister before I leave.'

'Yes, of course.'

Alma was sitting in the records storeroom, stiff and white-faced, her eyes looking glazed with terror.

Oscar went and knelt beside her, taking her hand. 'Alma. Alma, look at me.'

She stirred and did as he asked.

'Mr Neven has offered to take you to his home. His wife will be there and she'll keep you safe and—' He glanced sideways and received an encouraging nod, so continued, 'He's offered to help us both get completely away from Father.'

'You're coming with me?'

'Yes. One of the main reasons I've stayed so long was to keep an eye on you. I've even considered running away to Australia to avoid marrying that horrible woman. I think – no, I'm sure Father is insane, dangerously so.'

Alma shuddered and clung to her brother's hand, not wanting him to leave.

'I must go now. I daren't come to see you tonight, but I'll try to come tomorrow. You can trust the Nevens to protect you.'

She looked up at their host. 'Do you know where we can go to be safe, Mr Neven?'

'I have an idea. But I need to check out a couple of things first.'

Oscar gave her a quick kiss on the cheek and stood up. 'I really must leave.' He looked at Mr Neven and added in a choked voice, 'Look after her, please.'

The lawyer clapped him on the shoulder. 'I will. I give you my solemn word on that.'

Alma watched her brother leave, looking so bereft that Albert felt even more sorry for her. 'I won't be long.' He spoke to Penscombe on his way out of the storeroom, then went off down the corridor.

The clerk came into the doorway, and Alma looked at him apprehensively.

'You'll be quite safe with them, my dear young lady. Mrs Neven is as kind as her husband. They help a lot of people through their charity work.'

Alma could only nod. She felt lost and alone, but at least she'd got away from her father. She'd kill herself if anyone forced her to go back to him.

When Mr Neven came back to collect her, carrying a briefcase, she went outside with him, feeling numb.

'I phoned my wife, who says she'll be very happy to have you as a guest and will help you in any way she can. We can get into my car here, behind the building, and no one will see you. It'll be the same at my home, so you'll be quite safe, I promise you.'

'Thank you.' Her words were the merest thread of sound.

'I think it'd be better if you get into the back. You can crouch down as we travel through the streets, covering yourself with the travel rug. Just in case we pass someone who might recognise you.'

She did as he suggested, and felt safer when she was hidden from view.

She felt safer still when they arrived and she got out inside a big garage attached to the house. Mrs Neven took her straight up to a comfortable bedroom and gave her a big hug, just as Bella used to do.

'I'll bring your meals up here and you'll be the only person using the bathroom next door. Even the servants won't deal with you, then they can't tell anyone – not that they would, but I don't want to put them in a difficult position if the police come looking for you.'

'You're being so kind.'

'You and your brother need help urgently. We'll get you both away from here within a day or two, somewhere right away from London.'

'To Bella's new house?'

'Even that wouldn't be safe enough, I'm afraid. Your father can easily follow you there. And as you're under twenty-one, the law would be on his side.'

'It'll be over three years till I turn twenty-one. How can I be safe anywhere?'

'We'll make sure you are. My husband is looking into ways and means. He'll tell you all the details once he's worked things out, then he and your brother can make the arrangements.'

Mrs Neven started to close the door, then opened it again to add, 'You won't need to lock this door during the daytime. My servants are used to me giving shelter to vulnerable women and don't come near here unless I ask them to. But you may wish to lock the door when you go to bed, not because anyone is likely to come in, but because you'll probably sleep better if you do.'

After the door closed, the silence seemed to wrap itself around Alma. She went to check the window, but it only looked out on to the side of the next house, which was a good thing, she felt. She left the curtains open and when she lay down on the bed she found that her arm and one hand were in a patch of warmly glowing sunlight. It seemed like an omen and she played with the brightness like a child, making shadow patterns across it with the fingers of her other hand.

Perhaps, if she were very lucky, she need never see her father or mother again. That was her dearest wish.

She was quite sure Oscar would feel exactly the same.

But where could they go that was absolutely safe?

15

When Gabriel came back to pick her up as arranged, Bella asked him to drive her into Rivenshaw town centre to do a little shopping. She left him sitting in the van avidly reading a two-day-old newspaper that Wilf and Stella, his mother's employers, had kindly passed on to his family. Gabriel always seemed hungry for knowledge.

Bella strolled along the street, hesitating for a few moments outside the haberdasher's. She wasn't used to buying anything for herself that she didn't desperately need, but was rather tempted in by a brightly coloured scarf in the window. It would cheer up her dark brown outer coat. Yes, it looked lovely when she tried it, so she bought it.

Then a display of berets caught her eye and she bought one of those as well. The scarf was so pretty she couldn't help wearing it immediately, turning a few times to look at her reflection in shop windows as she passed.

At least she looked like a modern woman now, even though she wasn't all that smartly dressed because her clothes were obviously well worn. How she'd hated looking so frumpy all these years.

She felt like skipping for joy, but of course she couldn't do that at her age. She'd never have believed so many of her dreams could come true. She fingered the scarf again, adjusting it just a fraction to show the pattern to the best advantage. They didn't have to be big dreams to give you a lot of pleasure.

The weather was fine so she left the package containing her beret in the van and, feeling greatly daring, indulged in a stroll along the other side of the street. She stopped outside a small sweet shop, her mouth watering at the sight of the rows of big glass bottles full of multi-coloured sweets sitting temptingly across the back of the window.

Inside, it took her a few moments to work out whether to buy pear drops or humbugs, while the smiling shopkeeper waited patiently.

When she got back into the van, she held out the triangular paper bag to Gabriel and he accepted a humbug with a hum of pleasure.

His words came out slightly blurred by the large sweet, and so did hers.

'I like your new scarf.'

'Thank you. I couldn't resist it. But I suppose we'd better check how things are going at the house, now. They've had plenty of time to make a start on moving. I also need to find someone to scrub out the empty flats, especially the ground-floor rooms, and Mrs Tyler said she knew women who might do it.'

'She knows everyone in Birch End and a lot of people in the rest of the valley too. Nice lady, Mrs T.'

As they set off, Bella said, 'I'm hoping that horrible Goodby woman will have left by the end of today and that she'll stay away. I don't even want to see her again, let alone speak to her.'

'You won't be on your own in wishing to avoid her, but don't count on her staying away from you. If nothing else distracts her and she continues to feel aggrieved, she may do something to upset you, even if it's only arranging for little lads to throw muck at you in the street.'

Bella gasped. 'She wouldn't!'

'It's been known. It won't be anything serious with her.

She's too afraid of being arrested, but Welch might try something more, well . . . violent. Harmful even. There are rumours about his past. Nothing's been proved, but you'd better be on your guard and don't go out alone after dark till he's got past the worst of his anger.'

'Oh dear! I envy people who have vehicles to travel around in. It's been such a help having you to take me where I need to go. If I knew how to drive I'd be tempted to buy a little second-hand car. It'd not only be highly convenient, but I'd feel so much safer.'

He slowed down and stopped to let two old ladies with shopping baskets hobble across the road at one of the new pedestrian crossings, which had what people were starting to call a Belisha beacon on the footpath at each side. Studs marked a path across the road between the big yellow globes on poles.

He pointed to them. 'Some people complain that these new crossings are ugly, but I think they're a godsend for old folk who can't walk quickly.'

'I agree.' But her mind was still on cars.

'You know, you could always learn to drive.'

She gaped at him. 'Me?'

'There's a good driving school in town, run by Nick Howarth. Silas Johnson is starting to give lessons for him part-time, and I've heard that he's an excellent teacher. He learned to do it in the army. But there aren't enough customers yet for him to work there full-time as well as Nick.'

'Oh, gosh. I couldn't do that.'

'Why not? Driving isn't hard. Well, not unless you're absolutely cack-handed.'

She was amused by his picturesque phrase. 'What does that mean?'

'Clumsy. Are you?'

'No, I'm not. Um, is it expensive to learn?'

'It costs ten shillings an hour, which sounds a lot, but it only takes a few hours to learn enough to pass the new driving test. It'll soon be law that you have to take a test before you're allowed to drive. That comes in from March onwards. Why don't you try one driving lesson and see how you go?' He waited, as if expecting an answer.

'Me, learn to drive,' she said faintly. 'I'll, um, have to think about it.'

'Well, just in case you do pluck up the courage to try, the driving school has an office on Crimea Street where you can book your lessons. It's next to where Todd sells cars. He has them lined up outside, so you can't miss it. And he could find you a reliable second-hand car once you pass your test.'

She noticed that he wasn't short of words in discussing this. If it was shyness that made him so curt with other people, then his openness with her was a big compliment. She tried to think what to say next, but couldn't.

He chuckled. 'Don't look so shocked at the idea. Driving really isn't hard, I promise you.'

'I don't even know the road rules for vehicles – well, apart from a vague idea from a pedestrian's point of view, of course.'

'Buy a copy of the Highway Code and it'll all make sense. That only costs a penny from the post office, less than those delicious humbugs.'

He cocked his head on one side and eyed the crumpled paper bag, so she offered him another sweet. 'You should make them last longer than that.'

'I like crunching them.'

They both sucked happily for a minute or two, then she said, 'I'll think about it.'

He grinned at her. 'You do that. But I shall be disappointed if you don't at least give it a try. One lesson?'

'You're good for me in so many ways, Gabriel. I don't know how I'd have managed if Mrs Tucker hadn't introduced me to you. You're not only driving me around, you're putting good ideas into my head.'

'Well, you're putting money into my pocket and making my days more interesting, so we're helping each other. And Mam likes you, so you've got a friend in her as well. She's already told people you're a distant cousin, so don't you go contradicting her. It'd embarrass her.'

'I wouldn't do that for worlds. In fact, I wish I really were related to you all.'

'You are now, for all practical purposes.'

She gave him a grateful look then fell silent as she watched his hand and foot movements carefully. She'd hardly thought about the mechanics of driving before; now she was suddenly fascinated by them.

Eh! Her learn to drive. Did she dare?

She'd dared defy her cousin Thomas, hadn't she? If she could do that, maybe she could give driving a try? Maybe she should do it. Another test of her courage.

When they stopped in Daisy Street, Bella got out and paused as usual to stare at the outside of her house, still finding it hard to credit that she was the owner.

There was a lorry standing outside it today and people were carrying all sorts of oddments out to it and chucking them into the back any old how. These included quite a few bundles of sweaty, smelly bedding and she wrinkled her nose in disgust. Mrs Goodby came out with another bundle and stopped to scowl at Bella.

The expression 'if looks could kill' came suddenly to life even though the other woman didn't actually say anything. When Bella stared back at her calmly, her former tenant tossed her head, spat to one side, and carried on with what she was doing.

There was no sign of Welch today, thank goodness. Bella

was hoping he'd stay away, given that she had guards on the premises.

The hall smelled even more unpleasant now, and she grimaced at the odour.

'Mam would have a fit at such dirty ways,' Gabriel muttered.

'I'm trying not to have a fit, but I'm tempted to shriek at her.' Bella nodded to Ed, who was standing to one side with his arms folded. She mimed holding her nose and he nodded agreement, rolling his eyes. Then she remembered one of the main things she wanted to do, so headed for the stairs, beckoning to Gabriel to follow her.

On the first floor she unlocked the door of the room to the left where the miscellaneous objects were being stored. 'This all belongs to me too, apparently. I want to get some idea of what it contains so I'll know what else to buy to furnish my new home. There aren't any big pieces of furniture, but I think I saw a few smaller pieces like a bookcase last time.'

Oh, how she loved saying the words 'my new home'!

He stared around. 'Lucky you!'

They searched carefully, lifting aside bundles and boxes of who knew what, and found a couple of hard wooden chairs, a small side table, and the bookcase, which would all be very welcome. Her books wouldn't nearly fill its shelves, but she'd gradually buy more. It'd be wonderful not to have to hide them.

She took out the small notebook she kept in her handbag and began to make a list of the smaller pieces of furniture they'd found and a second list of the other things she'd need as an absolute minimum to start her off, like a bed, kitchen table, and an easy chair or two.

Gabriel continued to move the boxes about and his strength came in useful. Some of them were quite heavy, and several stacks were higher than her head. She couldn't have managed them on her own. She wondered what was in them, but there wasn't room to unpack them here. She couldn't move in till she had got the flat cleaned and bought some furniture, then she'd have these things brought down to explore at her leisure.

Gabriel scanned the room again after Bella had finished checking it. 'You're going to need cleaning tools. There don't seem to be any of those here.'

'Oh dear, I'd forgotten that sort of thing.' She scribbled that down, then put away the notebook. 'There are a couple of pans and some oddments of crockery, which will give me a start in the kitchen. I'm going to have to learn how to cook.'

She moved reluctantly towards the door. 'I'd better go and see Mrs Tyler about hiring these cleaners she knows before I do anything else. Maybe she'll help me work out exactly what I need to buy for them to do the cleaning with.'

He turned round on the spot. 'It's a strange mixture of stuff in here. There are things like books and a radio, cushions and vases, which are luxuries to most people, but not the basic items of necessary furniture.'

'I suppose someone just shoved what they didn't need in here and it was forgotten after Miss Chapman died – luckily for me.'

He shook his head. 'They didn't simply shove it in here, they packed it in boxes and stacked them carefully so as not to damage the contents.'

'So they did! I suppose we'll never find out who did it. Anyway, I shall have to concentrate on what I truly need first. You can't pull things out of boxes if you have nowhere to put them. Let's lock up again and call on Mrs Tyler.'

'Maybe you should think about getting something to eat first. It's nearly one o'clock.'

'Oh. Yes, of course. I was so excited I forgot, but now you come to mention it, I am hungry. Where should we go?'

'The village store in Ellindale has a little café with tables. Hikers eat there in the summer, but I'm sure Lily will be able to find you something to eat and make you a pot of tea. She's very obliging. Wouldn't take long to get there, and I can wait for you in the van.'

'Or we could both go in and have something to eat. I'm buying your midday meals when you're with me, and you're not to argue, cousin.'

'Thank you. I didn't want to presume.'

He drove her slowly up the valley and told her about a couple of places they passed, including the new stretch of wall that had been built after the locals helped bring a railway carriage up the hill for a man called Harry Makepeace to live in. Another name to add to her list, she thought. Gabriel knew so many people. How would she ever remember them all?

He slowed down to show her the railway carriage itself, which looked like a cosy place to live in, as big as some houses, really. Amazing what people would do to create homes for themselves.

As he'd said, Lily who ran the shop was happy to serve them and suggested meat pies followed by buttered scones with strawberry jam.

Bella's mouth watered at the mere sound of that.

They ate quickly, Gabriel drained the last of the tea, then avoided looking at her as he said, 'Lily will let you use the lavatory. She has one for the hikers, charges a penny each.'

Bella could feel herself flushing in embarrassment, but had been worrying what to do about that. She paid Lily a penny for each of them to have the privilege of using the facilities, then they went back to the van.

'You'll know where Mrs Tyler lives?'

'Everyone in Birch End does. She's probably at home now. She mainly works in the mornings and spends the afternoons with the baby they've adopted.'

'Do you think she'll mind if we simply turn up?'

'No, of course not. Especially when she knows why. She's a very kind and practical lady, helps a lot of people.'

The maid showed them into a cosy sitting room at the rear of the Tylers' house in Birch End. Mrs Tyler was playing with her baby son on her lap.

Bella's heart melted at the sight of the chubby, smiling little face. 'Oh, what a darling! Can I hold him for a minute? It's so long since I've been near a baby.'

Mrs Tyler held out the rosy-cheeked infant. 'Meet our Robbie.'

The baby gurgled and seemed happy to stay with Bella, but as they chatted she was aware of Mrs Tyler keeping an eye on her. She didn't mind that. If she'd had a child, she'd watch a near stranger holding it carefully too.

When she'd finished explaining why she'd come so soon after their previous meeting, Bella looked at her hostess hopefully.

'That's easy. I can find you someone straight away. Sounds like the place needs an extra-thorough cleaning out.'

'Yes. Frankly, it smells dreadful.'

'I'll get my maid to nip out and ask her two aunts if they can fit you in starting tomorrow. They only live just down the road and they don't work every day, say it's more interesting to do different jobs. They married brothers, and as both their husbands are in work, they're not desperately in need of money. Tyler's use them to clear up inside houses after we've done building jobs. I know other cleaners if they're not free, but those two are the best. They seem to hate dirt with a passion and they'll actually enjoy bringing your place up to scratch.'

'That'll be wonderful.' Bella played with the baby till Mrs Tyler returned from talking to the maid. 'Round and round the garden like a teddy bear.' She ran her fingers lightly around his face and he let out a gurgle of laughter. 'One step, two steps, tickle you under there.' She did the appropriate actions, then tickled him under the chin, making him give more of those delightful baby chuckles.

When she turned, Mrs Tyler was standing in the doorway, watching her and smiling broadly. 'I didn't know that game. I must remember it.'

'You didn't mind?'

'Mind you giving him pleasure? Of course not. Now then, my maid thinks her aunts are free for the rest of this week. She can nip round to see them straight away.'

'Thank you so much.'

Mrs Tyler called down the hall, 'Go and ask them now,' then as she sat down she said, 'You should make yourself known at the village shop when you leave here. Ask them to get you the necessary cleaning stuff from their supplier.'

'I was going to get it in Rivenshaw.'

'It'd be better to get it here in Birch End. They have fewer customers than the bigger shops in town so are more in need of your custom. They'll make sure your equipment is brought up here early in the morning together with tomorrow's deliveries to the shop, and someone will take it across to your house, if you like.'

'Will the shopkeeper mind going to all that trouble?'

'Mind? It'll make their week if you buy it all from them, make a nice difference to their takings.'

Bella knew she should have thought of that, but she wasn't used to organising the financial side of running a house. Of course it would be good to buy your supplies from nearby in such a small village. She would remember that from now on.

'When you go to the shop, tell them I said they're only to give the cleaning materials to Dolly Traske and her sister Gladys when they deliver them.'

'I'll do that.'

'And another thing. Charlie Willcox has a second-hand furniture shop in Rivenshaw with a collection of better furniture out at the back. Gabriel can take you there tomorrow morning and I'm sure you'll find everything you need. You won't have time to go there today after visiting the village shop, and anyway, it sounds as if your new home won't be ready for occupation for a day or two. It'd be better to go looking for furniture when you're fresh and alert. He has some good quality pieces that are much cheaper than new ones and you won't have to wait for delivery from a manufacturer.'

'Good idea.'

'Would you mind if my husband had a good look around inside your house while it's being cleaned tomorrow? He'll be able to measure up properly for when he starts putting in the bathrooms. I know you're in a hurry to move in.'

'No problem at all. And you're right. I am eager to move in.'

'And would you mind if we asked Ryan Cornish to work on the bathrooms? He's a good plumber.'

'Not at all. Why should I mind?'

'Because of him living there.'

'He seems a very nice person to me. He certainly loves his children. And I intend to move in as soon as I can – even before the bathroom is fitted.'

'Excellent. There might be some good news about reno-vating that part of the street after tonight's council meeting.'

When they got outside, Bella asked Gabriel if he knew what Mrs Tyler was hinting at.

He frowned. 'No one's quite sure what's going to happen. It'll depend how the councillors vote. The more reasonable people on the council have only a one-person majority, so if someone's ill, there could be trouble.'

'Are things that tight?'

'Unfortunately. Most of those who own rental properties in the Moss don't want anything changed if they can't use the grant money for themselves. They make a lot of money and rarely do repairs, you see. There are a few people who own their own houses on the outskirts of the worst part or have just one property to rent. They're mostly at your end of Backshaw Moss, and they'll be eager to improve the whole area. It'll be good for you in several ways.'

'What do you mean?'

'If they improve the houses nearby, yours will go up in value, I should think. If you ever want to sell it, that is. But we'll have to wait for the details of the council meeting to be released to find out.'

She hadn't thought of selling. She didn't really care about the value of her house, was just desperate to make it her home.

There were enough practicalities to take into consideration in her new life without wondering about the value of a house she didn't want to sell.

By the time Bella left the village shop an hour later, its owner was beaming at the size of the order and Bella's head was spinning with details.

'You look tired now,' Gabriel commented.

'I am, but I'm happy. Look, after you drop me at Mrs Tucker's, can you go back to the shop and get something for Ed and his friend to eat for tea? I meant to do it while we were there, but I forgot.'

He stared at her as if surprised, then said, 'You're far kinder than most employers to notice that.'

She shrugged, not used to compliments.

'They'll be grateful.'

'I'm the one who's grateful for their help. I want to keep my home safe.'

'Don't push what I said aside. You are being kinder than you need, to me as well.'

'I can't bear to see the hunger in some people's eyes. I wish I could help more of them, but I have to be careful with my money. I shall have a house to look after from now on.'

For a minute his eyes took on a dreamy look. 'Who wouldn't want to keep their very own home safe? If I ever get a place of my own, I shall look after it, I can tell you.'

'I'm sure you'll manage it one day.'

'Most folk don't. But I can dream, can't I?'

'That's what I used to do when I was particularly upset by my cousins' behaviour – dream of better times. They were so unkind to everyone, even their own children, but I knew if I protested or tried to prevent them, they'd keep me away from them. I used to complain a little now and then about having to look after them, and that made my cousins even more determined that I should do it, which is exactly what I wanted.'

'Not had an easy life, have you?'

Bella didn't like to talk about herself so much. 'No. But now wonderful things are happening to me. I'll wish for your life to change in the same way.'

'Thanks – Cousin Bella. Now, you go and have a restful evening at Mrs T's and we'll get you some furniture tomorrow.'

'As soon as I have the basics, I'm moving in, even if there isn't a bathroom yet.'

'I would too.' He chuckled softly as he walked away.

Bella sighed happily.

16

That afternoon when Albert Neven came home from work, he told Alma that when her brother visited her that evening, he'd like to talk to them both about their next step. His smile faded as she immediately began to look apprehensive.

'It's good news, my dear. At least I think it is. But I'd rather tell you both at the same time.'

She nodded, but hardly ate a thing, and his wife shook her head to stop him as he opened his mouth to urge their young guest to eat more.

When the doorbell rang they were in the sitting room and Alma jerked around to look in the direction of the hall, sighing in relief at the sound of her brother's voice.

The maid showed the visitor in and, once Oscar was sitting next to his sister on the sofa, Albert said, 'I won't beat about the bush. What would you think about emigrating to Australia – both of you, that is?'

They gaped at him, then Oscar said, 'I'd love to do that.' He took his sister's hand. 'How about you, Ally? What do you think?'

'We couldn't get any further away from Father, could we, so we'd be safest of all there?'

'I think so,' Albert said.

'I'd go to Timbuctoo tomorrow to get away from him.'

'Good girl.' Oscar patted her hand and turned to Mr Neven. 'What part of Australia were you thinking of?'

'Western Australia. Do you know anything about it?'

'A little. I've, um, looked at emigrating once or twice, but I was thinking more of Sydney or Melbourne.'

'I have a second cousin in the west and I'm sure he'd keep an eye on you and help you settle in. I doubt that your father would even consider Australia, and if he did – well, he too would probably think mainly of Sydney and the eastern states.'

'Then it sounds perfect.'

'I inquired about the airmail letter service, which was started recently to Australia by Imperial Service. I believe it costs one shilling and threepence per letter – or was it fourpence? I can't remember.' He laughed. 'I wish we could send you two by plane, but flights for people cost rather a lot of money, I'm afraid, and still take several gruelling days.'

Oscar gave his sister's hand a quick squeeze. 'We wouldn't expect you to spend that much on us, but if your second cousin could help us once we're there, we'd be grateful to have his advice. How soon can we go?'

'There's a ship leaving in three days' time. You'd have to share a cabin, though.'

Oscar shrugged and smiled at his sister. 'I think we get on well enough to do that.'

Alma looked rather panicked. 'Can we be ready by then? I don't have many clothes.'

'With my wife's help, I'm sure we can buy you enough garments. I'll have a word with the people at the Australian embassy that it'd be all right for you to go, but there aren't usually any problems about British citizens emigrating there. In fact, they encourage it, as long as you're in a good state of health.'

'What's the employment situation like there?' Oscar asked.

'They've been having hard times too, but my cousin will help you find something, I'm sure, and I'll give you enough money to tide you over for a year or so as long as you live modestly.'

Oscar frowned. 'I don't like taking so much from you. And

it's such a waste to buy new clothes when we both have plenty of clothes already – well, we would have if we could get them out of the house. We have possessions we love too, like our books and Ally's drawings. She's a talented artist, but our parents don't let that be known or even allow her to use her paints any longer because they don't think it's respectable.'

'You can't confront them and demand your possessions, though. They'd simply call the police if you tried and—' Albert broke off and suddenly began to smile. 'However . . . What if Lord Pesherton, who is a friend of mine, were to invite your parents to a country house party this weekend? Maybe you could sneak a few of your things out then.'

'Why would he do that?'

'To oblige me. Do they like the country?'

Oscar shook his head. 'Not at all.'

'Even better. I'll ask him to bore them to tears. He'll love that. They've certainly done that to him on more than one occasion. You're sure they'll accept?'

'They'll jump at the chance to visit a titled person, I'm sure.'

'I'll go and phone Laurence straight away. He knows your parents slightly and would never invite them to visit him off his own bat, but when I explain how it'll help you two, he'll love being part of the conspiracy and so will his wife. Come to think of it, they can't stand Maxwell Greene, either. Well, the thought of that nasty old man marrying an innocent young girl like Alma would sicken any decent person.'

While he was away phoning his friend, Mrs Neven asked, 'What about the servants at your parents' home? Won't they try to stop you taking your things?'

'I'll slip them some money to go to the cinema,' Oscar said. 'They all love that and even my parents daren't stop them going out on their days off. Everyone else allows their staff to do it and it's hard to find good help, so even they have to tread carefully.'

Alma swallowed hard and said in a breathless rush of words, 'Even if the servants aren't there, I still can't do it.'

'What can't you do, dear?' her hostess asked.

'I can't go back there. Not for anything. Not even if my parents are away and all the servants are out.'

There was silence, then Mrs Neven said, 'I could go with your brother and pack your things for you.'

Even her husband looked surprised at this as she gave them her gentle smile. 'I could take our chauffeur to protect me if necessary, Albert.'

'I don't like the idea of you getting involved at all, my dear.'

'Nor do I,' Oscar said. 'Send your chauffeur and car with me instead and I'll bring everything from Alma's bedroom.'

Mrs Neven pulled a wry face. 'I suppose I'm being a bit rash even to think of it, but I've never had an adventure. I really envy you two going out to Australia.'

'I'm afraid if I have my way, you never will have any adventures, my dear. I'd not want you to put your safety at risk.' They exchanged loving glances, then Mr Neven turned back to the young man. 'You must pack your things as quickly as you can, try to finish and get out well before the servants come back. Our chauffeur will be with you for protection and can also help carry the things out.'

He fell silent and started frowning.

'Is something wrong, sir?' Oscar asked.

'It occurs to me that if they wanted to be really awkward, they could claim you'd stolen their pieces of luggage, even though your clothes are your own.'

'They're mean enough to do that,' the young man said bitterly.

'I'll send some laundry bags with you,' Mrs Neven said. 'They'll be easier to stuff things into quickly, anyway. I know where to purchase second-hand trunks and suitcases for your journey, because I've done it before for others.'

'That's settled, then,' Albert said.

Oscar had been keeping an eye on the clock. 'I'll have to leave now, I'm afraid. I'll call in at your rooms during my lunch break tomorrow to find out if you've managed to arrange it all.'

Alma let out a whimper of protest as he stood up. 'Don't leave yet.'

'I must, Ally, dear. We don't want them to wonder what I'm doing. I do occasionally go to my friend's club after work just for an hour or so, and he's agreed to say I've been with him tonight if anyone asks. But we don't want to risk them suspecting something is going on if I get home later than usual, do we?'

She shuddered and turned so white Mrs Neven began to wonder what they could do to reassure her. She had rarely seen a young woman so terrified.

That same evening in Rivenshaw, the town council held a special meeting at which Roy Tyler was invited to speak about his investigation into how best to start clearing out Backshaw Moss's worst slums.

'The grant won't cover dealing with the whole of that area, not by a long chalk,' he began. 'So the best way to do it is to use the money to make a start in one area and do more later as finance becomes available.'

Higgerson let out a scornful snort, clearly annoyed when Tyler didn't even look his way, but continued speaking.

'In my professional opinion, we should start on the part of Daisy Street nearest to Birch End. If we ask some of the owners of the better dwellings to help finance the necessary improvements to their own properties, it will reduce the cost to us of the sewage system and make the money go further. Later we can work on the rest of the street and move towards Clover Lane, which as you all know is the worst of the slums. But it'll cost far too much to clear that part yet.'

Higgerson thumped one hand down on the table. 'Don't be ridiculous. You're assuming we'll get more money later,

which I seriously doubt. I'm a builder too and I've already
made a submission as to how the council can make the most
of this one-off grant.'

'Which had seriously flawed costings. Besides, we've already
agreed that none of the people on the council should benefit
directly from this grant,' the mayor reminded him.

'How do you intend to perform this miracle of keeping us
from benefitting?' Higgerson asked. 'We all live in the valley,
don't we? So we'll all benefit, whatever is done. I object strongly
to what Tyler has suggested, however, because it would—'

'Your objection is noted,' the mayor said in a disinterested
voice. 'Please continue, Mr Tyler.'

'I've already sounded out some of the people who own the
better houses on the upper side of Daisy Street, and they've
all expressed their willingness to share the cost of the suggested
improvements. This money will help push the new sewage
system further into the Moss, ready for the next initiative—'
He raised his voice as Higgerson tried to interrupt. 'Whether
it's council or government funded.'

Higgerson's friends interrupted with calls of 'Lies!' and
'Rubbish!' In the end Reg, as mayor, had to roar loudly that
anyone who didn't stop interrupting forthwith would be expelled
from the meeting and lose their chance to vote on the matter.

'I want it on record, Mr Mayor, that I'm trying to stop you
calling in your crony Tyler to do the work and overcharging
the town for these useless minor improvements.' Higgerson
folded his arms and gave them one of his sneering looks. 'And
renovating a few of the better houses at one end of a street
won't count for much.'

'We haven't come to the final part of the proposal,' Charlie
Willcox said. 'Stop interrupting and let Mr Tyler finish.'

Roy stood up again. 'Doing things this way will allow the
council to use the bulk of the grant money to knock down
that whole row of tumbledown dwellings along the lower side

of that end of Daisy Street and rebuild decent houses in their place. This will mean that a full half of one of the streets in Backshaw Moss will have been brought up to modern stand-ards on both sides. It'll also get rid of the danger to health from the present poor sewage arrangements, a danger which might cost the town dearly should it cause an epidemic. If that were to happen, we'd have to pay for improvements to it in full without the benefit of grant money.'

His face a deep red with anger, Higgerson's crony Cecil Pately stood up so abruptly he sent his chair flying and yelled, 'Those are my houses and they're all fully occupied. There is no need to do this. The tenants haven't complained about anything. I shall not agree to having my property knocked down.'

'You won't have a choice if it's voted through today,' Reg said in a mild voice.

'Even the council can't just steal a person's property,' Pately protested.

'Of course not. It'll be a compulsory purchase, for which you'll be compensated according to the values set on those dwellings for rating purposes.'

Reg waited till this had sunk in. He knew, as did most of the councillors present, that Pately had bribed a former plan-ning officer to value his properties far below their real price so that the rates he had to pay as owner would be lower. Unfortunately the man had moved away from Rivenshaw soon afterwards and they'd been unable to trace him, so they'd been unable to prove anything to the satisfaction of the law.

Now Pately was hoist with his own petard and would get far less than the houses' value in compensation.

Reg allowed himself a quick half-smile as they waited for a response. This couldn't happen to a more deserving rogue.

'Property values have risen since then,' Higgerson put in quickly.

He would say that, Charlie thought. Higgerson had also

done some undervaluing with his own properties in Backshaw Moss. He watched the mayor smile for a second time.

'If you wish to complain about the rateable value, we can revalue all the properties in Backshaw Moss and, if any are outrageously low, we'll be able to claim backdated payments. That would provide an increase in rates money that might allow us to extend the clearing of the worst slums in the valley a little further.'

The mayor let that sink in, then continued, 'Make no mistake, ladies and gentlemen, we are going to do it. Some of us care about our poorer citizens as well as about our own wallets.'

Higgerson breathed in deeply, but said nothing further on the topic.

'Let us put Mr Tyler's recommendations to the vote.'

'Standing orders say we have to allow time for thought and discussion,' Pately snapped at once.

'I vote we suspend standing orders, then, since we'll lose the special grant if we don't use it quickly,' Charlie said hastily.

'Those in favour of suspending it?' Reg looked around and, when the clerk had counted and reported the numbers, he said, 'Carried!' in a loud voice.

Leah Selby raised her hand and looked to Reg for permission to speak. 'I think we should vote immediately on starting the improvements, Mayor, and since no builder except Mr Tyler has tendered for the job, I propose that, given the exceptional circumstances, we also approve of him starting work as expeditiously as possible.'

'Seconded,' Charlie said at once.

That proposal was also carried, which brought an even deeper scowl to the faces of Higgerson and his coterie.

Todd turned sideways to wink at his wife. It had gone as expected and she'd wanted to be the person to propose this immediate action, because she thought it would be good for certain people in the valley to see women taking an active part in council business. He knew how deeply she cared about this sort of attitude, because she'd had to face a lot of prejudice after her first marriage, when she had started the fizzy drink business that was still providing a few jobs even in these hard times.

He didn't blame her for wanting to rub old-fashioned people's noses in the fact that women could be successful in public life. He remembered from his experiences during the Great War how women had made a difference, taking over men's jobs and driving ambulances through the worst of the battlefields. Yes, and some had died for their country doing it, just like the men. He had admired them greatly.

'A good night's work,' he said on the way home. 'But we'd all better keep an eye on Higgerson. He's the master of dirty tricks.'

'Just let him start on anything I'm involved with! I'm not the only woman in this town who's had enough of him. If I were not so close to my time, I'd do more than annoy him verbally, believe me.'

He grinned. She could be as fierce as a man in defending her own.

She was a wonderful woman and Todd felt lucky to have won her after she became a widow. He'd been happy to take on raising Jonah's child, and to help pay for her sister Rose's university fees if everything worked out as expected. And he was thrilled about the coming child, his first.

He stopped her outside their front door to give her a quick kiss.

'What's that for, Todd?'

'Because I love you.'

17

After breakfast, Bella went to stand outside her lodgings and wait for Gabriel to arrive. A sky filled with lowering dark clouds was threatening rain, but she wasn't going to let that spoil her day. She was so looking forward to buying some furniture. She'd be careful with her money, of course she would, but it'd be wonderful to choose her own comfortable chair, instead of the rickety wooden rocking chair she'd had to put up with in her London bedroom all those years.

Brr. It was cold. Without thinking, she swung around and started to walk briskly up and down. She moved just in time to avoid a soggy ball of mud that smelled foul and must have been hurled at her from behind a wall.

She darted quickly under the porch and tried to see who had done this, but footsteps clattering on the cobbles of the side alley told her they'd already run off. Gabriel had warned her about this sort of thing, hadn't he? She'd not believed it'd happen in public areas, though, and especially not in broad daylight.

Well, the incident set the final seal on her decision. She was definitely going to have a go at learning to drive. It'd be useful in so many ways in a valley with only an occasional bus service going up and down it. You could buy a small second-hand car for around twenty-five pounds, so it'd not make too big a hole in her savings. And the cost of petrol would be partly offset by not having to pay bus fares.

Did she dare do it – get behind the wheel of a car?

She stiffened, annoyed with herself for even thinking so timidly, and vowed to have a go at driving if it killed her.

She was glad when Gabriel turned up, and ran across to get into his van quickly.

'I called in at your house on the way and the Traske sisters have started work already. They said to come later if you can, because there will be nothing but dirt and dust for the first few hours.'

'Oh, that's good. We can take our time looking at furniture, then.' She sighed and checked that no dirt had hit her skirt, then turned around to see whether they were being followed.

'Something wrong?' he asked.

By the time she'd finished telling him about the attempt to upset her, they'd arrived at Charlie Willcox's second-hand furniture shop. She knew by now that Mr Willcox was a well-known figure in the valley and had a finger in all sorts of pies. But since Gabriel seemed to have a lot of respect for him, she was interested to meet him and was hoping he'd be here today.

So many things to do and learn now. How wonderful that was! She'd been very bored many a time, which was why she'd started writing her little children's stories. They were in her luggage, which was still waiting for her at the station.

They walked through the shop, moving past piles of miscellaneous goods till they got to the rear of the long, narrow space. It broadened out again at the back, where a plump, smiling man was standing. His round spectacles with dark frames made him look like a friendly owl. He was discussing something with a younger man, who looked like a shop assistant.

She didn't need Gabriel's whispered, 'That's Mr Willcox,' to tell her the bespectacled man was the owner. He looked to be totally at home and in charge here.

He came across when they stopped. 'How do, Gabriel, lad?'

'I'm well, thank you, Mr Willcox. I've brought you a

customer. Miss Porter is new to the valley and has just inherited Number 23 Daisy Street.'

'Hello,' she said.

He beamed at her. 'Welcome to the valley, Miss Porter. I hope you're going to stay here. I can tell by your accent that you're from the south, but the Ellin Valley is a grand place to live, and Lancashire folk are the salt of the earth.'

'I'm hoping to settle here permanently, but I'm going to need some furniture before I can move into my house, so Mrs Tyler suggested I come here. I have to be careful with my money, you see, so I'll only need the basic items to begin with, then we'll see what else I can afford later. But if I can, I'd like to buy things that look nice.'

He turned to the other man. 'I'll see to the lady, John,' then gestured to the area around them. 'You're in the right place for the very best second-hand furniture for miles around. I keep my really good stuff here at the back. How about starting with a bed?'

He gestured to his right and they followed him a few steps. 'We have some very nice sprung metal frames with headboards. You'll be delighted with the prices, but I'd advise you to purchase a brand new mattress. I keep a stock of them at very reasonable prices.'

'Oh yes, I will.' She took his advice on which bed frame and mattress to choose, bouncing solemnly on one he set out for her to try, and nodding approval. She was looking forward to sleeping on it, hadn't had such a comfortable bed for years.

He called out for his assistant to set the bed aside then turned back to her. 'Next, Miss Porter?'

'Some comfortable chairs for the sitting room, and a kitchen table with upright chairs. I think that'll do me for starters.'

'Won't you need a kitchen cabinet as well?'

'Oh! I never thought of that. Yes, of course I will. There is a cupboard I can use as a pantry, but I'll need something to prepare food on, won't I? I hope cabinets aren't too expensive.'

'I'll find you a special bargain, as a welcome to the valley – one with a modern, pull-out working surface.'

'Thank you so much.'

He asked how she came to own the house, so she replied with equal frankness, explaining what a wonderful surprise it had been.

'I remember James Beaton. Nice gentleman. He inherited all three houses from Miss Chapman about two years ago. She didn't live to make old bones, did she, poor soul? I heard he'd died recently too, and have been wondering who would inherit from him. Do you know who the other two houses were left to?'

'No. I didn't even know Mr Beaton owned them till I came here.'

'Well, you've arrived at an interesting time.' He lowered his voice. 'In confidence, the council is going to demolish that row of houses opposite, and about time too. They're on the verge of falling down and they're not even on mains sewage.' He mimed holding his nose. 'Has anyone spoken to you about your house?'

'What? Mr Tyler said they weren't going to demolish it.'

'No, no, I remember now. Of course we wouldn't knock any of those three down. The council is going to offer you financial help with renovations, if you pay half the costs.'

'Mr Tyler mentioned that it might be a possibility.'

He looked around to make sure no one could overhear, before adding, 'The measure to do this was passed at the council meeting yesterday, but it's not been announced yet.'

'Well, that's wonderful.'

He beamed at her again. 'Let's find you the rest of the things you need for your new home. But remember, not a word about this money to anyone yet. Gabriel, that means you, too.'

'You know you can trust me to keep quiet, Mr Willcox. I'm just driving Miss Porter around till she learns to drive herself and buys a car.'

'If you need a car as well, you should go to Todd Selby. He'll see you right about finding a reliable one, Miss Porter. I'm a partner in his business so I know you can trust him.'

They continued around the rear of the shop and found a lounge suite with maroon moquette upholstery that was hardly worn at all, and anyway, she could sew some arm rest covers to hide the slight signs of wear and tear at the front edges. It was so comfortable to sit on that she leaned back and sighed happily.

When she opened her eyes again she saw both men smiling down at her. 'I've been living in rather uncomfortable surroundings for a long time. This suite will be absolutely wonderful, Mr Willcox. I'll take it.'

She chose a kitchen table that came complete with six chairs, not four. Oh, good! She'd be able to use one beside her bed. And there was a lovely kitchen cabinet with a pull-out working surface, two drawers and cupboards below it, and glass-fronted upper cupboards. Then she saw the price on it and her heart fell. 'I'm afraid I can't afford that much.'

Mr Willcox smiled kindly and reduced the price by half. 'I'll let you have it at cost as a welcome to our valley. When do you want your things delivered?'

'Thank you very much, Mr Willcox. I'd like them as soon as the house has been thoroughly cleaned. It was left rather dirty. In two or three days, I hope. May I let you know? And I'll have to go to the bank to get money out to pay you now, because I don't have a chequebook yet. But I can put a deposit on the furniture.'

He laughed. 'No need to do that. I trust you to come back. Anyway, nobody with an open expression like yours could possibly be a cheat.'

Bella and Gabriel visited the bank next and when they left the shop for a second time, she stopped suddenly and took a few deep breaths. 'I can't believe this is happening.'

She let out a cry of shock as he suddenly shoved her to one side and stood in front of her, roaring, 'I saw you, Philip Little! I'll be telling your ma about this tonight.'

'That's the second time someone's tried to throw dirt at me today,' she said in a shaky voice. 'Thank you for pushing me out of the way.'

He hesitated and tried to distract her. 'Look. We're not far from the driving school. Let's go and book you a lesson now. In my opinion, the sooner you learn to drive and get a car the better.'

She stared at him, still feeling rather wobbly, but after a moment she drew herself up. She wasn't going to let anything stop her. 'Yes. Let's do that.'

'Good lass.'

Gabriel took her along two streets and stopped at an open space covered in tarmac, on which stood a neat row of cars. He gestured towards them. 'Useful arrangement, eh? The driving school's office is in the same building as the car sales and repairs. People can learn to drive, then buy a car.'

The door to the office was open and a man was sitting behind the desk, looking lost in thought. He suddenly realised they were there and jerked to attention. 'Sorry. Can I help you, madam? Oh, hello, Gabriel.'

'This is Miss Porter. Miss Porter, this is Silas Johnson, one of the instructors.'

Bella nodded, feeling nervous before she even started to discuss the lessons. It seemed such a big step.

'Have you started working here full-time now?' Gabriel asked Silas.

Did everyone know everyone else? she wondered.

'Just beginning to be here steady, like. Mrs Howarth is expecting and she gets tired quickly, so she's mostly leaving the office work to me, and I also do some of the teaching when her husband is busy.'

Gabriel grinned. 'From what I've seen, Nick's so thrilled about the baby he's hovering over her like a hen with one chick.'

Once again, Gabriel was chatting away. What made him tongue-tied with some people and not with others?

'Nick is definitely happy about it,' Silas said diplomatically. 'Now, how can I help you?'

'Miss Porter wants to learn to drive.'

'I'd like to try a lesson first to make sure I'm not – you know, hopeless at it,' she said.

Silas nodded. 'Very sensible. And I promise to tell you the truth. Not many people are hopeless, though some need more practice than others. There can be other reasons for problems. One of my customers did a lot better when she spent the money on bifocal lenses for driving spectacles. I had a lot of trouble persuading her to try it, but the newer types of bifocals aren't as fragile as the others used to be.' He smiled. 'Sorry. Didn't mean to bore you. It's an interest of mine, what makes some people good drivers and others not. Don't worry. We'll get you up to scratch before you arrange for your test.'

She felt embarrassed to have immediately found a gap in her general knowledge. 'What do you mean by saying I have to arrange for the test? I'd have thought you'd do that.'

'No, the one who's learned to drive has to arrange to meet the examiner somewhere to do a test.'

'Don't the examiners have an office like you do?'

'Unfortunately not. We usually advise our customers to meet the examiner at the park, and then we make sure they practise driving around the streets near it.'

'Ah. I see.' She'd had no idea about such details. 'Is the test hard?'

'Not really. We'd not suggest you arrange it till we're sure you can do all that's needed. You have to show you're in control of the car, can change gears smoothly, reverse accurately, and so on.' He looked at her expectantly. 'When would you like a trial lesson?'

'Um—'

Gabriel took over. 'As soon as possible.'

'This afternoon? Two o'clock?'

That was too soon for her. Even this short conversation had shown her how little she knew of the details. 'No, no! I need to buy a copy of the Highway Code first and go over all the rules.'

He grinned at her. 'That does help. When would suit you, then? Not Sundays, of course – the Sunday Observance Laws prevent us from giving lessons on that day.'

Gabriel continued to prompt her. 'Monday afternoon? It really isn't hard, Bella, and you want to get your first lesson in before you move into your new house, then one a day till you can pass the test. The sooner you're able to buy a car, the safer you'll be.'

'I suppose so.'

'Apart from anything else, I won't always be able to borrow Jericho's van, but once you're sure you'll be OK driving you can buy a car even before you pass the test. That way, if you need to go anywhere next week, I can drive you in your own vehicle whatever my brother is doing. Yes, and I can let you have a practice on a quiet stretch of road if you're feeling up to it once Silas says it's OK. You fell lucky this week that Jericho didn't need his van at all, but he and his wife will probably want to go out for a drive on the moors if it's fine tomorrow.'

'Can I ask why you're worrying about her being safe?' Silas looked from one to the other, frowning.

Bella was beginning to expect blunt questions even after

this short time in the north, but she didn't mind. She found it a lot easier to cope with than the sneaky tricks and lies hidden behind the insincere smiles of her Beaton relatives and their snobby acquaintances.

'She's inherited one of those big houses at the end of Daisy Street, turfed Mrs Goodby out for being dirty, and sacked Welch for dipping his finger in the till. Which has upset both of them.'

'Ah. Yes, it would upset Welch to lose a customer, but it serves him right. If he wants to turn into an honest businessman as he claims, he'll have to be honest. You definitely ought to be safer in a car than on foot, Miss Porter – well, unless you're an erratic driver. And I doubt you will be. Anyway, think of the sheer convenience of having a car. I've just bought one of my own from Todd. I had an old motorbike before. Not much fun in the rain, though she was very reliable. What sort of car were you thinking of buying?'

'I haven't the faintest idea.'

'Come and have a look at a few, get an idea of what's available.' He took her agreement for granted and gestured politely for her to go out to the line of cars first.

She felt as if fate was pushing her in a new direction. Before she could say anything, the two men had escorted her outside and introduced her to Todd.

He asked a couple of questions, studied her, and showed her three cars which might be suitable for a smaller person.

They persuaded her to sit in each car in turn, and she had to confess that the blue Austin 7 Swallow Sedan was rather nice, very comfortable to sit in, and small enough not to terrify her about driving it through the streets. After all, you didn't have to go fast, did you? And she really liked the colour, which made the three men chuckle.

'Women always care more about the colour than men do,' Todd said.

'I'll – definitely think about this one,' she said. 'But I need to try driving first, see how I go.'

At last Gabriel seemed to become aware of how rushed she was feeling and held up one hand to stop them. 'Right then, lads. Miss Porter will want to have a think about it. That's been a lot to take in. We'll see you on Monday afternoon for the first lesson, Silas. And if you put the blue car to one side for a day or two, Todd, she'll maybe come and have a try at driving it up and down that street next to the park once she's had a bit of practice, and let you know what she thinks.'

'I'll do that.'

When they were on the way back to the van, he said quietly, 'Sorry. I got carried away, it was all so convenient to arrange. A bit too much and too soon for you, perhaps?'

Perversely, she didn't want to admit that, didn't want to seem a coward. 'Not exactly. But that's enough for the moment. Apart from there being so much to learn, I'm not used to spending that much money – well, I'm not used to having any money to spare, and what with the furniture and – and everything, it's taking some getting used to. What I need to do before anything else is buy a Highway Code, see if the rules makes sense, and have a go at driving.'

So he took her to the post office, and after that they at last got back to the van. Sinking into the passenger seat, she let out a long whoosh of relief. She was glad when Gabriel didn't speak for a moment or two, allowing her time to recover from what was, for her, the most exciting morning she'd had for years.

When he didn't set off straight away, she glanced sideways. 'Where to, Miss Porter?'

She couldn't resist teasing him. 'You're supposed to call me Bella now, Cousin Gabriel, aren't you?'

'Bella, then. Do you want to go and look at your house,

see how it's getting on? I bet the Traske sisters have got stuck in and made a difference already.'

'Yes, let's do that. But on the way, can we stop next to a field and just sit quietly for a few minutes? Somewhere with a view of the moors, if possible. They make me feel peaceful inside.'

'I know what you mean, and I know exactly the place to stop.'

He went past the turn-off to Birch End and a short distance up the hill, before pulling in to the side and switching off the engine. There was enough room to park the van on a slant so that it looked across the road towards the moors.

The sudden peace and quiet seemed to throb around her. Across a couple of fields lay great stretches of moorland, rolling away into the distance. It was so spacious and serene, it made human troubles seem rather unimportant.

He gestured with one hand. 'There you are, lass. I stop here sometimes when I'm walking up the hill to Ellindale.'

'It's perfect. I'll get out and stand near that wall for a few moments, if you don't mind. There's a lovely fresh breeze blowing.' She'd spent too much time indoors in the past few years. And when a tiny bird landed on the wall nearby and stayed there only a handspan away as it preened its feathers, that made her feel even better.

He watched her, seeing a more relaxed look settle on her face, but he made no attempt to join her. She'd been thrown into the middle of a right old mess with her inheritance, but she had that house, and the interior could be sorted out bit by bit. Ah, how he envied her that!

When she came back, he was out of the van, leaning on the bonnet.

'I'm glad you don't smoke,' she said.

'I reckon it's a fancy way of burning money, and I don't have enough to do that.'

'I don't like the smell of it.'

'No, Mam won't have any smoking in her house, which upsets some folk.'

'I might do that too.' She gestured with one hand. 'I loved gazing into the far distance, can't seem to get enough of it.'

'Wait till you've tramped across the moors with the cloud shadows chasing you. That will make you feel on top of the world, literally. I'm sorry to have rushed you into things today, but I got excited for you.'

'I'm not sorry. I probably needed a bit of a push, but I enjoyed it too. Only afterwards I needed time to pull myself together in case we find ourselves confronting Mrs Goodby again at my house.'

'I doubt she'll come back, let alone shout at you. Besides, you'll be with the Traske sisters, and they're fearsome women when something makes them angry. I should think they'll approve of you, but be warned, they'll still boss you around!'

She was amused by that idea. She'd never met working women who stood up for themselves and what they believed in. She rather liked the idea of it.

Her amusement faded as she wondered if the servants at her cousin's house had felt scornful about her, underneath their polite exterior. They'd been helpful and polite, but not friendly, and had often stopped talking when she went into a room. She'd guessed they'd been talking about her or her cousins.

Ah, well. That was all over and done with now. Things had changed, and she'd changed with them. She was going to make sure she stood up for herself from now on, no matter who she was dealing with.

18

Oscar managed to catch the cook out shopping at the market. 'Mrs Baxter, I'm leaving London soon and didn't want to go without saying goodbye to you.'

She nodded. 'I don't blame you for leaving, Master Oscar. I'm going myself at the end of the year. I've told your father that I'll be getting married. He wasn't best pleased, but he can't stop me.'

'I hope you'll be very happy. Look, I wanted to give you and the other servants a farewell "present" of a visit to the cinema. Do you think they'd like that? You could all go together for once, while my parents are away in the country.'

She studied him, then said quietly, 'Get us all out of the house, do you mean?'

He didn't know what to say.

She patted his arm. 'I'll make sure everyone's out at the cinema tomorrow night.'

'Thank you.'

'Your father went through everything in your room and in your sister's, but didn't find anything amiss. They were in a mess by the time he'd finished, though, so don't be surprised.' She held up one hand. 'Don't tell me exactly what you're planning. I'll tell the staff it's me who's giving them a treat to celebrate getting engaged to be married.'

Oscar had never been as frightened in his whole life as when he used his door key for the last time to get into the house with Albert Neven's chauffeur, Davis, to retrieve the clothes and possessions.

He took plenty of laundry bags and simply stuffed clothes and other items into them. The chauffeur helped him by carrying each filled bag out to the car, and keeping an eye out for any of the servants returning early.

It wasn't until the two men drove away that Oscar was able to breathe more easily. Even so, he still kept peering behind the car in case anyone was following them.

There followed a frantic two days of preparations and packing for Oscar and Alma. With Mrs Neven's help, he and Alma divided their luggage up into groups of garments, so that clean ones could be brought up to their cabin partway through the voyage, and the ones they'd been wearing packed in one of the trunks till they arrived.

Mr Neven took charge of the final escape. He said he'd hire a car to take them to the Southampton docks, and they'd drive through the night, instead of taking the train. But he still hadn't arranged all the final details of how they'd leave London.

Oscar remained in a highly nervous state, because he was sure when his father found out that he'd taken their clothes away, he'd be searching for them both in earnest.

He was lodged in the bedroom next to his sister's at the lawyer's house and had taken to pacing up and down the corridor on that floor to use up some of his energy. He nearly bumped into the youngest maid a couple of times, but after her initial surprise, she simply nodded and passed by, so he didn't think any more about it.

Mr Neven didn't tell them the final details until the second day. 'You'll set off this evening, arriving in time to board the ship early the following morning.'

'Will it take that long to drive to Southampton?' Oscar wondered.

'If you look like arriving too early, the driver has orders to park somewhere off the main road till a suitable time. The main thing I'm concerned about is getting you away from this house without you being seen and pursued.'

'We're grateful to you for doing all this,' Oscar said.

'Keep your gratitude until we've succeeded. Your father came to my office yesterday to ask if I'd seen either of you. He was . . . rather uncivil, and didn't seem to believe me when I said I hadn't. Well, I'm not the world's best liar.'

Alma clutched her brother's arm. 'He'll find us, I know he will.'

'I'm planning it all very carefully,' Mr Neven assured her, but like her brother, she found it hard to believe that anyone could get the better of their father.

As it grew dark, his sister grew more nervous, and in the end, Oscar caught her on her own and scolded her. 'I know you're nervous, but I'm sure Mr Neven's arrangements are really well thought out.'

He gave her a big hug, then held her by the shoulders at arm's length. 'We'll soon be leaving. Don't give in to your nerves or you might do something stupid and let our father win.' As an afterthought he added, 'If Bella got away from him, so can we.'

Her face brightened at that thought. 'Yes, she did, didn't she?'

The older of the two maids knocked on the bedroom door. 'Mr Neven says you should go down to join him, then the chauffeur can load the final cases into the car.'

'Yes. We'll only be a minute.' Oscar gave his sister a stern look. 'Ready, Ally?'

She looked so young and fragile, he felt sorry for her, but was relieved to see her take a few deep breaths and straighten up.

Downstairs Mr Neven was pacing up and down, also looking anxious. 'Would you believe it, your father has paid someone to keep watch on this house? Good thing Davis noticed him.'

'How are we going to get out of here without being seen then?'

Mr Neven's smile was genuine. 'My wife and I will drive off in the car with all your luggage, and Penscombe has arranged for a van to deliver a couple of parcels at the rear entrance and collect you two at the same time. Davis will get out of our car in the next street and come back to join you while I drive my wife and myself to our friends' house. You'll have to crouch in the back of the van, but we're fairly sure they've only got one man watching the house.'

Oscar and his sister watched the Nevens leave, then went out to the kitchen.

It was longer than they expected before Davis came in, and he was looking worried. 'Good thing I went into the storeroom for something before I came into the house, because I heard voices. They've got two men watching the house now.'

'Oh no! What are we going to do?'

Oscar thought hard. 'They must have a vehicle.'

'Yes,' said Davis. 'It's parked behind the gates at the back. What's worrying me most is that someone must have told them you were here.'

'I bumped into the younger maid a few times outside my room yesterday.'

'She shouldn't have been on the guest-room floor. I'll mention that to Mr Neven. In the meantime, we have to find a way to stop them following us.'

For a few moments Oscar despaired, then he thought of one of his favourite detective novels featuring Hercule Poirot. The book was in his trunk now, together with a few other similar stories. He decided to live up to his hero and said slowly, 'Or we'll make sure they're unable to follow us. What if we can manage to slash their tyres?'

'Good idea,' Davis said.

'I'll do that, then.'

'We'll do it together, one keeping watch, sir. There are two of them, remember.'

Oscar nodded and looked at his sister. 'Stay strong, Ally! Tell the van driver we've got trouble and won't be long.'

'I couldn't bear to be taken back to Father now.'

They crept out and Alma looked at the driver, who was grey-haired and looked as nervous as she was. 'Better hide in the back of the van, miss.'

She did as he suggested, but wouldn't let him shut the door, wanted to see if anyone came looking for her. The driver went back to sit and wait, with the engine running.

She saw a tyre lever on the floor of the van and picked it up to defend herself with, more determined than ever that no one was going to take her back to her father.

The two young men crept out into the alley by unbolting a door at the far side of the garage.

'You keep watch. I'll puncture the tyres,' Oscar whispered.

He'd managed to damage two of them when a man suddenly pounced on him and yelled, 'Help! They're trying to escape.'

As Oscar dropped the knife and struggled with his attacker, footsteps thumped towards them, but to his relief, the chauffeur grabbed the second man.

Unfortunately the two watchers turned out to be experienced fighters and very quickly both Oscar and Davis were struggling to survive.

Suddenly Oscar's opponent grunted and fell to the ground groaning, only half conscious.

He looked across the body at his sister's white, terrified face, and saw a tyre lever in her hand.

He grabbed it from her and used it on the second watcher, who had his back to them and had already knocked Davis to his knees.

Oscar wasn't as lucky as his sister with his blow and though the man yelled in pain, he continued to struggle. However, between them, he and Davis managed to subdue the fellow.

'We need something to tie him up,' Davis panted.

'Here, use this.' Alma pulled off her scarf.

A final struggle ended with the attacker lying helplessly on the ground, glaring at them. He didn't yell for help or for anyone to call for the police, though, just said in a low voice, 'They'll come after you. Never saw a chap as determined as your father. You might as well give in now.'

Alma took an involuntary step backwards.

'Get in the van, Ally. Tell the driver I'll only be a minute.' Oscar retrieved his knife from the ground near the other car and used it quickly on the remaining tyres, then jumped into the back of the van.

Davis shut the second door and struggled to keep it closed as the van pulled quickly out of the backyard. The van driver took Alma and Oscar slowly along the back streets, making as little noise as possible. When they got to a backyard, he left the engine running and came to open the back door of the van. 'I'm to leave you here.'

He closed the back doors the minute they got out, then left without a word.

The Nevens' car was waiting for them. The lawyer and his wife were presumably inside the house.

'Come on!' Davis said. 'We need to get going.'

'They'll come after us,' Oscar said. 'They know what this car looks like. There aren't many people can afford a Lanchester.'

'Mr Neven's thought of that. Just sit tight. I have to drive fast.'

★

Later that evening, the police knocked on the door of the Nevens' house. 'I wish to speak to your master.'

The older of the two maids had answered it. 'He isn't home.'

'No, I bet he isn't. There's been a report that he's aiding and abetting a minor to escape from her parents. I'd like to come in and check what you say for myself.'

'I daren't let you in.'

The younger policeman pushed her aside, so sure of his information that he didn't call his superior.

A search of the house showed no sign of the lawyer and his wife, or the young woman they were searching for, and they couldn't get a word of sense out of the young maid, who looked terrified.

'I told you they weren't here,' the older woman said. 'They went out ages ago and they won't be back till nearly midnight.'

'Where did he say he was going?' the sergeant demanded.

'To Lord Melbrow's house, a dinner party,' she replied.

'Were they alone in the car?'

'No.'

'Aha!'

'The chauffeur was driving them.'

'No one else in the car?'

'Of course not. No one else lives here.'

'What's his lordship's address?'

'I'm afraid I don't know exactly. Somewhere in Belgravia, I think.'

When the police had driven away, the younger maid came into the hall to join her. 'You were so brave.'

'I liked that poor young lady, and anyway, Mr Neven told me exactly what to say and do, if necessary.'

'Can I go to bed now. Mrs Neven said I wouldn't be needed again tonight.'

'It's not like you to go to bed early. Don't you want a cup of cocoa first?'

'No, thank you. I might be catching a cold.' She hesitated, then asked, 'What do you think will happen to Mr and Mrs Neven?'

'Nothing. They really were going to a dinner party. This young lady who's run away has nothing to do with them.'

'But what about the one who was staying upstairs? Wasn't that her?'

'Miss Christie? No, of course not. She was another of Mrs Neven's rescues. Nothing to do with the Beatons.'

'There was a young man, too.'

She turned to stare at the younger woman. 'How do you know about him? You shouldn't have been on their floor.'

'Nothing. I saw him a couple of times. I was just – curious. About the police coming, I mean.'

His lordship didn't take kindly to having the police disturb his dinner party by insisting on speaking to two of his guests. He kept the sergeant waiting in the hall and stormed back into the dining room, explaining to his old friend in a loud voice what the police were asking.

Neven spoke in a low voice. 'Bring the sergeant in here. I'll complain to his superior tomorrow, but for the moment I want him to see us here with you.'

His lordship winked at him and went back to fetch the sergeant. 'Look for yourself.'

'How long have they been here?'

'Mr and Mrs Neven have been here for nearly two hours, if it's any of your business.'

There was dead silence in the room and the lighting was good enough for them to see the tide of colour that flooded the sergeant's face.

'May I ask who told you this faradiddle?' Neven asked.

'It was the captain he told it to, not me.'

'Who's "he"?'

'A Mr Beaton, I believe.'

'Mr Thomas Beaton?'

'Yes, sir.'

'Has the man run mad?'

'His daughter has run away from home, sir. And his son. He's very worried about their safety, especially hers.'

'What has that to do with me? I am no longer his lawyer.'

'He told the captain they'd taken refuge at your house, but we searched it and they weren't there. No sign of any other bedrooms being occupied, either.'

Mr Neven stood up. 'You searched my house? Did you have a search warrant?'

'No, sir. We were – in a hurry, thinking of the young lady, sir.'

'Nonetheless you had no right even to enter my house without official permission, and I shall be making a formal complaint first thing tomorrow.'

'I don't know what the world is coming to,' his lordship said angrily.

'I'm sorry, sir. I can see now that you've not been involved. Only apparently Mr Beaton was certain you must be, and he's a well respected gentleman.'

'Mr Beaton appears to me to have gone quite mad. Anyway, you can make your apologies to his lordship and leave us to enjoy the rest of the evening as much as one can after such an intrusion.'

When the police had left, the two men exchanged glances, then resumed their seats at the dinner table, chatting about the incident with their friends, then moving on to other matters of mutual interest.

A couple of hours later, the butler announced that Mr Neven's chauffeur had arrived to take him home, as arranged, and all the guests took leave of their hosts.

'Drinks at the club tomorrow?' his lordship asked his friend.

'Why not?'

The chauffeur sported a bruise on one hand big enough to be seen even by the dim light of the streetlamps.

Mr Neven waited till they'd set off to ask, 'Trouble?'

'Yes, sir. Two men were lying in wait outside your house. I'm afraid one of your servants must have been disloyal. But your fallback plan worked well after we'd dealt with them.'

'We'll check that they're no longer loitering around when we get back.'

'It's my guess they'll have gone, sir. They'd not want to be seen by the police.'

'We can only leave our young friends in the hands of fate now, and hope that Beaton won't even think of them going to Australia.'

'Well, they're not sailing under their own names,' his wife said in her calm comfortable voice.

'Unfortunately, I suspect Beaton will go after Bella next, expecting to find them taking refuge with her. He won't find any sign of Oscar and Alma, but I'd better warn her. He can be – difficult.'

'Oh dear! I hadn't thought of him trying to harm Bella.'

He leaned back and let out a long sigh. 'I'll contact her tomorrow and warn her. Thank you for your help tonight, Davis. You've more than earned your bonus.'

'I was happy to help them, sir. That young lady was terrified.'

When they got back, they found that the young chambermaid had gone missing.

'There's your informant, Albert,' Mrs Neven said.

'I doubt we'll see hide nor hair of her again.'

19

A short rest gazing at the beautiful view of the moors made Bella feel much better, and she was now looking forward to seeing her house again. She hadn't wanted to go back into that foul-smelling entrance hall till something had been done about it, and everyone had said the Traske sisters liked to be left alone to get on with a job.

As the van stopped in Daisy Street, a woman came out and grimaced in disgust as she threw a tattered object that looked like a ragged doormat on top of a pile of rubbish. She was about to go back inside when she saw Bella and Gabriel getting out of the vehicle, so waited for them, hands on hips.

'This is Miss Porter,' Gabriel told her. 'Miss Porter, Dolly Traske.'

The woman studied her carefully, then nodded as if satisfied with what she saw. 'Pleased to meet you, miss. Come inside and meet my sister Gladys.'

'I'll just nip into the village and buy some petrol, if that's all right,' Gabriel said. 'Don't go wandering off anywhere till I return, Bella.'

Dolly gave him a sharp look at his use of his employer's first name, but didn't comment.

Always that reminder to keep safe, Bella thought in annoyance, but when she looked across the road at the sleazy group of houses, she could see why. There were two men standing at the far end who looked like tramps, they were so poorly clad. They were eyeing her as if assessing the value of everything about her, ready to grab her handbag at the first opportunity.

If the council hadn't been going to knock those houses down, she might have thought twice about coming to live here permanently. But those men wouldn't be here for much longer, surely? Once the sagging buildings were demolished there would be nothing worth hanging around for.

It was no use seeing trouble everywhere she looked. She must concentrate on the positive aspects of the situation. She was suddenly eager to see what had been done inside the house so far. Dolly had already gone back inside so Bella followed her. Fresh air was blowing steadily through the hall from the flat and bringing with it that same horrible sweaty, dirty smell, though somewhat reduced now, thank goodness.

Dolly looked at her expression. 'Don't worry. We'll get rid of most of that smell by tomorrow, miss, then we'll scrub it again on Monday. But you'd be better leaving the doors and windows open tonight after we've scrubbed the whole of the ground floor out, and in the daytime, at least over the weekend. My hubby says it's going to be windy then, and that'll give this place a good blow-through.'

'Leave them open?!'

'Yes. Ed says you've hired him and his cousin to keep watch overnight, so it should be safe enough, and if it rains, they'll close all the windows and doors. He's around here somewhere. He was dozing in the scullery till we told him he was in our way. They're a good pair of lads, them two are.'

'What was he doing here in the daytime?'

'Looking for somewhere peaceful to sleep. They're crowded out in their house. I sent him to sleep up on the top floor out of my way. The tenants are out at work most of the day, even now. They daren't miss a day's wages. That was all right, wasn't it?'

'Yes, of course.' She could see what Gabriel had meant by saying the sisters were bossy.

Dolly led the way into the next room and introduced Bella to a woman who looked amazingly like her. They both seemed amused at her surprise.

'Gladys an' me are identical twins. Our husbands are brothers too, only they're not twins and don't look as alike as we do.'

'Goodness. I've never actually met identical twins before.'

'We used to get up to mischief with being so alike when we were kids, fooling people about which was which. I don't know how our mam stood it. She could allus tell us apart, though. We never once managed to fool her. But don't worry. We won't try that sort of thing on you. We've got a bit more sense at our age.'

'We were glad you trusted us to make a start here,' Dolly added. 'We know better than most how to clean up a place.'

Bella looked around, delighted with the progress they'd made. 'You certainly do. What an improvement! I didn't expect you to have done so much already.'

They nudged each other, clearly pleased by the compliment.

It was Gladys who spoke this time, and even her voice was similar to her sister's. 'It's interesting to bring a place back from filth to cleanliness. Makes you feel you've done something worthwhile. You won't recognise this flat once we've finished.'

'I'm sure I won't. Where did all that garbage outside come from? I thought Mrs Goodby and her lodgers had taken everything with them when they left. I glanced in and they didn't seem to have left any rubbish lying around.'

'That's because they stuffed all sorts of junk inside the cupboards. Some of the smell was coming from rotting food scraps. Dirty devils, they were. We're going to scrub all the cupboards out as well as the floors. Once we've finished the job, you'll have to get someone to cart the pile of rubbish away before you move in. You don't want to attract rats.'

'Ugh! I definitely don't. I'm dying to come and live here.' Gladys looked round. 'It'll make a nice home.'

Dolly murmured agreement, then said, 'We'll get the place thoroughly cleaned by Monday evening, but you'd better keep your eyes open once you move in. We've seen that Welch fellow walking past a couple of times today, an' a lad started throwing stones at the house earlier, aiming at the windows he was, the little devil. But Gladys went out and gave him what for. We know his granny, you see. She'll hit the roof when she finds out what he's been up to. He won't be trying that again. I warn you, though. He'd been offered money to do it.'

She guessed who had put the boy up to it, even before the other sister spoke.

Gladys joined in. 'It has to be Welch. He's a mean devil, an' everyone knows he's furious that you fired him. His wife was ranting on about it at the shops, silly creature. He might send someone else to get at you or damage the house, but forewarned is forearmed.'

'Oh dear. Well, I'll deal with it if he tries again. You will go on to sort out the top floor afterwards, won't you?'

'We won't leave till it's all sorted out, miss. We like to do a job properly. If you'll pay for it, we'll just run over Ryan's rooms as well. They're fairly clean, but Hettie's struggling to keep up. It'll only take us half a day or so.'

'Yes, please do that. But make sure you stay safe yourselves.'

Gladys laughed. 'That Welch knows better than to attack us. Our husbands are big chaps an' they won't stand no nonsense where we're concerned, not even a nasty remark. As for the top floor, we had a good look round up there before we sent Ed up to have a sleep. It's dirty, but not half as bad as this was.'

Dolly frowned. 'We'll need more cleaning supplies, though, an' you're going to need to change the doors and locks on the top floor. It's set up for two lots of folk to live in at the moment and share the sink on the landing. Not what you'll want if you're living here yourself. You'll be after a better class of tenant.'

'You're right. And I'd already decided that. Just tell me what supplies you need and I'll order them. I'm told you don't clean regularly for people, or I'd offer you an ongoing job for a day or two a week.'

'No, sorry. We like a bit of variety. An' since our kids are grown up now, we can please ourselves what jobs we take on. If you're needing regular help, though, we can help you find someone who knows how to do a thorough job.'

'That would be a big help. I'll need a week or two to get the place set up first. I'm just getting a few pieces of furniture to start me off.' She walked round the rooms, which had been swept, thinking where to place her pieces.

One room had already been thoroughly scrubbed and smelled strongly of carbolic soap. It wasn't her favourite smell, but it was better by far than years of dirt.

'On Monday we'll give them bare boards a bit of a polish till you can get some lino laid. Easy to mop down, lino is. An' we can get my hubby to clean the windows for you next weekend. He does a lovely job for a fair price. You should get a painter in, too, an' have another coat of distemper put on all the walls. They're looking a bit sad and scuffed. It'll brighten the place up and make it smell nice an' fresh.'

'I will do, but not till the bathroom has been put in.'

They perked up at that news, so she explained what was going to happen and asked them not to tell anyone till it was official. It seemed to please them to know before anyone else.

Afterwards she left them to it, delighted by their fierce attitude towards dirt, just . . . delighted generally.

'Home,' she murmured, spinning round and round in the empty, echoing hall for sheer joy, then feeling silly in case someone had seen her.

★

As Gabriel hadn't returned yet, Bella gave in to temptation and went up to see how the children were. She told Dolly where she'd be if he came looking for her then ran lightly up the stairs and knocked on Mr Cornish's door.

There were sounds from inside, but it took longer than she'd expected before the door opened a crack and instead of the old lady, Maddy was standing there, her head only a little higher than the door handle.

'Is Hettie in?'

The child put one finger to her lips. 'Shhh. She's asleep. She's not feeling well. We're trying to be quiet, but we're hungry an' we haven't been to the shops yet for today's bread.'

'Shall I come in and help you?'

The little girl looked her up and down as if working out what to do, then said, 'I remember you helped us yesterday. Daddy says only to let friends in, not strangers.' She held open the door.

Bella didn't know Ryan Cornish well enough to be called a friend, but hoped she would be on good terms with her tenants once she moved in. It'd be lovely to have children around. She didn't like to think of them going hungry, though.

She glanced quickly around, pleased to see that the main room was basically clean, if a little untidy, with some children's toys on the rag rug. 'Where's Hettie? Can I speak to her?'

Maddy opened the bedroom door and beckoned to her.

Bella went inside and found Hettie lying on a narrow single bed, looking flushed with fever. There was just room for a double bed as well, and a mattress was standing upright against one wall with bedding neatly folded over the top. Mr Cornish's bed, presumably.

The poor woman opened her eyes and stared blearily at her.

'I think you've got the same fever the children had,' Bella said gently.

Hettie tried to sit up and failed. 'Sorry, miss. I'm feeling that dizzy an' I keep falling asleep. Are they behaving themselves?'

'Oh, yes. How about I look after them for a while?'

'Really, miss? You don't mind? They can be a bit lively.'

She might have been offering Hettie a huge gift. 'Yes, really. I'll enjoy their company.'

'Well, I might feel better if I have a bit of a doze, miss, I will admit. They're good kids.'

'We'll go to the shops and I'll buy them something to eat. That'll give you some peace and quiet. Is there anything you need while I'm there?'

'Something for the mester's tea.'

It took her a minute to realise Hettie was referring to Mr Cornish as the master of the house.

'Some ham – just thin slices, mind – an' a couple of loaves. Shopping bags are under the sink. Money's in the jar on the mantelpiece.' She broke off to yawn, closing her eyes again, clearly finding it difficult to keep them open.

'I'll see to everything. You get some more sleep.' Bella went into the living area and explained to Maddy. 'Can you find all your coats and hats?'

'Yes, miss.'

'And scarves, too. There's a cold wind blowing. Do you have any gloves or mittens?'

'Devin lost his an' Nelly just pulls them off again.'

The children needed a piece of elastic attaching to the mittens, long enough to be threaded through their coat sleeves so that the mittens would hang out, but not get lost. She was surprised Hettie hadn't done that already – most mothers did – but perhaps the old woman wasn't good at sewing. Well, Bella could easily do it for them once she moved in downstairs. It'd only take her a few minutes.

She watched the little girl go to one corner and get their

outdoor clothes, which were piled neatly on an old pushchair. Maddy allowed Bella to help her with Nelly, but insisted on doing up Devin's and her own buttons, and pulling on their little knitted hats. Then she began dragging the rather battered pushchair out of the corner.

'We take her out in this because she's too heavy to carry now.' Maddy spoke as one adult to the other. 'I can't get it down the stairs on my own, though. Me an' Hettie usually do it together.'

'I can see to it on my own.' When she'd done that and carried Nelly down the stairs, Bella left Maddy fastening her little sister into the pushchair with Devin standing nearby, and popped into the ground-floor flat to ask exactly what cleaning things her helpers needed. She scribbled a list in the notebook she carried everywhere.

That delayed her a few minutes and when she went back into the hall there was no sign of the children. Her heart clenched in panic, then she heard the sound of voices outside and hurried out to look for them.

They were standing near the garden gate, with Maddy holding the pushchair handle. Nelly was sitting in it, bouncing up and down but held in place by a tattered strap. Devin was pushing his hands through the iron struts of the gate and rattling it slightly. All three were looking out like prisoners longing to be released from jail.

Bella had a quick look along the street for the two nasty-looking men, but there was no sign of them now, thank goodness.

'We aren't allowed to go past the gate on our own, miss,' Maddy announced.

'Well, that means you've been very good children and I'll buy you some sweets as a reward for that once we reach the shop. And since I'm here now, let's get on our way, shall we?'

She'd never been outside with three children in her sole

charge before and was a bit apprehensive about keeping them in order, but she needn't have worried. Maddy took charge of her little brother and left Bella to deal with the pushchair. All three seemed so happy to be out and about, they were no trouble.

'You walk faster than Hettie,' Maddy commented after a while.

'I'm not going too fast, am I?'

'No. Hettie goes too slow. Her feet hurt.'

At the shop Bella took them inside, keeping Nelly in the pushchair. 'What are your favourite sweets? Choose something.'

'Really?' Maddy asked. 'We can really choose anything?'

'Yes.'

The child pointed to the box of sherbet fountains, and Devin nodded his head vigorously. Bella bought them one each and one for herself to indulge in later. These sweets hadn't been invented when she was a child, and Thomas considered them vulgar, so she'd never tried one.

It did her heart good to see how their faces lit up as the shopkeeper handed them each a brightly coloured cardboard roll with a paper covering twisted to close off the top. A tube made of black liquorice was sticking out of the twisted bit.

Maddy tore open the top of the wrapping paper for the other two, then dealt deftly with her own. All three bit off the end of the liquorice and started sucking up the sweet powder, even little Nelly knowing how to manage, so clearly they'd had these before.

The shopkeeper smiled as she watched them. 'Isn't Hettie looking after them today?'

'She's not well. I'm keeping an eye on the children, and I have some shopping to do for her as well as for Dolly and Gladys.'

The smile broadened. 'More cleaning stuff for the twins, I expect?'

'Yes. They're doing an excellent job.'

'They'll be enjoying themselves. Never saw anyone who hates dirt as much as those two. Now, let's go through what you need, Miss Porter.'

The sherbet powder had been devoured by the time Bella had gone through her lists, and the three children were now sucking the remains of the liquorice tubes slowly. When the shopping was finished Bella started back to Daisy Street, walking more slowly because of the loaded sacking bags hanging off the back of the pushchair.

She stopped abruptly when she was nearly there because Mr Welch was standing just along from her house on the other side of the street. He scowled at her and put his hands on his hips in what seemed to be a threatening manner. Suddenly and for no reason she could tell, he shook his fist at her.

She felt her heart do a little skip of anxiety. She'd have to go quite close to him to get into her house. What if he came at her and hurt the children? There was no one else around on the street to come to their aid, and he was a big man.

She stopped moving, taking a firmer hold of the handle of the pushchair, uncertain what to do next. Oh dear, Gabriel had warned her to be careful. She should have waited for him to return before going out. She'd never forgive herself if the children got hurt.

Then Mr Cornish came striding round the corner opposite and, the minute he saw the children's father, Welch turned and walked away.

The children waved their sticky fingers and called out, 'Daddy! Daddy! Look what we've got.'

He didn't answer because he was watching Welch and, from the expression on his face, he wasn't happy to see him.

Bella let out a shuddering sigh of relief. The children didn't seem to have noticed anything untoward, thank goodness, being too engrossed in getting every single bit of slow pleasure from the remains of their treats.

Once Welch was out of sight, Mr Cornish came across the road to join them. He stopped on the pavement and held his arms wide. Maddy and Devin rushed to greet him and he swung each one round in a circle. Bella couldn't help smiling at this as she waited for him to finish cuddling them. After that he bent to kiss Nelly, with the other two still clinging to his coat from behind.

'Now let me go, kids,' he ordered as he stood up from the pushchair. 'I have to say hello to Miss Porter.'

'Look what she bought us.' Maddy brandished the mangled remains of the liquorice tube.

He smiled down at Bella. He wasn't a tall man, but he was still much taller than her.

'That was kind of you. They're mad for liquorice fountains.'

'You didn't mind me taking them out for a walk?'

'Of course not. You've already shown that you know how to look after children. Where's Hettie?'

'She wasn't feeling well, so I left her to take a nap in peace.'

He sighed. 'She's too old to look after them, really, but there was no one else available – unless I married some woman for convenience, and I definitely didn't want to do that. Poor Hettie was desperate not to be put into the old folks' home down in Rivenshaw after her daughter died suddenly. Well, they call it a home, but it's more like a prison. She treats my children kindly and does her best. What more can you ask of anyone?'

'No one can do more than their best. I'll be able to help out a bit once I move in. If you don't mind, that is?'

'Why should I mind? I'd trust you absolutely with them.'

She could feel her cheeks growing warm at this compliment and for a moment they stared at one another in silence. It was as if something was connecting them, something soft and lovely.

He broke the silence. 'I'll take the pushchair now, shall I? It looks heavy. You should have got the shopkeeper to deliver these things.'

'The children were hungry.'

'I usually buy the bread before I leave, but I had to set off really early this morning and it wouldn't have come into the shop by then. Eh, there aren't enough hours in a day sometimes.'

They had just set off across the road when Gabriel drove up in the van. He got out, looking annoyed. 'As I arrived I saw Welch standing watching you all from behind the corner of the house.'

Ryan spun round. 'Is he still there?'

'No, he left when I stopped nearby. Are you all right? You shouldn't have been out on your own, Bella.'

'I wasn't on my own. I had the children with me. Hettie's not well. There was no one in sight when I set off, but Welch was near my house staring at us when we got back. Luckily Mr Cornish came home just then and Welch walked off. I didn't think he'd still be hanging around.'

Ryan looked from one to the other. 'Is Welch causing you trouble, Miss Porter?'

Gabriel answered before she could. 'He might try, on account of her sacking him. Knowing him, he'll want to find some way to get his own back for that. Me and Mam are worried about her moving in here on her own.'

'I'll be able to keep an eye on you in the evenings, at least,' Ryan offered. 'You'll only have to shout for help and I'll hear you, Miss Porter. Even during the night, because I'm a light sleeper. I've had to be. The kids still get a bit upset sometimes about their mother.'

She nodded, but didn't say anything else. She blamed herself for not being careful enough today. That was another reason to learn to drive, however hard it was. And if Welch did anything else, gave her even half an excuse, she was going to report him to the policeman Gabriel had told her about. She didn't intend to be kept a prisoner in her own home because of the horrible fellow's spite.

Ryan took his children and the shopping upstairs, and Gabriel scowled at her.

Before he could say anything, she said it for him. 'I'll be more careful in future. I wasn't thinking of danger in broad daylight.'

'Why was it so urgent?'

'The children were hungry. I did a bit of shopping for Hettie while I was out because I had to get some more cleaning materials for the twins.'

'We're going to have to do something about protecting you if Welch keeps trying to get at you.'

'I'll be a lot safer once I have my car.'

'There's a rear lane behind your house for coal and other deliveries. I can put in double gates and you'll be able to drive your car right into the backyard. I'll fix a good strong lock on the gate while I'm at it.' He flushed. 'Well, I will if you'll let me have the money to cover costs. I can get everything I need second-hand, even some double gates. A friend of mine has started selling second-hand building stuff.'

'Good idea. I'd be delighted if you'd do that for me. I'll pay you day rates, if that suits.'

He hesitated as if he didn't want to charge her, then said, 'Agreed.' He gestured towards the two bags of shopping Ryan had left in the hall. 'Are these the cleaning supplies?'

'Yes. The bags belong to Ryan, though.'

'I'll take them to Dolly and ask her to return the bags once she's emptied everything out.'

When he came back, she was stroking the bannisters. 'I think these will polish up nicely, don't you, Gabriel?'

'Yes. But that's for another time. You need to get back to

your lodgings and start going through the Highway Code now, Bella.'

'Oh, my! I'd completely forgotten about it.'

As they sat in the van, she saw a child looking out at her from a first-floor window of her house and waved. 'Those are the best-behaved children I've ever met.'

'They've had some hard lessons since their mam died.'

'What happened to her?'

'She died in childbirth. Difficult birth and the doctor said she must have had a weakness in her heart. The kids have learned to be good because Ryan won't stand any nonsense from them. Well, kids are better with some firm discipline, as long as there's lots of love too – and anyone can see how much he loves them. That's how our mam brought us up, too.'

Bella had a sudden memory of her own father. 'My dad was like that. He was a lovely man, but you had to do as you were told quick smart. He was as unlike his cousin Thomas as chalk is to cheese. Living with Thomas was hard to get used to.'

'Well, you won't need to see him again, will you? Let's get you back to your lodgings now. You're looking tired.'

She smiled. 'Tired but happy. I haven't been bored once today.'

'Did you used to get bored?'

'Often.'

He didn't comment, but she could see him taking it in and feeling sorry for her.

What she felt sorry for was that she'd wasted so many years of her life. She should have risked leaving her cousin's house years ago, after his children left the nursery. But she wasn't going to waste a minute of her life from now on, if she could help it.

No use repining over the past. You couldn't change it,

however much you regretted what had happened. But it wouldn't be her fault if she didn't make a better future for herself now, thanks to kind Cousin James.

When they got back to her lodgings, Gabriel asked, 'Still want me to drive you around next week, as well?'

'Yes, please. But I'm going to take things easier tomorrow – I'm exhausted after such a busy time and I can't move in till the house has been thoroughly cleaned. I also have to learn my Highway Code. Will you be able to get the van again next week?'

'On Monday, yes, but not on the Tuesday. And Jericho will need it tomorrow.'

'Then I'd better buy that blue Austin 7, hadn't I?'

He looked surprised. 'You've definitely decided to learn to drive, even before you have your lesson?'

'Yes. I have to. Especially after today. Will you be able to continue driving me around in my own car until I pass my test? You can go home in it at night to save travelling time the next day.'

'Thank you. I shall enjoy doing that. Any idea where we'll be going on Monday?'

She shrugged. 'I have a driving lesson and I'll need to check on the Traskes, see if they've finished. And there will be some more shopping if I'm to move in soon.'

'Well, I have a message from Roy Tyler. He wants to see you about the bathroom in your new home at eight o'clock on Monday morning if you can manage that.'

'Lovely. I shall look forward to it. Can you pick me up in time to meet Mr Tyler?'

'Of course. Twenty to eight be all right?'

'Perfect.'

As he left Bella at her lodgings, Gabriel watched her go inside. She looked like a different woman from the one he'd first met. She'd done something to her clothes and hair, and she was absolutely sparkling with energy, getting enthusiastic at small things others would take for granted.

He'd been nervous about driving a stranger round, worrying that he'd get tongue-tied, but she'd quickly become a friend. He'd not felt at all shy with her, as he did with most strangers, especially women. The stutter he'd had as a child didn't seem to afflict him as much nowadays, at least not when he was with people he felt comfortable with.

Mam would approve when he told her what Bella had said about loving to be busy. She was just the same. She'd taken to the newcomer as quickly as he had.

Bella even felt like a cousin now! His mam had been worried at how quickly that had happened and had asked him bluntly if he was falling in love with Bella, which had made him laugh. Let alone Bella was far too old for him, she had never seemed like anything except an older sister or cousin, and he was quite sure she felt the same about him.

He didn't intend to let himself fall in love for a long time, not till he could support a wife and family, and especially offer them a decent home. He and his family had been forced by lack of money to live in the worst slums in Backshaw Moss for a few months, and he was never, ever going back there, or to any place like it.

His intention was easy to stick to because he'd never met a lass he wanted to go courting. The minute he got near a young woman he considered pretty, his stutter came back, so he mostly kept quiet.

20

When Bella went into the house, Mrs Tucker stopped her in the hall before she could even start up the stairs. 'There was a phone message for you from a Mr Neven.'

'Goodness! What did he want?'

'He wouldn't say.' She held out a piece of paper. 'You're to phone him at this number as soon as you get in and reverse the charges.'

'Oh dear. I hope there's nothing wrong.' She saw the curiosity on the landlady's face. 'He's my lawyer in London.'

'Ah. Well, you'd better not waste any time phoning him, then. It must be important.'

Bella got out her little notebook, just in case, took a deep breath and picked up the phone from the hall table.

While she was waiting for the operator to connect her to the long-distance number, she pulled the hall chair across to sit by the phone.

Mr Neven's clerk answered. 'Ah, Miss Porter. Mr Neven will be pleased you called back so quickly. Hold on a moment and I'll put you through. He was in court for several hours today, so he couldn't call until now, but the delay in speaking to you has been fretting him.'

There were clicking sounds, and Albert Neven said, 'Hello?'

'Bella Porter here, returning your call.'

'I'm so glad you did. Look, there's no easy way to say this, so I'll come straight out with it. Your cousin was angry with his daughter and was going to, um, spank her. Has he done that before?'

Disgust filled her. 'When she was little, but fortunately I managed to protect Alma from similar trouble as she grew older. Now I'm not there, he may feel free to, um—' She hated to say it, had noticed that Mr Neven had also hesitated to be frank, but this was no time to be timid. 'He might feel free to behave improperly again.'

'Again?'

'He did the same thing to a young maid. I, um, eavesdropped sometimes, to protect myself and Alma.' She heard a heavy sigh and there was a brief silence before he spoke again.

'That's disgusting! But I'm grateful that you're being honest with me. It's set my mind at rest about interfering.'

'What caused him to threaten it this time? His irrational behaviour usually only occurs when he's extremely angry.'

'Alma had refused to marry Maxwell Greene.'

Bella was so disgusted at the mere thought of this she couldn't speak for several seconds. 'How could anyone want their daughter to marry that strange, cold fish of a man? He has a terrible reputation with women, and some people won't allow him into their homes. His first two wives couldn't hide all the bruises, and both of them died young. Even I knew about him, and I didn't go out and about in society much.'

'Well, her father insisted she marry him and she ran away rather than obey him. Oscar brought her to me and I helped them both escape. Occasionally there is a higher morality than the law. Some things are – simply not right, they go against all moral canons of behaviour. I shan't tell you where they went except that it's not in England. They'll be safe, I promise you.'

'Oh, thank goodness. It was very kind of you to help them.'

His words came out in sharp staccato bursts, such was the vehemence of his feelings. 'I loathe men like Greene – and your cousin.'

'So do I.'

'The main reason I phoned you was that I'm rather worried for your safety. Since Thomas Beaton hasn't been able to find his son and daughter in London, I think he might come after you. As you've protected Alma in the past, he'll probably assume you're giving her and her brother shelter now.'

'Oh dear.' She didn't know what to say to that.

'I thought I'd better warn you. I'll get in touch again if I hear that he's left town. Should you need my further help, you've only to pick up the phone and I'll do whatever I can. Be very careful how you go.'

'I will. And thank you for warning me.' She put the phone down and stood by it for a while, feeling sick with worry. Even if Alma and Oscar had got away, Thomas would still keep his eyes open and go after them if he got the slightest hint of where they were, however long it took.

What foreign country had they gone to? She hoped it was far enough away for him never to find them.

'Everything all right, dear?'

She jumped in shock and turned to see Mrs Tucker standing nearby.

'No. It was bad news about a friend, I'm afraid.' She decided it would be best to make sure Cousin Thomas could get no help from Mrs Tucker. 'And, um, the cousin I used to live with is still furiously angry that I left his home and is vowing to come after me and make me sorry.'

Mrs Tucker gaped at her. 'What? In Britain? In this day and age? What does he think he can do to you anyway? You're long past twenty-one, and not dependent on him.'

'I don't know what he might try to do. He can be very nasty indeed.'

'What's his name?'

'Thomas Beaton. And please, if he ever tries to contact me here, don't tell him anything.'

'I won't.' Mrs Tucker hesitated and for once shared a confidence of her own. 'I had a cousin whose husband went after her when she ran away from him. He tried to strangle her, but a neighbour rescued her in time. I can't abide men who ill-treat women.'

She patted Bella's back. 'You can be sure I'll not tell this man anything at all if he phones me or turns up here. And I'll make sure everyone in my house knows not to speak to him, too.'

'I didn't want to tell too many other people.'

'Better safe than sorry, dear. You should tell the girls yourself this very evening at tea.'

Bella didn't answer, hated the thought of doing that. As she walked up to her room she felt as if someone had tainted her earlier joy. But there was nothing she could do for the moment except be on her guard. If she were very lucky, Thomas wouldn't come after her.

The trouble was, he knew where she lived – the town if not the street. It wasn't a big place. He'd only have to ask around to find her.

Oh dear! Just when she was starting to enjoy her new life.

Then it occurred to her that there were now two men who would hurt her if they could, and she shivered. What had she done to deserve that?

It was proving harder to set up an independent life than she'd expected. Much harder. Money wasn't everything. Did every single woman face such hostility, or was she just unlucky?

Bella fell asleep and had to be woken from her nap to go down and join the others for the evening meal. She planned to spend the next day reading through the twenty-four pages of the Highway Code leaflet and learning the rules by heart.

The other women were all looking so happy, she didn't like

to mention her problem, but when Mrs Tucker brought in the dessert, she looked across at Bella with a question in her eyes. When her guest shook her head, the landlady tapped on a glass with a spoon, her signal that she wanted to make an announcement. Everyone fell silent and looked at her.

'Miss Porter needs to tell you something.' She took a step backwards and gestured to her guest to speak.

So, Bella had to tell them about her cousin. Not the worst details – she couldn't bear to make that vile behaviour public – but just that he might come after her.

'Why would he do that?'

'He'd want me to act as an unpaid servant again and he'd take over my house.'

She waited as that sank in and elicited a few sympathetic-sounding mutters, then continued, 'Once he gets an idea fixed in his mind, he'll do anything to get his own way. So, if any strangers ask about me, could you please not tell them anything at all?'

There were nods from the other lodgers, so Bella sat down and finished her meal.

Afterwards, she was delighted to find that her second skirt had been shortened, and she gave her other skirts to Louisa to deal with, feeling that this money was well spent. Hettie was thrilled at the idea of having her other skirt, but Bella had always hated that one, so was equally thrilled to be getting rid of it. She'd keep the other scruffy one for doing dirty jobs in her flat.

She went up to bed intending to read through the Highway Code, but started nodding off after a few pages. Thank goodness she had a lovely long day with nothing to do but rest and go through it tomorrow.

She'd told Gabriel she didn't need him on the Friday, because she couldn't do much at the house till it had been thoroughly cleaned out. Besides, she was feeling exhausted after her busiest week in years.

After breakfast she went to rest in her bedroom and fell asleep on the bed, feeling guilty when she woke up to find the afternoon had nearly gone. Then she smiled at herself. She didn't need to feel guilty. She could do as she wished now.

On the Saturday, she asked Mrs Tucker's advice, then went out to do some personal shopping, things she'd feel embarrassed to shop for with a man. Well, the blue packaging of sanitary pads was such a giveaway. Even Muriel hadn't objected to providing her with those, because they were so much less embarrassing than cloths.

She felt quite safe walking round town with a shopping bag full of bits and pieces, and was happy that this time she was able to find her way round the centre without much trouble.

She also had another go at learning the Highway Code, and then went out for a short walk with Louisa.

On the Sunday it was fine enough to go for another walk, this time with three of the other lodgers. It felt wonderful to be with these women, to chat and gossip about the latest films or about which women's magazine they preferred. It was so long since Bella had had a chance to do that sort of thing.

When they got back she concentrated on the Highway Code again and by the time she went down to join the other guests for their evening meal, she felt she had a good idea of how the road rules for drivers and pedestrians fitted together.

On the Monday the busy times started again, but Bella was ready for it. She got up early and went down to the dining room where the gas fire was hissing away happily, to have an early breakfast.

She couldn't help feeling nervous about the coming driving

lesson. What if she made a pitiful mess of managing a car? But the lesson wasn't till later, so she put it resolutely to the back of her mind. Well, most of the time, anyway.

First she had to see what Mr Tyler wanted, and that would probably be an enjoyable meeting about the improvements to her house. Unless he'd found some serious problem there. No, surely not. Number 23 might be old-fashioned, but it was solidly built. Everyone she'd spoken to had agreed on that.

She was ready and waiting, but stayed near the front door until Gabriel drove up. He greeted her cheerfully. When she told him about the London lawyer's warning, his smile faded.

'Just let anyone try to hurt you when I'm around.'

Once they arrived at her house, she went in first, leaving him to lock up his brother's van carefully.

She stopped in the hall to listen, smiling. The Traske sisters sounded to be hard at work already. Before she could go and have a word with them, however, Mr Cornish came hurrying down the stairs.

'Miss Porter, have you a moment?' He put down his heavy bag of tools near the door and turned back to her. 'I'd like to thank you properly for helping Hettie with the children when she was unwell. You were a godsend for a second time.'

'I thoroughly enjoyed their company and they behaved very nicely, a credit to their upbringing, so it was a pleasure. How's Hettie today?'

'She's a lot better, but still feeling weak. She'll keep an eye on the children for an hour or two, but I want her to get a good rest, so I'm going to come straight home after my first job – luckily it's something easy that will only take an hour or so – then I'll be able to help out with the shopping.' He stepped back. 'I mustn't keep you, but I just, you know, wanted to thank you properly.'

'I love children and hope to see more of yours once I move in here. If you don't mind, that is?'

For a moment the world around them seemed to stand still as they stared at one another. It had felt like that before, as if they didn't need words to communicate that they liked one another – at least, she thought that was how they both felt. She certainly liked him and admired the way he cared about his children.

His expression softened. 'Mind? I'd be grateful. I don't have any close family nearby, and the kids don't have much to do with younger women since their mother died, so it'd be wonderful for them to spend time with you.'

She was delighted that he approved, and also that he thought of her as a younger woman. Was it the more modern clothes and hairstyle, or was it her happiness about the house brightening up her appearance? 'I'll have them to tea as soon as I get my flat set up to live in. We'll make a fun game of doing it in a fancy way, just like grown-ups. I used to enjoy doing that sort of thing with the Beaton children.'

'It'll be a real treat for mine.'

After a brief silence he gave her another of those quick little nods, picked up his tool bag and left the house. She heard his footsteps speed up as he strode off along the road. Was he always in such a hurry?

It was a few moments before she realised that Gabriel was standing in the doorway. He must have seen them chatting and waited to come inside. He was always polite and tactful like that.

She heard a car pull up and Gabriel glanced over his shoulder. 'Here's Mr Tyler.'

She moved forward to join him at the front door. Before she went out to greet the builder, she asked Gabriel, 'Could you please let Dolly and Gladys know that Mr Tyler will want to look around the house? And oh dear, I forgot to mention his visit to Mr Cornish.'

'I'll nip up and tell Hettie to expect him after I've seen Dolly and Gladys.'

'Thank you.'

Then she went outside, smiling at Mr Tyler and his wife, who were standing next to their car studying the outside of the house. 'Good morning.'

'Good morning to you, Miss Porter. I hope you don't mind, but I always bring Ethel with me when we're looking at putting in bathrooms. My wife has better ideas about how to fit them into older houses than anyone I've ever met, and she understands the plumbing needs, too.'

How wonderful to have a husband who appreciated you! Her cousin Thomas only appreciated himself and had openly derided the women in his household for their lack of skills, calling all women 'stupid and inferior to men'.

Ethel brought her attention back to the present. 'Shall we go and see where you're going to live, dear?'

'Of course. The Traske sisters are still finishing cleaning it, though.'

'They won't mind me turning up.'

Mrs Tyler greeted the sisters, admired their work, and was left to walk around the four rooms unhindered. When she'd seen everything, she went back to the kitchen and scullery and frowned. 'No room to put one here.'

She walked slowly around the other rooms again, then turned to her husband. 'The best thing would be to cut off a small part of this bedroom and use the corridor at the side of the house, if that will suit your plumbing and sewage needs, Roy love?'

'Perfectly.'

'Good. We can include the corridor space at the end in the bathroom and use the same window, then the reduced bedroom won't be too small.'

'Good thinking – as usual, my dear. All right with you to do that, Miss Porter?'

'Whatever you think best, Mr Tyler. It does make sense

to me, though. I shall still have four rooms, and a big kitchen.'

'That's one floor settled, then. Let's go upstairs and inspect the middle floor. Is Ryan Cornish still living here, Miss Porter?'

'Yes. He's the only tenant still left. The rest of the house was filthy, so I threw those tenants out. I don't want anyone living here who doesn't look after my home.'

'I'd feel just the same,' Mrs Tyler said approvingly.

Ryan came back through the front door as they were still chatting in the hall and was happy to take them up to see the flat where he lived.

They walked around the two rooms, which were quite large, but both the Tylers shook their heads.

'This flat isn't as easy, being so small. Where does that other door on the landing lead, Miss Porter? It seems an anomaly.'

'It's a room that's being used as a storage area. The previous owner seems to have left a jumble of stuff behind, and the lawyer said everything I found here would belong to me. I haven't had time to look at what's in all the boxes, let alone clear them out.'

'Can we see inside the room, please?' Mrs Tyler asked.

Bella got out her key ring, enjoying the cheerful jangling sound, and opened the door. 'As you can see, the room is full of boxes, but who knows what's in them? I haven't opened many of them yet.'

Ethel looked inside the room, then walked to and fro on the landing, went back into the flat and came out again looking thoughtful. 'This storeroom would be perfect for a bathroom if you wanted to make it part of the flat, Miss Porter. You could get another small bedroom out of it, too, if you were careful.'

'Could we really do that?'

Mr Tyler went to rap on the wall of the flat that abutted

the landing, then tapped on the storeroom wall, getting a hollow sound from both of them. 'These are only stud walls, not brick ones, so they'll be easy to take out or change. Can we get this stuff out of here quickly? I want to start work on all three bathrooms as soon as possible so that I can get them done before I start building the new houses across the street.'

'I, um, well—' Bella broke off for a moment, annoyed at herself for dithering. 'I'm sure we can. There's plenty of space downstairs in the flat I'll be occupying. Could you hire someone to carry everything down and put it in the room on the left as you go into the flat? I'll pay them for their time, but I'm not strong enough to carry the heavy boxes myself.'

'If you'll trust me with a key, I'll get it cleared out straight away and it'll only cost you a few shillings.'

'I shan't mind that. I'll be able to go through the boxes at my leisure then.'

'You'll have an exciting time opening them, won't you?' Ethel Tyler said with one of her warm, motherly smiles.

'Yes. But if the boxes are going to be lying around without me knowing exactly what's in them, I'd better arrange to move in quickly, hadn't I? If someone broke in, I wouldn't even know what had been taken. I'll contact Mr Willcox and get him to deliver the furniture I've bought.'

Excitement ran through her, and trepidation too. She'd rather have waited to see if there was a problem with her cousin Thomas before she moved to live on her own, but on the other hand, it'd be good to be on her own territory if she had to confront him. She might keep Ed on as a night watchman for a while, though. Just till the bathrooms were finished and the top-floor flat occupied.

Mrs Tyler murmured her approval. 'Well, you can guarantee the place will be clean if the Traske sisters have dealt with it, so in that sense you'll be all right to move in. Now, let's go up to the top floor.'

The two families had moved out now, but it still smelled bad up there because it hadn't been cleaned yet. She opened the cupboard doors, relieved to see that the tenants hadn't left stinking rubbish in any of them.

'We'll need to turn it back into one flat,' Bella said. 'Could you do that for me as well, Mr Tyler?'

'Easily.'

Mrs Tyler looked around thoughtfully. 'Actually, we can make the sink on the landing part of the kitchen, and put the bathroom next to it at the other end.'

'Please do!' Bella said recklessly. She was determined to have it done properly.

'I think this house will be a much better place after the changes, and should bring you higher rents.' Mrs Tyler moved towards the top of the stairs. 'Sorry, but I must go now. I shall watch what my husband does here with great interest, and in the meantime I'll order some simple fittings for your bathrooms. I know where to get the best bargains for you.'

Her husband watched her go, then turned to Bella. 'I need to speak to Ryan about something else, if you don't mind, Miss Porter.'

'Of course not. Stay as long as you like. I'll go back to see Dolly and Gladys. I need to make sure they'll still be able to finish the ground floor cleaning today.'

The Traske sisters listened intently to her plans. They were sure they could finish today, and Dolly's husband could come the following weekend to clean the windows properly, as long as it wasn't raining.

'There's a storeroom on the middle floor, and Mr Tyler is arranging for the boxes in it to be brought down here today. I've told him to put them in that room.' She pointed. 'Is that all right? I think you've already finished in there, haven't you?'

Dolly waved one hand encouragingly. 'Yes, and we lit a fire

so the floor's dry now. You go ahead and arrange to have your furniture delivered tomorrow, Miss Porter. The other floors will dry out properly overnight, and we'll be upstairs cleaning if you need any help arranging your things tomorrow.'

Bella didn't let herself smile. She was sure what they really wanted was to see what was in the boxes, and what furniture she had. They'd be disappointed in the furniture, but what she'd bought would be enough to manage with for the time being.

She had met some really kind people in the Ellin Valley, was so glad she'd come here, in spite of the problems of setting up home.

But oh, she hated even the thought that her cousin Thomas might come here and try to spoil it all. He seemed to spread misery wherever he went, had only to enter a room for the atmosphere to change. And he could be unscrupulous when he wanted something. She'd definitely keep Ed on as night watchman.

21

Bella smiled ruefully at Gabriel as she joined him outside. 'I'm still being whirled about by fate.'

He listened as she told him what she had to arrange, and all within a few days. 'Better than having nothing to do. Now, I've been keeping an eye on the time for you. The driving lesson comes next, and then buying the car.'

'Oh. Yes. I suppose I still ought to . . .' Her voice trailed away.

He looked at her suspiciously and she hurried on before he could stop her. 'The thing is, considering how busy I'm going to be moving into the flat – perhaps I'd better leave the driving till another day.'

He suspected she was still terrified of making a fool of herself, so said firmly, 'I'm speaking to you as my adopted cousin here. You need to have at least one driving lesson to make sure you can do it, and you're going to need that car even more if you're moving into that flat. And by the way, I'm sure you'll manage the driving just fine.'

That surprised her. 'Why?'

'From the way you move, sort of balanced and graceful. And as we said before, I can drive you around in your car till you pass your test and feel confident about doing it your-self. You'll be wanting to nip into Rivenshaw for things the shop in the village doesn't sell.' He waited, watching her expression.

She nodded, but the fear was lurking in her eyes, the lack

of confidence this cousin of hers had given her, damn him. Well, Gabriel wasn't going to let the bully win and keep her timid for the rest of her life.

'Think on, Bella, you'll be buying all sorts of things for the house, and you'd have difficulty carrying your purchases back by bus. Or are you going to keep taking taxis? That'd be expensive.'

She shook her head, so he continued, 'And then, after you've got the flat sorted out, you'll want to get out and about, meet people, go to the cinema, all sorts of things. From what I've read, it's different in London, which is what you're used to. It has plenty of buses, trams and taxis, not to mention the Underground. There simply aren't such things here. There are three or four buses a day going up and down the valley, a couple of taxis, and that's all.' He waited again, head on one side, giving her time to think about what he'd said.

At last she said, 'I suppose you're right. I hadn't really thought that through, I was so excited about moving into my house. Driving and owning a car are such big steps for me. Do you think I can do it, though, Gabriel: learn to drive, buy a car and move in, all in one mad scramble?'

He felt sorry for how alone in the world she was. He'd never had much money, but he'd always had his two brothers and his mother to encourage or comfort him. Families were worth more than money to him, far more! And Jericho's new wife was part of the family now as well. Frankie was a lovely woman, a superb cabinet maker, which some men hated, but Jericho was proud of her beautiful work, and so were the rest of the family.

'I definitely do think you can, Bella. Actually, I was talking about it to Mam last night, because she's such a wise person.'

He shared his own longings. 'Eh, I often wish I could give Mam some money of her own. She's had such a hard life, always having to make each farthing count, let alone each penny. You have the chance to get a car, and the freedom that will give you is priceless. Grab it with both hands, lass. You're one of the lucky ones.'

There was silence and he waited, giving her time to pull herself together, which she did. He could see the way she straightened her back and gave a few little nods, as if answering her own questions.

'You're right. Let's go and get that driving lesson over and done with, Gabriel.'

He chuckled. 'It's not a torture session. You'll enjoy it once you get going.'

The look she gave him said she didn't believe that, but she'd do it anyway.

It was ironic that Bella had made Gabriel feel more capable and confident about dealing with strangers, especially women. She didn't realise that, but he'd tell her one day.

When they pulled to a halt next to the row of cars, Bella looked for the blue car, but it wasn't there. She clutched Gabriel's arm, disappointment running through her. 'It's gone! Oh, no.'

He scanned the workshop behind the row of cars. 'Is it my imagination or is that something blue inside?'

She followed his pointing finger and let go of his arm, beaming at him. 'Yes. Come on!' She led the way across to it, almost running in her eagerness.

She saw Todd straighten up from the car he was working on, his overalls covered in smudges of oil and what looked like smears of paint. 'Are you here for your driving lesson, Miss Porter? The office is over there.' He pointed towards the house.

'Yes, and I wanted to confirm that I'd definitely like to buy the blue Austin.'

'You've decided that already, then, before the lesson?'

'Definitely. I'll be back afterwards to sort out payment.' She wasn't stupid, had never been clumsy, so she could do it. She had to keep reminding herself of that.

The two men watched her hurry across to the office, then exchanged grins.

'She's coming out of her shell,' Gabriel said.

'It's lovely to see. Your doing.'

'Only partly. No one could help her if she didn't have the courage. All she needed was a nudge or two. Now, can I watch you work while she's away, and will you tell me exactly what you're doing? You never know when a piece of information will come in useful, and one day I'm going to get a van of my own, whatever it takes.'

'Happy to have you watch me any time. You don't pester a person with idle chat. When you do talk it's worth listening to.'

Gabriel kept that compliment close to his heart. It meant a lot coming from a capable man like Todd.

Bella arrived at the office just as Silas came to the door.

'Right on the dot. Come along, Miss Porter. Your chariot awaits.' He flourished a bow to her and gestured towards a shiny black Austin Seven.

She studied it. Not a big car, which would have frightened her. She had a sudden thought as she got into the passenger seat: how outraged her cousin Thomas would be if he knew what she was doing. That made her smile.

'I'll drive us out of town to a little road where I've hardly ever seen another car, and you can have your first try at driving there. We don't want to perform for an audience, do we?'

She smiled at him gratefully. 'No. It'll feel better to try it in private the first time, in case I do something silly.'

'You won't. This car is easier than most for a beginner to drive. And if you buy that small blue Austin, we can do your lessons in that later on, and you'll feel quite at home in it when you start driving on your own.'

He looked at her earnestly. 'You'll soon know what you're doing when you're behind the wheel. Trust me.' He grinned as he added, 'Think about it. You're not the first beginner I've taught. I do understand how terrifying the first time behind the wheel can seem. But it isn't all that difficult once you get going and the more you drive, the more of a habit it becomes, something you do automatically. You'll see.'

'It's all happened so quickly. But it will be wonderful to have a car. I'll be truly independent then.'

'There you are. Keep your mind on that.'

He drove up the main valley road and turned off to the right just after Birch End, stopping on a street which seemed to have no purpose because there weren't any houses there, and it curved slightly across waste land to a dead end.

'Why doesn't this street lead anywhere?'

He stopped and waved one hand as if inviting her to look round. 'Because this is a prime example of Higgerson's planning. He was going to build a lot of fancy detached houses on what had been a field, so he put in the roads first to tempt people to buy. But typical of him, he reduced costs by only putting in the services like gas, electricity, and sewage to the first couple of streets. He'll have to dig this road up again if he ever gets started on the grand houses that are supposed to go here.'

'What a strange way to go about things.'

'He's a strange man. But he offered to build at good prices, and had some pretty pictures drawn to go with the plans, so people signed up with him. I'd never buy a house he's built because he cuts corners wherever he can. You're lucky that your house was built in an era where they did things properly, even if it does need modernising now.'

'I am, aren't I?'

'Right then, enough chatting. Let's make a start. We'll begin with changing gears, and then you can have a very slow drive to and fro along this road to practise doing it. Luckily there's room to turn round at each end of this street, because we don't want to start you on reversing yet.'

It wasn't nearly as hard as she'd expected. She drove back and forth, and at first she found that her feet didn't always move as quickly as she needed them to. But she'd felt herself improving even in that short time. She clashed the gears a couple of times at the beginning when trying to change, but after she'd had a few goes, she managed not to do that again.

She was surprised when Silas said, 'Can you stop driving now? It's time to go back, so we'll need to change places.'

'Already?' She felt disappointed. How quickly the time had passed!

'First, let me set your mind at rest: you're going to make a good driver.'

She gaped at him as she got back into the car at the passenger side. 'How can you possibly tell? This is my first lesson and I've hardly gone above a crawl.'

'I taught hundreds of chaps to drive in the army in the last couple of years of the war, and I'm back to doing it again, this time with ladies as well as men from the valley. Believe me, I can spot someone who's hopeless, and I don't tell any lies about how they're going on. Lives depend on my teaching people to drive properly, pedestrians' as well as drivers' lives. There are a shocking number of accidents on the roads of this country, you know. If you ask me, the Government should have brought in a driving test sooner to weed out hopeless folk.'

As he drove them back down into Rivenshaw, she watched him carefully, understanding what he was doing with the gears this time.

'It truly was an excellent start,' he said when they got back, and he had such an honest face, she believed him.

She couldn't stop smiling.

When they got back, she saw Gabriel leaning against a wall in the workshop, chatting to Todd and watching intently what he was doing. He looked up at the sound of the car arriving and said something to the other man before walking across to meet her.

'How did it go?'

Silas answered for her. 'It went very well indeed. She's going to make a good, steady driver. It'll only take about half a dozen more lessons to get her ready for the test, I should think. They only check the basic skills, after all, and she's already changing gears smoothly. Tomorrow at the same time all right for you, Miss Porter?'

'Yes, please.'

'I'll go and write it in the book.'

Gabriel grinned at her. 'Doing well, eh? I told you so. And what's more, you look as if you enjoyed yourself.'

'I did, once I got the hang of changing gear. But I haven't driven in traffic yet.'

'You'll cope with that as well. Now, let's go and finish buying your car.'

'Yes, let's.'

Gabriel stayed out of the discussion, letting her find out from Todd what she needed to do in order to buy the car and legally drive it. Then he went with her to the bank and the little office where they sold car insurance, keeping an eye on who was nearby all the time. He scowled at one lad who seemed to be following them, and jerked his thumb to indicate the lad should stop that, but managed not to let her see what he was doing.

After that, they went back to pay Todd.

When Bella had counted out the money and accepted a receipt, she turned to the car and pressed her hands over her cheeks, staring at it for a long time as if she couldn't believe what she was seeing.

'It's yours now,' Todd prompted gently.

'I know. It's just – I still can't believe it.' She turned to Gabriel. 'Will you please take me out for a drive?'

'With pleasure. Where do you want to go?'

'I don't care, as long as it's in my car. My – own – car!'

So he took her up to the top of the valley, got out, and stood beside her as she sat in the driving seat, stroked the dashboard and traced around each dial with loving fingertips. Every now and then she beamed at him.

He could see that she didn't want to go back to the passenger seat, but in the end he took the wheel again.

'Let's stop at that nice café and celebrate with a ginger beer,' she said as she settled in. 'Didn't you say they make it up here in Ellindale?'

'Yes. And very good ginger beer it is, too. Todd's wife started the business. She's a clever woman.'

'She must be, to start her own business.'

'That's what you'll be doing.'

'Pardon?'

'You'll be starting a business when you rent out your flats.'

That didn't seem to have occurred to her, and it was a few seconds before she said faintly, 'I never thought about it that way.'

'Well, you should. I'll park the car right outside and you can sit looking at it through the café window for as long as you like.'

She insisted they have an iced fancy to go with their ginger beer.

Gabriel looked at her more often than the car. It wasn't often you saw such happiness glowing on someone's face. It warmed his heart even to see it, let alone feel part of it, as he did today.

He hoped nothing would happen to spoil it. He'd have a quiet word with Ryan Cornish about the danger she was in so that the other man would keep a close eye on her when he was at home.

From what he'd seen, Ryan wouldn't find that an unwelcome chore.

After Miss Porter had gone off with Gabriel for her driving lesson, Roy only had to wait a short time for Ryan to return. 'Have you got time to discuss a job, lad?'

'Always ready for a bit of work.'

'Let's go up to the top floor to talk. There's no one up there at the moment.'

'There's Ed, but he'll be asleep.' Ryan followed him, and gestured to one of the two bigger rooms there, then waited.

'How would you like to work for me?'

'Any time, Mr Tyler.'

Roy smiled. 'How about all the time?'

'You mean – a permanent job?'

'Yes. I'm going to be doing a lot of building around here in the next few years, which will involve plenty of plumbing work, both inside and outside on the sewage system and connections. Are you up to that?'

'You know I am.'

'Yes, I do. You've done a few jobs for me over the past year, and they've all been done well. I'm sure you won't mind doing other odd jobs for me in between the plumbing, whatever is needed?'

'I'm not too proud to shovel muck, if there's no other work. My main concern is not my own pride, but to put bread on the table for my children and pay my rent on time.'

'Good lad. So, how about it? Will you come and work for Tyler's?'

Ryan's voice was shaky and his eyes over-bright. 'I'd love to. When do I start?'

'How about this afternoon? Your first major set of jobs will be to put three bathrooms into this house, one in each flat. And you can hire who you want as a temporary labourer when one's needed. I'll pay them too.'

He had to be sure. 'Do you mean my own flat is going to have a bathroom as well? How will we fit that in? We use every bit of the space in our two rooms at the moment.'

'The box room will be added to your flat, so you'll get a small bedroom as well as the bathroom – it'll be very small, I'm afraid. We're in a hurry to get the job done, so I have to get the place cleared of boxes today. That'll be your first job, taking everything down to one of the rooms in Miss Porter's flat.'

'I'll enjoy doing that.'

'The next job will be putting in her bathroom, and that wants doing as quickly as possible. Ethel will go over the plumbing needs and layout with you, then order what's needed.' He smiled proudly. 'She always runs everything past me before starting a job, but she's better than me at that fiddly stuff and paperwork.'

Ryan had to swallow hard before he could speak. 'Eh, it'll be grand to have a bathroom. Hettie will think she's gone to heaven. It'll make her life easier, that's for sure.'

'So you see, your first job isn't plumbing, it's lugging boxes around. After you've taken everything from the storeroom down to Miss Porter's flat, someone will need to keep an eye on it tonight.'

'That'll be easy enough. She's hired Ed to act as night watchman here already.'

'Good. Know a chap who'll help you this afternoon? Some

of those boxes are heavy, and we want to get them down intact for Miss Porter to open at her leisure.'

'Yes, I know someone.' Ryan grinned. 'In fact, he's sleeping next door, as I told you.' He poked his head into the next room. 'Ed lad! Wake up! Got a minute?'

Roy took the big key out of his pocket and handed it over to Ryan. 'I'll leave you to it. Don't lose this. I'll need it back at the end of the day. I'll be popping past to collect it and check that the boxes weren't hiding any surprises in the storeroom.'

'I'll look after it carefully.'

'I'll leave you to tell Ed about this afternoon, then.'

Roy trusted Ryan to do things properly. He only took on permanent staff after he'd observed them for a while and given them odd jobs. He'd rarely been let down.

He and Higgerson differed greatly there. The other builder had hardly any permanent employees, except for his office staff. He treated his workmen like dirt, because he said they weren't to be trusted. So he didn't get the best work out of them.

Roy moved towards the stairs, trailing words after him. 'Go and ask the Traskes to show you the room you're to put the stuff in, then you and Ed can make a start. He'll get a bit of extra pay for helping you.'

And then he was gone. Ryan took a minute or two to smile about his new job and dash away the tears that would well over from his eyes. He didn't want anyone to see him, because men weren't supposed to cry, were they? Even for happiness.

Eh, it'd make such a difference to know how much money was coming in from a permanent job. Well, it would once he found out what Mr Tyler would be paying him. But the Tylers always paid decent wages, so he wasn't worried about that.

Ed came into the room, looking sleepy and yawning. 'Something up, lad?'

'Something good. Tyler's just taken me on full-time.'

His companion let out a long, low whistle. 'Eh, he must think a lot of you. But it couldn't happen to a better man.'

'I think a lot of him, too. One of the best bosses in the whole valley, he is.' Ryan took a couple more deep breaths, then said, 'You all right to work this afternoon? You'll get paid extra for it. And you'll still be wanted to keep watch tonight.'

Ed brightened. 'I'm always ready for paid work. What do you need doing?'

'We need to take all the stuff in the storeroom down to the ground-floor flat. Then the storeroom is going to be added to my flat.'

'Eh, she's not wasting time improving the house, is she?'

'No. And even if the rent goes up, I should be able to afford it if I have a permanent job. I won't have to move house again, thank goodness. Any road, let's have a look at what there is in that box room and get started.'

He unlocked the door and the two men studied the contents.

'There's a rare lot of stuff,' Ed said.

'Aye. And she doesn't even know what's in it. It's part of her inheritance.'

Ed let out a low whistle. 'She's fallen lucky, hasn't she?'

'She has. But she's had some hard times, from what Gabriel said. She doesn't look down her nose at you, even though you can hear how posh her family was by how she speaks. You should have seen her with my kids when they were ill. They took to her at once. And she always treats Hettie nicely too.'

Ed stared at him, then looked quickly away to hide his surprise at the warm way his companion had spoken about the new owner of the house. Ryan didn't often seem to notice women. He'd noticed Miss Porter, though.

'Nice voice, she has, for all she's so small. I can't be doing with shrill women,' Ryan went on.

Ed hid a smile. Who'd have thought it? Ryan didn't seem to realise it yet, but he was falling for her, if ever Ed had seen a chap fall.

Ryan stood thinking for a moment or two, then indicated a pile of boxes near the door. 'We'll take this pile down first to clear the way. Eh, I'm looking forward to having my own bathroom. Kids get so mucky when they play.'

'Who wouldn't be happy about that?'

22

When Gabriel took Bella home to her lodgings, he parked the car nearby. 'I'll walk back to Todd's to pick up the van and return it to my brother. It's not far. I'll come back down for your car later this evening. My brother will probably be able to drive me here. If not, I'll walk down the hill. It's only a couple of miles, and it's not going to rain.'

'Thank you. It's a lot of trouble for you. You're sure you wouldn't rather leave it here all night? After all, this is a respectable neighbourhood.'

'Even so, your car will be much safer outside our house after dark than so near to the town centre.'

'I suppose so.'

'I'll be able to pick you up as early tomorrow morning as you want. And you won't need to worry about your car. Everyone on our street keeps a careful watch on what's going on inside and out. They're really good neighbours. A couple of people have dogs that bark at passers-by, but not at residents. I often wonder how they can tell which is which from a distance.'

She was pleased at how careful he was being. After he strode off into the dusk, she lingered outside, looking at her car, running one hand along the side. He'd parked it right under the nearest street lamp.

She didn't want to go inside and leave it out here on its own. Which was silly. Cars didn't get lonely, as people did. But there you were. If you couldn't be silly on such a special day, when could you?

Of course, Mrs Tucker appeared within minutes to ask her what the car was doing there and why she was standing outside on such a cold evening.

When she found out Bella had bought the car, she gaped at her. 'You must have a lot of money to spare!'

'Not so much now,' Bella replied prudently. How much money she had was one secret she intended to keep from everyone.

But she couldn't refuse when Mrs Tucker asked if she could have a sit in the car, because people often wanted to do that. Some of the other lodgers heard their voices and came out to see what was going on, and then they had to take turns at sitting in it too.

When they all went inside, Bella sat near the dining-room door, which was always left half open to let people bring trays of food or dirty dishes in and out. She wanted to be able to hear the van's engine when Gabriel came back. She ate her meal quickly, not really interested in food tonight, too excited about the coming changes in her life.

It was fully dark by the time Gabriel returned, and the women were now in the sitting room, from whose window Bella could peep out if she lifted the side of the heavy winter curtain. Yes, it was Jericho's van. His brother had indeed driven him down from Birch End and, when she hurried outside to give him the key, he introduced them.

The two men resembled one another and you'd have guessed them for brothers: tall, dark and not exactly handsome, but attractive, with lovely warm smiles. Jericho seemed as friendly and easy to like as his younger brother, and treated her in a similar manner.

'I gather you've joined our family now, Cousin Bella.'

'You don't mind – Cousin Jericho?'

'No, of course not.' He glanced round to check that his brother wasn't within earshot, and added in a low voice, 'Your friendship is helping Gabriel come out of his shell. It's so good to see that.'

When the two brothers drove away, Gabriel in her little blue car following the van, she felt nervous, as if someone was watching her, so hurried back inside. She heard Mrs Tucker finishing clearing up the dining room, so went to tell her she needed to leave really early the next day.

She hesitated, then took a risk. 'And maybe once I get my flat properly furnished and the bathroom finished, you'd like to come and have tea with me? You've been so kind.'

She didn't get the polite refusal she was half expecting, but a big smile and an instant acceptance.

'I'd like that, Miss Porter.'

'Bella.'

'Bella, then. And I'm Viv.'

They both smiled at that transition to first-name terms, then Mrs Tucker added, 'I try to look after my ladies, so I'd have done what I could for you whatever. But I must admit I enjoy your company. You're a sensible woman. And I'm a nosey one. I'd really like to see inside your house.'

'I'd be happy to show you around.'

'Good. I shall be delighted to have tea with you any time, my lodgers' needs permitting, of course. And you must come back for tea here every now and then, too.'

It made Bella feel so good to have taken the first steps towards making a female friend. Viv Tucker was older than her, but that didn't seem to matter once they got chatting.

After that she went into the sitting room with the others and said her goodbyes, especially to those who'd been helping her improve her appearance. She made sure to pay for the skirt alterations while she was at it, and Louisa said she'd leave the skirts with Mrs T so Bella could pick them up when they were ready.

Bella went up to her bedroom earlier than usual because

she had to finish packing her suitcase. Doing that felt so good, a visible sign of progress.

Tomorrow Gabriel could take her to the station to pick up her trunk and the other suitcase before they went up to the house. Only . . . Oh, no! It suddenly occurred to her to wonder whether the huge, old-fashioned trunk would fit into her little car. She didn't see how it could. Oh dear, she should have thought of that and told him how big it was.

Well, she'd find out tomorrow, wouldn't she? If necessary she'd pay to have the trunk delivered to Daisy Street.

So many details to think of. It had been another lovely day. She hadn't felt so alive for years.

She stretched out in bed, intending to lie and think about the following day, and her new home . . .

When she was woken by her little alarm clock, she realised with a start that it was morning already. She was amused at how quickly she'd fallen asleep the previous night and how soundly she'd slept.

Getting up straight away, she finished packing her suitcase and went down for the early breakfast she'd asked for last night, energy surging through her.

She was moving into Daisy Street today. How wonderful was that?

When Gabriel arrived at Mrs Tucker's, he was driving the van again. She rushed out to see what was wrong with her car.

He grinned at her anxious expression. 'It's all right. No trunk that I've ever seen would fit into that little car of yours, so I've borrowed Jericho's van. We'll have to get a move on because he needs it back as quickly as possible. Where's your suitcase? We need to hurry.'

She'd brought it down to the hall already and she left him to put it in the back of the van and fasten it to one of the side hooks.

After popping her head into the kitchen to say a hasty goodbye to Mrs Tucker, she ran out to the van, beaming at the world even though it was a chilly grey morning.

The left luggage office wasn't officially open so early, but Gabriel found the deputy station master, who let Bella retrieve her trunk and suitcase and even helped Gabriel and a porter load the heavy trunk into the van. And then they were off, driving up the valley to Backshaw Moss, and Bella was trying not to show how childishly excited she was.

Ed was waiting at the house to help Gabriel bring her luggage in, and the two men struggled with the weight of the trunk. After that Ed took the van back to Jericho and said he'd return with her car.

'Don't look so worried. Ed's a good driver.' Gabriel led the way inside her flat to where her three pieces of luggage were standing to one side of a totally bare room, which would soon become her bedroom. It was clean now, no trace of that horrid smell, but the luggage looked lost on its own.

'Come and look at this,' Gabriel said to Bella, and flung open the door of the room next to the entrance.

'Oh, my goodness! What a lot of boxes! Are they all from the storeroom? I didn't realise there were so many.'

'They were packed in very skilfully, piled on top of one another. You're going to have fun opening them.'

'Yes, I am.' She patted the nearest one, made of stout cardboard, and found that a flap at the top was loose. She couldn't resist tugging the other flaps open as well to see what was inside. 'These look like curtains. I do hope they fit my windows.' She wriggled a hand down the side, pulling one corner of the curtains back. 'And there's at least one blanket. Oh, good!' She'd been planning to use her dressing gown as an extra cover if she wasn't warm enough in bed, but now she wouldn't have to.

'What time is Charlie Willcox sending up the furniture, Bella?'

'He said he'd send it first thing.'

'Then we won't have long to wait. He gets to work well before his shop opens, and he doesn't usually promise what he can't do.'

At the sound of another vehicle stopping outside, she ran to look out of a front window. 'It's Dolly and Gladys.' She watched them get out of a shabby little van, carrying what looked like more cleaning materials. Dolly blew a kiss at the driver, who must be her husband, and both women waved as he drove away.

They put down their burdens in the hall and came to join Bella in her flat, calling, 'We're here!' and peering into the box she'd opened.

'Come in useful, them curtains will,' Dolly said. 'Hope you don't mind, but we picked up a few more things from the shop. They said you could pay for them later. Your top floor hasn't been cleaned properly for a while, so it'll need a good old scrubbing out.'

'I'm glad you did that. You'll know what cleaning materials are needed better than I will.'

They nodded complacently in acceptance of this compliment.

After the two of them had taken their bags upstairs, Dolly came clattering back down to find the big old kettle they'd brought with them when they first started work. As she carried it upstairs to heat some water on the old-fashioned gas stove up there, Bella remembered that she still had no kettle of her own. She'd have to boil the water for pots of tea in her small saucepan for the time being. She got out her notebook to add it to her list.

Gabriel leaned against the wall, watching her pace up and down. Clearly, she couldn't stay still for sheer excitement.

'Do you want to open more boxes while we wait?' he asked after a few minutes.

She had a quick think, then shook her head. 'No. It's tempting, but not till I have somewhere to put whatever's in them. Besides, my furniture may arrive any minute now.'

On one of her walks out into the hall, she said good morning to Ryan Cornish, who was coming downstairs, on his way out to work, judging by his overalls and big canvas holdall of tools.

'How are you today?' she asked.

He looked as happy as she felt. 'Very well indeed. I had some good news yesterday: I was offered a job. I'm going to be working permanently for Mr Tyler from now on.'

She knew how important it was for people to find steady jobs, so she congratulated him and asked after the children.

'They're still asleep. I told Hettie to have her breakfast in peace till they wake up. She was looking a bit better this morning, I thought.'

'What will you be doing first for Mr Tyler?'

'I already did it yesterday afternoon. Me and Ed carried your boxes down.'

'I hope everything goes well today.'

'Thank you. I hope your move goes smoothly, too.'

They beamed at one another and she thought he looked every bit as excited about his job as she felt about her new home.

He was, she decided, as easy to talk to as Gabriel. And his children were darlings. She was so glad to have them as tenants.

It seemed a long time till a big removal van drew up outside. Bella glanced at her watch, surprised that it was barely nine o'clock because it felt later. She hurried to the front door to watch them unload her furniture.

'This is where we start to turn your flat into a home,' Gabriel said quietly from behind her. 'I'll tell them where to put things, shall I?'

Bella knew the men would take orders from another man more easily than from a woman, so she gave in to the inevitable and nodded. 'Yes, please.'

He went out to see the two men who'd brought her purchases and, in a shorter time than she'd have believed possible, her furniture was in place. Which just showed how little she had.

The men went back to the van and started to unload something else, which puzzled her because everything she'd bought was there. They came back puffing and panting with a battered tallboy, which was higher than her head. It had five drawers, topped by a small two-door cupboard about eighteen inches high, with oval mirrors in each of the little doors. It had quite a few scuff marks, but was still very handsome.

'Mr Willcox said to tell you it's a present for your new home,' the older man said. 'It's been bashed around, but he's sure it'll come in useful. Where do you want us to put it?'

She whispered to Gabriel, 'Do I accept this?'

'Of course you do. Charlie Willcox is known for little acts of kindness. He's going to be very rich one day, but he won't have trampled on ordinary folk to make his money, unlike some.'

'This way.' She led the men back to her bedroom and worked out quickly where the tallboy could stand. She now had a wardrobe and two chests of drawers, one large and one smaller. But the room was so big it still looked half-empty and of course she didn't have carpets or rugs on any of the floors – or curtains at the windows. Well, they would come later. She'd have to get dressed and undressed in the dark or in the corridor until she could get someone to put up a new curtain rail, because the one there now was sagging markedly at one side.

When she'd said goodbye to the men she went into the sitting room and stopped in surprise when she saw a faded rug spread out neatly in front of the fireplace.

'Where did that come from? I didn't buy any rugs.'

'Charlie being generous again. If you look at it carefully, you'll see that it's well worn, nearly threadbare in places, and you might want to mend that fringe where it's loose at the far end.' He pointed.

Tears came into her eyes at this extra kindness from a man she'd only met once, and she scrubbed them away, resolving to pop by his shop and thank him as soon as she could.

Dolly came in just then and looked at Gabriel suspiciously. 'What've you been doing to her?'

'It's not me; it's Charlie. He gave her a battered old tallboy and this worn rug, and she started to get weepy.'

Dolly's plump arms came round her and one big work-worn hand patted her back. 'There, there! That's not anything to cry about, is it, love?'

'It's just – I've never met such kind people in my whole life.'

'Ah, we look after our own in the valley. Even them in the slums of Backshaw Moss do what they can for each other most of the time.'

'But I'm a stranger.'

'You won't be for long now you own a house here. Besides, Ryan told folk how you helped look after his kids when they were sick, so word has spread already that you're all right.'

Bella mopped her face and blew her nose a couple of times, then gave them both a watery smile. 'Thank you, Dolly. You and your sister have been kind as well.'

The older woman went pink and began to back out, saying gruffly, 'Happy to help. Just need that carbolic soap from under your sink.'

Gabriel went back to his favourite position, leaning against the wall, smiling indulgently at her.

'I was silly to get upset, wasn't I?'

'No, just a normal human being. Think of it this way, Bella. One day, you'll be able to help others in return for the way people have helped you. Even a tiny bit of help can make a big difference in hard times.'

She nodded, mopped away a final tear, and stuffed her crumpled handkerchief up her sleeve.

'Now, lass, do you want me to help you make the bed up? You bought a double bed, so it'll be easier with two of us doing it. They left the bedding you bought from Charlie's on the kitchen table and we can pull that blanket out of the box we opened as well.'

She looked at him in surprise. 'Men don't usually bother about making beds.'

'Me and my brothers had to do everything for Mam while she was recovering from her operation, and she sat watching us, making sure we learned to do it properly.'

'She brought up three lovely men – at least, I'm assuming your other brother is as nice as you and Jericho.'

'Our Lucas tries to hide it, but he's a big softie. He's the cleverest of us all, can add up huge sums in his head just like that.' Gabriel snapped his fingers. 'Eh, it was such a pity he couldn't go to grammar school. He passed the eleven plus exam, but Mam couldn't afford the fees. She sat and cried about that. Someone else won the fee-paying scholarship for boys that year, you see. Must have been a good year for brainy babies for someone to have beaten our Lucas.' Or else, as he and Jericho had long suspected, that particular family had had friends in high places.

'I was sent to a small private school for young ladies, which was all my parents could afford. I was supposed to study embroidery and playing the piano as well as the three Rs.'

He grinned and began to chant what these were, so she joined in, 'Reading, writing and arithmetic.'

'They're not really the three Rs, are they? I like the joke version in *Alice in Wonderland*, "reeling, writhing and fainting in coils".'

'The Mock Turtle's story,' she said. 'You read a lot, don't you?'

'Anything I can lay my hands on. You'll have to get a piano later and play it to us.'

She laughed at that. 'I can't. I wasn't good at music. In fact, I was so terrible they stopped even pretending they could teach me. I still can't sing a tune properly. It all comes out wrong.'

'What did you like about school? Anything?'

'Oh, yes. I had one or two special friends, only Thomas wouldn't let them visit me at his house after my parents died, said they weren't our sort of people. So I lost touch with them.' She scowled at that memory.

'And?' Gabriel prompted.

'I loved reading books about the real world outside London. In fact, I was like you, would read anything and everything I could lay my hands on, including the old daily newspapers before the servants used them to light fires. I soon knew more than my teachers about some topics. As a result, I know a lot about the history of our country – and about foreign countries, too. But nothing much about science.'

'Did you play sport?'

'Not really. It was too small a school to field teams for netball or hockey, and I wasn't interested in playing tennis. It always seems silly to me, bashing a ball to and fro.'

He chuckled. 'Not as silly as golf. I've watched them playing at the golf course on the other side of Rivenshaw, and it beats me how they get pleasure from it.'

It was her turn to smile.

'What were you most interested in of all? At school or at home?' Gabriel asked.

'Children. How they grow and develop. They're such complex little creatures. I found some books, read them more than once, wanted to become a teacher, only my parents were very much against that. They wanted me to marry someone suitable, insisted I'd remain a spinster if I became a teacher. But they died before my mother could introduce me to any suitable young men, and here I am, a spinster anyway.'

She didn't say 'with no children of my own', but it was as if he could hear the sad thought echoing behind what she'd told him. Strange how she really did feel like a cousin.

Bella shrugged away the sadness and looked around the bedroom. 'Thank you for helping me move the furniture. I'll unpack my clothes later. I have plenty of drawers for them now. As well as a wardrobe. Isn't that a marvellous start?'

When Gabriel went home for the day, he took her car with him again, but he was only a few streets away from her this time. They had to keep it safe until the backyard could be made secure, because although the council had just started to demolish the small row of houses opposite hers, there were still some scruffy families living at one end. And men still stood on the pavement staring at Bella when she came out of her house.

As she was waving goodbye to Gabriel, Mr Cornish came striding along the street and smiled when he saw her, so she lingered to greet him. 'Did you have a nice day?'

'Very nice indeed. I enjoy keeping busy and there's work of all sorts at Tyler's. I don't mind what I do as long as it's useful to someone.'

'I like to keep busy, too.'

He didn't carry on into the house, but stood beside her and pointed at the mess across the street, which sent one of the scrawny, ragged men edging back into his house. 'It'll be good to see that lot demolished, won't it? They've moved some people out already. Mr Tyler isn't wasting any time.'

'I didn't notice much about what was going on over there. I've been too busy setting up my new home.'

'I'm sure it'll be very nice by the time you've finished.'

Bella chuckled. 'I won't be able to get things really straight till Tyler's have installed the bathroom, will I? That's bound to make a lot of mess.'

'Um, actually, fitting out a bathroom will be my responsibility, and I'll do my best to keep the mess down. Wilf Pollard will be popping in and out to keep an eye on what we're doing. He's the foreman now. He's another person you'll like.'

'What will you be doing first of all?'

'We have to dig the outside connections to the sewage lines first, then put your bathroom in and connect it to them. While we're doing that, Wilf will bring in a couple of men to change the storeroom upstairs so that it's part of my flat. Eh, it'll be good to have another bedroom, even if it's only a small one.'

She murmured agreement.

He looked at her rather shamefacedly. 'You must have seen the mattress that I put down in the kitchen area at night.'

'Yes.'

'I've been meaning to ask you how much the rent will go up once the bathroom is installed? I think I'll still be able to afford it now that I have a permanent job.'

'The same as you're paying now, eight shillings a week.'

He looked at her in puzzlement. 'I've been paying ten shillings a week, not eight.'

She stilled, then decided to be honest with him. 'Welch was stealing two shillings a week from me. You're listed in the accounts as paying eight shillings a week, and that's fair as far as I'm concerned.'

He looked at her in shock. 'You have to report this to Sergeant Deemer. It's outright theft.'

'Welch is already furious at me because I sacked him. Maybe I should just let sleeping dogs lie. I'll have to think about it.'

'But with a bathroom and extra bedroom—'

'Mr Cornish, I'm not out to grasp as much money as possible. I want to rent out the two flats in my house to honest people I can respect and trust.'

'You won't regret it, Miss Porter.'

She let out a sudden gurgle of laughter and he smiled at her. He loved the way she did that sometimes. Such a merry sound.

'You might. If I could ask your help with little jobs that are too big for me, just small things, that'll more than make up for the bathroom.'

'I'm at your service any time.'

'Thank you.'

'There's the top floor to deal with, too. Wilf will make the changes into one flat with a bathroom, and Mrs Tyler has already drawn out the way they'll do it. He's a good chap, Wilf is. Everyone likes him. Well, everyone except Higgerson and his cronies.'

'People keep mentioning this Higgerson man, and never in a positive way.' Bella looked at him, head on one side.

'And with reason. He calls himself a builder, but doesn't do a good job. Only cares about making money. And he's not a good person in any aspect of life. Never trust him, not about anything.'

There was another of those wordless moments where they exchanged glances and she could feel herself flushing, she didn't know why. She said a hasty goodbye and whisked back into her flat, hoping he hadn't noticed her blush.

She didn't hear him walk up the stairs. He must still be standing there in the hall. Why?

She heard him go upstairs a couple of minutes later as she was walking round her flat, touching pieces of furniture, going to stand and stare out of the windows. It'd soon be dark and she wished she had curtains. It made her feel nervous to be on view to people, especially those opposite. She'd be glad when the rest of the houses were demolished.

Goodness, what was she standing there for? It was time she got her tea ready. It was ages since she'd done any cooking. It'd only be boiled eggs and 'soldiers' of toast to dip in them tonight, which wasn't at all fancy, but it'd do her. She would have an apple to follow. It didn't matter that the ones she'd bought from the village shop were a bit wrinkled. Apples were past their best by this time of year.

She got her food ready, sat down at her own table and ate her meal slowly and happily, dreaming of the day her flat would be properly furnished.

Only – what would she do with herself then? How would she spend her days?

She pushed that thought to the back of her mind. Time enough to worry about that when she'd got everything sorted out.

This was more than she'd ever hoped for – far more. A real home and, she hoped, real friends. But a little shiver ran down her spine. She'd be happy as long as Thomas left her alone. Surely he wouldn't bother to come all this way just to get back at her? And how could he, anyway? She had friends now to help her. And Ryan was living in the same building. He'd come running if anyone tried to hurt her.

23

The following day a well-dressed gentleman got off the train at Rivenshaw in the late afternoon and looked round the open space outside the station disapprovingly. What a horrible little town, even worse than he'd expected! That was the north for you, a very inferior part of England.

His clerk had already booked him a room in a small hotel near the station. He'd been very apologetic about the standard, but it wasn't his fault. It seemed to be the only hotel in the district that was even remotely suitable for the better class of traveller.

When the taxi deposited him there, he found the hotel every bit as bad as he'd expected, a nasty little place with not even a pageboy to hold the door open for him. Still, he hoped not to spend more than a couple of nights here. Bella had been easy to control before, and would be again. She'd regret defying him for the rest of her life, by hell, he'd make sure she did.

Arthur Thornlee stiffened as Beaton glanced round the bedroom and wrinkled his nose as if it smelled bad.

'Is this your best room?' Beaton asked.

The owner, who'd shown him up and carried his bag, had met this type of person before, so stifled a sigh. 'Yes, sir.'

'I suppose it'll have to do. It's only for a couple of days, after all. What time do you serve dinner?'

'We serve the evening meal from six to eight o'clock, Mr Beaton.'

'I'll eat at seven, then, and don't try to fob me off with a table in the corner.'

'No, sir. I'll make sure you have the window seat, which is our best table.'

'See that you do.'

Arthur couldn't manage any polite response, had trouble even making himself incline his head politely as he turned to leave the room.

'Just a minute. I'm expecting someone to call on me here at six o'clock. I clearly can't see him up here. Is there somewhere downstairs where I can speak to him in private?'

'I could light a fire in the breakfast room, sir. But it'd cost you extra.'

Beaton waved one hand dismissively. 'Add it to my bill. Show him in there when he arrives and then call me.'

'And the gentleman's name, sir?'

'Is irrelevant. He's not a gentleman; he's someone who's going to do a job for me. He'll ask for me by name, which should be enough for you to identify him. In the meantime, bring me up some tea and biscuits.'

Arthur didn't say anything about the encounter till he got back to the small office behind the reception desk after popping into the kitchen and ordering a tea tray to be sent up to their guest. He closed the door and leaned against it for a moment, looking at his wife and shaking his head slowly.

'Bad one, is he?' Susan asked. 'I saw him looking down his nose at our hotel when he came in. Who does he think he is?'

'King of the dung heap, that one. Doesn't even know the words please and thank you. Apparently, someone's coming to see him at six o'clock and he wants a private room to speak to them in. I suggested lighting a fire in the guests' breakfast parlour.' He winked at her. 'I told him it'd cost extra, so it'll be two shillings and sixpence added to the bill when you make it up.'

'I'll make that five shillings.'

She was still frowning, so he asked, 'Something else the matter, love?'

'I watched from the office as you signed him in. I not only don't like the looks of him, Arthur, I got one of my feelings. He's here to cause trouble for someone, I just know he is.'

Arthur became suddenly very alert. His Susan was never wrong when judging a guest who needed a close watch keeping on them. Her instincts had kept them and their hotel out of trouble a couple of times before.

She spoke quietly, 'Snob or not, that man is definitely up to no good, love, so you'd better eavesdrop on his conversation with this anonymous visitor.'

He shrugged. 'I was going to do that anyway. He said this person coming to visit him here isn't a gentleman, but someone doing a job for him. What sort of job would that be, do you think? It sounds suspicious to me. As far as I know, this Beaton is a complete stranger to the valley, and his business card said "Accountant" on it. What sort of job can he need doing?'

'Keep your eyes open. And so will I.'

At two minutes before six o'clock a short, thin man came into the hotel, still wearing his cap, and asked to see Mr Beaton.

'People usually take their hats off inside our hotel,' Arthur told him. 'It's called good manners.'

'Oh, sorry.' He took it off, but hunched up his shoulders and kept his gaze mostly downwards as if not wanting to show his face, let alone meet anyone's eyes.

That made Arthur take another good look at him so that he'd remember him again. He'd certainly not forget his voice, which had a distinct London accent, if he wasn't mistaken, and not an educated one either. He showed the man into the small parlour, but left the door wide open so that he could keep an eye on him.

His wife went up to inform their guest that his visitor had arrived and was waiting for him downstairs.

Arthur stood in the hall until Mr Beaton came down. He showed him into the room and waited for him to acknowledge his visitor, but he didn't. He indicated a table to one side that had been quickly cleared of tomorrow morning's tablecloth and cutlery, and covered with a maroon velvet cloth. The visitor was fidgeting around near it, looking uncomfortable.

Beaton waited for the manager to close the door and leave, before turning to the man. 'And your name is?'

Biff used his false name. 'Smithers, sir.'

By that time, Arthur had hurried around to the spyhole in the office, which had an adjoining wall. That gave him a clear view of the chosen table and most of the room as well.

Beaton had left the man standing. Their voices came through clearly to the office because of a usefully placed air vent, and also because Beaton spoke so loudly.

Arthur didn't like what he heard. He wished this so-called gentleman hadn't come to stay at his hotel.

Thomas Beaton studied the man who had been sent ahead by the London detective agency he'd consulted. He was a nondescript little chap, which was just what was needed, he supposed. No one would notice someone like this fellow wandering around the town, he felt sure.

The agency had found out that Bella was indeed here, and had furnished him with her exact address before he wasted his time coming north.

'What did you find out?'

'She's inherited a big house—'

'Big house? The will said it was a cottage. You must have got the wrong address.'

'No, sir. I went to see Number 23 Daisy Street myself this afternoon to check it out. It's a big, three-storey house. Old-fashioned, though, and not in a good district. It was split into four flats but she's planning to make that three, modernise the place, and occupy the ground floor herself.'

'We'll see about that.' Wasting family money on renovations that the sort of tenants from a town like this would not appreciate – or pay extra for. She was not going to do that if he had any say in it. Which he soon would. 'Tomorrow you can fetch me a taxi and take me to see this house.'

Biff Higgins looked hard at the man who was paying him. Was he really so stupid? No, perhaps not stupid, but arrogant, which could sometimes amount to the same thing when dealing with people outside his own class.

'I've come up north in my own car, sir. It'll be better if I drive you round. It's not a fancy car, but it's comfortable enough. You don't want a taxi driver poking his nose into your business, after all.'

'Hmm. Sensible. You can bring the car round to this hotel at nine o'clock tomorrow morning and we'll go and visit my cousin. She's not fit to be let loose on her own, and I'm going to do something about it straight away, pull her into line again.'

If you asked him, Biff thought, it was this toff who wasn't fit to be let loose. His employers hadn't given him nearly enough information about what needed to be done and why.

'Could you please explain what you mean?'

'Didn't they tell you?'

'I don't think you told them the details, sir, but I want to do the job properly.'

'I suppose you'd better know the general details. She inherited a cottage and has run away from home to live there. I'm here to take her back, by force if necessary, which is where you come in. She's rather simple-minded, not fit to live on her own, let alone manage anything.'

Biff didn't like the sound of this. Simple-minded? That remained to be seen. And in any case, did Beaton think people wouldn't notice and ask questions if he took this woman away by force? And if someone had left her a house, other people mustn't think she was simple-minded. What if she wasn't and this sod was just claiming it was so? No woman in her right mind would willingly submit to giving up her inheritance and being bullied.

This could all lead to big trouble. And they'd know who to blame for it, because Beaton would stick out like a sore thumb in this town, with his fancy clothes and posh London accent. And if he behaved in this arrogant way with everyone, people would take offence and then at the first sign of trouble, they'd be on the woman's side.

Biff didn't like the sounds of it at all, but he'd worked for posh sods before, and there was nothing much he could do to change such insulting behaviour except be ready to get away quick smart himself if trouble erupted.

'You can go now.' Beaton waved one hand. 'Don't be late tomorrow.'

'Yes, sir. I mean, no, sir.'

Biff went outside, seriously worried. For a while he paced that big square near the railway station, which was well lit. Then he went back to his lodgings, a small room over a nice, cosy pub a few streets away.

He lingered in the bar, ordering a pint and a pie for his evening meal, not liking the way the other customers stared at him. He couldn't always work out what they were saying with their comical northern accents, and he tried to say as little as he could because he couldn't help speaking differently from them.

The pie was good, and so was the beer. He'd ordered jam roly-poly for afters and the man behind the bar sent his barman out with it when Biff had finished the first course. You couldn't beat good, solid food in your belly.

The main consolation for putting up with this arrogant sod was that he'd earn some nice money by finding this poor woman. The more he thought about it, though, the more uneasy he felt. He didn't want to do anything that would land him in trouble. He'd looked after himself since he was ten years old and his mam had dropped down dead one day. He'd run away, determined not to go into that miserable children's home. And he'd done OK.

He ate the last of the roly-poly, scraped the plate clear of custard, then raised one finger to indicate to the landlord that he'd like another pint.

The man nodded.

Just this one more pint, Biff decided regretfully as he savoured the first mouthful of it. He'd have to make it last while he sat here in the warmth with nothing to do but listen to the conversations around him. He didn't intend to be foggy-brained in the morning from too much booze.

As he was sitting there he heard the name of the woman his client was after and stilled, listening very carefully. What a bit of luck! The man going on about her didn't seem in a good mood and had been sitting with a couple of strong-looking fellows, pouring down the beer.

'She's a bitch, she is, sacking me and turning Pammy Goodby out like that. I'll pay her back for that, though. See if I don't.'

A sharp-faced woman came into the pub just then and went over to the fellow. 'I knew I'd find you in a pub, Vincent Welch. Stop drinking all our hard-earned money and come home this minute. Your tea's ready.'

The other two men edged away, Welch drained the last of his beer and went off meekly. For all his ranting about this Bella Porter, he seemed to be under his wife's thumb.

Catch Biff ever getting married again. Wives and kids spelled trouble.

He finished his drink, then went up to his room. Might as well have an early night.

He'd leave his ratty old suitcase here to show he hadn't done a runner. Well, he'd booked for two nights and had had to pay for them in advance. But there was hardly anything in the suitcase. His spare clothes were in his car boot in case he needed to make a quick getaway.

Surely it wouldn't come to that this time? His client was supposed to be a gentleman.

Biff wasn't going to enjoy this job, he just knew it.

If this female didn't come quietly, he decided suddenly, he wasn't going to be the one to force her. He'd stayed clear of trouble with the law and he was going to continue to do that. He earned a nice living working for the detective agency, had a very pleasant life in between jobs.

No, he definitely wasn't going to do anything dodgy. But he'd wait to find out exactly what was going on before he took action.

24

When Bella woke up after her first night in the house, it was still dark. She'd roused briefly a couple of times in the night, not used to the creaks and other faint sounds this house made, let alone the occasional yells and crashing sounds that came from down at the far end of the street, as well as occasionally from opposite her house.

She didn't linger in bed, but got up and slipped on her old dressing gown, shivering her way into the kitchen from where she could reach the outside lavatory. Ugh! She was already hating using it. She felt it necessary to lock the back door of the house behind her while she attended to her needs by the light of a flickering candle. It took her three matches to light the cheap, nasty thing. She'd have to buy a torch and batteries.

She hurried back across the yard to unlock the door, dropping the key in her haste, terrified of someone from across the road attacking her. As she got inside and locked the door again, she let out a soft groan of relief.

By now she felt frozen and stiff. She put a full pan of water on the cooker and lit the gas. By tonight she hoped to have a kettle and would leave it ready, lighting the gas under it before she went outside. That would give her warm water to wash in as soon as she returned. She doubted anyone would be peering in through the window, but because she had no curtains, she still switched off the electric light, dim as it was. The gas burner gave her some warmth and just enough light to see by. It'd have to do for today.

She could never bear to skimp on cleanliness, but she reckoned today was the fastest all-over wash she'd had in years. She must make it a priority to get some curtains in here and in her bedroom.

She switched on the kitchen light again and put the pan on for a pot of tea. In her bedroom she dressed by feel because the window faced the street. Wrapping her old grey shawl round her shoulders, she went back into the kitchen. Was that a faint glow among the chunks of ash in the grate? Yes, it was.

Thank goodness she managed to get a fire going from it at her first attempt, and stood warming her hands at the cheerful flames. Oh dear, she'd organised things badly this morning. She'd do better when she was used to being here. And, of course, she'd be able to develop a far more pleasant routine once she had curtains and a proper bathroom of her own. Ah, that'd be bliss.

Pouring a mug of tea, she walked around her flat, cradling the warmth in her hands and sipping occasionally. She switched on all the lights and stayed by the door of the room that was piled with boxes, contenting herself with looking inside, not wanting to fall over something.

She couldn't unpack the boxes in here because she had few places to store the contents, though the extra tallboy would help. She'd peep into any she could reach, though, to try to get some idea of what they contained. Even if the contents had to be put back again, at least she could label the outside. She must buy a pencil and some sticky labels.

It was infuriating that the electric light bulbs were so dim they left spooky shadows in the corners of the two echoing rooms she couldn't afford to furnish at present. She didn't linger there, but once she got back to the kitchen, she took out her notebook and added brighter light bulbs to her list. She'd buy some this very day, along with the kettle. Ooh, and a torch.

The other thing she had to buy urgently was food staples. She had no stocks to fall back on, just one shelf containing the oddments of fresh food and a few tins she'd bought from the village shop. Porridge would be good for breakfasts. She also needed a meat safe to keep vermin away from certain foods. She did hope there were no mice or rats here, but wasn't taking anything for granted.

While sipping a second cup of tea and eating her third slice of toast and jam, she went through her day's plans mentally, continuing to add to her list.

Gabriel was coming at nine o'clock and they were going into Rivenshaw again. They'd have to visit several shops because there would be a lot of different things to buy that she couldn't get in the village store, but they'd call there on the way home as well. It was so important to shop locally in a small place. She'd realised that the first time she'd seen the owner's face brighten at her big order.

She would be having her second driving lesson today, and felt excited at the mere thought of it. Would she do well again? She hoped so.

It was a relief when it grew fully light, even if it was still the cold grey light of a winter's dawn.

March was such a chancy month for weather. Fine one day, stormy the next. Thank goodness it wasn't snowy or icy, because the men would apparently have to dig a trench from the house to the sewage system. Only the outside lavatory was linked to that at the moment.

She'd never expected to have to face all these renovations.

She smiled as she mentally added up the costs, but then she'd never expected to inherit a house, let alone such a big one, or the money to improve it.

Her cousin Thomas would be furious if he found out how big it was.

★

At just before eight o'clock Mr Cornish tapped on the door of her flat. 'I'm sorry to disturb you, Miss Porter, but I forgot to arrange what time we could start working here in the mornings for the next week or so. The noise is bound to disturb you, I'm afraid.'

'You can come as soon as it's light. I'm an early riser and I'm dying to have a proper indoor bathroom.' She shivered involuntarily at the memory of how cold she'd felt after going outside this morning. Yes, and how nervous.

He must have noticed her shiver because he said, 'You should get a gas fire fitted in here. It'd soon warm the room up and save you all the trouble of having coal delivered and cleaning out the fire each morning.'

It took only a minute for that suggestion to sink in, then she beamed at him. 'Thank you. I will do that. I don't know why I didn't think of it myself. At least we have gas and electricity connections already.' She saw a dubious expression on his face and added almost pleadingly, 'Don't tell me something's wrong with them.'

'The gas should be all right, but you'll need a more modern electricity connection and system if you're going to use many appliances, and probably the whole house will need rewiring, to be safe. You've got a very old system at the moment, and there isn't any electricity at all on the top floor. And while you're at it, you should run some power down into the cellar.'

'Oh dear! That's going to be expensive, isn't it?'

'Don't forget, the council will be paying half of the modernisation fees, as long as you allow them to run their various connections along the back of your property. You should get your rewiring done while they're offering to share costs. Mr Tyler explained all the details to me yesterday. It's such a good offer you should snap their hands off.'

'I'll do that. I've been too cold this morning to think straight,

I'm afraid. I have one other urgent problem.' She hesitated. Did she dare ask his help?

'And that is?'

'I need to put up some curtains quite quickly in here. I had to wash and dress in the dark today. There are some curtains in one of the boxes you brought down. I'm hoping there will be another pair in the box as well. People usually pack similar things together, don't you think?'

He nodded.

She took a deep breath and said it. 'Um, would you have time now to help me check whether the curtains fit the bedroom or kitchen windows? I shan't care what colour they are or what material they're made of, as long as I can be private.'

'Of course I have time. Won't take us more than a few minutes. I can stand on a chair and hold them up to the top of the windows while you check the length.'

She went to get the curtains, but was glad he followed her into the other room to help, because they were heavy. She couldn't help muttering, 'Oh, thank goodness!' when they found another set underneath them. She got the blanket out as well, to put on her bed tonight. Please let them fit! she pleaded with fate.

They measured the curtains together, both laughing when she tugged too hard and pulled them out of his hands while he was standing on a chair and they fell down on her head.

'Are you all right?' he called as he jumped down.

She burst out laughing and was still chuckling as he pulled the heavy mass off her, which left him standing very close. 'I'm dusty but unbowed.'

The way he smiled down at her made her feel – a little breathless. How strange.

'Let's start again, and lift them up more slowly this time.'

She fumbled for a better grip. The curtains were a dark

brownish colour, not a cheerful shade, but at least they would fit adequately in both rooms.

'Get Gabriel to take you to buy some rods to hang them from while you're in town. I'll measure the windows now and tell you the width. And don't forget the gas fire.'

He went to get his measure from his toolbox, which he'd dumped in the hall, then came back and told her the dimensions, which she wrote down in the notebook that was proving invaluable. Never had twopence been better spent.

He pointed upwards, frowning. 'Look at that! What's left of the original rods is falling to pieces and insecure. Someone must have been behaving roughly when opening and closing the curtains, in the kitchen particularly. I used to hear what sounded like fights and arguments and I bet they grabbed the curtains then.'

'And Welch said they were excellent tenants!'

'He was in cahoots with Mrs Goodby. Look, if Gabriel will stay late to help me, we can put the rods and curtains up tonight after I stop work. Don't forget to buy the wooden rings to hang the curtains on the rods. There are hooks in the tape already. See.'

He looked down at her. 'Just a minute. You've still got cobwebs in your hair.' He pulled some from the side of her face.

She looked up into his eyes as he did so, and felt something shiver through her even more strongly than before.

He stared back at her for a moment or two, then stepped hastily away. 'There. That's better. I'll help you fold up the curtains again, then I must get to work. Mr Tyler's sending two labourers to help me, and I think I heard someone outside in your backyard. He wants to get your bathroom done quickly and a proper sewage connection set in place all along this end of the street. I'll be at your service later, though.'

'I'll be very grateful for your help. Thank you.'

Only when he'd gone did she release the breath she'd been half holding, letting it out in a long whoosh of air.

She'd read enough novels to realise that she was attracted to Ryan Cornish, that her body was reacting to his closeness. Some of the books she'd borrowed from the penny library had been rather racy, by her standards anyway, and had had descriptions of people getting together and . . . well, starting to show their love for one another by kissing and fondling.

But she hadn't had any real experience of being courted, so couldn't work out whether he was as attracted to her as she was to him. No, he couldn't be. She was too old now to attract a man, too plain in appearance, as her cousin hadn't scrupled to point out many a time.

Only . . . Ryan Cornish had stilled and stared down at her in the same way she'd been staring up at him, without saying a word, just . . . feeling something.

What did that mean? Did it mean anything?

Oh, she was being very foolish this morning.

She had to admit to herself that she did find him attractive: tall, with deep blue eyes, regular features, and a warm smile. His dark brown hair was slightly wavy and lightly touched with grey at the temples, so he must be in his thirties, surely? Had he married later than most other folk?

His children obviously adored him, and Hettie thought the world of him.

She must be careful not to make a fool of herself over him. He was probably just being kind to an old spinster.

She clapped her hands to her burning cheeks and muttered, 'Stop it! You can't let yourself get silly about him.'

Only, she couldn't seem to help how she felt. All she could do was try to hide it.

A boy came panting up to the front door just then with a message from Silas about the driving lesson. Could she possibly come a bit later this afternoon instead? Something had cropped up. The boy would take her response back to the shop.

'Yes, I can come later.' She gave him a penny for his trouble and he ran off again.

Gabriel arrived just then in her car. She was longing to be able to drive it herself. She didn't go out to greet him because it was still very cold. And anyway, she needed a few moments to pull herself together. By the time he came in, she was calm enough to greet him cheerfully, tell him about the change of driving lesson time, and discuss what they'd do today, then show him the curtains.

'I'll be happy to stay later tonight.' He looked up as there were sounds from the group of men outside, and moved across to peer out of the window. 'It's good that they've started work. You'll want that bathroom putting in quickly before we get another spell of icy weather. Now, have you got a list of shopping? What exactly do you need to buy today apart from food and curtain fittings?'

They got all the shopping done and even managed to buy a gas fire with the promise of having it delivered and fitted the following morning.

They set off home from Rivenshaw at just after eleven o'clock, with a car full of parcels and carrier bags, including a fine new kettle. The two curtain rods were sticking out of the rear window, wedged under the dashboard near her right leg.

When a policeman flagged them down, she asked, 'What's wrong, Gabriel?'

'They're probably going to warn us about the rods sticking out too far.'

A young constable approached their car and a much older sergeant got out of the police vehicle, leaning against it with arms folded to watch him.

'That's Sergeant Deemer!' Gabriel exclaimed. 'You can tell him about Welch cheating you while we're stopped.'

'I wasn't going to say anything.'

'Mam said to tell you that whether you want to press charges or not, you should let our sergeant know what's been going on. No detail of what's happening in the valley is too small to interest him. He's a grand chap.'

He turned to listen meekly to the young constable, who warned them not to drive again with the curtain rod or any other pole sticking out so far, because it was dangerous. What's more, it should have had a piece of cloth tied to the end of it to warn other drivers not to get too close, and if they had anything at all suitable they should tie it on now.

Bella fumbled in her pocket and pulled out a handkerchief. 'Will this do?'

The constable nodded.

'We won't make that mistake again,' Gabriel promised. He took the small square of fine lawn from her and stared at it dubiously. 'This is too nice to use. I'd offer you mine, but I was fixing something for Ma and used it to mop up a spill, so it's filthy. I forgot to get a clean one this morning.'

'Then this is all we've got, and we don't have far to go.'

He got out of the car. 'I'm sorry for forgetting the cloth, constable. But Miss Porter is desperate for some curtains putting up in her new house.'

By the time he'd tied the little piece of white lawn to the curtain rods, Deemer had moved closer, so Gabriel turned to him. 'Miss Porter has something you might like to know about, sergeant. Do you have a minute or two?'

She shook her head at Gabriel, but it was too late to deny what he'd said, so she let herself be introduced to the sergeant and explained about Welch and why she'd sacked him.

'I'm glad you told me that,' he said. 'I've had my eye on that chap for a while. He kept telling everyone he was going to become very respectable when he started up as a rent collector, but I had my doubts. And that wife of his is as bad, if not worse. She's got a really nasty streak, too. One day I'll get some proof and pounce, then the Welches will wonder what's hit them.'

He snapped his fingers to illustrate his point, then stepped away from the car. 'You'd better get off home now while the roads are fairly quiet. I hope the handkerchief doesn't get damaged, Miss Porter.'

Gabriel drove away. 'He's a clever chap, Deemer is. Some folk underestimate him, including Higgerson, because he's so quietly spoken and looks like a kindly grandfather, but still waters run deep is a good way of describing our sergeant.'

She was glad when they got home without her handkerchief blowing away. Gabriel suggested she go inside and put the new kettle on while he unloaded the car.

When he came in with the last load, he held the little piece of material out. 'It's a bit dirty, but I don't think it's damaged.'

After she'd put her purchases away, she offered to make him a sandwich.

'You're sure you've got something to spare?' he asked.

'Of course I am. I bought some potted beef. I couldn't eat my own food knowing you were hungry.'

'Thank you. We'll have to keep an eye on the clock, though. You don't want to miss your driving lesson.'

Bella stared at the battered little alarm clock she'd managed with for several years in London. If there wasn't a nicer-looking clock in one of those boxes, she'd buy herself a new one for her sitting room.

The Traske sisters came downstairs as she and Gabriel were finishing their hasty meal to say they'd finished the top floor, so she had to go up and admire their handiwork.

'Would you have time to do Mr Cornish's floors today?

Hettie's been ill, you see. I've got to go out, but I'll pay you to do it.'

'You'll pay us to do his flat?'

'Yes. He's going to put up a curtain rail for me tonight, so I thought I'd do something for him and the children in return.'

They nodded but didn't comment further. She hoped they weren't thinking she and Mr Cornish were . . . well, getting involved.

'We could put in half a day on the hall and landing and stairs tomorrow as well, if that's all right?' Gladys suggested. 'They need a thorough cleaning. Just look at the dust and dirt on those bannisters.'

'Oh, yes, please do. And there's the cellar, too. I'm not even sure what's down there, but it doesn't smell very nice.'

'We'll go down with you to have a look at it tomorrow, as well.'

Dolly turned to go, then spun round. 'Ooh, I nearly forgot to tell you. A gentleman called here this morning. Said he needed to see you.'

'Did he give you his name?'

'No.' She hesitated, then added, 'He didn't give his name and said he didn't need to leave a business card, just said you knew him. We didn't like the looks of him, so we said you'd be out all day.'

'Then he said he'd just have a quick look round the house for the time being,' Gladys put in. 'I told him he'd do no such thing and we thought for a minute he was going to push his way in, but I told Gladys loudly so that he could hear it to fetch the workmen if he tried anything. He glared at us, but went away.'

Bella's heart lurched as she began to wonder— Oh, no! Surely Thomas wouldn't have followed her up to Lancashire already? 'What did this man look like?'

'Tall, thin, bald with a nasty way of talking down to you.'

She felt so upset she had to lean against the wall, and all three of her companions looked at her in concern.

'Are you all right?' Gabriel asked.

'No. It must be my cousin Thomas, and if he's come after me there will be trouble. I knew he might follow me one day, but not so quickly. I wanted to – to get ready for it before he had the chance to upset things here. What can he want?'

Then she answered it herself before they could try to guess. 'He wants to get his hands on my house, of course. And wants me back as his family's unpaid servant.'

'Well, he can't drag you back by force,' Gabriel said.

She hesitated, then told them a secret she'd never revealed to anyone else, because she didn't dare. 'Thomas is quite capable of arranging to have me kidnapped. He did that to one maid who'd run away from working for him before seeing out her notice. He didn't know I'd overheard him talking to his wife about it.' She sighed. 'There was nothing I could do for her. I was helpless, not a penny to my name and nowhere to go if he threw me out.'

The two sisters exclaimed in dismay.

'What happened to her?' Dolly asked.

'Her brother helped her to escape. I don't know where she went, but Thomas was in a foul mood for the rest of that week, so I assume he never found her. Well done for keeping him out of the house. Not many people manage to stand up to him. Don't let him come in if he returns this afternoon.'

'We won't,' Gladys said grimly.

'I can't abide bullies,' her sister added.

Bella drew herself up. 'Gabriel, I'm not giving up my driving lesson, but afterwards, well, I shall need to hire both Ed and Steve to keep watch until we find out for certain that my cousin has gone back to London.'

'He won't be able to kidnap you here in our valley,' Dolly protested.

'He's very cunning – and unscrupulous. He usually finds a way to get what he wants. Please keep your eyes open.'

They both nodded vigorously and Dolly said quietly, 'We look after our own in the valley, don't you worry.'

Bella was very quiet as she and Gabriel went out to the car.

When they got to the driving school she said, 'I meant what I said. I'm not letting him stop me doing anything, not if I can help it. If I vanish suddenly, remember that I won't have left willingly, and ask Sergeant Deemer to come and look for me. I'll give you the phone number and address of my London lawyer when we get back. No, I'll do it now.'

She took out her notebook, scribbled on a page as they drove along, and tore it out of the book.

'Your cousin must be bad to make you so afraid of him. Tuck it in my top pocket.'

She did that. 'He is utterly ruthless when he wants something.'

'Well, I won't lose the piece of paper. I'll put it in my inside pocket when we stop. In the meantime, let's carry on as planned. Is it all right if I go for a walk round town while you're away? There are a couple of things I need to buy for myself.'

'Of course it's all right. I don't expect you to stand outside the driving school on your own for an hour.'

Mr Johnson came out of the office just then and she greeted him quietly but calmly.

She was still changing, she decided, as she got into the other car. She wasn't paralysed by her fear of her cousin this time, and she had friends to turn to for help – as he would find out if he tried to do anything to her. She would never obey him again as long as she lived.

Perhaps it was a good thing she'd met the sergeant today. She'd found him a very direct but likeable man. In fact, if

Thomas threatened her, she'd tell Sergeant Deemer and ask his help, not wait till something went wrong.

After Silas had driven off, Gabriel strode across town to the police station and was lucky enough to find Deemer there. He'd only pretended to have shopping to do, wanted to make sure the sergeant knew trouble was brewing.

'I thought I'd better tell you something about Miss Porter.' He explained about her cousin coming after her. 'I have no idea what this Thomas Beaton is planning to do, but she's obviously afraid of him, and says he can be very cunning.'

'But she's not a child, not even a young woman,' Deemer exclaimed. 'What does he think he can do to her?'

'She's afraid he might kidnap her, or – or try some legal trickery. So I wanted you to know her side of things, just in case.'

'I'll keep my eyes open. But I think you're worrying over nothing. Anyone can see she's a sensible woman, with all her wits about her.'

'You should have seen how upset she was at the mere thought that he'd come here, and if a sensible woman like her is that upset at the thought of someone, it won't be for no reason.'

Gabriel made his way back to the driving school, where he got talking to Todd. He found himself sharing his worries about Bella's cousin with his old friend as well. The more people knew about her problems, the better. That way they could all keep their eyes open.

When he'd finished, he said, 'Eh, I don't know what's got into me today, Todd lad. It's just – he must be a really horrible man, because Bella's not the sort to exaggerate. Nor are the Traske sisters, and they didn't like him at all. The trouble is, rich people can get away with bending the law more easily than poor ones, sadly.'

'He must be bad. It's not like those two to take a dislike to anyone.'

'Aye. Dolly said she'd never taken against anyone as quickly before in her whole life, and that I should look after Miss Porter.'

'Well, I'd trust their judgement. If I see anything, I'll let you know, Gabriel. Or if you think I can help in any way, you have only to send word.'

'Thanks.' Gabriel went back outside to lean on the wall of the building in which the driving school office was situated, to wait for Bella to come back. He didn't want her to be on her own for one minute while that fellow was in town. Just in case.

25

Sergeant Deemer left his constable in charge of the counter at the police station and strolled across to the hotel.

He was lucky enough to catch Arthur and his wife taking an afternoon tea break, and readily joined them in a cup.

'You've got a so-called gentleman staying here.' He watched their reaction carefully.

They stiffened and exchanged quick frowns.

It was Mrs Thornlee who answered. 'So-called is right. He might have money, but he's a bad man, if ever I've met one.'

The sergeant was surprised by the vehemence of her tone, but knew she was a good judge of character. 'You sound very certain.'

She nodded. 'I am.'

'Do you have any proof?'

'Not exactly. But he's hired a man to do a job for him here in Rivenshaw,' Arthur said. 'Little snirp of a fellow, shifty sort, came here to report to him. You wouldn't look twice at him if he didn't have such a strong southern accent. I eavesdropped on their conversation because I have my hotel and reputation to think of. They're here to see a Miss Porter. Do you know her?'

'Slightly. Gabriel Harte introduced me to her. He's doing some work for her. Seems like a nice lady. She's inherited one of those big houses at the end of Daisy Street. He came to see me today to tell me he's worried about her safety – because of your guest.'

Arthur let out a soft whistle of surprise. 'Well, Mr Beaton was asking particularly about Daisy Street – what it was like, who lived there. I've been wondering whether to come and tell you how uneasy we both feel about him, only we've no proof that he's here to do something bad.'

'You should have told me anyway, just in case. Where is he now?'

'Beaton went out this morning and hasn't come back since. Shortie picked him up in a car.'

'I think I'll take a drive out to Daisy Street myself,' Deemer said thoughtfully. 'Make sure the lady is all right.'

'Wouldn't hurt,' Arthur said. 'He's only booked to stay here till tomorrow. I shall tell him all my rooms will be occupied for the rest of the week if he tries to stay longer.'

When Sergeant Deemer arrived in Daisy Street, the three end houses looked peaceful enough. He could hear the sound of men working at the back, so drove around and stopped in the little laneway to get a feel for things.

It couldn't hurt. They might have heard or seen something.

Ryan looked up as a car stopped near where he and his men were working. When he saw that it was the police car, he went out to see what the sergeant wanted.

Sergeant Deemer got out and nodded a greeting. 'Is Miss Porter at home?'

'No. She's having a driving lesson.' He couldn't help worrying about her, but if Silas was teaching her to drive, she would be all right at the moment, surely?

'I hear some chap turned up here asking after her.'

Ryan nodded, frowning. 'Yes. I overheard him talking to the Traske sisters. He sounded arrogant and patronising, tried to bully his way in. But they weren't cowed, and they didn't let him inside.'

He and the sergeant grinned at one another because they

both knew the feisty women he was talking about. Salt of the earth, those two were.

'Is something wrong, sergeant? Bella's all right, isn't she?'

'As far as I know. How do you get on with her?'

'She's a very nice woman. The kids like her too, run to her when they see her. I'd not want anything to happen to her.'

'Everyone who's met her says that she's a decent sort, and I liked the looks of her, too, when I spoke to her. They say the exact opposite of this other chap. Arthur Thornlee didn't take to him at all and, in his job, you need to be able to judge people. It seems this Thomas Beaton is Miss Porter's cousin.'

'He left her a message that he'll be back later, even though Dolly told him she'd be out till teatime.'

'Will you be around for the rest of the afternoon?'

'Yes. And she's hired Ed and Steve to act as night watchmen until we've finished working here and got the back more secure.'

'That's good. Look, I can't do anything officially unless this Beaton puts a foot wrong, but don't hesitate to call me in if you think she needs my help.'

'I won't, but the trouble is, we haven't got a phone here and the nearest one is at the village shop. She's afraid of him trying to kidnap her, told Gladys he did that to a maid who left his house without working her notice.'

'Hmm. I'm glad she's got you and the Traskes on the premises, then. Keep your eyes and ears open. Beaton is supposed to be leaving town tomorrow. I'll check that he does.'

When Bella finished her driving lesson, she looked at her instructor. 'Was I – all right?'

He studied her thoughtfully. 'More than all right. You're one of the fastest learners I've ever dealt with. You're a natural.'

She could feel herself flushing. He didn't seem like the sort of man to offer empty compliments. 'I'm feeling a lot more confident about changing gears and steering accurately now, and am really starting to enjoy driving.'

'Good. How about more lessons at two o'clock every day this week and next? By then you should be ready to take your test. I know it's voluntary till July, but I think it's worth taking anyway. People can be rather rude about women drivers, unfairly so.'

'You should hear my cousin ranting about them.'

'Captain Spenser is the local examiner. He lives a bit out of town, but you said you hadn't got a phone nearby, so as soon as you're ready you can use our office phone to book your test with him and arrange to meet him near the park, probably by the middle of next week.'

Bella couldn't help beaming at him. She didn't think she would go to the expense of having a phone put in at her new home. Who would she need to call except for the occasional tradesman or shop?

'We'll see if my colleague Nick can take you for one of the lessons early next week. It'd be good to get another opinion.'

'Whatever you say.' She hugged the warmth of his compliments to herself.

'I'll take over now. You can try driving in town next time. I'll stay with you till we find Gabriel. We don't want you standing around on your own, do we?'

His last remark made all her happiness vanish like a balloon being popped. She could guess why he'd said it.

'Has my cousin been here?'

'No, but Gabriel told me he intends to warn everyone to keep an eye on you till that fellow leaves town.'

She shuddered.

'We'll look after you,' Silas said gently. 'Word will go out to the lads as well.'

'Who are they?'

'Some of us were in the army during the Great War. We

keep an eye on one another, as we did then. It's nothing official, just . . . friends watching out for friends.'

'But why should you care about me?'

'Because you fitted in here so quickly. And if the Hartes like you, you must be all right. People think well of that family. Ah, there he is!'

Gabriel came out of the workshop and walked across to her. 'You look upset. Didn't the lesson go well?'

'She drove really well,' Silas said. 'It's this cousin of hers she's worried about.'

'I haven't clapped eyes on him yet, but he sounds a nasty bit of stuff.'

'He is,' she said.

'Well, let's get you home and check that he hasn't turned up there again. If he comes when I'm there, I'll throw him out for you. We'll see if he bounces.'

But even that little joke didn't raise a faint smile.

Biff could see at a glance that Mr Beaton was furious at being turned away from the house in Daisy Street. He watched him get into the back of the car and slam the door shut.

'They have no manners in the north. Drive somewhere I can sit and think without people gawping at me.'

Only, as they were driving up the hill from Rivenshaw, they saw a car being driven slowly along a little side road. It had a sign on the back saying the name of a driving school and, in larger letters, 'Learner Driver'.

At the sight of a woman driver behind the wheel, Beaton scowled, then blinked and exclaimed, 'Stop!'

They watched the car for a couple of minutes, then he exclaimed, 'That's her! My cousin. Whatever will she do next? Women should never have been allowed to drive cars. They're not capable of logical behaviour. It's putting us all at risk letting them on the roads.'

Biff blinked in surprise but didn't say anything about this ridiculous, old-fashioned comment because he'd already found that his client didn't like to be interrupted when he was having a rant. Well, Biff had seen women drivers during the Great War who were just as good as men. Better than some, in fact.

After a few moments Beaton's harsh voice ordered, 'Carry on. Find somewhere quiet we can stop for a while. I need to work out how to proceed.'

Biff stopped before they got to the next village, on a level patch of ground near the road, but with a wall between it and the field.

'This do you, sir?'

'Yes. You stay in the car.'

Beaton got out and began pacing about in a way Biff reckoned would have made anyone in his household shiver, the man looked so vicious. He was not enjoying this job.

After a while, Beaton came back to the car. 'We'll go back to Daisy Street and wait for her to come home.'

Biff didn't say anything, but he wondered what his client was planning. Surely he wouldn't try to kidnap a grown woman in broad daylight?

He stopped further along Daisy Street, turning the car so that they were looking towards Number 23.

Then they waited, with his passenger getting more and more fidgety, muttering to himself.

It was well over an hour before she came back, getting out of a little blue car, smiling at the driver.

'There! Didn't I say she was immoral? She's found herself a man. Already! I always knew she needed keeping on a tight rein. And I'll do that better once I get her back.'

Biff risked asking, 'How will you get her back, sir?'

'If she won't come willingly, I'll send for my doctor. He used to be her doctor, too. In fact, I'll send for him anyway.

He'll be well placed to help me.' He glanced round, wrinkling his nose as if there was a bad smell. 'It'll mean staying on in this damned town, but it's my duty to do it, for the sake of the family. Go and see what's behind that house. There might be a back lane. I might have to break in to get to her.'

Biff got out and did as he was told. This was getting worse and worse. He didn't mind bending the law a little, but he wasn't getting involved in actual crimes. And his employers wouldn't want him to, either. They were detectives, who got information or found lost people for clients; they didn't break the law, and because of that they had built up a good reputation. Besides, they sometimes needed police help.

Back at the hotel, Beaton didn't offer him any thanks for his day's work, merely said, 'I shall not need you again today. Come and collect me at nine o'clock tomorrow morning.'

After which he simply walked into the building and left the detective to drive away.

Biff went to the train station and found his memory hadn't failed him. There was a telephone box there and, after a lot of hanging around, he managed to be put through to his employers and tell them what he feared.

There was a lot of muttering, then the senior partner came on to the phone. 'Tell him we'll charge him double for such activities. But if he looks to be taking this too far, get out.'

'What do you mean by too far?'

'Murder.'

'I don't think I want to be involved in a kidnapping either, sir.'

'We'll pay you double too. He said the woman was unstable, after all, so it's probably better for her to be looked after.'

'Oh. He didn't tell me that. I'll see how it goes.'

When he put the phone down, Biff sighed. If he upset his employers, that would be the end of his job. But he'd meant what he said. He wasn't getting involved in kidnapping, either.

What if there was nothing wrong with her? What if it was Beaton who was a wrong 'un?

That night at the pub he watched the same chap come in and have a couple of pints, then start cursing Miss Porter and waving his fist, saying he'd make her regret it. He didn't say why exactly, just that she'd cheated him.

Biff ordered an extra drink. He needed it.

All he could decide was that he wasn't handing over a perfectly normal person into the power of that arrogant sod, nor would he stand by and let the man from the bar hurt her, or any woman.

Beaton told the landlord he'd be staying on for a few more days, and was surprised when Arthur looked regretful.

'I'm sorry, sir, but we're fully booked for the rest of the week.'

'You can't be. You haven't had any other guests while I've been here, and hotels in little out-of-the-way towns are never full in winter. If you try to deny me accommodation, I'll complain to the council about you not being fit to hold a licence.'

Arthur froze. He happened to be on bad terms with a couple of officials at the town hall and didn't want to give them an opportunity to cancel his licence.

Behind him he heard his wife come out of the office and turned to greet her.

'I heard that Mr Beaton wants to stay on. I know we'd planned a little winter getaway, dear, but we can postpone it for a day or two.'

'I, um, didn't want to let you down.'

'We'll do it later.'

She turned to Mr Beaton to say in a colourless voice. 'If you could pay for the two nights first, I'd be obliged, sir.'

Her eyes met his, and Thomas tried to stare her down, but

for some reason he failed. He was surprised Thornlee let his wife be so pushy. But there you were: some men were weak.

He shrugged and pulled out his wallet. 'Doesn't make any difference to me, Mrs Thornlee.'

Afterwards he said, 'I need to use the telephone. I can reverse the charges.'

He had to make his phone call from the office and, although Arthur tried to eavesdrop, he could only hear part of the conversation and couldn't make sense of what their unwelcome guest was arranging. Whatever it was, he was rapping out more orders.

When he'd left the hotel to take a walk around the town centre, Susan Thornlee took a deep breath and scowled after him. 'He is one of the most horrible guests we've ever had. I think you should go and mention this to Sergeant Deemer. I still think there's something wrong with him, something nasty. I wonder what he's planning to do to this woman he's trying to find. Have you met her?'

'No.'

'She stayed at Mrs Tucker's first, I gather. I think I'll go and have a chat with my old friend. See how she found this Miss Porter.'

'Good idea.'

26

Late the following morning Bella was chatting to Ed, who'd just woken up and come down from the top floor. It was a quieter place to sleep than his own home during the daytime, but now he wanted to get some fresh air and buy something to eat.

His cousin Steve came strolling along the street and stopped to say hello to her as well.

There were some lovely friendly people in Ellindale, she thought. Then she looked towards a car that had just driven along the street and stopped near them and exclaimed involuntarily, 'Oh, no!'

'What's the matter?'

Ed and Steve both turned to look at the car and the man getting out of it, then glanced back at her in concern.

'That's my horrible Cousin Thomas. He can only have come here to cause trouble. I don't know who the other men are. Can you please come back into the house and stay a little longer, Ed?'

'Of course.'

She turned to Steve. 'And would you go and fetch Mr Cornish, please? He's working in the backyard.'

Steve hurried off round the side of the house.

Thomas got out of the car and stood staring at Bella with a distinct look of triumph on his thin features. The driver and the other man remained in the vehicle.

Bella took a deep breath and stared back at Thomas. Just

when she thought she couldn't keep up a calm expression any longer, he moved towards her, stopping at the gateway, still wearing a sneering smile of triumph.

Typical of him, he didn't attempt to offer a greeting, just rapped out an order. 'You and I need to talk, Bella. In private, if you please.' He jabbed one forefinger towards the house.

'I have nothing to say to you.'

He stopped smiling, but before he could snap out any more orders, the sound of approaching footsteps made him swing round and frown as two men came round the side of the house to join them.

Steve hung back, but Ryan went to stand next to Bella, studying the tall man with the thin, vicious face. 'This must be that cousin you were telling me about.'

'Yes. Unfortunately.'

Thomas scowled at them all. 'Send these men away, Bella. You'll regret it if you don't because what I have to tell you is something you'd prefer to keep private, believe me.'

'I'm not sending my friends away and I don't wish to talk to you, not now, not ever again.'

'I'm afraid you'll have to.' When she shook her head and opened her mouth to refuse again, he said even more loudly, 'Very well then. If you wish to be embarrassed, you have only yourself to blame. I have legal custody of you and have had for years, because you've been deemed mentally unstable, so you have no choice but to do as I tell you.'

She folded her arms. 'I don't believe you. You kept me in your house because I was useful. You never had custody over me.'

'I can easily prove what I say. A doctor certified this and it was registered legally.' He beckoned to a man who'd been sitting inside the car and waited as he got out.

This man was plump and seemed nervous, with straggly grey hair, and he was clutching a doctor's bag in his hands.

The sight of that bag upset Bella. Did Thomas mean to drug her now? Why else would he bring a doctor with him? She clutched Ryan's arm involuntarily and he looked down at her, then put his arm round her shoulders.

'Get your hands off her, fellow!' Thomas exclaimed sharply. He turned to the newcomer. 'Come and tell them, Dr Farrow.'

The doctor swallowed hard, stumbling over his words, looking like a man who hated what he was doing. 'I, um, certified this woman many years ago as needing careful supervision for the rest of her life, due to mental instability. She cannot cope with any stress or make sensible decisions about important matters.'

Thomas smiled. 'Since then the good doctor has been proved right, because leading a quiet life has kept her reasonably stable.'

'How could you have done that? I've never seen you before in my whole life,' Bella said to the doctor, quite sure of that.

'You weren't in your right mind when he attended you, but I was there. I have the certificate he wrote then in my pocket and when I show it to them, the authorities here will have to back me up.'

Thomas patted the chest of his coat and a paper crackled inside it. He smiled at her, the gloating smile he used when he was about to force someone to do something they really didn't want to do.

Only she wasn't going to obey him, whatever he said or did.

Ryan didn't believe what either man had said because he knew Bella. What's more, these men both had a strange look in their eyes, the one menacing and the other distinctly fearful. He made no attempt to take his arm away from Bella's shoulders. She was trembling, clearly terrified, though she was trying to hide it. He definitely wasn't going to let them take her away.

'The paper must be a forgery,' she said in a low voice.

He nodded. 'We'd better send for Sergeant Deemer, I think, and Dr McDevitt.' Arrogant rich men could get away with things ordinary folk couldn't, but he trusted both those local officials.

'There is no need to send for anyone to come here. Did you not hear what I said, fellow? She's mentally unstable. Dr Farrow can sedate her, and we'll take her home, where she'll be safe. You can't possibly have the money to look after her.'

Ryan gave him a disgusted look. 'I don't believe a word you say, but I do believe Bella. You could produce a dozen London doctors – if this man is even a genuine doctor – and I'd still not believe what you're saying about her. I've seen Miss Porter coping admirably with difficult situations, looking after my three children when they were sick, being kind to my children's nanny, and organising her new life.'

'You're only doing this because you want to get hold of my inheritance, Thomas, but you're not getting away with it.' Bella tried to sound as calm as Ryan, and somehow that arm around her shoulders, that tall figure standing close to her made her feel stronger, as did the house behind her.

Ryan continued to scowl at Thomas. 'Bella will not only be safe here with her friends, but happy. Which she wasn't in your household.'

'How dare you speak to me like that, you impudent rascal?' Thomas darted forward so quickly that before they'd realised what he was doing, he'd grabbed Bella's arm and jerked her forward. As he tried to pull her further away, Ed stepped forward and took hold of him in a grip of iron, so that he had to let her go.

Being the largest man there, Ed easily pushed Thomas back to stand near the car, then remained where he was, partly blocking the entrance to the bare little garden.

Bella moved back hastily to stand on the other side of Ryan from her cousin.

It seemed natural that Ryan would take charge. He turned to Steve. 'Would you please go to the village shop and phone for Sergeant Deemer to come and help us sort this out? And ask him to bring Dr McDevitt with him. Tell him it's extremely urgent.'

'Aye. Gladly.' As he passed the group, he forced Thomas to take a step to one side, and Steve stopped to scowl at him. 'I don't care who you are, mister. Miss Porter is a nice lady and doesn't deserve to be treated like this. Nor I don't believe what you said about her, either. I'd believe it of you, though. By hell I would.' He tapped his forehead to emphasise what he meant.

While Thomas was almost gibbering with fury at this impertinence, Steve ran off towards the village with an easy lope, his footsteps soon fading away.

'I think we should continue this discussion inside, Bella,' Thomas said. 'There is no need to involve these people and make a further spectacle of yourself.'

'I don't want you setting foot inside my house.'

He rolled his eyes and turned to the doctor. 'See. She's still totally irrational.'

The doctor mumbled something indistinct.

Thomas turned back to her. 'You will regret your incivility and disobedience, believe me, Bella.'

'No, she won't,' Ryan said at once.

'Stay out of this, fellow. This is none of your business, as this police officer will confirm. You've tripped yourself up sending for him, which just shows how stupid you are.'

'Bella is my business, actually. Not only would I not desert a friend in need of help, but she and I are engaged to be married.'

His words surprised her, but she hoped she'd hidden that fact. They also made her feel safer, just as the arm around her shoulders did. How kind of him to pretend that they were engaged.

'Have it your own way,' Thomas said scornfully. 'I have the law behind me. You're only saying that to get hold of her inheritance.'

It was cold, but they remained where they were, waiting. A breeze blew around them, sucking the warmth from their bodies, and Bella couldn't help shivering. But she wasn't letting her cousin into her house. She felt that his mere presence would taint the place.

After a few minutes, Thomas muttered something that sounded like a curse, and said abruptly, 'Get out and keep an eye on them, Higgins. Dr Farrow, let us sit in the car out of the wind. She may be foolish enough to stand outside in weather like this catching her death of cold, but I'm not.' He got into the back of the vehicle but didn't shut the door – or stop glaring at her.

Farrow stared round as if he'd like to run away, then shuffled round the car and got into it from the other side.

'Why don't you go into the house, Bella love,' Ryan suggested. 'It's a cold day. I'll wait here and keep an eye on him, then call you out when Sergeant Deemer arrives.'

'I'd rather stay with you.' In a whisper she added, 'It was kind of you to say that about us.'

'I meant it. I don't want anyone to take you away.'

Still speaking quietly because the driver was now standing next to the vehicle and keeping an eye on the people in front of the house, she asked, 'How can you prevent them if they really do have a doctor's certificate saying I need looking after? Sergeant Deemer won't be able to tell whether it was forged, will he?' Bella frowned, trying to work it out, then continued slowly, 'He must have got it soon after the death of my parents. I had a mild dose of the Spanish flu and, as I began to recover, they told me Mother and Father had died. I was very upset, naturally, couldn't stop crying. But grief at losing both your parents is normal, surely? I can't understand why Thomas would go to such extremes to get control of me when I had nowhere else to go but to live with him.'

Then she gasped as something occurred to her. 'He only does things for money. He took over the business side of selling our house and getting rid of their possessions, told me he'd been appointed executor by my parents and would deal with everything for me. But what if he hadn't been appointed? What if he got me certified to get legal control over my affairs? I'm certain my parents didn't like him, and they hardly ever saw him, so why would they have appointed him? They weren't old; they died so quickly from that horrible influenza, like many others, that they wouldn't have had time to make a will.'

'Would he go that far, break the law?'

'Oh, yes. He'd do anything he thought he could get away with to obtain what must have been a tidy sum of money by the time he'd sold our house. It was quite big, in a nice area. He wasn't always as rich as he is now, has been building up his fortune over the years. He's what people call a self-made man. And I was so naïve he got away with it for all these years.'

'Did you never think of leaving his house?'

'Oh yes, many times. If it hadn't been for looking after the children I'd probably have found a way to leave. I didn't have any money at all, but I was younger then. Only, they needed me, had no one else to love them.'

'You love children, don't you?'

'Very much.' She went on thinking aloud. 'I've overheard him now and then boasting to his wife about cheating someone, or as he always called it, "getting a better payment". He's utterly without morals, believe me.'

'Well, he'll not get you or this house, if there's any justice in the world.'

They stood waiting in silence, then a few minutes later Ryan whispered, 'If he persists with this ridiculous claim, I think we should get married. Who better to look after you than a husband?'

She gasped and stared up at him. Oh, the kindness in his face. He really meant it. She could think of nothing she'd like better than to be his wife.

'I won't take advantage of you, Bella love. This house and any money you have would still be under your control. A lady like you would never choose to wed a rough plumber like me, I know. I think you're already fond of my children, though, so they wouldn't put you off, and I'd trust you with them absolutely, so I don't think you'd have a bad life.'

'I love them already. I've always wanted children of my own. But you're wrong: I would happily choose to marry someone as kind and loving as you, Ryan, with or without children.'

'Really?'

'Oh, yes.'

'I'm glad of that. I'd really like to marry you, too.' He gazed at her, and then slowly a smile creased his face. 'If this isn't the most ridiculous way to propose to someone!'

She smiled, too, sharing a similar sense of the absurd even now. Then she grew serious again. 'It's the only proposal I've ever had or am likely to receive given how old and plain I am.'

'Now that I've met your cousin, I can see why you lack so much confidence.'

Bella gazed involuntarily towards the car.

'There's something vicious and unwholesome about him. But you're a good woman, and pretty too. Any normal man would be happy to marry you.'

She blurted out her thoughts before she could stop herself, 'Would you really – not mind?'

'Mind? I'd be happy to do it, Bella. But I'd want a wife in my bed as well as a mother for my children. Could you want me in that way? Even though I'm just an ordinary working man who doesn't talk posh?'

'I'd love to marry you in every way – because you're Ryan.'

'Then we'll do it, whatever happens with him. There's been an attraction between us since the first time we met. I was fairly sure you'd felt it too.'

'Yes, I did. I—' Then a car turned into the street and stopped behind the vehicle in which her cousin was sitting. She could have wept at the bad timing of Sergeant Deemer's arrival.

Ryan really wouldn't mind marrying her. She'd be over the moon to marry him, as well as to mother his children, couldn't imagine anything she'd like better – or any man she'd like better than him.

But she might not have the chance to do what her heart wanted, so she took a deep breath and turned towards the sergeant, praying he could sort this out.

Sergeant Deemer scanned the group quickly, noticing that Ryan Cornish had his arm round the shoulders of Miss Porter and that she wasn't pulling away. Well, well! Rumour was right about them.

He also noticed the disgusted, sneering look on the face of the ugly man who had just got out of the back of the parked car.

Interestingly, the passenger from the other side of the vehicle looked extremely unhappy and was still sitting inside it.

The man called, 'Come along, Farrow!'

The other man got out of the car wearing the sort of guilty expression the sergeant had seen on the faces of many minor criminals, but not usually on the face of a man clutching a doctor's bag. And he still kept his distance from Beaton, which was also puzzling since they seemed to have come here together.

As Sergeant Deemer opened his mouth to greet Miss Porter and Ryan, the sneering man said loudly, 'I'm very glad to see you, sergeant. I am Thomas Beaton, my poor cousin's guardian.'

'Poor cousin?' the sergeant queried.

Beaton gestured towards Miss Porter. 'This poor lady. And I've brought along Dr Farrow, who certified her as mentally incompetent and in need of supervision in 1919. He will be happy to confirm his diagnosis again.'

Sergeant Deemer glanced at Miss Porter in puzzlement. Mentally incompetent? Not her!

'This fellow,' Beaton flapped one hand towards Ryan, 'is trying to prevent me looking after my cousin, and you've been sent for because he's defying a legal order.'

Miss Porter spoke in a firm tone of voice, looking the exact opposite of what the thin fellow had claimed. 'My cousin Thomas has pursued me from London and is telling lies about me, sergeant. Absolute lies.'

'I have the signed paperwork to prove what I claim,' Thomas said in a gentle, patronising voice. 'You really should resign yourself to letting me continue to look after you, Bella. You know you can't manage business matters or run your own life.'

The way he spoke to Miss Porter annoyed Sergeant Deemer, and he saw it was having an even stronger effect on Ryan Cornish.

'I can manage my own business matters perfectly well. You have no right to try to take over my affairs.'

'You are so forgetful, Bella. Which only proves my point.'

He took a piece of folded paper from his inside jacket pocket and held it out to Sergeant Deemer. 'If you'll look at this, sergeant, you'll see that I have every right to take charge here, not only to help my poor cousin, but to prevent opportunists like this fellow from taking advantage of her weakness.'

The sergeant took the piece of paper, read it, and frowned. Then he studied the date. He turned to Bella. 'Do you know what this is, Miss Porter?'

'No. I've never seen the piece of paper before, and I only heard an hour or so ago my cousin's ridiculous claim that he is responsible for me. What is the date on that paper?'

'1919.'

'The year my parents died. Like them, I was suffering from the Spanish flu; unlike them, I recovered. I wasn't mentally incapacitated in any way; I was ill. My cousin told me he'd been given power of attorney in their will and that unfortunately my father had made some unwise investments and incurred debts which would wipe out my inheritance almost completely. When he offered me a home with him, I still hadn't recovered properly, wasn't thinking straight, so I went with him, thinking it would just be temporary. I should have found a lawyer, checked the facts properly, but I was still very young and naïve.'

The sergeant looked at Beaton's smug expression and the increasing distress on the other stranger's face. Now, why was that?

For some reason, he believed Miss Porter's version of the story. He had seen for himself the havoc wreaked in people's lives by the dreadful flu epidemic at the end of the Great War. It had destroyed lives with brutal suddenness, and some people had taken a while to recover from losing their loved ones.

He had to make an effort to speak mildly to the cousin, who clearly looked down his nose at the rest of them. 'I've spoken to Miss Porter before and it seems to me that she is perfectly capable of managing her own affairs.'

'There I must differ from you – and I have both the law and this doctor on my side.'

Fear settled in Bella's belly like a heavy weight. Surely this claim couldn't be true? She couldn't bear it if Thomas got control of her again.

27

Another car drew up just then and, as a man got out of it, Ryan whispered, 'Remember Dr McDevitt? You can trust him.'

Bella's panic eased a little at the mere sight of the newcomer, because he looked so friendly and normal compared to the doctor her cousin had brought with him. He'd been lovely when the children were ill. She had to keep calm, she told herself, not let Thomas panic her. She could only rely on the truth.

Ryan gave her hand a quick squeeze and that also helped give her the courage to stand her ground.

When Dr McDevitt asked what was the matter that he had to leave his morning surgery and come here so urgently, the sergeant took charge. Under his questioning, they went through it all again. The two officials listened carefully, but they didn't scowl at Bella as Thomas was doing, not even slightly. In fact, their faces remained mostly expressionless.

The doctor's eyes went to Bella more than once, however, so she tried to return his gaze steadily.

After they'd finished their story, he announced, still in a calm, reasonable tone, 'I'd like to speak to Miss Porter on her own, if you don't mind.'

'But I do mind,' her cousin said at once. 'In fact, I'll not have it.'

Dr McDevitt looked at him incredulously before turning to the policeman. 'Sergeant?'

Sergeant Deemer said, in his slow, quiet way, 'You go into the house with Miss Porter, doctor, and I'll stay with these gentlemen.'

Beaton took a hasty step forward. 'No! If you must go through this ridiculous charade, I insist that Dr Farrow go with them. He was the one, after all, who made the initial diagnosis, and I doubt he'll have changed his mind. I can assure you, Dr McDevitt, that my cousin is not stable mentally, as we in the family have known and seen for many years. You have only just met her, after all.'

The doctor didn't even attempt to respond to that patronising tone, but turned to Farrow. 'Come with us, then.'

After what the sergeant considered a panic-stricken look at Beaton, Farrow shuffled off to join the others. If ever a man was radiating reluctance to do this, it was the doctor from London.

Dr McDevitt waited till they'd all three entered the hall to close the front door and say to him, 'Please do not interrupt my questioning of the lady, Farrow, or I'll have to ask you to leave. Miss Porter? Is there somewhere we can sit to chat in comfort?'

She inclined her head and went past them towards the entrance to her flat, hoping neither of them could see how shaky she was feeling inside. To her relief, she was still managing to speak quietly and calmly. 'Please take a seat, gentlemen. I'm sorry to have to bring you into the kitchen, but I've only just moved in and there isn't a fire lit in the sitting room.'

'I shall be quite happy to sit here.' Dr McDevitt sat down and, after a slight hesitation, Dr Farrow took a place at the far end of the table.

Bella sat down near Dr McDevitt because she didn't trust the other man. She didn't wait for the two doctors to speak, but began the conversation by saying, 'Dr McDevitt, I swear that I had never seen that piece of paper before today, nor had I ever been told that I had been committed to my cousin's care in such a dreadful way.'

Dr Farrow would have spoken, but Dr McDevitt gestured to him to be quiet. 'Why do you think your cousin made this claim, then?'

'That's easy. In the first place to get hold of my inheritance from my parents after the war. He told me they had debts and there was nothing left but some cheap jewellery of my mother's. I've recently found out that the jewellery was quite valuable, which doesn't make sense if there were debts. I'd guess he now intends to do the same with my new inheritance and take this house from me. He is . . . ever greedy for money.'

Again, Dr McDevitt held up one hand to stop the other man speaking. 'Tell me briefly about this house, who you inherited it from, and what you intend to do with it.'

She was a little puzzled that he'd want to talk about this, had expected him to ask about her health, but did what he'd requested.

He asked her a few more questions, then looked at his colleague. 'If you wish to ask anything, now would be a good time.'

Dr Farrow shook his head, looking even more uncomfortable than when they'd come in.

'Perhaps my colleague and I could go into the next room and speak privately, Miss Porter? Would you mind?'

'If you think it necessary.'

'It is necessary, but we won't be long.'

The two men went away, and Bella tried to think what to do if they agreed with the unjust diagnosis and Thomas attempted to take her away by force. Only, if the law proved to be on his side, what could she do? She had nowhere to run to, and wouldn't ask Ryan to break the law, because those dear little children were totally dependent on him.

Sitting by herself, she found it hard to cling to hope, so got up and put some more coal on the fire, then swept the hearth. Anything to keep herself occupied. Anything to keep the fear at bay.

In the next room, Dr McDevitt looked at his colleague. 'Miss Porter seems perfectly normal to me. Quite a sensible woman from her answers.'

'Yes. She was – upset and incoherent last time I saw her.'

'She'd just lost her parents and was recovering from the influenza, I gather.'

'Yes.'

'You haven't seen her since then?'

'No.'

'And you only saw her the once?'

'Yes. But Beaton said she was often like that, incoherent I mean. He thought it'd upset her even more for me to question her again.'

Dr McDevitt frowned. 'There must have been a review of the case by another doctor since then, surely? And that doctor would have spoken to you before coming to a final decision.'

'There's been no review that I know of.'

'That's rather unusual, isn't it?'

'Mr Beaton was in charge of her. I am not his family doctor, and haven't been for many years. I moved away from where he lived shortly afterwards.'

'Then we shall consider this a review. I find Miss Porter perfectly sensible, and she seems as capable as the next person of managing her own affairs.'

Dr Farrow opened his mouth then closed it again, looking panicked.

Dr McDevitt waited and, as the seconds ticked slowly away and the other man didn't speak, he said sharply, 'Let me make one thing clear: I shall take it very much amiss if you don't agree with my conclusion, because it's clear to me she is not and never could have been half-witted, which is exactly how you described her on the certificate. Indeed, I'm not sure I shouldn't report this case to the medical authorities, because it was clearly a miscarriage of justice.'

There was a pregnant silence, then Dr Farrow said, 'Well, um, you're right about her now. She, um, does seem perfectly normal . . . now.'

'Then let us start making amends by putting her out of her misery. Oh, and one other thing: I shall look forward to hearing about your retirement soon.'

Dr Farrow gasped and clapped one hand to his mouth.

'Need I say more? Do more? I will if I have to.'

Dr Farrow saw the look of distaste on his colleague's face and shook his head. 'I'll retire.'

'I shall check on that, believe me.' With a final scornful look at him, Dr McDevitt led the way back into the kitchen.

They found Miss Porter filling the kettle. She set it down and turned off the tap as they entered, staying where she was next to the sink, staring at them anxiously.

Dr McDevitt hated to see people so afraid, but took it as further proof that she was capable of excellent self-control when she didn't burst into tears. 'You have nothing to fear, Miss Porter.'

She stared at him for a few moments longer, then swallowed hard and gestured. 'Please sit down again, gentlemen.'

'No need. This will be very brief. We don't find you in any way incapacitated mentally, Miss Porter and,' he fixed the other man with a stern gaze, 'that is a unanimous decision. I don't believe you ever were.'

Her words were barely above a whisper. 'Oh, thank goodness!'

'I shall be happy to inform your cousin and the sergeant of that, as well as to provide any necessary paperwork. If Mr

Beaton doesn't leave you to manage your own affairs from now on, if he tries to make any more ridiculous and unlawful claims about you, you can call on me for support. Do not under any circumstances ask Dr Farrow for help. He is about to retire.'

The other man's gulp was audible and he was pale and sweating, in spite of the coldness of the day.

This was puzzling, but she was so relieved at Dr McDevitt's pronouncement that she didn't speak to the other doctor. She'd never seen him before today, and hoped never to see him again.

All that mattered was that she was legally free of Thomas!

When they went outside, Ryan immediately came across to put his arm around Bella again, and she gave him a brilliant smile.

Dr McDevitt raised his voice slightly. 'We find Miss Porter to be perfectly normal and quite capable of managing her own life and affairs.'

Beaton stepped forward. 'Surely you didn't agree with this, Farrow?'

Dr Farrow hesitated, then glanced at Dr McDevitt's stern face and said, 'I d-did. She is – quite obviously – fully recovered now.'

'I doubt she was ever in any way incapacitated,' Dr McDevitt said slowly and clearly. 'And if there is any attempt to go against my decision, I shall raise the matter at the highest levels in the country, both medical and judicial.'

Beaton's face was a mask of hatred for a few seconds, then he took a deep breath and turned to his cousin. 'I still think you need my help, Bella, and you would be wise to take it.'

Ryan had had enough of poorly masked threats and bullying. He gave Bella a questioning look and said, 'Let me remind him.'

At her nod he said firmly, 'Let me assure you, Mr Beaton, that Miss Porter is not on her own and never will be again, God willing. We shall get married as soon as possible. You may therefore set your mind completely at rest about her welfare and go back to London.'

'I cannot allow this! Bella, you need to stay with your family. This man is only after your money.'

She stared coldly at him. 'You are the one who's after my money.'

'But it's family money.'

Sergeant Deemer gave him a scornful look. 'Enough of this. Didn't you hear what the doctor said, Beaton? You have no further say in Bella's affairs.'

Ryan nodded. 'I shall look after her in any way she needs from now on, as she'll look after me and my children.'

The sergeant turned his shoulder on Beaton and smiled at Bella and Ryan like a benevolent grandfather. 'Congratulations. I hope – indeed I'm sure – you'll both be very happy.'

Beaton took a hasty step towards his cousin, caught the policeman's eye, and stopped. His voice was even harsher. 'Don't be a credulous fool, Bella! You can't possibly marry him. He's not even a gentleman.'

She raised her chin. 'If you're an example of a gentleman, Thomas, then that's the last sort of person I wish to marry.'

He sucked in his breath audibly, then forced an unconvincing smile. 'I am still your cousin, your closest living relative, so don't forget that you may turn to me if you're ever in trouble.'

'I shall have Ryan to turn to.'

'Well, I shall still be keeping watch over you—' he paused, glanced at the sergeant, then ended, 'mindful of your welfare.'

'And you'll be doing that from London?' Sergeant Deemer asked quietly. 'Bit difficult, eh?'

Beaton ignored him. 'I can do it from anywhere I choose.

I would spare no expense, believe me, because family is very important to me, as you are aware, Bella.'

When she would have spoken, he held up one hand. 'Did you know my younger daughter and son have run off, Bella? A childish folly. Alma and Oscar will not settle easily in such an uncivilised place, and will live to regret it, I'm quite sure. People usually do when they go against my advice. I shall find a way to keep an eye on them as well as on you.'

With that he got into the car and after an unhappy glance at the others, Dr Farrow joined him and they drove away.

'That man is dangerously arrogant,' Dr McDevitt said. 'Keep an eye out for him, Cornish. I think he could be very close to a breakdown, and he looks unhealthy to me, with that unnaturally high colour when he's angry.' He pulled out his watch and made a tutting noise. 'Look at the time. If I'm not needed any longer here, I must get on. I have other patients to see.'

'You're sure this decision will stand legally?' the sergeant asked.

'Very sure. Farrow knows I'll report him to the medical council if he doesn't support my conclusions. He was . . . very lax all those years ago, to put it mildly, taking Beaton's word for it about Miss Porter and not getting a second opinion.'

Sergeant Deemer moved closer and whispered, 'Was he over-persuaded perhaps?'

'Or even bribed.'

'What about Beaton? Should we not bring him to account?'

'I wouldn't advise it. I can see no benefits to be gained, and it'll upset Miss Porter unnecessarily. For all his threats – did he think we didn't understand that he was threatening her? – he's far away in London. Still, perhaps we should ask her.'

He went across to Bella. 'Miss Porter, what do you wish to do about your cousin?'

She shuddered. 'I don't want anything to do with him ever again, Dr McDevitt.'

'Then I suggest you hire a lawyer and leave the paperwork with him, just in case.'

'I already have a lawyer in London, Mr Albert Neven. He helped me escape from Thomas, so he'll understand the situation. I'll tell him what happened. Thank you for your help.'

'I don't think Farrow will give you any more trouble. And he's retiring from medical practice quite soon.'

Her expression showed that she guessed exactly what he'd done.

Ryan joined in. 'I'll make sure Bella's not left in a vulnerable position from now on.'

'Congratulations on your engagement. How are your children now, Mr Cornish?'

Ryan smiled. 'Fully recovered. See for yourself, doctor.'

Hettie was approaching along the street with the youngest child sitting in a pushchair. The other two had been holding on to its handle, one on either side, but when they saw Bella, they let go and ran along the pavement to throw themselves at her and hug any part of her they could reach.

'We've found our ball.'

'You said you'd play bat and ball with us when it was fine.'

'It's not raining today.'

'Can we play out, Dad? Can we? It's not dark yet.'

Bella took over. 'I'll play ball with you later, but first I'm going to make us all a cup of hot cocoa. Would you like some? And a biscuit?'

They nodded vigorously.

She smiled at the old woman. 'Will that be all right, Hettie? I can offer you a cup of tea if you'd prefer it.'

'I do love a cup of tea, miss. Puts heart into you, tea does.'

The children were jumping up and down shouting, 'Hurrah! Cocoa!' Then they grew impatient and each grabbed one of Bella's hands, pulling her towards the house.

'Calm down, you two,' Ryan said sharply.

They quietened down at once. But they didn't let go of Bella's hands, or she theirs, and his face softened into a fond smile at the sight of that.

The sergeant winked at the doctor. 'They say children can tell what a person is really like.'

'Yes. And they're usually right, too.' He doffed his trilby to the ladies and got back into his car.

Sergeant Deemer touched Ryan's sleeve, then lingered till everyone else had gone inside to say to him, 'Watch how you go for a while. Beaton is the one who needs taking care of, if you ask me. There's something very strange about him. He might try to get his own back on her.'

'I'll be very careful.'

'And congratulations again on your engagement. Bella's a nice lass, will fit in well in the valley.'

'She's more than merely nice; she's utterly charming. I shall do my best to make sure she doesn't regret marrying me, even though she's bringing me far more than I can give her.'

'I don't think so, from the way she looks at you, and at those children. What a lovely warm smile she has when she's not worried or upset.'

Beaton dropped Farrow at the station and when he would have hurried off, grabbed his arm for a moment. 'You'll be hearing from me.'

Farrow dragged his arm away and made his way quickly into the station.

Laughing loudly and ignoring Biff's surprised glance, Beaton left Farrow to wait two hours for the next train to Manchester, before returning to the hotel. He'd intended to be on that train himself, with Bella in his charge, but he now thought he'd stay a little longer, see what he could arrange.

No stupid bitch was going to get the better of him!

He said, 'Wait!' when Biff would have got out and opened the car door for him at the hotel. He sat in the car for a good ten minutes, not attempting to move or speak, then asked suddenly, 'Did you meet anyone in that pub you're staying in who might be amenable to making a little money on the side?'

'Most of the chaps I met there would be happy to earn some extra money. What did you want doing?'

'I want someone to give Miss Porter a little trouble, enough to make her change her mind about staying here in this ghastly town. And I want to see it happen.'

'What do you mean?'

'I want to see them hurt her, just a little, because she's an ungrateful bitch.' He paused to take a few deep breaths. 'They're to tell her there's worse to come if she doesn't go back to where she belongs.'

'What if she doesn't change her mind?'

'In that case we shall have to kidnap her and take her back to London.'

'I don't think I—'

'Your employers would want you to assist me in this, given the amount I'm paying them.'

Unfortunately Biff knew he was right – well, they'd want it as long as he didn't get caught out in a crime and drag them into the mess. 'It might help if I knew what sort of trouble you want to cause her.'

'Attack her when she's out of the house, maybe knock her over and give her a kick or two.'

'Will that change her mind, do you think?'

'It's worked on other people.'

Another of those strange pauses and an expression of satisfaction on Beaton's face, then, 'But if more severe measures are needed, they are to break into the house during the night and make themselves free of her body. That always upsets women. I don't want her badly injured or permanently incapacitated, though.'

Biff didn't know how to respond to that, so made a noise that could be taken any way, and it seemed to satisfy Beaton.

'I'm a gentleman, not a crook, so I'll leave the detailed arrangements to you.'

Biff was amazed yet again at his arrogance. 'I can ask around, see if I can find you the help you need.'

'You're not to give anyone my name!'

'Of course not.' Biff hadn't even given his own name when he booked the room at the pub. 'Mr Smithers' was good enough for him whenever he was away on a job.

'See if you can arrange for it to happen tonight. I don't want to have to stay too long in this ghastly town. Come and get me from the hotel when you know where it's going to happen.'

'Yes, sir. I'll need money to encourage someone to help you.'

'I suppose so.' He felt in his pocket and took out a coin purse, handing over two half crowns.

'That won't be nearly enough these days, I'm afraid, sir.'

Beaton muttered something and gave him a pound note.

Biff took it, thinking what a stingy devil this man was. 'You'll need two men and that'll take two pounds.' Another was doled out, which he would keep for himself.

He didn't like the expression on Beaton's face, didn't like it at all, wished he didn't need to get involved.

The fellow might call himself a gentleman, but he didn't seem to understand any way of getting what he wanted except brute force. Actually, he sounded to enjoy hurting people.

Biff decided to continue keeping his personal possessions in the car, so that he could leave the area at the slightest sign of trouble. If he wasn't worried about losing his job, he'd have left straight away.

When he went into the pub, the first thing Biff did was buy a drink using a pound note to pay for it. That made the landlord complain about taking up all his change.

'I can't help it,' Biff said in a voice loud enough to be heard by all the early drinkers. 'I did a little job today an' the chap paid me with a couple of pound notes. I wasn't going to turn them down, was I?'

'Sounds like a good sort of job to me if you got that much for it in one day,' a man over by the fire said.

'Yeah. Easy money, too.'

The man he'd seen before was standing next to him at the bar. He waited till everyone was chatting again to say in a low voice, 'Mind if I ask exactly what you were doing?'

'You can ask. I ain't telling because you never know who's listening.' He tapped his nose and looked around suggestively. 'He wants me to do something for him tomorrow an' I'll probably earn as much again. I'll buy you a drink if it works out, because you're the first person to speak to me civilly in here.'

He picked up his glass of beer and went across to sit on the bench he'd used the previous night, watching the fellow who'd spoken to him go back to a group over by the fire. All the while, the fellow was still watching Biff carefully.

Later Biff ordered a meal and ate it with relish. And still that chap was keeping an eye on him.

As he drained his second glass of beer and stood up, he saw the same man slide forward quickly to the edge of his seat and meet his eyes, giving a little jerk of his head towards the door to the backyard. So Biff gave the tiniest of nods in return and went outside as if to relieve himself in the stinking privy there. Luckily there was no one else using it.

The chap followed him inside and shut the door. 'Any chance of another job like yours coming up?'

'Bound to be, from what he said. It's just a pity I have to leave and go back down south. I've got more work than I can cope with there, only came with him for a few days as a favour.' He rubbed his fingers together to signify money paid.

'What was involved in this job?'

'Frightening someone so that they paid up. That chap came all the way from London to do it, he was owed so much. And I doubt it's finished yet. Pity. He said it'd only take a couple of days, and now he doesn't know how long it'll take. Trouble is, I've got useful things happening in, um, Birmingham, so I can't carry on working with him.'

'I'd be interested in taking over from you. I've done that sort of work before.'

Biff nodded. 'You look like a chap as can handle himself. I could put in a good word for you if you like. As long as you slip me a few bob for the favour, that is.'

'Happy to do that.'

'How do I get in touch with you?'

'Tell the landlord and he'll send a lad to fetch me.'

'Your name?' Biff wasn't doing anything with a Mr No-name.

'Just say you want to see Vince. He knows me.'

'Vince who?'

His companion sighed. 'Vince Welch.'

'All right.'

Biff went back into the pub, smiling. He reckoned he'd found someone to help Mr Beaton, and he wasn't going to wait long to hand over to him. He did not want to get involved any further himself.

Then his smile faded as he worried about how far Beaton would actually go. He had a bad feeling about the whole affair. And what made it worse was that the woman seemed a nice sort. He'd seen her with those kids.

He didn't usually care what happened to people after he left a job, let alone get involved in whether it was right or wrong while he was doing it, but then he didn't usually get involved in crimes against women. Besides, Beaton had got right up his nose, treating him as if he was dirt.

Just occasionally the money wasn't worth it. Or the risk.

28

Bella went up to Ryan's flat to help give the children their tea. Afterwards they all went downstairs again and she invented a game of rolling the ball to and fro between goalposts made of books in one of her nearly empty rooms, even Hettie joining in the fun. The only large item there was Bella's trunk, so there was plenty of room to play.

When it came time to put the children to bed, they protested and while Bella was giving Devin the cuddle he demanded before he would climb the stairs to his own home, Maddy went to peep into the trunk.

'What's this, Bella?' She waved some papers and then began to study them. 'They're pretty pictures.'

Ryan hastily took them from her, but when he saw what was on them he stared at Bella, then repeated his daughter's question. 'Yes, what is this?'

She could feel herself flushing. 'Just some silly little stories I wrote to keep Alma and Penelope quiet when they were small.'

'Who did the drawings?'

'Um, well, me.'

'They're charming. Why did you let them get so crumpled?'

'Muriel Beaton found them, screwed this one up, and tried to throw them all away, but I got them back again. I know they're only amateur efforts, but I like to keep them because they remind me of some happy times.'

'We borrow books from the library, and I've seen a lot of children's stories that aren't nearly as good as these.'

'Don't be silly. I'm only an amateur.'

'I'm not being silly. They're lovely. Can I borrow them?'

'Why?'

'I'd like to show them to someone. I'm going to prove to you how skilled you are.'

'Why would you want to do that?'

'I want to do it because this is another thing that shows how clever you are. I'm not going to let you continue putting yourself down.'

'Who do you want to show them to?'

'Charlie Willcox's wife. Marion Willcox draws too, but hers are pretty designs for personal stationery and note cards, not pictures of imaginary creatures. But she makes money doing it, and gets a lot of satisfaction, too.'

'I don't want to waste her time with my amateur efforts.'

'Please let me show her. She'd love to see them, I'm sure. I did some plumbing work for her and her husband, and she was really nice to chat to.'

Bella shrugged. She didn't see the point, but it seemed to matter to him so she agreed he could do it. It'd be nice if someone said her drawings were good. She had quite a collection of these little illustrated stories at the bottom of her trunk.

After she'd helped Hettie put the children to bed, she invited Ryan to come down and share her evening meal.

'I'd love to.' He looked at Hettie. 'Will you be all right? I'll only be downstairs in Miss Porter's flat if you need me.'

Hettie smiled and flapped one hand at him. 'We'll be fine. The children are nicely tired out after playing ball, then listening to the stories. I'll have to remember that ball-rolling game for wet days. It kept them happy for ages.'

'Thanks, Het. I'll get my bed out now so that I don't have to disturb you if you're asleep when I come back.' He went into the bedroom and came out with the mattress. After going back for a neat pile of blankets, he turned to Bella, offering his hand without a word.

Hettie nodded as if in approval of this gesture.

Bella took his hand, loving the warm feel and the touch of another human being. She'd been starved of that ever since the Beaton children were taken from her charge and discouraged from seeing her.

They passed Ed, who was in the hall, sitting on the chair she'd lent them. He and Steve took it in turns to keep watch inside and out during the night. She'd decided to keep them on for a further night or two, till the bathroom was finished and she could get some extra bolts fitted inside the back door.

'We'll not let anyone in, miss,' Ed had assured her, and she'd believed him.

When she was alone with Ryan in her flat, she watched him draw the curtains, feeling suddenly nervous. What if he'd changed his mind? What if he didn't really want to marry her, but now felt obliged to?

He came back and took her hand again. 'Stop it!'

'What do you mean?'

'I want you to stop worrying about you and me. When I marry you, I'll not be doing anything I don't want to. You're a grand lass and we get on well, even laugh at the same things. That means a lot to me. Deirdre was a good woman, though a bit slapdash around the house, but she had no sense of humour and used to tell me to stop being silly if I made a joke.'

'You must miss her, though.'

'If I'm honest, I don't really, except to look after the kids. I'm sorry she died, mind, don't mistake me there. Really sorry. But I should never have married her.'

'Why did you?'

'The usual tale of a young fellow's stupidity: she was pretty and willing, so we made love. When I found out I'd got her pregnant, I wasn't going to abandon my own child, so I married her. I like kids. I'm hoping you and I will manage to create at least one more baby. I'd love to have a little girl with your pretty hair and warm smile.'

Bella could feel herself blushing and was sure that showed under her new brighter light bulb, but he was waiting for an answer and she couldn't pretend. 'I'd like that too. Or a little boy with your blue eyes. I gave up hope of becoming a mother years ago. Only – don't you think I'm a bit old for it to happen?'

'Who knows? Some women go on having children into their forties and you're what – twenty-one, no, twenty-two? Really old.' He knew she was much older than that, but liked teasing her.

She chuckled. 'I'm thirty-six. Well past my prime.'

'And I'm thirty-four. There are only two years between us and I consider myself, and therefore you, still in my prime. Why should you not have a baby, two even? I've proved I can father them easily enough, and you seem healthy.'

Hope turned Bella's face beautiful for a few seconds and she said in a hushed voice, 'It'd be like a miracle, a wonderful gift nearly as good as you marrying me.'

'Miracles sometimes happen. I met you, didn't I? A woman I like, someone I can really talk to and laugh with. That's so rare. I enjoy us playing with the children together as well. Deirdre didn't do that much, either. She said my games were silly.'

'I love playing with them.' She loved him too, but didn't dare say those words in case that was a step too far. 'Are you hungry?'

He grinned. 'I'm always ready for my food. You'll find that I have a hearty appetite.'

'It's only bacon and eggs. I'm not very good at cooking.'

'Get Hettie to teach you. She gets too tired to do anything

fancy, but she knows how to. With you to help her around the house, she'll be happy to take over most of the cooking and share her skills with you, I'm sure. You'll let her stay on with us, won't you? She's become part of the family now and the kids love her nearly as much as she loves them.'

'Of course I will.' But still, for all the fine words, she had to ask him again, 'You're absolutely certain you want us to get married? I won't make a fuss if you don't.'

He put one finger across her mouth. 'Don't keep asking me that, love. I'm very sure I want it. It's the other way around. A lady like you doesn't usually marry an ordinary chap like me, but I shall make a big, loud fuss if you try to wriggle out of it. I'll probably stamp my feet and throw a tantrum all over the place.'

She had to chuckle at the image he conjured up. 'I can't imagine you losing your temper.'

'I don't often, but I would if someone tried to hurt you or my children. My dad made sure I learned to control it when I was a lad, but I have a fiery temper and if I see someone being cruel to a child or animal it still boils up sometimes.'

She could understand that. She hated to see children hurt, too. Only the knowledge that Thomas would act even more viciously if she protested at what he used to do to his children had kept her silent sometimes. But she'd wept herself to sleep afterwards.

'Where shall we live after we marry?' he asked.

'Would there be room in my flat?'

'Yes, of course. You don't mind me taking advantage of your inheritance? It's not the reason I'm marrying you, I promise.' He looked round. 'This would be a fine place to live.'

She smiled. 'Then that's settled.'

'We'll discuss details another day. We're wasting valuable time alone together doing it now. Come here, love.' He took her hand and pulled her into his arms. 'We haven't even sealed our bargain with the customary kiss yet.'

She had been kissed a time or two before she went to live with her cousins – quick furtive kisses in the garden with young men as inexperienced as she was. It had never been like this, though, so soft and yet urgent. She was sorry when he pulled away, but he was smiling at her tenderly, cupping her face in both his hands now, and she couldn't help but smile back.

'Very nice. I knew you'd be a good kisser.'

'I haven't had much practice.'

'I'll be happy to remedy that.' His stomach rumbled and he rolled his eyes, giving her a rueful smile. 'I think that's a sign that we'd better get something to eat before we do anything else. A gurgling stomach isn't at all romantic.'

She loved the way he found amusement in the smallest thing. She'd tried to be like that with the Beaton children, but they'd lost all signs of humour once they passed from her into their parents' hands. The girls especially had become so wooden and proper they were hardly recognisable.

Which reminded her that Alma and Oscar had got away from their father without having to marry people they disliked. How wonderful!

'Now what are you thinking of?'

She told him, ending thoughtfully, 'I must learn more about Australia, so that I can imagine what sort of life Alma and Oscar will be leading there. I wish I knew where in Australia they'd gone. It's a big country, I do know that, so I won't be able to find them again. And I doubt they'll dare try to find me. I expect they'll have changed their names even because they'll be scared of their father finding them again.'

'Let's hope a miracle occurs and you do hear from them one day.'

'Ah, yes. It'd make me happy and set my mind at rest.'

Then she realised he was waiting patiently for her to cook him some food, so she didn't say any more about Alma and Oscar.

Ryan helped her without being asked by setting the table with her mismatched crockery, then cutting and buttering a few slices of bread.

'I've never met a man who shares the housework before.'

'I've had to do some of it for the past few months or my kids would have suffered, and I wasn't having that. And I helped out when Deirdre was expecting, even she let me do that. I did a lot of it this last time because she got more tired than she had with the other babies. Actually, it can be fun to do things together. You should see how well Maddy wipes the dishes and how carefully Devin puts away the knives and forks – one at a time. It takes him three times as long, but he's so proud of himself.'

He gave a wry smile. 'I should explain that as soon as the babies started arriving, Deirdre had little interest in anything but them. Some women are like that. And though she loved the children, she was terrified of us losing them as some of her family had done. Only it was she who was lost, poor lass.'

He cocked one eye at her. 'Do you mind me talking about her? Only I can't pretend she didn't exist.'

'No. I'd worry if you didn't.'

'That's all right then. Now, we're doing too much talking. Let's get those eggs fried and happily settled in our bellies.'

As he began to clear his plate, making happy noises of enjoyment, she found she'd regained her appetite.

They sat chatting for quite a while after they'd finished, before he insisted that he would dry the dishes for her.

But somehow, they didn't get round to that because she found herself in his arms again. It was so lovely to be held like that.

When he kissed her she felt as if they were actually connecting to one another, not just mouth to mouth but soul to soul. It was strange and wonderful to be so close to this man.

After a while he pushed her away and turned around abruptly.

'Is something wrong?'

'No, love. It's just – we don't want to take it too far yet, do we? Not till we're well and truly wed.' He adjusted his trousers and took a few deep breaths.

She didn't know what she wanted, only that she hadn't wanted him to stop cuddling her.

'Come on. Let's do those dishes,' he said.

When he left after another gentle, dreamy kiss, she had to sit very still for a few moments to calm herself down. She had never felt like this before.

She fell asleep thinking of him, and woke doing the same thing.

As she brushed her hair she smiled at the realisation that in one sense, Thomas had done her a favour. He'd given Ryan a reason to break the barriers that life and their class differences might otherwise have set between them.

But it was Cousin James and his godmother she had to thank most, for leaving her the house, which in turn had given her the courage to stand up for herself.

The next day passed uneasily. They didn't go to church, and Bella didn't set foot outside her flat.

At one point Ryan felt he'd seen someone watching them from one of the partly demolished houses across the street, but he didn't tell Bella, who was a bundle of nerves.

Luckily it was fine, with people walking about, no chance of anyone sneaking up on the house, in daylight at least.

But as it started growing dark, he saw the same man again and warned Ed to keep his eyes open.

★

Bella had only just finished getting dressed on the Monday when there was a knock on the door of the flat. She opened it to see Ryan smiling at her.

'Good morning, Bella.' He plonked a quick kiss on her cheek. 'I'd give you a better good morning kiss than that but the lads have arrived. You told me you wouldn't mind us disturbing you early, and I thought I'd heard you stirring. We'd like to make a start on installing your bathroom, if that's all right with you.'

'I'm eager to have it done.'

'Good. Mr Tyler will be bringing the bathroom suite today and some stuff to make a new wall and doorway in that part of the house. Can we put everything in one of your empty rooms till we've got the pipes laid?'

'Yes, of course.'

'I'll bring in the lads then, and we'll make a start. I apologise in advance for the noise.'

'It'll be well worth it.'

When the men started hammering, adding their noise to that coming from across the street, where other men were demolishing the derelict houses, Bella decided this would be a good time to walk to the village shop and buy some food. She was very careful about going out on her own, keeping watch for a while before risking it. But it wasn't far and it was broad daylight, and other people would be around, going shopping.

Gabriel wouldn't be coming to pick her up till ten o'clock, so she could get some food in for the children and Hettie before she left. Dear Gabriel. She was glad he got on well with Ryan.

Still in a blur of happiness, she left with the sound of banging beating in her ears.

She was only halfway there and had just turned a corner when someone pounced on her from behind and when she struggled, clouted her on the side of the head. That sent her stumbling against a high wall that blocked off someone's backyard.

She screamed at the top of her voice, but the sound was cut off abruptly when the attacker yanked her to her feet and put a hand over her mouth. Whoever he was towered over her and was so much stronger she could only struggle feebly.

Then suddenly the person roared in pain and let go of her. As she rolled away she saw two youths hitting him with sticks.

'Run, missus!' one yelled as another man appeared at the far end of the alley.

She was already struggling to her feet. She ran out into the street, pounding along the pavement towards the shop, shouting for help as loudly as she could.

A car screeched to a halt and terror washed through her, then she realised that it was Mrs Tyler, who was beckoning her urgently. Bella opened the passenger door, scrambling desperately to get inside because she could hear footsteps running down the alley she'd been dragged into.

The two lads burst out of it and ran off along the street in the other direction, then the tall man came running after them, saw the car and turned towards it. Another man appeared next to him, and they watched the ladies in the car from the end of the alley.

'Hold tight!' Mrs Tyler set off driving with Bella clinging to the door handle still trying to close it properly.

They reached the shop in a couple of minutes and the men didn't pursue them to the area where there were other people. A couple of women had turned around to see what had made Mrs Tyler, normally the most cautious of drivers, screech to a halt.

'They've stopped following us,' Mrs Tyler said, looking into the rear-view mirror that was a feature of her fancy modern car.

'Thank you!' Bella's heart was still pounding.

'What happened?'

'I was walking to the shops when someone grabbed me
from behind and shoved me into that alley. It was the man
who ran out chasing those two lads who came to the rescue.
They hit him and made him let me go. I ran away as fast as
I could.'

'I know one of the men who came out of the alley by sight,
but I can't quite place him. I know who the lads are, and I'll
tell their parents how proud of them they should be. One of
them's Dolly Traske's nephew. After you've done your shopping I'll drive you home again, just in case they're still around.
What were they after, do you think?'

'I can only think my cousin from London hired them. He
tried to claim I was mentally deficient and take me back to
his house so that he could get his hands on my inheritance.
Ryan saved me and then called Sergeant Deemer, and Dr
McDevitt said it wasn't true that I couldn't look after myself.
The Traske sisters told me the doctor who came here went
back to London, but that my cousin had stayed on.'

After a brief pause for thought she added, 'I've also upset
Mr Welch by sacking him as my rent collector.'

'You did right there. He's a rogue.' It was her turn to pause
and look at Bella. 'And is it true what I hear? That you're
engaged to Ryan Cornish?'

'Yes. How on earth did you hear that so quickly?'

'The Traske sisters, of course. They find out everything
before anyone else does, heaven only knows how. Look dear,
the valley isn't usually dangerous, I promise you, but I think
you'd better not go out on your own for a while. Someone
definitely set those men after you. Do you really think your
cousin would do that?'

Bella's shiver said more than words.

Mrs Tyler clicked her tongue in annoyance. 'I do wish I

could remember that man's name. I caught a glimpse of a car at the far end of that alley where they ambushed you. It was blue, or was it black? I'm not sure. I didn't recognise the make, but I'll tell Sergeant Deemer about it being there. Oh dear, you're bleeding. Here, give it a wipe.' She passed across a clean handkerchief.

Bella touched the side of her forehead, which was throbbing, and her fingers came away with a smear of blood on them, so she used the handkerchief.

'You need to wash that graze properly and put some Germolene on it. How did he do that to you?'

'I was hit on the head and then thrown against a wall. It was horrible to feel so helpless.' Then they heard footsteps running towards the car and Bella stiffened.

'Shut the car door, quickly!'

But it was Ryan who came into sight. He ran up to the car and peered inside. 'What happened? Dolly Traske's nephew came to fetch me, said you'd been attacked.'

She nodded. 'He and another lad saved me. I'm so grateful to them.'

'I'll slip them sixpence each next time I see them and they'll be happy,' Ryan said. 'But Bella love, you can't go out on your own at the moment, even to the village shop, even in daylight. I thought you understood that.'

'I thought I'd be safe here. The shop's only just down the road, and it's broad daylight, after all.'

'I'll spread the word that she's been attacked and people round here will watch out for strangers,' Ethel Tyler said.

'What did you want to buy?' he asked Bella.

'Just some food for the children. I'm going shopping with Gabriel in Rivenshaw soon, and after that I have a driving lesson – it'll be my first time driving in the town. I'm going to be very busy. There's so much to buy for the house, and I want to arrange to have a gas fire put into the sitting room.

I've already arranged for one to be put in the kitchen, as you suggested, but said to wait until you'd finished putting in the bathroom.'

'I can install them for you. It'll save you some money.' Ryan was glad to be able to contribute.

'All right.'

'I shan't worry about you if you're out with Gabriel. He'll keep you safe. And so will Silas. They both know how to take care of themselves. Nip into the shop now and buy what you want, then I'll walk you home.'

When she had gone inside, he looked at Mrs Tyler. 'That cousin of hers must be mad as a hatter. What good will it do him to hire someone to attack her?'

'He may be doing it to pay her back for defying him – or to soften her up, in which case this won't be the end of it.' Then she snapped her fingers. 'I've just remembered something about her attacker: he works for Vincent Welch. He's been known to terrorise the slum dwellers in Backshaw Moss if they fall behind with their rent.'

'I'll have a word with Welch and warn him off.'

'Better let our good sergeant deal with that. I've heard him say more than once that he doesn't trust Welch and hopes that one day he'll catch him out. Look, I'll drive along the street beside you and Bella. One man might not be enough to keep her safe if those two are still lurking nearby.'

'Thank you.'

'And I'll mention this attack to Roy. He'll spread the word among his men.'

'Good. I'll phone the sergeant and tell him about it.'

'I'll do that for you.' She saw the expression on his face and said sharply. 'I saw more of what happened than you did. Don't think of going after them yourself. Your job is to protect her when she's at home. It's the police's job to catch villains.'

'I suppose so, but I won't be answerable if I catch them attacking her again.'

Bella came out of the shop just then, carrying a loaded shopping bag, so he took it from her and they set off.

'Mrs Tyler is seeing us home,' he explained as the car set off slowly, staying beside them.

They walked in silence for a couple of minutes, then he said gently, 'You have to be a lot more careful, love. I hate to see you hurt.'

'I know.' She sniffled and wiped away a tear with one fingertip. 'I was feeling so happy.'

'Don't cry. We'll keep you safe.'

'I expected you to shout at me for being stupid.'

'I'm not like him.'

'No. You're the nicest man I've ever met.'

This time it was his turn to blush.

29

Biff had been parked at the opposite end of the alley from which the two hired bullies Welch had found attacked Miss Porter. It was a stupid place to be seen, not even good for ambushing someone. As for letting the men scramble into the car afterwards, that was even more stupid.

What had upset Biff most had been the smile on Beaton's face when he saw that poor woman thrown against the wall. When he saw she was bleeding as she was yanked to her feet he said, 'That'll teach the bitch to defy me.'

Biff had been glad when two lads came to her rescue.

The way the two men talked about how to get to her next worried Biff too.

'She'll have a rare old bruise where I thumped her against the wall,' one of them crowed. 'At least I managed to do that.'

'You didn't keep hold of her, though, did you?' Beaton said sharply.

'Well, who'd have thought them two lads larking around in the street would have come to her rescue?' he protested. 'They should mind their own damned business an' leave grown men to get on with theirs, lads should.'

Biff didn't say anything, but when Beaton went upstairs at Welch's place of business with the two men, he slipped up the stairs after them to eavesdrop. It was strange how eager Beaton was to hurt Miss Porter. His own cousin! Very strange.

The men went over it all again for Welch, who cursed them for their incompetence. 'If I didn't intend to pay that female back, I'd give up now. But I do intend to. I always do if someone upsets me. You'd better be more cautious next time and choose your moment more carefully, even if you have to wait longer.'

'We'll get her next time, Mr Welch. You know you can count on us.'

'I thought I could, but you just let me down, didn't you?'

'It was them damned lads who spoiled it all,' the man insisted.

The other said eagerly, 'It'd be better for us to get a bit rougher with her next time. That'll make her really sorry she upset you.'

Beaton didn't say anything, but Biff heard the man mutter to his friend, 'I'm going to have first go at her. She's not bad looking for an older woman. Still got some use in her, I reckon.'

'You're welcome to her.'

Beaton didn't seem to have heard that exchange, just said, 'I'm not paying till after it's been done properly.'

Welch said, 'We'll get it right next time, Mr Beaton. I want her out of the valley, too, whatever it takes. She's bad luck, that one is, hasn't been good for my business.'

Biff was sickened by Welch's indifference to them hurting the poor woman and surprised at him talking about bad luck. You made your own luck as far as he was concerned, mostly by being careful and working hard. Nobody handed things to you on a plate. They were more likely to take your plate away from you.

He wasn't going to let on about how he felt while he was still here in Rivenshaw, though, because those two might turn on him. Welch clearly wasn't much use, but Beaton didn't seem to see that.

Biff had met people like Welch before. The man talked big, but he'd left attacking one small woman to someone else, hadn't he?

He made sure he was sitting in the car when Beaton came

back. As he took the man back to the hotel, he heard him still muttering under his breath about 'incompetent idiots' and all he said to Biff as he got out of the car was, 'I'll send a message to you when I need you again.'

He didn't even look at you as he spoke, the arrogant sod. Biff sighed as he drove away. The more he had to do with Beaton, the less he thought of him. And fancy risking being seen by going along to watch her being hurt. There was something loathsome about the man that made Biff not even want to brush against him.

Needing to think about what he should do next, he drove the car over to a little park he'd found yesterday and stopped in the street next to it, glad of a bit of peace and quiet before he had to do something else for Beaton.

He came to the conclusion that he didn't just want to leave Rivenshaw; he wanted to stop what these vile people were planning to do. He was a proper detective, not a bully who beat up women. Beaton must have offered a lot of money for his employers to take on a nasty case like this one.

Apart from anything else, Biff couldn't see how getting his own back on his cousin would gain Beaton anything. She wasn't going to part with her inheritance, because she wasn't nearly as meek as he'd described her. Anyway, she was now engaged to a chap who was well thought of in town from the scraps of conversation Biff had overheard. Cornish would go after her if she was kidnapped, he was sure.

Ah, he hated it here. When he talked, people looked at him strangely, and one woman in a shop had asked him straight out which foreign country he came from. That was another thing, he'd decided. He wasn't going to work in the damned north again. He stood out like a sore thumb among the slower-speaking locals, and he didn't like to be noticed when he was working.

Someone tapped on his car window, then opened the door

before he could stop them. He looked up to see that old policeman scowling down at him, and his heart sank. What now?

'I'd like a word with you,' the sergeant said. 'Would you get out, please . . . sir?'

Later that afternoon, still feeling happy from her driving lesson, Bella heard a car draw up nearby, so naturally she peeped out of her sitting-room window. It hadn't stopped outside her house, but a bit further along. Three well-dressed people got out of it, two men and a woman.

Talking and gesticulating, they walked up and down the row of half-demolished houses opposite, where some dust-covered workmen were just finishing for the day. As he turned, she recognised that nice Mr Willcox, who unrolled a big piece of paper and the other man held the other end of it. They all studied, pointing and talking animatedly.

Could it be the plans for the new houses? If so, Bella wished she could see what they'd look like. She was so hoping they'd be nicely built.

They nodded to one another, looking pleased, and Mr Willcox rolled up the paper again, after which they vanished around the rear of the site. Two of the workmen threw some more rubbish from the demolition into the back of a lorry and then they got in and drove off.

Bella was curious enough to keep on watching and her patience was rewarded because a few minutes later the trio came back into the street. This time they stood looking across at the three houses of which hers was the middle one, pointing now and then.

As they started to cross the street, she guessed they were coming to see her so she moved away from the window. Well, the two other houses were unoccupied, so where else could they be going?

Oh, goodness, where would she take them if they needed

to come inside? She might have a suite and chairs to sit on, but the living room and kitchen were full of empty boxes and piles of small items because she'd been giving herself a treat by unpacking some of the big boxes from the storeroom.

One in particular had clinked slightly when she tried to move it, and she'd wondered if it contained crockery, of which she was desperately in need. To her delight she'd already found various plates and dishes, and was planning to wash them and put them away once she'd finished unpacking these few boxes.

Someone knocked on the front door and she pulled off her pinafore and threw it on to the nearest box. One hasty glance into the mirror had her trying to smooth down her hair as she hurried towards the door. Taking a deep breath she opened it.

Mr Willcox smiled at her. 'Ah, Miss Porter. Nice to see you again. I wonder if we could come in and have a word with you?'

'Yes, of course.'

'You and I have met, but I should introduce my companions. This is the mayor, Mr Kirby, and this is Mrs Selby, one of our councillors – you bought your car from her husband.'

'Pleased to meet you.' She gestured to them to enter. 'I'm afraid the place is in a bit of a mess because they've started work on the new bathroom and I'm unpacking some boxes I've found in the house.'

'That sort of mess is bound to happen when you move into a new home. It must be exciting to find out what's in the boxes.' Mrs Selby had as friendly a smile as her husband.

Mr Willcox took over again. 'Your new bathroom is partly why we're here. Mrs Tyler said we might like to look at how Ryan is fitting bathrooms into small spaces. She's very good at working out that sort of thing herself and she thinks he's doing an excellent job.'

The mayor added, 'And the other reason we're here is because Mrs Selby thinks you might like to see what the new houses we're going to build across the street from yours will look like.' He smiled and brandished the rolled piece of paper.

'That's a kind thought. I'd love to see the plans.'

A door opened and Ryan appeared. 'Good morning, Mrs Selby, gentlemen. I heard voices and wondered who it was. Miss Porter has had a bit of trouble with Welch's bullies, you see, so I'm keeping an eye on her.'

The mayor frowned. 'I hope you told Sergeant Deemer about it. We don't like that sort of thing to happen in our valley.'

'Mrs Tyler was going to report it for me.'

Bella flashed a quick smile at Ryan, who was wearing overalls and was covered in dust and debris. She couldn't resist stepping forward to remove a few small lumps of plaster from his hair.

He winked at her, then turned to the others. 'Please excuse my appearance. We've been knocking down part of a wall and putting up the framework for another one nearby to create a bathroom.'

The visitors took it in turns to stand in the doorway of the new bathroom, nodding as Ryan explained where each of the three pieces would go.

'Now, I need to get on with this bit so that we can lock up safely tonight, but Bella can show you the suite we're going to install. It's in that room.' He pointed to a door. 'We're going to put ones like it on each floor here.'

'Roy Tyler said the suites were very good value for money,' Charlie Willcox added.

Ryan nodded. 'They're nice sturdy pieces. You can always trust the things you buy from that company.'

As he went back to work, Bella took them into the next room. She'd sneaked in here earlier this morning and sat in the bath to see how it felt. She was absolutely dying to use it.

Charlie took over. 'Plain and simple but perfectly functional, as you see. We can buy these suites for all six new houses at a nice discount.'

His two companions nodded, then Mrs Selby smiled at Bella. 'Now for the plans. Do you have a table we could spread this out on, Miss Porter?'

She hesitated, then took them into the kitchen. 'I'm afraid this is the only room with a table, and though I've got the fire going, it's a bit draughty with all the coming and going.'

'It'll be worth it, I'm sure, and none of us mind that.'

Bella moved some piles of crockery from one end of the table and Mrs Selby spread out the architect's drawing. It showed a row of six houses. Bella liked the simple lines and also the way each house had a little open porch over the front door.

'Do you understand plans for interiors?' the mayor asked her. 'I must say I find it a bit difficult to visualise the end result from lines and squiggles.'

'Yes, I can make sense of them.' She studied the plans, half-closing her eyes to imagine the rooms. There was one thing missing, to her mind, and she mentioned it without thinking. 'What about a pantry? That makes such a difference to the women dealing with the household chores. Oh, sorry. It's not my business.'

Charlie looked at her in surprise, then turned back to stare down at the drawings, pushing his spectacles up his nose and leaning closer. 'What do you think, Leah?'

'I think Miss Porter is right.'

'We'll have to chat to the architect, see if he can find a way to put in pantries without too much extra expense. We want these to be known as good houses to live in.' He began to roll up the paper. 'Thank you for letting us come in and see your bathroom, Miss Porter. And congratulations on your engagement.'

'Oh, er, thank you.' She couldn't believe how quickly everyone seemed to know about it.

Ryan came back. 'Oh good, you've not gone yet. We got the pipes in more easily than I'd expected and I was just wondering: what time does the town hall marriage department close today, Mr Kirby?'

'The register office? Five o'clock.'

Ryan glanced at the battered clock on the mantelpiece. 'Then I reckon if we hurry we'll have time for me to get out of these overalls and then drive into Rivenshaw in your car, Bella. After we book our wedding, we have to wait a week to get married, you see. Stupid rule, that. Are you all right to come with me now?'

She forgot the other people in the room and looked at him in delight. His impatience with red tape seemed further proof that he really did want to marry her. 'Yes, of course I am.'

'We'll leave you two love birds in peace, then.' Charlie beamed at them both.

Bella saw them out and ran into her bedroom to put on her coat and beret. It was only a couple of minutes before Ryan clattered down the stairs and burst in, the first time he'd done that without knocking.

'Come on, love. I've told the men to lock up carefully at the back before they go, and Ed will be here in a few minutes to keep watch inside the house.'

As they got into the car, Bella's heart soared with joy. She was going to do it, get married to this lovely man, bring up his children, and make them hers too. She really was. It would be a dream come true.

And Thomas could do nothing about it.

She'd no sooner thought that than she shivered. Surely even he would see sense and leave her alone now?

Not only would she never give in to him again, but she now had Ryan and various others keeping an eye out for her. Her life had changed so much, and for the better.

★

As they drove away, the two workmen began to pack up their tools and set the house to rights as much as they could.

Ryan had made it very clear that he expected them to leave things as tidily as possible and to wait for Ed to arrive before they left, keeping their eyes open for intruders.

'She's a nice woman, isn't she, Trev?' one of them said. 'It was kind of her to bring us mugs of tea. They don't all do that.'

'Very kind.' Then he clutched his friend's arm. 'There was a chap looking over the back fence just now. He bobbed back quickly and I don't think he realises I saw him.'

'Anyone you know?'

'It was that chap who does odd jobs for Welch. Eh, I've forgotten his name. Can't mistake that scar on a bald head, though, can you?'

They looked at one another in consternation. Ryan had made them aware that he was worried about someone getting at his family and the woman he was going to marry.

'Oh, hell! We'd better tell someone, and we can't leave the house unattended because Ryan's children and the old lady are upstairs. Look, I'll stay here, Baz. Your young legs are nimbler than mine. Go and phone Sergeant Deemer from Mr Tyler's office. I'd not like to see Miss Porter get hurt, and Ryan's had enough trouble in his life lately.'

'Lock up carefully behind me.'

'I will.'

Roy Tyler listened carefully to the young man who'd rushed into his office and told him some rough-looking men were watching the back of 23 Daisy Street. 'Wait in the other room while I phone the police station.'

Baz nodded and went to warm himself in front of the fire.

Roy came in a couple of minutes later. 'Sergeant Deemer asked if I'd go and keep an eye on the place with you. He's going to find his constable and come out here as soon as he can. But he wants to pounce on them, so we're not to let them know we're there if we can help it.'

'What if Ryan comes back before Deemer gets there?'

'He won't. They never do anything quickly at that town hall.' He smiled. 'It'd be easy to slow things down, though. I'll just tell my wife what I'm doing and she'll get in touch with the mayor's secretary.' He went across into his wife's little office space at the other end of the room.

Ethel listened carefully, then waved him on his way and phoned her friend, asking her to slow down Ryan and Bella's application and promising to tell her why another time.

Her husband had left by then, but she didn't like how things were going, so she took a quick decision before she put the phone down. 'I'm coming into Rivenshaw to see if I can catch up with Ryan, so stop him if he tries to leave.'

'How can I do that?'

'Tell the clerk at the registry office to delay him, but if you have to tell him I'm on my way to see him, then do that. We need to leave dealing with such things to the good sergeant. Ryan is a man in love and his woman is being threatened, so he may do something stupid.'

Sergeant Deemer insisted Biff go with him to the police station, promising that if he helped the police, they'd let him go. He was talking to Biff there when the call came in from Roy Tyler. He listened carefully, nodding once or twice, then went back out to where his unwilling guest was sitting.

'I need you to do me a favour.'

'A favour?' That meant he wasn't going to be arrested. Biff sagged in relief. 'What sort of favour.'

He listened carefully, stared at the older man unhappily, then made a couple of suggestions.

'Good idea. We'll do it that way. If it all works out as I hope, I'll turn a blind eye so that you can slip away afterwards.'

'What if it doesn't work out as you hope, sergeant? That won't be my fault, I promise you. I want to stop them.'

Another of those penetrating stares and the sergeant nodded. 'Yes. I reckon you do. But I'm relying on you to be clever about how you play your part. Come on, lad. Tell me your real name.'

Biff gave in. He hated his real name. 'Nelson Higgins.' He didn't reveal it normally, but there was steely determination in the sergeant's eyes. If the police were all like this man, there would be a lot fewer villains around to catch, he reckoned, and less work for private detectives.

Sergeant Deemer pointed outside to the car. 'Right then, Higgins, time for you to get started. Beaton will want picking up again soon, I reckon, if he's got men posted at her house.'

He waited till Biff had driven off, then tried to phone Tyler again to ask him to watch out for Beaton, but the man must have left.

The sergeant joined his constable in the car.

'Drive up to Backshaw Moss as fast as we can. We have some criminals to catch.'

'Yessir!'

The constable was young enough to find this exciting. The sergeant was old enough to pray that no one would get hurt – unless it was one of Welch's bullies, or even that Beaton fellow. Nasty, greedy sod he was. Look at all the trouble he'd caused in the valley in such a short time. They wanted rid of his sort, and the sooner the better.

30

Ryan drove into town and Bella watched how well he handled the car, driving faster than she'd dare, but seeming perfectly in control of the vehicle the whole time. Would she ever be able to drive as effortlessly as that?

She had another lesson booked and was looking forward to it, though she'd had to concentrate hard to drive around Rivenshaw town centre, even at a time when there were fewer people about. But oh, she loved the freedom of driving.

The town hall was quite a large older building with a big car park in front of it. She'd only seen it in the distance until now and would have stopped to admire it if they hadn't been in a hurry.

Ryan stopped the car and switched off the engine. 'Come on. The registry office is at the rear. It shouldn't take us long to fill in a form or two.'

The reception area in the foyer was deserted and it was clear that business was winding down for the day.

'This way,' he said.

'Did you get married here last time?'

'No. We got wed in her church. I didn't like the priest, who did nothing but talk about our sins and make Deirdre cry. I've been here a couple of times for friends' weddings, so I know my way round. Apart from it being simpler to get wed here, I prefer it for us. I'm never going back to that church, and neither are my children.'

Bella suddenly thought of how Thomas would have an even

bigger fit about her marrying someone brought up a Catholic and couldn't hold back a gurgle of laughter. When Ryan asked what had amused her, he chuckled at the thought of it too. She loved the way he shared her sense of the ridiculous.

A smiling clerk greeted them inside the narrow reception area of the registry office with, 'Nice to see a couple looking so happy.'

As Ryan closed the door behind them, a phone rang somewhere in the back and the clerk said politely, 'Please excuse me but I have to answer that because there's no one else around at this time of day. I'll only be a minute.'

She went away and they could hear her voice but not make out the words. She was away for a lot longer than a minute, though.

'You've still got time to run away and escape my clutches,' Ryan joked to Bella.

'So have you.'

'Not a chance.' He took her hand till the clerk came back to join them.

'Sorry about that. It was the mayor's office, and you can never hurry them.'

It seemed to take a long time to go through the paperwork for booking a wedding, or maybe it was just that the paperwork was fiddly. Only, the clerk seemed to be working particularly slowly, fiddling with her pen to adjust the nib, and then having trouble finding one of the forms, which proved to be in the wrong file.

Or so she said. Ryan frowned at her as she shoved the paper she'd retrieved underneath the others spread out on the counter. If it had been so urgent to find it, why wasn't she using it?

Before they finished, she insisted on showing them the room where the ceremony would be performed. He'd not have bothered, had already seen it, but Bella had said yes before he could stop her, and he didn't want to take the smile from her face.

It was only an oblong space, with six small rows of hard wooden chairs. It looked unwelcoming without people sitting on them. A table and two larger chairs stood at the front, and a jar of stiff paper flowers graced a stand to one side. They looked dusty.

'It's very nice,' Bella said.

It wasn't all that nice, but Ryan didn't contradict her and turned to leave. 'We've seen it now, and to tell the truth, miss, I don't care where we get married as long as we do get married, so can we get on with filling in the forms, please?'

Back in the office, the clerk managed to knock the pile of loose papers off the counter and immediately squatted down to pick them up. It seemed more and more as if she was trying to do this as slowly as she could.

At one stage she left her place behind the counter to lock the door that led out into the corridor and turn the sign from OPEN to CLOSED. 'I have to do that at five o'clock precisely each day. Don't worry. I can let you out of the building when the time comes.'

'Surely we've nearly finished?'

'Um, let me see.'

He'd had enough. 'I can tell when someone is deliberately delaying, and I want to know why.'

She looked at him in dismay and then let out a big sigh. 'Mrs Tyler rang the mayor's secretary and asked her to tell me to delay things because she's on the way here and needs to see you.'

'Did she say why?'

'There's some trouble in Backshaw Moss apparently.'

'What sort of trouble?'

'She didn't say.'

'Well, I've had enough delays. Get this finished and let us

out. I have three kids in Backshaw Moss and if there's trouble there, I want to be with them, not hanging around here.'

But it still took a few more minutes to finish.

Arthur Thornlee knocked on Beaton's door at the hotel. 'There's a Mr Smithers downstairs. He says he got your message and has brought the car.'

'And about time too. Tell him to wait for me, and hurry up about it.'

'I'm just passing on the message, sir, and I do not appreciate the way you're speaking to me.'

Beaton gaped at him as if unused to this sort of reaction.

Arthur let it sink in, then said smoothly, 'He's waiting outside for you. I'm sure you can find your own way out.'

Beaton muttered under his breath but got his overcoat and hat and went out to the car.

'What's kept you, Higgins? Couldn't you arrange things more quickly than this?'

'I arranged it as quickly as I could.'

Beaton's tone was gloating. 'What is Welch planning to do with her next?'

'He said they'd have to check things out before they decide that. They're not taking any chances this time, but if she's at home, the other houses nearby aren't occupied so there might be a chance of getting in and getting hold of her.'

Biff watched Beaton hesitate, but he didn't intend to get out and open the car door for him. It took a minute or two for the sod to work that out and open the car door himself.

He scowled at Biff, but who cared? He wasn't working for the man after today, and was only doing it now because the sergeant wanted his help to ensure Beaton was personally involved as a condition of letting Biff escape.

As soon as he was in the car, Biff set off, driving so fast it threw his passenger back in his seat.

Once Beaton was upright again with his hat straightened, he ordered, 'Drive more slowly, Higgins. Why the big rush?'

'Sergeant Deemer has been told about the previous attempt to capture Miss Porter, so Welch reckons they need to act fast in case he turns up.'

'Well, in that case, you be careful how close you get to the action. You know I don't wish to be seen to be personally involved in this.'

Why was he here, then? Biff wondered, but answered it himself: Beaton had enjoyed watching them hurt Bella last time and wanted to see it again. What a nasty sort he was!

Biff made up some more details so that his passenger didn't try to go back to the hotel. 'At this time of day, the sergeant always takes afternoon tea, sir. He lives next door to the police station, you see. Welch thinks this will be the safest time to do it.'

Beaton grunted. 'It might be better if you took me back to the hotel and then returned to check that it gets done properly.'

Biff had had enough. 'If you insist on doing that, I'm leaving for London straight away. I'm not risking my neck later on when the sergeant is out and about. I don't know why you're so eager to see them hurt her anyway, but we're nearly there now. Make your mind up whether we turn round and leave them to it.'

'It's because I know her that I need to see it happen. She's easier to persuade once you prove she'll suffer if she doesn't obey. I want to make sure she's nicely upset.'

Nicely upset, indeed! What a way to talk.

But Biff didn't say anything, and his passenger stayed in the car.

He just wanted to get his part over and done with. For some reason, he was quite sure Deemer would keep his word and let him get away. He was not at all sure of what this chancy sod would do, though.

★

In the end, the clerk couldn't think of any more ways of delaying things, so she had to let Ryan and Bella out of the town hall. She hid behind a big pot plant in the foyer and watched them drive away.

Oh dear, they'd taken the back way out of the car park, which she knew was a short cut that used rough, bumpy side roads and alleys to get up to the eastern side of the valley to Backshaw Moss and Birch End.

Just as she was about to return to her office to pick up her outdoor things and go home for the day, she saw Mrs Tyler turning into the car park and rushed out to speak to her.

'I tried to keep them here longer, but Mr Cornish isn't a man you can fool easily, is he? As soon as I said there was trouble in Backshaw Moss, he started worrying about his children.'

'They must have taken the back way to the main road because I didn't see them, and I was keeping a careful lookout.'

'Yes, they did. I saw them go.'

'Will you please phone my husband's office and see if anyone is there. If they are, tell them to get word to him that I missed Mr Cornish. If not, try the village shop and ask them to tell him.'

Mrs Tyler took a deep breath and drove off as fast as she dared, taking the main road because she didn't trust herself to drive the twists and turns of the narrow back roads in the fading light. Older eyes weren't as sharp as younger ones after dark.

31

As they turned into Daisy Street, Beaton said, 'Stop! If you wait behind that pile of rubble, we'll see if we can spot her inside the house. There's a light on upstairs and the curtains aren't drawn.'

They did this, then Beaton spotted a woman passing an upstairs window and jabbed his forefinger in that direction. 'Aha! There you are. She's at home.'

If she was, then where was that blue car of hers? Biff wondered. And that hadn't looked like Miss Porter to him. The figure had seemed much older, just from the way it moved. But he didn't say anything. He hoped Beaton had made a mistake, hoped he'd get caught. He had to persuade him to get out of the car, though, so that he could drive off and leave the fellow to incriminate himself.

'Drive further on down the street, Higgins.'

'You won't be able to see anything if I do that, sir. How about we turn into this little side street. We should be able to see down the back alley clearly from there. When Welch and his men arrive you can take a stroll along it to watch what he and his men are doing.'

'It's your job to check that before I go anywhere.'

'I'm not leaving my car to be stolen in a slum like this when I might need it to get you away.'

Just then a car cruised slowly towards them and Biff called, 'Duck down, quickly!'

★

When Welch took his two men up to Backshaw Moss, he checked the parked cars they passed to make sure none of them were occupied. Only when he felt certain of that did he turn into the alley behind Daisy Street and stop.

He looked round at his two passengers and said emphatically, 'Do not let me down this time.'

'No, sir. Do you want us to get out now and break into the house?'

'Don't go inside yet, you fool, till you've made sure there's no one keeping watch at the back of the house. If there is, you'll need to get rid of him, then it'll be a quick in and out to get hold of her. We'll slap her around a bit, then dump her out on the moors. That should be enough to persuade her that Beaton means business. The moors can be spooky after dark and there won't be anyone around to help her.' He chuckled at the mere thought of that.

'Aw, can't I— ?'

'No. We're doing this quickly.'

Beaton sat up again and said in an aggrieved tone, 'Why did you want me to duck?' He pointed down the alley. 'That's Welch's car. He's on our side.'

Biff managed not to smile at that stupid remark. Men like Welch were only on their own side.

'Well, sir, I wasn't sure, and better safe than sorry, eh? Since that was Welch, you only have to go and ask him what's happening. I'm not driving my car down that narrow alley. I need it to earn a living.'

'I still think you should be the one to reconnoitre. I shall complain to your employer. You're supposed to be working for me, doing whatever I tell you.'

Biff prayed for patience. 'I am working for you by looking out for your interests. We'd both be in serious trouble if someone stole this car. You're in a slum now, Mr Beaton. You have to be careful. And apart from anything else, there isn't room for two cars to pass in that alley.'

'Hmm.'

'Go and join him, sir. You'll see a lot more about how they deal with her from there, and you'll be safe enough with him. A man like Welch wouldn't be staying there if it looked risky.'

'I suppose you're right.' Beaton opened the rear door carefully, hesitated, then sat back again.

Biff held his breath, but his passenger hadn't shut the door, so there was hope.

A minute later Beaton grunted and got out. 'Turn the car round so that we can get away more easily, but do not move away from this spot afterwards! If things go smoothly, I may take a quick look round the inside of that house. Once I've got her back, I shall, after all, be managing it for her, or selling it, whichever will be more profitable.'

Biff couldn't believe how over-confident this idiot was. 'Good idea, sir.'

He watched Beaton walk down the street, mentally urging him to hurry up and go inside the house. Deemer might want to catch the fellow in the act of breaking and entering to be sure of being able to make the charges against him stick, but Biff just wanted to get away.

He reckoned Deemer might be being a bit optimistic about charges sticking, though. Rich sods could get away with things ordinary folk couldn't, in Biff's experience.

On the other hand, this particular rich sod was stupidly blind to anything but his own interests and hurting his cousin. These weaknesses were likely to be his downfall. Biff didn't intend to wait around to find out.

Sergeant Deemer would protect the lady, if anyone could. She'd be in safe hands, so Biff's conscience would be clear.

He waited till Beaton had got into the front passenger seat next to Welch, then started the car, letting it move forward slowly and quietly down the slight slope, breathing a sigh of relief when he left the alley and Backshaw Moss – for good, he hoped.

He drove down the hill towards Rivenshaw as fast as he could without attracting attention. He was never, ever coming back to this stupid valley again.

He wasn't working for any arrogant chaps like that one again, either, whatever anyone offered to pay him. Stupidity could land you in deep trouble if you were working on the edges of what was legal.

He smiled as he saw the police car coming up the hill towards him, then laughed aloud as it passed, because no one in it seemed to have noticed him.

That old sergeant couldn't complain. Biff had played his part, persuaded Beaton to go up to Daisy Street to watch the capture. It was up to the police now to step in and nab them.

His main regret was that he wouldn't see Beaton's face when that happened. Pity.

The two bullies got out of the car, moving quietly along to the back of Number 23. One grabbed the other's arm and they stopped. Sure enough, there was a fellow keeping watch. Welch had been right to tell them to be careful how they went.

By good luck the fool went into the privy. They grinned at one another and crept into the yard. When he came out they were standing ready to thump him, after which they tied him up and gagged him.

They left him out of sight inside the privy, then one of them said, 'Count of sixty for you, forty for me?'

His friend nodded, so he went around the house, finished counting up to forty, then knocked on the front door to distract the people inside. By the time his companion had counted up to sixty, he'd be out of sight of whoever answered it.

He ran back, grinning. Piece of cake, this.

In the downstairs flat, Trev hesitated at the sound of the front door knocker, then opened the door of the flat cautiously to see if Ed had come to answer the outer door. It was that young man's job to keep watch, after all.

Ed came running down the stairs and opened the door with the safety chain on. Trev waited to see who it was.

Ed looked out, took the chain off, and peered around to each side, then shrugged. 'No one there. It'll be a lad playing knock and run. I used to do that myself when I was a kid. I didn't see anyone at all. Well, there are fewer people hanging round now they've started to knock the houses opposite down.'

As Trev smiled and nodded agreement, there was the faintest sound of breaking glass from the back of the house. It was so faint that if they'd been chatting, they might not have noticed it and even so, it took a moment or two to register what the sound meant.

Trev cursed. 'Someone's getting into the flat through the kitchen, damn them. I thought your cousin was keeping watch outside at the back.'

Ed frowned. 'He was. I'd better go and check he's all right. If they've hurt Steve, I'll make them sorry.'

Trev grabbed his arm 'No, don't go into the flat on your own. They've already broken in and I'm not going to be much good to you in a fight. I'm too old for that sort of thing. Baz has gone for the police. They must be on their way now. He'll be back soon, but he'll know to be careful.'

'Then I reckon the most important thing for us to do is keep an eye on the kids and the old lady till help arrives. Come on upstairs.'

Trev hesitated, then followed Ed. Ryan had told them Miss

Porter's cousin, who was from London, was after her inheritance, but that didn't make sense to him. You couldn't just
walk off with a house, now, could you? And she wasn't likely
to hand it over meekly to him, let alone she was engaged to
Ryan and he'd look after her. So why the hell was someone
breaking into the downstairs flat?

He tiptoed up the stairs, didn't want whoever had broken
in to hear them. He let Ed knock on the door of the flat there
and tell the old lady what was going on. 'Can you keep the
kids quiet? We'll stay up here on the landing. Leave the door
open in case we need to take refuge inside. We don't know
how many there are, but it sounds like more than one person.'

She nodded. 'Just a minute.' She darted back inside and
returned with a cosh, which she handed to Trev. 'Just in case.'

He took it so as not to offend her, but wasn't sure he could
hit anyone, had never been a fighting man, even when he was
young.

Then they all listened. Even the littlest kids knew to be
quiet when the grown-ups looked so sternly at them.

Sergeant Deemer drove as fast as he could, but slowed right
down as they passed through Birch End. He stopped just
before Daisy Street to look around. Everything was quiet, and
there were no cars near the three big houses at the near end.

There was no sign of the blue car, either, so Ryan wasn't
back yet, thank goodness. Unless he'd parked it at the back.

He said quietly to his eager constable, 'We'll drive slowly
and turn left on the little street that leads to the back alley.
Thank goodness the moon's rising. If we see any strange cars
parked in the alley, I'll stop just past the entrance to it, then
you can get out and take a better look at whoever it is. The
back alley's not well lit and your eyes are young. You'll see
what's going on better than I would. Be sure to nip back and
tell me straight away. Do not do anything without my say-so.'

'Yes, sarge. I mean, no, sarge.'

But the constable had no sooner peeped into the alley than he jerked back and came to whisper that some men were just opening the doors of a car. Deemer joined him to take a careful look, grinning as he recognised one chap in particular.

'It's him. Beaton. And he's the main one we want to catch, the ringleader. Remember that, lad. You're to catch him at all costs, even if it means letting the others get away. We'll stay here and watch them.'

But Beaton stayed in the car.

After a few moments, the sergeant said, 'I know how to get into the back from next door, and there's no one living there at the moment. I'll show you where to get through.'

They did this and saw no sign of the men at the rear end of the yard.

The constable led the way, then stopped and looked towards the outhouse. 'Is it my imagination, or is someone inside there banging?'

The sergeant had heard it too. 'You're right. Take a look. Be quick, though. We need to let Beaton and Welch get right inside the house and hopefully incriminate themselves. I don't want that fellow getting away with encouraging crime in my valley.'

The constable went to open the outhouse door, and beckoned. 'There's someone tied up.' He was getting out his penknife as he spoke.

Steve groaned as he was released.

'Shh. Follow us when you can,' Sergeant Deemer told him. 'We're about to catch the villains who did this to you.'

Just then, they heard the sound of glass breaking.

Ryan drove up the back roads as fast as he could, startling a couple of straying sheep at one stage and nearly ending up in the ditch. After that he slowed down slightly, but not much.

When they arrived at some tumble-down houses Ryan said they were in Backshaw Moss, but it was a part of it Bella didn't recognise. Was it her imagination or did the people standing around under lamp posts or in doorways look more worn down and hungry than anyone she'd seen in Rivenshaw or Birch End? There were children on the streets, but some weren't playing, just sitting listlessly on doorsteps or the edges of footpaths.

'Poor little devils. The sooner the council knocks these slums down, the better,' Ryan muttered, swerving to one side to avoid a mangy dog that was barking furiously at them.

When they got to Daisy Street, there were no people to be seen. 'Let's keep out of sight.' He turned up the side road, stopping when he saw the police car parked a bit further up the slope. There was no one in it.

'They must have gone inside the house,' he said. 'Look, Bella, you need to stay in the car and lock the doors from inside. I shan't be able to defend you and my family.'

She sighed but agreed.

He parked the car a little way down Daisy Street, switched off the engine and got out. 'Stay in the car!'

Bella watched him go, feeling mutinous at being left behind, and also worried about his safety. Still, Ed and Steve would be there to help him, wouldn't they? But when Ryan vanished up the little side street that led to the alley, she was tempted to follow. No, she might hinder him more than help.

There was no one around at all and as the minutes ticked slowly past, she couldn't help wondering how strong the locks were on car doors. The remains of the demolished houses had a threatening air after dark. Could you smash car windows easily? How would she defend herself if anyone managed to force their way into the vehicle?

She didn't know, so fumbled around on the floor in the darkness for some sort of weapon. When she found a lump behind her seat under a screwed-up rag it turned out to be a spanner. Not a big one, but big enough to hit someone with and make them sorry.

She'd seen people do that in films on the rare occasions she'd visited the cinema. She hefted it in the air. Could she use it to protect herself?

She got annoyed for doubting herself again. Ryan was right. She had to trust in her own abilities.

Suddenly, there were shouts from her house and she leaned forward to peep out of the car window.

Someone switched on a light inside the building, then switched it off again. What was going on?

In the distance a deep male voice yelled, 'This is the police. Give yourselves up.'

There was a further chorus of yells and crashing sounds.

Just then a man crept around the side of her house and out on to the pavement. When he stopped right under a streetlamp, she realised it was Cousin Thomas. He cast a panic-stricken glance over his shoulder as a whistle shrilled from inside the house then moved along the street, stopping dead when he saw her sitting in the car.

She thought he'd be trying to get away, so was puzzled when he darted across the road and picked up one of the bricks that were lying around. Then he came back to the car and raised it.

'Unlock that car door, you bitch!'

She shook her head.

He crashed the brick down on the window of her door, fracturing the glass, sending cracks across it, then smashed it down again and again in a frenzy of fury.

There was nothing she could do to stop him, could only hope the window would hold. It certainly didn't break like a house window would have done. All she could do was hold the spanner concealed in the folds of her skirt and hope someone would hear the noise.

The window fell apart suddenly and she put up her arm instinctively to shield her face. Shards were sticking out round the edges of the hole, which was big enough for him to put a hand inside and though she hit out, trying to stop him, the angle was too awkward to do so easily. He was so much stronger, he shoved her hand out of the way and managed to get hold of the handle and unlock the door.

He dragged her out, slapping her cheek. Fury boiled up and she raised the spanner, hitting him with it as hard as she could on the shoulder.

He yelled out, so she hit out at him again, aiming for his head, but he grabbed the spanner with one hand and took it from her, throwing it away so violently he staggered back against the car.

She tried to run past him, but he grabbed her coat, yanking her backwards, smiling now. His free arm rose to thump her, as he'd thumped her before.

She tensed, trying to kick him, expecting to be hurt at any moment. Only, his arm didn't descend on her because it was grabbed from behind and he was jerked backwards.

'Ryan!'

'Move back, love.'

Beaton struggled, but Ryan managed to twist his right arm behind him. The older man began to struggle frantically, but she saw the spanner on the ground and picked it up again, smashing it down on Beaton's arm.

He howled in pain and Ryan seized the opportunity to kick his feet from under him and kneel on one of his arms.

Bella was just raising the spanner ready to hit him again if he tried to get away, when another man joined them, a man in uniform. There was a click as a handcuff was clamped to

Thomas's free arm, which was then dragged round his back to click on to his other wrist.

The young constable was panting. 'I've got him – now – sir.' He yanked Beaton to a sitting position.

'Thank goodness you're here, constable,' Thomas panted. 'These people attacked me for no reason.'

Bella was so surprised by this accusation she could only gape. There was dead silence. Had the constable believed him? Surely not?

Only, the policeman hadn't been there when Thomas smashed the window of her car and dragged her out, had he? How would he know who was telling the truth?

'Take these things off my wrists this minute!' Thomas ordered in that upper-class voice. 'You've got the wrong man.'

He sounded so calm and assured, the constable started to do as he asked.

'That's not true,' Ryan said. 'He attacked my fiancée. See how he's broken the window of her car.'

As the constable hesitated, uncertain who to believe, another man stepped out of the shadows, a shabby stranger. 'No, they didn't attack him. I saw what happened. The other man was telling the truth.' He pointed at Thomas. 'That one smashed her car window, trying to get at her. And when he got his hand in, he unlocked the door, dragged her out and slapped her face. I bet her face is red if you look at it in the light. An' he might have a cut on his wrist from the broken glass.'

'He's lying!' Thomas said, sounding suddenly desperate.

'I ain't lying. Why should I? I was about to help her when I saw you slap her. I can't abide men who knock women about like that. An' she's only a little 'un, you bloody coward.' He pointed to Ryan. 'But he came out of the house and stopped the old man thumping her again, so I didn't need to do anything.'

From one side a voice said, 'Well done for speaking up, lad.'

The man spun round. 'Sergeant Deemer. You know I don't tell lies. You've given me a sandwich once or twice for helping you out.'

'Yes. Danny Green, isn't it? I remember you. Will you come down to the police station and sign a witness statement, lad?'

'Might as well. I haven't got a roof over my head any more.' He gestured across towards what had been a row of houses. 'I was going to sleep in the coal house.'

'No one will take this man's word against mine,' Thomas said loftily.

'I will,' Sergeant Deemer's voice was quiet, 'because I saw what happened too. You'll get in big trouble for the things you've done here, Beaton.'

'She is the one who should be in trouble.'

'What on earth for?'

'Disobeying me, taking the family's money away from us, and living immorally on it.'

The sergeant gave another of his gentle smiles. 'No one who's ever met the lady is going to believe that she's immoral. And if I have my way, you will end up in jail – or in the lunatic asylum – for what you've done. I am not having people stirring up trouble in this valley. So you're under arrest.'

Beaton's voice came out choked with rage and it was a minute before he managed to put words together. 'You can't – can't do that. Not to a gentleman – of my standing.'

'Oh, can't I? You're still bound by the rule of law. Everyone in this country is.'

'But I am—' The words cut off abruptly and there was a sudden choking sound. Beaton's knees crumpled under him and, before anyone could catch him, he'd fallen to the ground.

He was totally silent now.

'Get those cuffs off him.' The sergeant knelt down beside him, but though the constable quickly did as he asked, Beaton still didn't stir.

'He's not breathing. Run and call an ambulance, lad. The nearest phone is at the village shop.'

Bella moved closer to Ryan, who put his arm around her. 'He can't be dead,' she whispered.

'His chest isn't moving. And he's got that look to him. You can't mistake it. I reckon he's had a seizure.'

She shivered, and Ryan said, 'Sergeant, can I take Miss Porter inside, please? She's upset and she's feeling the cold.'

'Yes, of course. But be ready to talk to me in a few minutes.' He turned to the man who'd spoken out. 'You stay with me, Danny lad.'

The man nodded. 'I've nothing better to do. Eh, it don't matter how often you see it or who it is, death's still a sad thing, isn't it?'

Inside the house, the furniture had been knocked around in the struggles, but the two bullies had been captured and tied up with Bella's brand-new washing line. The two night watchmen and the plumber's labourers were still there, looking as if they didn't quite know what to do.

'I think we should all have a cup of tea,' Bella suggested, and they nodded eagerly.

Ryan laughed softly. 'It's the answer to everything, isn't it, a cup of tea?'

She smiled back at him. 'Not to everything, but it can help quite a lot when things aren't going well.'

Ryan looked around. 'Ed, will you build up that fire? Trev, how about you fill the kettle and put it on the gas burner? We'll make the tea. I'm going to get Bella a blanket. She's frozen cold, and that sod of a cousin just dropped dead at her feet.'

He made his way into her bedroom, a large space with only a few bits of furniture, and took a blanket off the bed, returning immediately to wrap it round her shoulders.

She sat on a chair and watched the men fumble around making a pot of tea. She was still trying to take in what had happened, unable to believe that Thomas could be dead.

She'd never wish anyone dead, but if he was, she'd be free of his bullying for good and would be able to live her life without feeling insecure all the time.

Feeling washed out, she watched the confusion as the men decided her teapot was too small, so found her biggest saucepan. She didn't laugh at their clumsiness but once her eyes met Ryan's and they exchanged a brief smile.

By the time the ambulance arrived, they'd drunk all the tea, and the two labourers were fretting to be off home.

'If you're all right, Bella, I'll go out and see what's happening,' Ryan said.

'I'll be fine.'

He came back a few minutes later. 'Beaton is definitely dead. They're taking the body away. It'll need an inquest to find out why he died, but they think he had a massive seizure, from the twisted look of his face. The ambulance was about to set off.'

There was the sound of a vehicle driving away, then the two policemen and their witness came in to join them. By that time the kettle had boiled again and Ryan took charge of making another panful of tea.

She saw Danny hesitating in the doorway and stood up, going across to him. 'How long is it since you've eaten?'

He shrugged. 'Yesterday morning, I think.'

'The bread's a bit stale, but I can make you a sandwich.'

'Eh, missus. I'm that hungry, it'd be a godsend. I'd be that grateful.'

Ryan gave her a quick smile of approval. 'I ought to go and tell Hettie what's happened.'

He came back not long after to say, 'You wouldn't believe it, but she and the kids are all sound asleep.'

'They said they were tired,' Ed told him.

'Yes, but how anyone could sleep through that racket, I don't know.'

Ed lowered his voice to ask. 'All right if I let Danny sleep on the top floor, miss? Only he's got nowhere to go, and I've got a spare blanket.'

'Of course it is.'

By the time everyone left, Bella was half asleep herself.

Ed smiled at her. 'We'll still keep watch, miss.'

'Thank you.' She knew she'd have felt unsafe without them around tonight, because the police hadn't caught Welch, who hadn't even waited for her cousin, and had somehow managed to get away.

She turned to Ryan. 'You're tired too. Get off to bed.'

'You're sure you'll be all right?'

'Yes, love.'

'Just one goodnight kiss, then.' He pulled her into his arms and she went willingly, not caring who saw them.

32

There followed another of the busy times – and yet such a happy one. Bella was definitely feeling the happiest she could remember for a good many years.

It had been decided by Mrs Tyler and Gabriel's mother that the wedding should go ahead, so they took her shopping to buy a pretty new outfit, and Ethel bought her a hat as a wedding present.

Gwynneth Harte insisted on making her a wedding cake, and Hettie said she could ice it in a pretty pattern.

Apart from the shopping, Bella spent a lot of her time going over the living arrangements, unpacking more boxes, and working out with Ryan where his family would sleep. In the end they decided that the children would share one bedroom and Hettie use the smallest room, but could stay upstairs till the downstairs rooms were ready for them, which would mean buying a few more pieces of furniture.

When the other bathrooms were finished they could find suitable tenants for Ryan's old flat and the top floor.

She and Hettie took the children to buy new outfits, and she insisted on Hettie also having some nicer clothes, which reduced the kind old lady to tears of joy.

That evening Ryan seemed a bit upset about something. He waited till they were alone to say stiffly, 'You must let me pay you for the children's clothes.'

Something about his voice made her feel wary. 'There's no need. I enjoyed taking them shopping.'

'Nonetheless, I'm not intending to sponge on you. If I can't afford to clothe my children, then they must manage with what we can find on the second-hand stall at the market.'

The way he'd said 'my children' upset her. 'Aren't they going to be my children too from now on?'

He didn't answer, just frowned at her.

She didn't know what to say, how to make him see that the money she'd spent didn't matter. And then she knew that the time had come to tell him the truth about her money.

'Sit down, please, Ryan. I ought to have told you sooner but I was afraid you'd be – well, upset.'

'Upset? What about?'

'Money. It seems to be more important to you than to me.'

'I'm not marrying you for your money. What you have is yours and will remain yours. It's up to me to support my children – and my wife too, as much as I can.'

She took a deep breath and said it baldly, 'Well, before you go deciding that sort of thing for me without asking me what I think, I need to tell you that I have some other money, more than you realise. I inherited some jewellery, you see, only I don't need jewellery, so I sold most of it. I only kept a couple of my mother's pieces.'

'How much money do you have?'

'I had four hundred pounds, but—'

Breath whistled into his mouth and he didn't seem able to speak.

'I spent some of it. On the car and – and the furniture and repairs on the house – and now the clothes for the wedding.'

'But you'll have at least three hundred pounds left. More.'

It wasn't a question, just a slow statement, and he got a sad look on his face as he stared at her. 'You should have told me sooner. You shouldn't have let me hope.'

'What do you mean by that?'

'How can I marry you now? It's bound to come out about the money, and people will say that's why I married you. I can't even put a roof over your head.' He gestured upwards. 'This is your roof.'

'It'll be ours – our home.'

He shook his head. 'I could cope with the house being yours, because I can do a lot to help, to make it better, but I can't cope with the thought of all that money.'

'Why on earth not?'

'I can't face being a kept man, a sponger on your money. I just can't. I've always looked after my own. Always. Maybe not as well as I wanted to, but there has always been something to eat, somewhere to sleep. What can I bring to you? I don't even talk properly. I had a rough upbringing. You were brought up to be a lady.'

'Ryan, I don't care about that. It's you I want to be with, and your children.'

But he continued shaking his head. 'Three hundred pounds. It's more than most men dream of ever having in the bank. And you didn't even tell me about it. You let me think I'd be looking after you. But I'd be like a dog on a lead, a dog you could tell what to do, pull up, and say stop or go.'

'I didn't think that way about you. I couldn't.'

'And I didn't think of being a kept man. I can't face that. I'm sorry but we'll have to cancel the wedding tomorrow.'

He turned and stumbled from the room, and Bella stood there, feeling as frozen as any statue, her dreams smashed, her happiness destroyed.

And for what? For Ryan's stupid pride.

She walked slowly across to the sofa and sat down on it, heedless that the fire had burned low and the room was growing colder.

Her whole life and happiness had frozen into nothing.

★

It was dark but it wasn't late yet and Bella couldn't bear being alone. She had to talk to someone kind, because Ryan had been unkind tonight. Brutally unkind.

She stumbled along the streets, not consciously thinking where to go, but ending up outside the Hartes' house. She didn't hesitate, but went round to the back.

When she knocked on the door Gwynneth opened it, took one look at her, and said, 'Come in and tell me what's wrong.'

'Are you – alone?'

'For a little while. The lads have gone out for a glass of beer. They're not boozers, but they enjoy the company of friends at the pub.'

She drew Bella inside and put her arms round her, rocking her slightly. 'Tell me what's wrong.'

So it all came out in jerky bursts of pain.

'Ach, men. They can be fools to themselves sometimes. He'll come around.'

'He said he'd cancel the wedding tomorrow.'

'I'd like to take my rolling pin to him for even thinking it. Look, I'll make us a cup of cocoa, then I'm going around to give him what for.'

Bella shook her head. 'It won't do any good. He was like a stranger. He can't really have loved me, can he?'

Gwynneth busied herself, putting on a pan of milk to heat up and making the cocoa.

Bella held the mug in her hands because the warmth was comforting, but she couldn't choke much down.

When Gabriel and Lucas came bursting in, laughing about something, Gwynneth told them to leave her and Bella in peace for a while.

'What's wrong?' Gabriel asked. 'I'm not going anywhere till you tell me.'

She cast a quick glance over at Bella, still hunched over the lukewarm cocoa, hardly seeming aware of what was going on around her.

'She and Ryan have had an upset.'

'Bella? She's a gentle soul. What's he done to her?'

'You leave it alone, Gabriel. Some things can't be sorted out by outsiders.'

He gave her a dubious look and she gave him a quick shove. 'Leave us,' she insisted. 'Go to bed down in the basement and don't come up till I say you can.'

Bella sat there a little longer, saying nothing, then stood up and gave Gwynneth a hug. 'I need to get back now. Thank you for listening to me. It was – comforting.'

She walked out before Gwynneth could stop her, so the older woman went to the basement room where her sons slept and said urgently to Gabriel, 'She's gone off home. Go after her but don't catch up with her. Just make sure no one tries to attack her or take her purse.'

He nodded and moved towards the door.

Gwynneth burst into tears. Eh, what a thing for Ryan to do. She'd thought better of him than that. Poor lass. She didn't deserve it.

What did money matter? It was people who mattered most.

Bella had felt vaguely comforted by Gwynneth's presence, but now she wanted to go home. It was all she had left, her house. She only hoped it'd be enough.

But before she'd gone more than a hundred yards, a man came running along the street, calling her name. It wasn't—
It couldn't be—

Only when he grabbed her, she saw that it really was Ryan.

He rained kisses down on her face. 'I'm the biggest fool in the world. How you ever put up with me, I don't know.'

She stared at him, not daring to hope till he pulled her close and buried his face in her hair, rocking them slightly to and fro.

'Can you ever forgive me?'

She moved her head back to stare at his face. The old love was there again, you couldn't mistake it. 'Ryan?'

He kissed her again, this time on the lips, so of course she kissed him back.

After a long embrace she had to ask it. 'Why did you say those things, though?'

'I think it was the shock. I've always been – well, short of money, having to be careful, worried about staying in work. And I've always been proud of managing to put bread on the table.'

'And now?'

'I sat down in the outhouse. Of all the romantic places! But I couldn't think where else to go that I'd not be disturbed. And the thought of not having you, well, that was worse than anything. Even in this short time, I've grown used to having you to turn to and love, to you looking after my children, and Hettie too. You're such a kind, caring woman.'

He sucked in a deep, anguished breath. 'It didn't take me long to realise that the money didn't matter nearly as much as being with you. Can you ever forgive me, Bella, my love? I don't deserve it after such stupid behaviour, but oh, I can't bear to be without you.'

'Of course I can forgive you, as long as you don't think or say such things again.'

'Never, never.' He kissed her.

When they came up for air, she said, 'I just want to be with you, to be your wife, the mother of your children and, if you run a business of your own one day, I want to be like Mrs Tyler and help out. I'm greedy, you see. I want to be in all parts of your life from now on.'

'I don't deserve you, but I'll try my hardest, with all that's in me, to make you happy.' He pulled her close and they stood there for a few moments. Then, without needing to say the words, they turned as one to walk slowly home.

Maybe you had to nearly lose it, Bella thought, to truly believe that a man could love you so much.

She had no more doubts, none at all.

Gabriel watched them go, smiling. His mother would be so pleased about this. So was he. If anyone deserved to be happy, it was Bella.

He whistled cheerfully as he walked home. Sometimes fate did the right thing by you.

The next few days passed peacefully. Bella had felt hassled before, worried something might go wrong, but she felt serenely happy most of the time as they waited the requisite week and made their final preparations. There were so many details to sort out.

She hadn't heard from Muriel, hadn't expected to, but she did receive a brief note from Stephen, who said he was sorry for the trouble his father had caused her, and informing her that the family were burying him the following week at a private ceremony.

Bella wondered how the others were, the two in Australia, and poor Penelope still married to a man she hated.

She managed to keep those worries to herself, but going to the court had brought them all back.

Bella had been asked to answer the magistrate's questions about her cousin Thomas, but with Ryan to one side of her, Gwynneth and Gabriel to the other, it didn't upset her as she'd expected. It seemed more like tying off loose ends. 'All right?' Ryan asked as they left the court.

'Yes. It's good to get it over with. I just, you know, worry about the others.'

'You can't do anything about them.'

'No.' She forced a smile. 'Worry about things you can change, eh?'

'Yes, love.'

'Now about moving down to our flat . . .'

Planning for her new life cheered her up. There wasn't a lot of furniture to bring down from Ryan's flat, and they agreed to do most of the moving the day after the wedding, which meant the children would be upstairs for their wedding night, to Bella's relief.

She'd written to her lawyer to tell him she was getting married. To her surprise, she received a warmly approving letter from him by return of post, in which he said that Mrs Beaton seemed to be suffering from shock at her husband's unexpected death, but that her eldest son and his wife had moved back home to look after her.

He also gave her some more information about Oscar and Alma. They were on their way to Western Australia, and he said he'd pass on to them her new address and marital status once they let him know where they were, as they'd promised to do.

The thought of being in touch with them again cheered her up immensely.

The worst news was that Welch had got away with his involvement in the break-in, because he'd slipped away during the fighting and his two men had flatly denied that he'd been there at all, while someone else said he'd been drinking with Welch all that evening.

'It's a battle for another day,' Sergeant Deemer said philosophically as he gave Bella and Ryan the news. 'I reckon he'll live very quietly for a while, though. Well, he will if he knows what's good for him. I shall not forget. And one day I'll snabble him, you see if I don't.'

She chuckled. 'Snabble? What does that mean?'

The sergeant slapped one hand down on the table to illustrate catching something. 'And Welch won't get away next time. He'll stay snabbled.' He grinned at them.

★

And then at last the big day came. Bella got up early and took a bath in her newly finished bathroom. Oh, it felt so wonderful.

When she was dressed, she stared at herself in the mirror as she adjusted her new hat. She'd never be beautiful, but she thought she looked quite pretty today, she really did.

Then she heard footsteps in the stairwell and rushed out to greet her new family.

'Oh, my goodness, don't you all look fine in your new clothes?'

Maddy twirled round and stroked her skirt. 'It's pretty.'

Devin clutched Hettie's hand and jigged about, staring down at his shiny new shoes, which seemed to fascinate him.

Ryan was holding Nelly in his arms, but his eyes were on his bride. 'You look lovely, Bella darling.'

Maddy giggled and nudged Hettie's arm, as she did every time her father used that endearment.

Then they all got into the blue car, with its new window, and Ryan drove them down to the town hall.

'By next week, you'll be driving us all around,' he said to Bella.

'Yes. I'm looking forward to that.' Because if she could win the love of this wonderful man, she could do anything.

When they went into the register office, Bella was surprised to see quite a lot of people there – in fact, all her new friends from the valley. It made the day feel even more special.

'We're having a meal at my house now,' Mrs Tyler said firmly once the brief ceremony was over.

Bella exchanged smiles with her husband, who had clearly been in the know about this. 'That'll be wonderful. Thank you.'

In fact, everything that day went past in a blur of happiness until they got back and were left alone in her flat, when Bella could feel herself starting to worry.

Ryan looked at her. 'Nervous about tonight?'

She could only nod.

'I think, from the way you react to my kisses, you'll rather enjoy making love. I must admit I do.'

'You do?' She'd thought it something women endured for the sake of having children.

'Yes. And a woman can enjoy it too if the man loves her and provides for her happiness as well. Bella darling, I love you dearly, and I'm quite sure I can make you happy in bed as well as in the rest of our lives.'

He took her hand, raised it to his lips, and said softly, 'Come to bed, my dear one. Come and find out how much I love you.'

And oh, she did!

When she wept in his arms afterwards, he grew anxious.

'It's happy tears,' she told him, nestling closer.

'Ah. That's all right then. You carry on crying.'

She chuckled. 'No. That's enough.'

Yes, she thought as she snuggled up to him, everything was all right. More than all right. Simply wonderful.

This is another drawing from my great-aunt's autograph album, which was given to her as a school prize in 1898. Most of the entries in it are hand-drawn sketches, some really superb. This one of the ice-cream seller really caught my eye. Towards the end of her life she added a few entries herself, giving her thoughts about the world, in beautiful handwriting.

This is me and my grandma. It's about 1943 or 44, and I'm about three. It looks as if we're walking along the seafront in Blackpool. We went there a lot from our home in Rochdale because my grandma's sister lived there and let out rooms to family members for inexpensive holidays.

CONTACT ANNA

Anna is always delighted to hear from readers and can be contacted via the Internet.

Anna has her own web page, with details of her books, some behind-the-scenes information that is available nowhere else and the first chapters of her books to try out, as well as a picture gallery.

Anna can be contacted by email at
anna@annajacobs.com

You can also find Anna on Facebook at
www.facebook.com/AnnaJacobsBooks

If you'd like to receive an email newsletter about Anna and her books every month or two, you are cordially invited to join her announcements list. Just email her and ask to be added to the list, or follow the link from her web page.

www.annajacobs.com

This book was created by
Hodder & Stoughton

Founded in 1868 by two young men who saw that the rise in literacy would break cultural barriers, the Hodder story is one of visionary publishing and globe-trotting talent-spotting, campaigning journalism and popular understanding, men of influence and pioneering women.

For over 150 years, we have been publishing household names and undiscovered gems, and today we continue to give our readers books that sweep you away or leave you looking at the world with new eyes.

Follow us on our adventures in books . . .
 @HodderBooks /HodderBooks @HodderBooks

HODDER &
STOUGHTON